Burning Bridges

Burning Bridges

Shiloh J. Manley

Tiki Press

Burning Bridges is a work of fiction. Any similarity to actual persons or events is purely coincidental.

Tiki Press, Westbank, BC, Canada
tikipress@shaw.ca

Original Cover Art by Tammy Turner

ISBN-10: 0986526908
ISBN-13: 9780986526909

Many people pass through one's life. Every once in a while you find one that is special. Having hidden away my love of writing from most people, I started a novel. When I finished a rough draft, I decided to ask an avid reader, my mother-in-law to read it and comment. It never got that far. On the trip from Alberta to Vancouver, we stopped in the Okanagan, to spend the night with our best friends. I hesitantly took my book out and asked her to read it. We sat by the kitchen table while she did so. I squirmed and twiddled my thumbs nervously until she finished. I was shocked when Joy said she liked it. It would of course need polishing up but she asked if I would allow her to be my agent in trying to get it published.

I was thrilled, and shocked, and trembling down to my boots, but agreed. Joy did indeed become my agent, my editor, my taskmaster in getting this book done.

Without her this book would never have been published. Therefore it is my greatest pleasure to dedicate this book to her. Love you Joy!

Chapter 1

Jenny held trembling hands to her aching head. "What ever possessed me to make this trip now?" Here she was, trapped in a confining railway car, hot, dirty, and very tired. She berated herself for her impulsive move to buy an economy ticket rather than wait the few days it would have taken to purchase the first class fare. She was paying for her foolishness now.

Anxious to start her new life, she'd plunged ahead. For five days it didn't seem to matter what train she transferred to, the continual noise of recalcitrant children filled the air. Shrieks, squeals and screams of cranky, restless juveniles and the more recent smelly crate of chickens she was forced to share the train car with, were causing everyone's ears to ring. She was not happy and she let the long faced conductor know of her irritation.

"Why are these chickens not in the baggage car?" she inquired distastefully.

"They're only goin' to the next stop. I saw no reason to waste time putting them into the baggage car for this short trip. You'll just have to put up with them," he said impatiently.

A whiskery, tanned farmer, who was keeping a wary eye on them, grinned at her discomfort. He kept wiping his sweating brow on his shirt sleeve. His faded shirt and coveralls were covered in dirt and dust. It was indeed hot. The windows were all open, but all that seemed to do was allow even more dust into the railcar. The clucking and cackling chickens tried their best to outdo the bored children. Jenny grimaced, the noise was deafening. Small children kept squalling, while harried mothers' yelled at them with threats of mayhem if they didn't settle down.

Jenny sighed in relief when the next stop arrived and the farmer along with his chickens left the train. In fact even the children it seemed had settled down, most were napping. Their careworn mothers were valiantly trying to do the same. Jenny hoped she would never have to travel with children or chickens again, at least not any great distance.

In the relative quiet, Jenny's headache started to subside. She gamely tried to force herself into a better frame of mind. "I have certainly met some interesting people travelling this way," she reminisced. "I would probably have been bored silly in first class anyway."

Staring out the train window, she leaned back in her seat. The landscape was a monotonous scene of grass-colored plains broken only by the odd river, gentle hills and a few water-starved trees. The rhythm of the wheels clicking over the track was mesmerizing. She closed her eyes and let herself relax. Her mind wandered, inevitably following its own course back in time.

She began to think of her parents. Her father, John Richard Stockton, had been president and chairman of one of the largest banks in America. He was a handsome man, but of a one-track mind. Outside of his business friends and acquaintances, his world revolved around the bank. He had worked hard, rarely taking time for any leisure past-times.

Even his marriage was arranged. John was acutely aware of his low class heritage. He was the grandson of English working class immigrants, who had done well when they came to the United States. They were goldsmiths, crafting exquisite jewellery. John's father had added to the family fortune by working hard and making sound investments. He taught his son the business, and how to invest in stocks. His life was prematurely terminated by a heart attack in his early forties. His new found wealth was left to his only son. John vowed to add to his wealth and was not slow to realize he needed social prestige to go along with it. It was essential that he marry well. His alliance with the Avery family was very important to him and designed strictly to enter him into a higher social stratum.

His wife, Mary Pauline Avery, had been the incomparable of her debut year, and daughter of a wealthy high-class family originating in Philadelphia. John was lost to all domestic and family pleasures. It was a mistake of nature when his wife got pregnant. On March twenty-first 1874, to top off his displeasure, his wife had the nerve to bear a daughter instead of the expected son that could take over the family business. John was furious and disappointed. He never even went up to see the tiny baby, and ignored both his wife and daughter except for the rare occasions when the picture of a loving family was needed for business to further the myth of the happily married family man. If his wife accompanied him on business trips, it was only for appearances. He did make sure his wife and daughter never lacked for any material possessions, but that is as far as his acknowledgement of the women in his life would go.

Mary Avery was a beautiful petite lady who hid the loneliness of a loveless marriage by becoming one of the leading ladies in Boston Society. This endless round of business duties mixed with social engagements left a lonely little girl by the name of Jennifer Louise Stockton to be raised by an attentive household staff.

The indulgent retainers delighted in their young charge. They treated her more like their own kin. Jenny's avid curiosity and general good nature had her pursuing activities in the kitchen, laundry or sewing room. The daily running of the household held just as much fascination, as did her studies, which were inexhaustible. Governesses' found her to be extremely studious, often amazing them with her insight to the world around her and her knowledge of obscure trivia. To be sure, the governesses' made certain she knew the correct behaviour for a young debutante. She was musically inclined, and learned to play the pianoforte and harp. She was told she had a pleasant Alto singing voice as well, and was welcomed by the church choir when she was twelve. She also enjoyed doing embroidery and water color painting. But above all these accomplishments, she loved to read. It was the passion in her life.

Her early years did not feature much socialization, as custom dictated children remain seen but not heard outside the nursery. As Jenny grew up, she gradually became a part of this socialite society, starting off with a debutante ball at the age of sixteen. She made some friends and tried hard to please her parents by becoming an incomparable of the social elite. Unfortunately her parent's ambition to increase their consequence with a huge Boston wedding was doomed to failure. Jenny did not oblige. She became bored, and she whole heartedly disliked being put on the marriage market. She found most of the young men snobbish and the girl's lives seemed narrowly focused on getting married as soon as possible. Jenny had fretted over these social restrictions. She wanted more.

When Jenny expressed her desire to become a teacher, her parents were scandalized. John immediately quashed the whole idea. She was going to be married if he had to drag her to the altar.

At one point her father was all for sending her to England, so his business friend could introduce her to London's Polite Society. Fortunately for Jenny this never came about.

Jenny's reluctance to find a beau wore on her father's patience, although he did go along with her refusal to marry any of her avid suitors. Most had something wrong with them, according to John. Lack of wealth or in most cases, they didn't cater to John's every wish. That is until William Randolf Worthington the Fifth came on the scene. He was smitten by Jenny's beauty, and had a good eye to the fortune that went along with marriage to her.

John Stockton liked this new young man. He was image-perfect of his ideal for a son, or in this case son-in-law. William could trace his roots back many generations and was the cream of the Boston elite. He also had a head for business and stock market. All in all, perfect for Jennifer.

When Jenny rejected this offer of marriage, John flew into a rage. He sent Jennifer to her room and vowed she was not to come down until she was able to see reason.

John did not leave the situation alone though and arranged with the Worthington family, to have Jennifer become engaged to William by proxy. A written contract was made. This announcement was proclaimed at a ball held at the Stockton home unbenounced to his daughter.

Jennifer was ordered to dress for the ball and attend. No excuses would be accepted. Mary persuaded Jennifer to listen to her fathers order so reluctantly Jennifer attended. Her engagement was announced to everyone by John, just before the dance was to start. A stunned Jenny went into shock. She never objected when William led her out for the first dance. Her face was ashen, and she longed to tell her father exactly what she thought of William and his idea. Protocols and politeness kept her silent until after the ball.

John was well pleased, the silly girl didn't know her own mind. What woman did? He had sat in his easy chair after the ball drinking some port. The door flew open and Jenny strode in. She was furious and hurt.

"Father, how could you humiliate me like that? I will never marry that insufferable man. Never!" Jenny said firmly. "This is not the Seventeenth Century where a woman could be forced to marry by her parents. I will not! "

John stood up, and roared. "You live in this house, you are mine to do with as I see fit. You will marry William and you will like it. Now go to your room and stay there!"

Jenny fled, sobbing uncontrollably, "What am I going to do?" She thought as she threw herself onto the bed.

Frances Rutherford came into the room and was astonished to see Jenny sobbing on the bed. Due to financial circumstances, Frances had taken the position of Governess when Jenny was ten. It was Frances who taught Jenny that it was no shame to work, and that there was nothing Jenny couldn't do if she put her mind to it. She was Jenny's inspiration, confidant and friend. When Jenny turned sixteen, Frances had become Jenny's personal maid. It was either that or seek a new position, but Frances had not wanted to leave the Stockton employ. Frances was ten years, Jenny's senior, but the age difference was negligible. She rushed over and sat beside her. "Jenny, Jenny what on earth has happened?"

"Oh, Frances, I am so miserable," she said, tears streaming down her cheeks. "Father is forcing me to marry William Worthington! I can't stand him Frances, what on earth am I going to do? I want to leave, but I have no money. Where will I go? What will I do?" Jenny wrung her hands in despair.

"This is indeed a terrible situation Jenny, we must settle down and think and plan, I'll help you if I can."

Jenny stopped her crying and tried to get herself under control. Frances's calm behaviour had a steadying effect on her. "When is the wedding to take place?" Frances asked.

"I don't know," Jenny replied.

"Then let's hope we have some time. What to do? Hmm..," she said thoughtfully. "I have an idea, but it will take plenty of courage on your part," Frances stated.

"What is it? I'll do anything, Frances, anything!" Jenny said.

"You *will* have to play along with your father, like you have accepted the situation. We need to lull his fears and doubts. We can do nothing without money. I do get paid, and between us we will save all we can. Before the wedding date arrives we will leave Boston for parts unknown. You've always wanted to be a teacher, it would be a good start. You will need to study to take the test for a teaching certificate. Both of us have a lot of work to do," she said.

Time passed and her father was thrilled over Jennifer's apparent capitulation over the idea of marrying William. Her mother was worried, she didn't quite trust Jenny's new attitude. She would not put her position in jeopardy by defying her husband, even though she secretly sympathized with her daughter. A loveless marriage was not an easy one.

Jennifer was guilty at putting on an act for her father, but they needed money, so Jenny acted like she was looking forward to the wedding. All she needed to do was mention "wedding preparations" and her father gave her permission to get what she needed. Since any purchases were charged to the family account, she and Frances bought many items which Frances then took to the second hand emporium and resold for cash. Time was passing too quickly. It was coming up to the spring and her wedding had been announced for June. Jennifer was starting to panic, but Frances kept her on an even keel. Little by little their small horde grew.

Just as Jenny and Frances's plans were about to be implemented, her father announced that he and her mother were taking the train to New Orleans. It was an extremely important business trip. They would be back in two weeks, and then the final plans for the wedding could be completed.

Jenny was happy for the respite. She was conspiring with Frances to leave Boston as soon as possible while the parents were away when the Butler brought Jenny the telegram. The train that her parents had been travelling on had derailed. Many crew and passengers were killed, including Jenny's parents.

Jenny was shocked. She mourned her mother and felt guilt that she could not call deeper feelings toward her father. This puzzled and worried Jenny: her reaction to the death of the aged gardener, who had been like a father to her had devastated her two years previously. Frances tried to put Jenny's feelings into perspective. She had barely known her true parents. Until she had turned sixteen she had rarely seen them. After that she associated mostly with her mother. Her father had only recently dipped into Jenny's life when suitors for her hand in marriage began to come around. Still Jenny felt horrible about the deception she had been playing on them. Guilt left her depressed. She was not sure what to do with herself.

She threw herself into funeral preparations following the rituals of the day. She settled the affairs of her parents and learned she was the sole beneficiary to the estate. Although in deep mourning and wearing the traditional black she was incensed when her fiancé started to come to her home every day. He gave her advice constantly, possibly trying to get her to see his wisdom and superiority. He would look at the house and its contents with a possessive eye.

Finally Jenny had enough. The next day when the odious man came to the house to tell her what to do, she rose up to her full height and told him to leave, the engagement was at an end. Jenny was two inches taller than William. He started to rant about the contract that her Father had signed and that he had all rights over her. When he made the mistake of shoving the agreement in her face, she had grabbed it and threw it in the fire. Spluttering in rage, William Randolf Worthington struck her. It was hard to say who was most shocked, Jenny or William. He blanched.

Furious, Jenny called the butler and with the help of the cook and gardener, who happened to be in the house at that moment, physically removed the frantic man out of the house. He had been counting on this marriage to make his fortune. Of course the marriage would have had to be postponed for a year, but he was still counting on the cash inflow. In the coming weeks, rumors spread, no doubt started by William that she was crazy and tried to have him killed. How much society really paid attention to this is hard to say.

Convention required a period of mourning. The time passed slowly for Jenny. She would visit her parents' grave every Sunday after church, always bringing flowers. In spite of not really knowing her parents, she was left with a deep rift in her soul. She felt extreme guilt over the deception she had played out.

As the year of mourning finished, she began to get invited to various parties and fetes. Young men started to try and wiggle their way back into her life. Undeterred, suitors seemed to crawl out of the woodwork renewing their acquaintance with her, or making sure they were introduced to her. It was pathetically obvious that her wealth had become a magnet for every single male in Boston and not a few married ones. She rejected everyone firmly. She stopped going to these entertainments. Envious women labelled her as "on the shelf" according to society, she was now an old maid. They would, snicker and whisper behind her back. It hurt her a bit, when she heard one newlywed say to another, "Three times a Bridesmaid, never a bride," and then laughed.

Stung Jenny snapped. "I would rather remain single and happy, than be sold to the highest bidder like you!" She walked away head held high.

The shocked girls watched her leave, their mouth's agape, while they digested what Jenny had said. Her former shallow friends grew cold to her, but Jenny ignored them.

Jenny was determined to leave Boston, she didn't really care where she went, she just needed to go. That following fall she and Frances took a short holiday to New York, and while she was there sat for the examinations to get her teaching certificate. She passed easily and enrolled in a short course for new teachers, on how to handle and discipline students and learned the current curriculum.

Once that precious piece of paper was in her hands, she returned to her home. Jenny knew she wanted to put her education to good use. Smiling to herself, Jenny thought how scandalized her society acquaintances would have been, if they heard of her decision to answer a small advertisement in the Boston Gazette.

WANTED
Teachers for Small Country Schools.
Must have a Teaching Certificate
Apply to Montana Board of Education

She wrote to the Board of Education by sending a letter in care of the Gazette. She was thrilled when she was accepted to teach in the tiny community of Water Valley, Montana.

The conditions were certain to be primitive to what she was used to in Boston, but she had always loved a challenge. With her final decision made, Jenny's first priority was to sit down with her long time servant friends. They had always shown her the love and dedication that made her what she was. Most of the retainers were elderly, and her generosity extended to making sure they had a place to live and an adequate pension for their retirement. In her heart these folks were her family. Younger staff members were helped to find new positions.

Her hardest decision was what to do for her friend. Jenny wanted Frances to come with her, but it was Frances who told her she needed to spread her wings, be by herself for a bit. So it was with great reluctance then that Frances took the position of a companion to a feisty Octogenarian lady. It was an easy position that paid well. The two of them vowed to keep in touch by letter. If Jenny ever married and had children, Frances would drop everything and come to work for her again. Jenny laughed and thought that might be a very good idea, but not something she thought was in the cards. They hugged each other hard, sweeping tears of sadness away at their goodbyes.

The house itself and all the furniture had meant little to her so she sold them keeping only a few mementos of her previous life. From now on things would be very different. Jenny was burning the bridges to her past life, revelling in her independence. She was determined to rely only on herself and on her knowledge to cope with whatever life dealt her.

The trip so far had been interminable. The train cars were often suffocating in the extreme heat of the day and cold of night. Billows of dust surrounded the travellers. At times she had a hard time seeing the far end of the rail car clearly for the dust in the air. She never felt so filthy. Meals in the dining car were mediocre at the best of times. The noise of the train combined with the shrieking of fussy children and often having to share her seat with unsavoury persons, had made her outlook on travel rather dismal. The sleeping car with narrow bunks was not too bad if one didn't count the lack of privacy.

Jenny had dozed off, and was roused by a gentle voice. She looked up and saw an old man, with two long braids of hair, silvering with age, staring questioningly at her. "Excuse me sir, but did you say something?" she asked groggily.

The elderly man smiled and repeated his question. "May I share your seat, ma'am?" He asked.

"Certainly you may", Jenny said, removing her hat from the adjoining seat. She observed the man as he made himself comfortable. His leather clothing was stained with age, giving off a rather pungent but not unpleasant odour. The delicate beadwork around the collar fascinated Jenny. It was Indian in design but the man was obviously white.

"What beautiful beadwork," she said admiringly, "such intricate detail."

The man smiled, "My wife made this for me to celebrate the occasion of my daughter's wedding. She was a Sioux Indian maiden, and I lived with them many, many years. She passed away two years ago," he said sadly. "It took her a year to make this outfit. I only wear it for very special occasions. This trip is one of them. I travel now to see my new great granddaughter," he said proudly. "It's a rare treat to travel by train, and I'm looking forward to seeing my family."

They passed the time by talking of the old days. He was a hunter and trapper, and a wonderful storyteller. His way of life was fast disappearing and as they crossed the plains, he spoke to her of the buffalo that used to roam across the land like a living dark brown carpet. He spoke of the horror for his Indian friends as they were forced to give up their land and freedom, to live on reservations.

"The buffalo are all gone now and with them went the Indian people's way of life. However their free spirit will always remain," he said with his face wrinkled in sadness.

Throwing off his melancholy mood, he pointed out a small herd of pronghorn grazing near the train. The noise of the chugging engine didn't seem to bother them. A couple of young ones did buck and jump, racing away at incredible speeds. They circled around, and came back to the adults. They both laughed at the youngsters exuberant antics. Jenny enjoyed her time with him and she was sad when he reached his destination. She wished him Godspeed on his journey.

Jenny sighed and looked through the window. Outside the flatlands had given way to the larger foothills. More and more trees were dotting the hillsides. Pines and Poplar were now visible. The terrain was climbing and the day time temperature dropping a little.

"What a blessing!" she thought. The odd deer fled the noise of the train and once she saw a coyote looking for his supper. She found herself attracted to this beautiful unspoiled country. There was something satisfying about seeing land untouched by human hands.

Jenny looked down at her handbag. Opening it, she saw the letter that had changed her life right on top.

January 15, 1896
Dear Miss Stockton:

It is with great pleasure that we inform you, of your acceptance as the new school teacher for the community of Water Valley, located in the State of Montana. This school is expecting an enrolment of fifteen to twenty students in varying grades ranging from one to nine. As it is a new district the school has few resources in the way of books or equipment. The people in Water Valley want to be guided by you and what you require for the school.

You will report to the Mayor of Big Rock, no later than September 1st of this current year. He will give you further information and directions to your final destination. It is my understanding that a small house has been provided for your use next to the school. We hope that you will enjoy working for our Department. I will attempt to visit your school at least once in the coming year and look forward to meeting you in person at that time. If you have any problems, please do not hesitate to contact me.

Sincerely,

Ben Moss

Superintendent

Montana Board of Education

It was much the worse for wear from frequent reading. The severely creased letter was burned into her memory anyway. She carefully refolded the dog-eared letter putting it back in her handbag.

Jenny sighed, Big Rock was the train's final destination and the terminus of the railway line. According to the conductor they would arrive in a couple of hours. She looked down at her dark green traveling cloak and her light green gloves. She saw how soiled they were and noticed their mangled look.

"I must be more nervous than I thought," she grimaced. She had unconsciously been twisting them between her fingers. Her hat, a jaunty little item in forest green with a spray of light green feathers, lay on the seat beside her. It too had a coating of dust on it. A quick look around showed her that everyone else in the car was in a similar condition. When she looked out the window, a huge dust devil whirled its way across the land. It was unusually dry out west.

Jenny was glad that she would have a chance to get herself cleaned up before taking the last part of her journey to Water Valley. She patted her deep auburn hair and wrinkled her nose. Her petite heart shaped face had a dusting of freckles that were her bane in life. Her lovely green eyes had attracted the young porter, and she had taken advantage of his interest by questioning him about her ultimate destination, Water Valley.

"Well, uh…I don't rightly know Ma'am! Uh, I never been past Big Rock." The flushed young man said. "I only travel the rails, so what I heard be just hearsay. Those folk said there be a new town by the name of Water Valley a growin' west of Big Rock. Round thirty miles accordin' to them!" he ruminated.

There was no public transportation, so she would have to rent a wagon and driver to take her there. It was late summer, and she had just a few weeks before her first classes were due to start. She wanted to be able to get settled, and accustomed to the area before the start of the school year.

Chapter 2

At long last the train came to a halt with screeching wheels and burst of steam. Jenny gathered her personal items together and along with the other travel worn people made her way to the exit. A cacophony of sound assaulted her ears as she stepped down onto the wooden platform. The shouts of men were heard over bawling cattle. Startled, she looked to her left just beyond the station and saw what seemed to be hundreds of milling long-horned steers being herded into the corrals. Clouds of dust hung in the air as the cowboys whistled, chirped and yelled at the stubborn beasts. She noticed several well-dressed men gathering on the other side of the station. They were the buyers, sent from the city to purchase cattle to feed the multitudes of residents that could not produce their own. The cattle would be loaded onto special livestock cars, which stood waiting on a second set of tracks.

Jenny started to cross the platform to the ticket window of the stationhouse. A burst of hot steam escaped from the train's engine. She involuntarily jumped. The noise out here was worse than inside the train if that were even possible.

"I much too tired," she thought to herself, "My nerves are frazzled." She needed to ask directions to the boarding house she previously arranged to stay at. Jenny moved toward the ticket masters window. In spite of all this chaos, she could not help but notice the tall dust covered man chatting with the ticket master.

His clothes were the well-worn leathers of a cowboy. She noted his rugged appearance and appraising eyes, as he caught sight of her approaching. He stood aside, letting her address the ticket master. A little self-consciously Jenny found her self practically shouting to be heard over the din. When he caught the gist of her question, the cowboy volunteered to take her to the boarding house. She was startled at his open friendliness, a true mark of the west. In the east a man would not presume to address a lady before being introduced. The stationmaster interceded by performing the introduction.

"This here is James Borland, Ma'am. A bit forward perhaps, but a good enough fellow. He's the owner of all those cattle yonder," he said.

James grinned and swept off his battered hat revealing dark blonde hair damp with perspiration. A scar marred his face just above the eyebrow but vivid blue eyes sparkling mischievously far over-shadowed this flaw. His grin was a bit lopsided, but was completely genuine.

Jenny hesitated, looking dubiously at him. He certainly was different in appearance from the men back in Boston. His grin widened, his eyes grew challenging. This forwardness was not something Jenny was used too. Yet in a way James attitude was refreshing from the wishy-washy ways of Boston males. First meetings between men and ladies were always under the strict eyes of a chaperone.

Seeing her hesitation James apologized. "I'm sorry Ma'am, I didn't mean to butt in, but this town is quite large and has many side streets.   It can be confusing to a new arrival," he said persuasively.

Jenny slowly nodded agreement yet remained rather apprehensive. She was alarmed at his boldness. When she decided to accept the escort of a man without supervision, her heart fluttered a bit. She found herself inexplicably attracted to this stranger.

"Would you mind waiting a couple of minutes while I give instructions to my men before we go?" James inquired.

She acquiesced, as she had to arrange for her trunks to be stored at the station anyway. Everything she needed for the night was already in her oversized carpetbag. Jenny was just completing these details when the man returned. She noticed out of the corner of her eye James's long, firm stride. Here was a man who looked in control of any situation. Picking up her bag, he politely gestured for her to precede him toward the street. As they crossed, puffs of dust rose up around them. He moved along side her so he could engage her in conversation.

"I know Mrs. Shouldice's Boarding House well," he stated. "She's a good friend of mine, runs a very clean place. And..." he continued, rolling his eyes a little in memory of some culinary delight, "she serves the most delicious food you will ever taste!"

"That sounds just fine," she replied. Jenny was unaccountably shy for some reason and she found herself rather tongue-tied.

James did not seem to notice her lack of conversation as they moved quickly to the boardwalk. They passed a couple of hotels along the way. Each had a saloon attached and although it was fairly quiet at the moment, Jenny shuddered at the idea of what it was probably like in the evening. It would have noisy drunken rowdy men, intermixing guffaws, with the shrill laughs of loose women and loud music. Even now the scent of alcohol, sour sweat and overpowering perfume wafted out of the open doors. Jenny wrinkled her nose in distaste. She was very glad she was not staying at one of these establishments.

They turned around the corner onto a side street. The noise of the busy town centre died away and Jenny sighed in relief. Passing several cottages, they came to a lovely yard. They entered, and Jenny admired the oak trees that shaded the huge house. They crossed a large veranda and with a perfunctory knock, he opened the front door.

"Dora! I have your new boarder here," he called out.

The woman that came from the back of the house had a blue kerchief over her dark brown hair. Her red gingham dress had a white apron sprinkled with flour.

"Oh hello, James" she said as she glanced appraisingly at Jenny. A warm welcoming smile crossed her face.

"You must be Miss Stockton?" she asked, and at Jenny's nod, she continued. "I have a room all prepared for you, I heard the train arrive so I had my helper Tommy Spinks heat enough water for a bath. I know what train trips are like. Do follow me."

Throwing a thank-you smile James way, Dora turned and started up the nearby stairs.

Turning quickly, Jenny smiled and softly said," Thank you Mr Borland, you have been most kind." With that she turned and followed Mrs Shouldice up the stairwell. James stood at the foot of the stairs, staring up after her. There was a rather vapid grin on his face.

At the top of the stairs, Jenny noticed a long hall with several doorways at intervals along it. There looked to be another staircase at the back of the building.

She showed Jenny the tiny but neat room. The bed took up most of the space. A dressing table and wardrobe stood against one wall. Dora also led her to the back staircase and told her the bathing room was at the bottom to her right. The back door revealed a path to a treed area. That was where the outhouses were situated.

"Shall I have Tommy fill up the tub with the hot water in a few minutes?" She asked.

Jenny smiled gratefully, "That would be lovely, Mrs. Shouldice. I look forward to feeling clean again. May I be so bold as to ask your advice in finding someone to take me out to Water Valley? I have several trunks," she said.

"Oh most certainly, Miss Stockton. Do call me Dora. How did you come upon young James, and why Water Valley, if I am not being too nosey?" she asked curiously.

"Call me Jenny please. James was talking to the Station Master, and volunteered to escort me here when I asked directions. As for your second question," she said smiling, "I am the new teacher in Water Valley." Jenny was soon to find out that Dora rarely stopped talking.

"Oh Water Valley, how wonderful! It's a very new community situated in the most gorgeous valley. It is quite a distance between towns here, and I believe James and his family decided to start a small village so folks didn't need to travel so far for supplies. There are many families in that area and a school teacher was one of James's ideas." Dora rambled on. "Most of your students will have folks that work for him, or at least know him because he is the owner of the Rocking B ranch," she stated. "I haven't been out there myself, but I heard that he and his men built the schoolhouse and a teacher's cabin as well. Oh and please don't mind me, everyone says my mouth runs on wheels," Dora grinned engagingly.

Dora's soft brown eyes twinkled as she asked, "Does James know you are the new school teacher?"

"No, the subject never came up," Jenny said. Jenny smiled at Dora, but her heart was giving funny little leaps. "That is indeed interesting. What a coincidence," she mused to herself.

Jenny's face must have showed her intrigue, because the grin widened on Dora's face. She excused herself and left Jenny with a parting thought.

"You'll see him again at supper, as he always stays here when he is in town. Supper is at six o'clock and I'm sure you won't be late," Dora laughed, for she was an incurable romantic at heart and a born matchmaker. She closed the door leaving Jenny to herself.

Jenny sat on the bed and willed her fast beating heart to behave itself. She smiled a little at her reaction. "He really is handsome in a rugged way and so tall!" she told herself. Jenny herself was five foot six and he had towered over her.

With that, Jenny put her few belongings away and when Tommy let her know that the bathtub was ready, she took some clean clothing and descended the stairs to the bathing room. She noted the immaculate little room with ceramic tub. Towels were laid out on a chair. Jenny set aside her dirty clothing and stepped into the hot water. She soaked in it, revelling in the luxury of being clean again. She made herself at home and spent time on her appearance. She returned to her room, and noted that was only an hour until supper. She very much wanted to be on time. She wore a bronze colored dress, with a cream collar and pearl buttons down the front.

At five minutes to six, there was a soft tap at her door. A young girl's voice said "Supper is ready ma'am."

"I'll be right there," Jenny acknowledged. She took one last look in the mirror, smoothed her hair and left the room.

At supper Jenny enjoyed meeting the other lodgers, but her natural outgoing personality was a bit curtailed. The presence of one young man made her uncharacteristically nervous. She remained fairly quiet while the other three ladies and six men bantered and chatted away with the ease of good friends. Jenny found herself glancing sideways at James, because he was at the opposite end of the table. She would invariably blush when she found him looking right back. He laughed and joked with the rest of them and Jenny was impressed by his pleasant voice and friendly attitude.

After the delicious meal was finished, the guests sauntered either to the sitting area or the veranda while Tommy Spinks and Greta Lund, Dora's employees cleared the table and cleaned up. Some of the guests played quiet games or chatted amicably with each other. James hesitantly approached Jenny. Willing herself to remain calm, she smiled at him. Gesturing for her to take a seat in a comfortable chair, he sat down near her. Another couple joined them and they all talked about interesting happenings in and around Big Rock. All of them were curious about Jenny of course, but she was reticent regarding talking about herself. A couple of hours passed with general pleasantries. The guests began to retire as most of them worked early the next morning.

Jenny too rose and bid everyone a good night. She was looking forward to laying in a bed that didn't move for a change. James stood and wished her pleasant dreams and escorted her to the stairwell. He watched her ascend the stairs with admiration. In her room, Jenny vainly tried to read, but found herself daydreaming about the blue-eyed man. After attempting the same page five times she gave up and prepared for bed. She scolded herself severely, not willing to admit she was definitely smitten with a total stranger. With that she closed her eyes and willed herself to sleep.

Chapter 3

The next morning she ate breakfast with Dora, as the other boarders had already left for their places of work. Jenny apologized to her for being tardy, she was not usually a late sleeper. Jenny had donned an attractive apricot walking dress as she had some errands to run in the town.

Dora smiled and said, "I know you were tired from your train ride and I don't mind the company at breakfast. I'm always too busy serving the others to sit down and eat breakfast myself until later."

Jenny found herself vaguely disappointed to find that all of the tenants were gone. She had secretly hoped to see James again. Dora told her that James had left early that morning for the ranch.

Dora explained the layout of the town, admitting to her that the nicest time to shop was morning as it would probably get very hot by afternoon. She also told Jenny to buy everything she would need or wanted here in Big Rock, as the General Store in Water Valley carried mainly basic necessities.

She suggested seeing John Frost at the livery stable. He would find a trustworthy man to drive her to Water Valley. Dora also told her where to find the town offices and the Mayor, Dan Rowley.

Jenny left the boarding house for Main Street, stopping to admire Mrs Shouldice's flower garden. It was a beautiful sunny day and already the temperature outside was rising rapidly. There was no wind at the moment, so the only dust rising was the small puffs being kicked up by horses or men walking in the street. The boardwalk she was on had been swept clean. Shop proprietors did this ritually every morning. She decided to see the Mayor first making her way along the smooth weathered boards toward a tree covered park in the centre of town. Crossing it she approached a two-story building that held the Sheriff's office and the town hall. According to a small sign beside a staircase, she realized that a Dr. David Foster M.D. resided upstairs on the second floor. She chose the door to the Town's Office and entered. A young man greeted her from a paper-cluttered desk. She introduced herself and he promptly got up and tapped on the inner office door. A voice answered from the other side and the clerk ushered her into Mr. Rowley's Office. The young man then retreated to his own office, quietly closing the door.

Mayor Daniel Rowley was a portly man of medium height. He stood until Jenny was seated in a chair facing his desk. Seating himself he observed her for a moment, then smiled. He welcomed her to the town and proceeded to tell her about her new duties. He also asked her about getting supplies in for the school. "What will you require?" he asked kindly.

Jenny said, "I have taken the liberty of purchasing many things the new school will need. I have brought books, slates, and other items. More than half of my luggage coming here is school supplies," she said candidly.

"My goodness," he said. "I am impressed by your initiative in bringing supplies with you!"

She smiled in return at his amazement and told him, "After reading the letter from the School Superintendent, I only did what needed to be done. Much time would be wasted if I waited until getting here before ordering supplies. It would take precious time in arriving. Time that is better spent on studies."

Mr. Rowley smiled at her evident enthusiasm. "Supplies can be ordered anytime through Ray Brown, the Water Valley General Store proprietor. Give it a few weeks, as they will have to come in from Butte. A school account has been set up at the store as well for simple items. I hope you'll drop by whenever you visit Big Rock, to tell us how you're doing. You can leave an accounting letter for your purchases with the clerk outside, you will be reimbursed very shortly."

She nodded and said, "Thank-you Mr Rowley, you have been very hospitable." Rising from her chair, she accepted his escort to the door. She found her account paper and gave it to the clerk.

Daniel Rowley said, "I do wish you all the best with your new position, I've heard nothing but good about the community you're going to. If you need any assistance please do not hesitate to call on me. Your key to the new school and your home is with Ray Brown, the proprietor of the Water Valley General Store. He will see to your getting settled there. Good bye Miss Stockton and good luck to you."

She left the Office, unaware that both men were watching her walk gracefully away with very appreciative looks on their faces. The Mayor mused out loud, "I wish I had a teacher that looked like that when I went to school." They then glanced at one another, grinned sheepishly and scuttled back to their work.

Mr. Frost the liveryman was next on Jenny's agenda. When she arrived at the stables, her keen eye noticed the cleanliness of the barn. The straw bedding under the animals was fresh and the horses had healthy, shiny coats. Two small boys were busy carting out soiled straw under the supervision of a short gaunt little man. His hair gleamed silver, when a shaft of sunlight from the barn window illuminated his head. His face was weathered, and his clothes were faded from frequent washing. He came right over to Jenny as soon as he noticed her arrival.

"Good morning! My name is Jennifer Stockton, the new teacher for Water Valley. Dora Shouldice recommended your establishment. She was sure you could help me," she said with a smile.

He beamed with pride. "I'll certainly try, Miss Stockton. What can I do for you?"

Jenny thought for a second. As today was Thursday, an early start the next day would be best, so she asked him "Can you find me a reliable driver to take my trunks and myself to Water Valley tomorrow morning?"

John's nod was assuring, "I have a good fellow in mind. He's strong enough to help you with the heavy trunks. Benny York is a good horseman and he'll get you safely to your destination. He is an excellent worker." John seemed over anxious to expound on Benny's virtues. He explained. "Ma'am, Benny is a little slow. He was thrown from a horse when he was a youngster. He is very trustworthy though," John said hopefully.

Jenny smiled. "If you trust him, I'm sure we will get along just fine. Thank you, I would like to leave around seven o'clock tomorrow morning. Can you have Benny retrieve the trunks from the train station and pick me up at the boarding house when he is ready to leave? I will be prepared with lunch for the trip as it will take all day. Is that correct?"

Mr Frost nodded, "Yes, with the heavily loaded wagon, it will likely be evening before you get there. Lunch would be appreciated, but Benny will bunk with the livery man in Water Valley so you needn't worry about him."

Assured that everything would go as planned, Jenny left with a light mind. She was excited and looking forward to this new adventure. A corner of her heart leapt a little knowing she would most likely see James again. After all if he lived in the area, built the school and cottage, he was bound to come for a visit. Wouldn't he?

After learning that there was no bank in Water Valley, Jenny visited the one in Big Rock. She asked to speak to the manager, Jackson Troy. She was ushered into the office of a grey haired, gentleman in a business suit. He stood up when she entered, and waited until she was seated. Jackson looked at the cut of her dress and easy manner, and decided to await her wishes before passing judgement on whether this woman was worth his valuable time. He was a hard man, refusing many people loans and this lady would be no different... however her hat had a rather expensive look to it. He looked at her dubiously.

"I would like to open an account," Jenny said coldly. She had seen his dismissive look. She vowed she would be at her most officious. Just because she was a woman, there was no reason for him to look at her in that manner.

Jackson looked at her and said. "If that was all, you could have seen one of our bank tellers..."

Jenny never waited for him to finish but she stood up and said "Well if that is your attitude, I will take my account to a bank in Butte. Good day, sir." Then she added in extreme annoyance. "In fact it would please me to start up my own bank in competition with yours. I may just do that, and for your arrogant information, I could well afford to do so!" Jenny exclaimed. She strode toward the door. Jackson realizing in his jumping to conclusions may have just lost him a client.

Apologizing, he rushed around his desk to detain her before she got to the door. "Please, ma'am, I am truly sorry, please come back and I will be happy to take care of your account myself," the man grovelled. "Please do not go."

Jenny observed Troy with distaste. Dealing with this man made her feel dirty. However as much as Jenny disliked the man, she didn't want to go to Butte for her banking. She liked Big Rock in general, and decided to let the begging man talk her into staying. "I *will* make him sweat for a few minutes though," she said to herself.

Pretending anger and snobbishness, soon tired her, and she allowed the man to hold her chair as she was re-seated.

The thankful Manager was visibly perspiring as he took out the necessary paperwork to open an account. When Jenny handed him the draft from her Boston bank, the man visibly whitened. He handled Jenny like she was made of gold from that point on. This woman's wealth rivalled some of his largest ranching clients. She had not been joking about starting up a rival bank. She had the financial backing to do it.

Jenny arranged for him to contact her accountant for any future communications. With all the arrangements made, she thankfully left the humbled man and his officious local bank. He was the first person in the west that she found easy to dislike.

Her duties done, she spent a couple of hours browsing around the various shops, getting to know the people and the types of goods they offered. She enjoyed herself tremendously, especially at the Dress Maker's. Jean Drummond took her measurements for future purchases. Jenny was overjoyed to find that Big Rock had a good seamstress. She was capable of making her own dresses but she much preferred to have an expert make them. She also met Jean's business partner Samantha Riggs who designed the most intriguing hats and accessories.

Jenny stopped at the telegraph office and sent a telegram to Frances, telling her that she had safely arrived at Big Rock. She was missing her friend and mentor. "One day I'll get Frances out here. Maybe as my companion." She grinned at the thought. "We can be old maids, together," Jenny laughed.

The heat of the day was increasing as she sauntered back to the boarding house for lunch. She was the only person there so Dora joined her. They sat on the shaded veranda, eating sandwiches and sipping cold drinks. All too soon Dora would have to start on supper. Jenny found that she was drawn to Dora and that they were becoming good friends.

She asked, "Dora, can I get a large packed lunch for tomorrows travel? Benny is going to take me to Water Valley in the morning."

"Of course," Dora said. "I'm sorry you're leaving so soon, but I know I'll see you again at least a couple of times before snow and avalanches close the road between us." Then Dora laughed. "If Benny is driving you it had better be an extra large lunch. I'll have it ready tomorrow morning."

After supper Jenny retired early, with Dora's assurances that she would be awakened in plenty of time to meet with Benny. Jenny had a hard time getting to sleep because of her excitement over the last stage of her journey to her new home. She started to recite poetry, until her body relaxed, and she drifted into a dreamless sleep.

Friday morning Dora awakened Jenny. It was just getting light outside as the sun was just peaking over the horizon. The clouds were a mass of pink and golds. It was spectacular. Dora began to make breakfast for her tenants. Jenny yawned and stretched. She hurried outside to use the facilities. It was a little chilly this morning, so she didn't delay in returning to the house. Nights were starting to get cool. It was a hint that winter was not far off. She swiftly got herself washed and dressed. She packed her things and looked around to make sure she didn't leave anything behind. Taking her carpetbag downstairs, she placed it on the veranda out of the way.

She heard the early morning greetings of sleepy tenants, as they descended to breakfast. Sitting down at the table, the boarders greeted Jenny cheerfully. Dora had made stacks of pancakes, sausages and bacon. Plenty of coffee assured that all would be wide awake in no time. The food as usual was delicious and Jenny ate her fair share. Her elite acquaintances in Boston would be scandalized if they saw her devour food in such a manner. Jenny grinned at the thought.

After breakfast, most of the tenants left for work. Dora gave Jenny a huge picnic basket. It was so heavy; that Jenny laughed, "There must be enough food for twenty people in it."

Dora returned her laughter, "Well feeding Benny is like having twenty people with you. Next time you come to town you can return the basket," she said with a smile.

"Thank you Dora, you've been most kind to me. You have become my first friend in the west!" Jenny spontaneously hugged her. Dora's eyes registered surprise and then filled with unexpected tears. She wordlessly returned the hug.

Jenny continued, "I probably will be back soon because I will invariably forget something I'll need." Jenny glanced at the time on the huge grandfather clock that stood in Dora's Parlour. It was ten minutes to seven o'clock and she already heard the horses and wagon coming to a halt in front of the house.

A minute later, Dora answered the knock on the door. "Good morning, Benny," she said. Turning, she beckoned Jenny. "This is Miss Stockton. Now I want you to take good care of her, Benny!" she exclaimed.

"Ah, Miss Dora, you know I will!" Benny replied, his face turning an interesting shade of red. He was a huge, bear-like man, with a tattered hat that he twisted in his huge hands.

Dora grinned and relented, "There is her bag, Benny, and you better take this picnic basket too." Turning she gave Jenny a spontaneous hug. "You take care, Jenny, and return to see me soon."

"I will Dora, thank-you again for being so kind to me," Jenny said, and followed Benny to the wagon. Her trunks were all there: three on the bottom, two stacked on top. Ropes tied them on for safety. Jenny awkwardly scrambled up on the seat and Benny climbed up beside her.

Taking up the reins, Benny slapped them down lightly on the horse's backs and they started off. Jenny turned and waved at

Dora. Dora waved back, watching until the wagon turned the corner before retreating into the house.

Benny drove carefully along the street, but once out on the road he urged the horses to a faster walk. "This is going to be a dusty trip," Jenny thought.

Dick and Dan, the horses, kicked up clouds of dust as their hoofs shuffled along the road. Jenny sneezed. She had worn a lightweight grey cloak to protect her dress from becoming soiled. She tried to make light conversation with Benny, but he seemed to be very nervous when talking to her.

Rarely had any woman ever talked to him, and certainly never one this pretty. He was embarrassed that his replies were short and accompanied by stuttering and blushing. Whenever he did speak Jenny noticed Benny's discomfort and decided to limit her conversation with him. She did not want to cause him further embarrassment. Instead she looked around at the scenery and admired the horses. Dick was a sorrel, with a white blaze on his face, and a white right foreleg. Dan on the other hand was a bay, with a black mane and tail. He too had a blaze, but no other white, on his body. They kept up a steady fast walk while the road was level, but slowed down on the hills. She knew her trunks were heavy and she felt sorry for them.

They had to cross several streams. There were no bridges so the horses splashed across. Jenny had no idea if it was the same stream or a totally different one. There were many cliffs and valleys and the wagon was climbing steadily into the foothills. She saw some rather spectacular waterfalls. As the day progressed the sun's heat started to make them uncomfortable. The mist from these waterfalls became very welcome. In the higher elevations, Jenny noticed that bushes and scrub brush along the creek were already putting on their autumn colors. There were varying shades of red, pink, gold, and yellow. It was an awesome sight. Being a city bred girl, Jenny thought that this was the prettiest country she had ever seen. Deep forest greens of the spruces, the lighter greens of the pines and cedars contrasted with the crowning glory of the various deciduous trees. Birch, poplars, oak and maple, caused Jenny to catch her breath in wonder. What a change this was from what she was used to.

"Right now I could yell my head off and with the exception of Benny, know that no one would hear me." Her heart soared with wonderful feeling of freedom. "All of this is a bit overwhelming though," she thought. "Can one be too alone?" She could not remember a time in her life when she was not surrounded by people. Jenny wondered what her new community would be like. "Will they accept me as their new teacher?" Jenny's biggest fear caused her to shiver. "I know that ninty-nine percent of the teachers in America are men. What if Water Valley is expecting a man and they don't like me?" Jenny spent several more miles trying to calm her fears.

Benny was a conscientious driver, and stopped the horses frequently for a rest. Jenny memorized their route, although it was scarcely necessary as they came across very few turnoffs. In some places the road narrowed dangerously with terrifying drop offs. Cliffs on one side, plunging rocky gorges on the other. The gorges were almost without exception full of rushing white water. There was barely enough room for the wagon. Jenny convulsively held onto the seat railing. Her heart remained in her throat until the narrow passage was passed.

Jenny looked ahead and saw a huge mountain. It still seemed quite a ways away. Benny when questioned said that Water Valley was at the foot of that mountain.

Most of the trip was accomplished in silence. They stopped where a stream and the road converged. There was a small grassy meadow that seemed perfect for having their picnic. The hot sun beat down unmercifully but was negated by a huge oak tree right next to the road. Benny first looked to the horses, unhitching them so they could graze or drink water as they pleased. He put a set of hobbles on their front feet and removed the bits so they were comfortable.

Jenny was also glad for the break because she was becoming very sore from the bouncing on the hard wooden seat. The buckboard didn't have any springs so she felt every bump. Dora had packed fried chicken, much to Benny's delight. He enthusiastically worked himself through the generous meal. Water to wash the lunch down was retrieved from the pure clear stream, which tumbled down from the nearby mountain range. To both Benny and Jenny's delight, chocolate cake had been placed in a special wood box to keep it from getting too crushed. It was a heavenly way to end a meal.

They delayed an hour to let the horses rest. Benny re-hitched the refreshed team to the wagon and they carried on. The hills grew higher the closer to the mountain they got. It was nearing evening when the road again was crossing between two high cliffs, Jenny thought they must be at least one hundred feet high. The road was near the bottom of the canyon, and the rapid stream paralleled the narrow trail. Jenny closed her eyes, terrified that they would careen into the water. Benny volunteered the information, that this stretch of road was known simply as "The Pass".

The "Pass" proved to be worst part of the trip for Jenny. She found that the end of the canyon opened up into a wide gorgeous valley. The mountain she had seen from the distance towered to her right. The valley was enclosed by a second mountain to the west and a tree covered hill to her left. The sun was touching the horizon, showing off the valley to perfection. Jenny could see the sparkle of a river near the bottom. They then followed the rushing stream on down into the valley. When they arrived in the tiny village, Benny pulled up beside the General Store and Jenny got down to talk to the couple that came out to greet them.

Jenny smiled. "I am Jennifer Stockton, your new school teacher," she said to the delighted couple.

"And I am Janet Brown, and this here is my husband Ray." Janet said. Ray Brown was a short plump, balding man. His wide friendly grin lacked any guile. Jenny was instinctively drawn to him. Her immediate reaction was to trust him. No doubt he was secure in his own business, leaving Jenny with the impression that he would be easy to talk to by anyone in the valley. Janet too, gave Jenny the idea that she was very self confident. Physically she was Rays exact opposite being tall, thin, with a wealth of black hair tied severely into a bun. Both of them gave her a friendly smile.

"Welcome to Water Valley!" they said in unison.

"Thank-you," Jenny said as she straightened her wrinkled cloak. Before she could continue Jenny had another greeter, a huge black and white dog that had the look of a Collie mix. He came racing up the street to inspect her. Jenny stood perfectly still while the dog with hackles raised looked her over very carefully. Jenny held her hand out to be sniffed and the hackles lowered and the tail began to wag. Jenny breathed a sigh of relief.

"I believe I have just been welcomed formally into this community," Jenny said.

Ray and Janet laughed in delight, "This is 'Mayor'," Ray said. "He kind of belongs to everyone but lives with Joe Walters down the street. The name suits him because there is not much happening in town that this dog doesn't know about. He leaves the community feeling fairly safe for he lets the town know when something is amiss. Wild animals are greeted with barks and strangers are always observed until he either approves or disapproves of them. If there is a threat, his barking alerts the towns' folk of the trouble and it gets taken care of. Mayor knows everyone that belongs here and who doesn't."

Janet asked Ray to get the keys to Jenny's house and school. While he was doing her bidding Janet explained the need for locking the buildings up. "It is necessary to lock up in this little town, not because of the residents, but because we are the only town between Big Rock and Butte. Big Rock is fairly decent, but Butte is a transient town and fairly wild. Travellers often stop here for the night. Normally they bunk down at the mill, but any of us could come out and find someone sleeping in any unlocked building.

Jenny nodded in understanding. "I heard that people rarely locked their doors in the country. People usually have respect for other folk's properties.

"That is true too, in most cases. I am afraid we are the exception." Janet said, turning toward her husband who was coming back outside with a couple of huge iron keys. He beckoned for Jenny to follow him, pointing out the side street for Benny, telling him to follow it. They would meet him in a minute. Jenny and Ray followed a tiny footpath beside the store to the property directly behind. They passed Ray and Janet's home which was attached to the store. They walked about a hundred feet, through a hedge finding themselves in front of the school. It had freshly white washed walls and the door was recessed into a tiny covered porch. Her first glance made her heart thump with pleasure. This was her school now.

Ray, Jenny and Mayor hurried to the door. One of the keys opened the door and Benny pulled up as close as he could with the team. Jenny went inside. It was warm and cheery, the setting sun glowed off the wood giving it a cozy look. Ten double desks were arranged in two rows facing the teachers' desk. Jenny stroked the shiny wood of the desks possessively. An iron stove stood in one corner, near the teacher's desk. A wood box next to the stove had birch firewood chopped and ready for use. A portable blackboard stood on the other side of her desk. There were three windows on either side of the room. Jenny loved it.

Jenny turned with a big smile to Ray, and said. "This is wonderful, what a beautiful school."

Ray beamed. Jenny then gave instructions for the two trunks of school supplies to be brought inside. Benny, with Ray's help did so.

Jenny's heart beat with excitement as they all turned their attention to her new home. A white picket fence marked the boundaries of her property. "It is so small," she thought. "They told me in the letter that this was a house, but it is just a cabin." She was a bit dismayed. They opened the gate and she did admire the flat rocks that had been placed carefully to create a stone sidewalk up to the front stoop. The veranda was one step up from the front yard with a sloping roof to keep the rain off of anyone coming to the door. The veranda was big enough to accommodate two chairs that beckoned invitingly. Ray opened the door for her and she stepped into what appeared to be a two-room cottage. Jenny spotted a lantern on the table. In spite of the two windows in the main room, the setting sun caused the interior to be somewhat dim. What she wouldn't give for some of those new electric lights that were fast becoming popular in Boston. Jenny knew it would probably be years before electricity became available in this remote area. Lantern light would have to do. Jenny examined the glass lantern. It had a pretty design on the bowl. There was a small metal lid covering the opening where coal oil could be poured in. There was a box of matches beside the lantern. She took the clear glass chimney off, noting that the wick had already been trimmed. She turned the knob that allowed the oil to saturate the wick. She struck a match and the resulting light allowed them all to see fairly well. Her new home glowed in the soft yellow light. She realized that she would have to have at least two more to give her adequate lighting. The sun had completely set now but the temperature outside was still warm.

The main room had a fireplace, with a modern wood cook stove. It was obviously new as the shiny black of the caste iron did not have even a scratch on it. The cream ceramic sides also shone. There were two chairs, made of birch wood facing the fireplace; they had leather cushions and back. Jenny did not know what stuffing the maker had used, but it looked soft and comfortable. There was a table also made of birch. The shape was rectangular with legs that were square on each corner. Someone had gone to a great deal of trouble to make the wood this smooth and shiny.

Benny and Ray had brought in her three trunks while she was looking around. Mayor remained on the veranda looking in on the excitement but knew he could not come in unless invited. Ray then started a fire in the stove. She was grateful, because she did not want to embarrass herself by trying to start it while the men were with her. She was proud and didn't want to be thought a greenhorn. The fireplace would not be needed until later in the fall, as the days and evening were still warm. Jenny was a little over whelmed and hoped she could pull off her deception.

"Someone has gone to a lot of work, in making this cottage nice," she said to Ray.

He replied, "Well James, the boss of the Borland Ranch wanted to make our new teacher at home in the village."

Janet arrived at the door. She held a lantern in one hand. "Miss Stockton, I have supper just about ready would you like to eat with us? You too Benny," She added.

Jenny's face lit up in thankfulness. "That is very kind of you Mrs. Brown, I would be very happy to join you for your supper. I have not had the chance see what supplies I have to make my own this evening. Benny and I ate every bit of the lunch that Dora Shouldice in Big Rock made for us. Also please call me Jenny."

Janet beamed, "I'm Janet to you Jenny and he's Ray." Everyone in the valley calls us that," she stated with a wide smile. "Why don't you explore your new home? Come over to our house in half an hour." Noticing that Ray had finished stoking the fire up in the stove she added, "Come on Ray, Benny, lets leave Jenny to do her exploring."

They left none too soon. Jenny emotions were pushing to the surface of her mind. Jenny felt awfully close to tears. She was exhausted from her trip, yet was happy to reach her destination. On impulse she invited Mayor to come in and the delighted dog came over to her for petting. She tried to sort out her feelings. True she hadn't known what to expect for a home here, but it did seem cozy and nice. It was very small, but when she really thought about it, the size was perfect. She was by herself, no servants' quarters or special rooms for privacy were needed. She decided it was really quite nice. In fact it was just right for her. Ray and Janet were so friendly, that it was a revelation to her. What a difference from Boston, where you were lucky to know anyone by first name, unless they were in the same social strata. Even then etiquette forbade you use it. If most of the people here were of the same mold as the Browns, she would be very happy indeed.

Jenny walked slowly around the room followed closely by Mayor. A kitchen hutch with counter, cupboards and drawers stood next to the stove. She looked in the various drawers and cupboards, finding all kinds of basic supplies ready and waiting for her use. Bins on the lower half of the hutch contained sugar (both white and brown), flour, dried beans and rice. There was also a table that had a large ceramic sink on one end. It had an interesting ceramic addition, angled slightly, that could be used to place clean wet dishes. Dripping water would flow easily back into the main part of the sink. Jenny had never seen anything like that before. The drain at the bottom of the main sink emptied into a tin pail placed precisely underneath. A blue linen cloth skirt hid the pail. As she touched the table she realized a master carpenter had made this furniture, with a loving hand.

Taking the lantern with her, she crossed the hardwood floor to what proved to be her new bedroom. The door was opened but could be closed to give her privacy. The same carpenter must have made the bed as well. It had a birch bark head and footboard. The frame she found out on inspection was iron. It was covered with a huge feather mattress. There were white linen sheets, a goose down pillow and wool blankets. A hand made colourful quilt, filled with goose feathers covered the bed. There was a washstand along the wall sporting a blue ceramic basin and matching pitcher. A wardrobe stood next to the window. It had two doors and a large drawer on the bottom. She looked dubiously at the size of it, hoping it was big enough for all her things. There were white muslin curtains covering the window. She noticed they had tiebacks, so they could be opened to let in the sun. Returning to the main room, Jenny went to the back door. Opening it, she was surprised to find another room. It was now quite dark, she was glad she took the lantern with her. It was filled with shelves and barrels.

"A pantry!" she exclaimed. She didn't stop to explore, as she realized time was running out before supper. Opening the door at the back of the pantry, she discovered it led outside. An outhouse was about twenty feet away, down a slight angle. It was tucked amongst some trees. She was kind of glad to have Mayor's company, as the tiny building was even darker than the night sky. She knew it was new because the only odour associated with it was the smell of new wood. It had not gained all the spider webs and other insects that would no doubt invade the premises attracted by the odours. Jenny hated spiders. In fact she disliked most insects. To the left side of the exterior pantry wall, a cord of wood was stacked neatly. A small building was also to her left. It proved to be the pump house. A hand pump was the only thing inside. It had a wooden floor, which she realized must cover a well that could be dozens of feet deep. Going into the pump house would always give her the feeling that the boards would give away and she would fall into the well. A shiver crawled up her spine. A pail hung on the spout, waiting to be filled. Jenny hurried to fill it before her slight phobia took over. She quickly took the water into the house. Hanging her dusty cloak on a peg near the door, she went into the bedroom, she poured the cold water into her washbasin. She hastily cleaned her hands and face. Fortunately her dress protected all day by the cloak was not too dirty. She had no time to change because she would have had to dig in her trunk for a clean outfit. All the ones she had with her in her carpet bag were soiled. There was no mirror in the room, so she patted her hair into place by feel. She smoothed her dress, took a deep breath, and left the house for the Brown's residence.

Janet met her at the door, "Come in Jenny, supper is on the table and our impatient men are ready to eat."

It was true, Ray and Benny's plates were mounded with food, and only politeness and the threat of Janet's ire kept them from digging in. Jenny and Janet hurried to seat themselves. Janet quickly passed the food to Jenny and took some herself. The steaming pot of stew, with fresh made biscuits was quickly devoured. It was delicious and Jenny was very thankful for the invitation.

After supper Jenny helped Janet with the dishes. They asked her to join them for a card game but she shook her head, promising both of them that she would be happy to play with them some other evening. She was very tired and her body was beginning to ache. She left the Browns residence very thankful for the lantern. Unused to the natural sounds of western nightlife, she found the walk home rather spooky. Fortunately Mayor had remained close, and escorted her home. Once inside, she prepared for bed. She sighed with happiness, as she sunk into the comfortable bedding. She found herself still a little nervous about the future, but she determined to try and not think about it. She blew the lantern out, but found herself staring at the ceiling. All her life she had been surrounded by people. Her little cabin was quiet, too quiet. Crickets chirping just outside her window finally soothed her into sleep. Once she finally did drop off, she slept deeply with no dreams to disturb her rest.

Chapter 4

James Borland awoke early Saturday morning. The sun was rising over the Eastern Mountain Range. He rested a minute, letting his eyes adjust to the dim light. Stretching, he got up out of the huge bed that was the focus of the master bedroom. It was a masculine room and the dark mahogany furniture reflected the personality of the owner.

He made his way to the water closet. It was a large room, but it had no window, so a lantern light was needed. He examined himself in the mirror, and rubbed the growth of whiskers on his jaw. He disliked whiskers as they itched in the heat of the day. Besides that, if he did not shave Grandma Alice would send him back to remove them like a naughty child. He smiled at the thought. Grandma Alice in spite of her diminutive size was not a lady you wanted to cross. She had a way of cutting the most arrogant of people down to size with just a few quietly spoken words. He hastily stropped his razor to its accustomed sharpness. He lathered up some soap with his shaving brush and proceeded to carefully remove the offending stubble.

He noticed his hair was getting a bit long too. He'd have to get Rick Mead the handyman, to shear it off pretty soon. He sighed studying his face. He had to admit that it was not a very handsome visage, but showed a rugged leathery look from years of work outdoors. Laugh lines around his eyes and mouth showed that he had a great sense of humour. It was true that he laughed a lot. He thought his nose was a bit too long. The scar above his eye marred an otherwise undamaged appearance.

Grudgingly, in his own opinion James resigned himself to the fact that he was not likely to impress the ladies. He would never admit that contrary to his thoughts, it was he who was not impressed by them. Most of the women he had met were either gushing in girlish behaviour, or sadly already married. Some of them were nothing but fortune hunters as well. He shuddered. Firmly directing his thoughts from those kinds of women he could not help but carry on with his current train of thought.

He cocked his head to one side and then laughed. "Obsessed with ladies are we lately?" he asked himself, "What on earth has brought this on anyway?" He stared hard at himself and sobered. "I'm feeling my age, that's what." He thought ruefully. "Grandma Alice's prodding and hints are finally getting to me! She's always trying to get me to marry and start a family."

"I am not getting any younger, I want to see my grandchildren before I join your grandfather in the churchyard!" he mimicked his beloved grandmother. "Good Lord, she'll probably out live me," he stated to his mirror image.

"Goodness knows finding a wife isn't easy. Single ladies are few and far between, I refuse to settle for just anyone either!" he vowed. "Most single women are either taken or are of the more crass variety in these parts. I want a woman who is intelligent, has a sense of humour and would be my partner. Humph! Anyone marrying me would have to have a sense of humour," he snorted.

James briefly recalled, the young lady in Big Rock that he had escorted to the Boarding House. "She seems really nice. Pretty too but she's probably engaged or something even if I could find her again." He laughed. Firmly he put her out of his mind. "I'll have to go east, or to San Francisco to find the one I want." He frowned at the prospect.

Completing his ablutions, James strode out of the bedroom and down the stairs. This commiseration was not getting him anywhere. He entered the dining hall.

Sleepy eyed men were sauntering in and he joined them for breakfast. Today would be a busy day. Once the breakfast was finished, James stood up. His men instantly ceased their chatting to pay close attention to him.

James spoke. "Every man not involved with a specific job, is to go to the work shed. Load a wagon with hammers, saws and any other implements necessary. We're going to finish the boardwalk in Water Valley. Prepare two other wagons to help haul the logs and lumber to various points within the town." He left the dining hall. It would be up to his foreman, Bruce McMillen, to give more specific orders. Bruce was well prepared because James and he always got together the night before to plan out the next day's work.

James paused only to get a few carrots from the cook, and then went outside to check on his special horses. His hobby, the pride of his life, were the beautiful Morgan horses his family had spent a small fortune acquiring. As he entered the horse barn, he saw the stable boys hard at work cleaning stalls.

He called. "Toby?"

Toby Wells, an elderly man hurried out at the sound of the boss's voice. "Mornin' Boss!"

James asked. "Is the little black mare designated for the school teacher ready?" When Toby nodded a quick assurance, James continued. "Hitch her up to the old buggy in the corner of the Carriage House. I'll drive the buggy into town. I need Twister saddled as well for the ride home.

"Immediately sir," Toby said and hurried to do James bidding.

Leaving this to Toby's efficient hands, James went to look in on his stallions and broodmares. They whickered and nudged him affectionately searching for the carrots they knew he carried with him. James observed the shine on their coats and approved of the tender care Toby was giving them. One by one he gave them their treats, while petting and talking to them.

At the sounds of men gathering outside, James reluctantly left this pleasant communion and joined them.

He tied Twister to the back of the buggy and got in to drive the teacher's mare to the Water Valley livery barn. He clicked to her, "Gitty-up." They started off at a fast walk. The wagons and men on horses filed in behind him.

James watched the mare's paces with great pleasure. Perhaps he should keep her at the ranch after all. A hard-handed teacher whoever he was, could spoil her irreversibly. The dainty little mare was half Morgan and half Ranch stock. It had turned out to be a pleasant combination.

Well he didn't really have to make that decision yet. He would meet the teacher first, and then judge. James had other horses that could be given to him. He just hoped Ben Moss would find him someone suitable for his brand new school.

During the drive, James thought about his pet project, Water Valley. It had been his father's idea to build a settlement near the ranch, because of the long distance to the nearest towns. It was decided that the beautiful valley six miles north of the ranch would be perfect. Thinking of his father, James grew sad. James Senior had been killed trying to save a horse that had fallen through the ice the spring before last. The horse had been pulled out but the man himself was swept under the ice. James missed him greatly. He took over the Water Valley Project with as much enthusiasm as his father had. James's mother had died at his birth.

A widowed Grandma Alice was all he had left now for family. She was the driving forced behind the Borland Ranch. Stricken with arthritis, the lady rarely left the house. She was strong of mind though and if James had any problems he could always count on her advice and help. She had never been tall, but the crippling effect served to shrink her even further. She refused to use the wheelchair James's father had given her. She proudly walked everywhere using a cane.

When the wagons reached the lumberyard the men loaded up the boards and logs, that Cyrus the mill owner had waiting. Starting at the church the men spread out dividing the work party into sections. Many folks from both the town and rural areas were there to help. These men were absorbed into the various work parties.

James dropped in to the general store and learned that the new schoolteacher had arrived. Ray and Janet were not beyond priming the surprise. They never said a word about the teacher being a lady.

James was elated that the schoolmaster had arrived. Now he could judge whether to leave the mare in town or not. He drove the mare over to David Olson the blacksmith and liveryman. Leaving her in David's capable hands, he decided it was the right time to go meet the teacher. He wondered what the man would be like. He started up the lane beside the store with anxious anticipation.

Chapter 5

A sharp pain in her lower back awoke Jenny on Saturday morning. With a groan, she forced her aching muscles to move. She hoped that if she ever had to do a similar trip again, the wagon would have a much more comfortable seat. She sat up on the side of the bed and donned her sheepskin slippers. Forcing her sore legs to move she hurried outside to the outhouse. The cool of the morning caused her body to shiver by the time she got back into the house. The fire had gone out during the night. She fought to relight the wood in the stove. It was one thing to help someone start a fire, quite another to do it all by yourself. A half hour later she was still not successful. Tears of frustration and anger moistened her cheeks. She was going to have to break down and ask for help.

Still shivering, she hurried into the bedroom to dress. At least she would be warmer. She was frustrated, having watched the cook's helpers make a fire countless times, the knack of creating it was beyond her. It hurt her pride to have to ask for help. She had a feeling if word got around about it, her humiliation would be assured. Ray and Janet were the only folks she knew here. She would just have to humble herself. She threw on a cloak and made her way to the General Store. She knocked on the back door of the residence. When Ray answered Jenny's face became more and more flushed with embarrassment, as she asked. "Ray, I'm sorry to bother you but I find myself in difficulties. I can't manage to get the fire started in my stove."

Ray never hesitated. He knew was how embarrassed she was. He turned to his wife who was making breakfast in the kitchen. "Janet, I'll be back in a few minutes," he called to her. He grabbed a jacket from the peg, donned it and took Jenny by the arm, escorting her back to the cabin.

"Don't you worry about a thing, my dear. I guessed last night you weren't used to the country," he said. Jenny flushed even redder if that was possible. Ray continued, trying to make Jenny feel more at ease. "I should have shown you last night how to bank the coals so the fire wouldn't die before morning. There is a trick to it."

Arriving at the cabin, Ray was an extremely good teacher. He did not make the fire but guided Jenny as she did the work herself. When a small blaze was going, Jenny breathed a sigh of relief. It really was not that hard, but her accomplishment seemed enormous. Ray explained to her how to properly bank the coals so that they would glow all night, making it easy to restart the stove in the morning.

Ray said, "I really have to be getting back home, Janet is not the most patient of women. Breakfast was almost ready." He looked at Jenny's and continued. "Jenny, I know what you're feeling. You needn't be embarrassed by your lack of knowledge in building a fire. It's no crime. Many many people have difficulty doing it." Jenny's face still reflected her embarrassment, so Ray continued. "I'll never tell a soul, Jenny, especially my wife!" he said with an encouraging grin.

Jenny looked into Ray's eyes. "Thank-you Ray, you don't know how much this means to me." Her face registered her relief.

Jenny put the kettle on, knowing it would take a while to get hot. She opened one of her trunks. Right on top, the china was wrapped carefully against breakage. She took out a cup, saucer and teapot from the trunk. Jenny then rummaged in her carpetbag, for her small tin of tea. It was a special blend, available only in Boston, travelling across America with her. She knew she would be sad when it was all gone and she expected it would be a long time before she would be able to get some like it. The water was not boiling yet so she spent time putting her clothes away. One trunk held all her dresses. These she hung up in the wardrobe. She noticed that there was not much room left after all of them had been hung. Perhaps she had brought too many? Grimacing a little she continued. A drawer built into the bottom of the wardrobe, was used for all her undergarments. Shoes fit nicely on the floor of the closet with the top shelf perfect for her hats.

Jenny had brought a few dresses that she thought may be appropriate for a country teacher to wear. Jenny felt it was important to dress as a dignified and serious lady, as her new profession dictated. Jenny laughed at the thought. "Serious and sober, me? Not likely!"

Jenny had brought beautiful outfits with her as well. Nice clothes were her passion and she just couldn't resist bringing some of them. Jenny hung her winter coat and cloaks on the pegs near the front door. Boots she placed on the double shelved boot rack on the floor under the coats. Remembering the chill of that morning, she realized the time to use them might not be all that far away.

The water was boiling merrily now, so she poured some in her teapot. While waiting for her precious tea to steep, she decided to carry on putting things away. The third trunk contained all her precious mementos and items to make life comfortable here. She carefully finished unwrapping the china set. It had been made in England. The beautiful blue pattern added a splash of color to her otherwise plain hutch. The hutch had many drawers, large and small. She chose one and used it for her silver cutlery. Noticing the tea was ready she sat at the table and drank it. She was hungry and tried to think of something to make with the supplies she had been given. Her store of knowledge and recipes was found to be inadequate, as she just couldn't figure out what some of the implements in the hutch were used for. She explored the pantry and saw several jars of preserves. To her delight she spotted a jar of canned peaches. She helped herself to a generous bowlful. They were wonderful, abating the hunger of her rebellious stomach. She would need to visit the Brown's store to get her fresh supplies.

Using the rest of the hot water, she poured it into the sink she gave herself the best washing she could. Jenny could feel the grime of travel still on most of her body. She needed a bath. She washed her dishes, dried and put them away.

She delved into her trunk again withdrawing a hand made rag rug. She was proud of its multicolored braids, as she had made it herself. This she took and placed next to her bed. This rug had been over a mirror, protecting it from getting broken, a knitted coverlet did the same from below. She took the mirror into the bedroom and hung it on a peg with some hair ribbon she sacrificed for this purpose. The knitted coverlet was not big enough for the bed, but fit beautifully on one of her new chairs adding a cheerful spot of color to her living room. Her housekeeper had spent hours knitting it for her. A set of candlesticks came next. They had belonged to her grandmother and she placed these on the dining table. She unwrapped a wooden box of candles putting two of them in the holders. The rest she placed on one of the shelves in the pantry. A multitude of small doilies, embroidered runners and tablecloths protected breakable items, including a portrait of her parents. Most were gifts from her staff in Boston.

Jenny placed the portrait on the mantle above the fireplace, she looked at it for a minute. The photographer had them pose. Her father stood behind her mother's chair, with one hand on her shoulder. He had his usual sober demeanour. Her mother beautiful face held no hint of a smile. Jenny thought of how sad her mother must have been. Rousing herself from her melancholy she continued to unpack.

She found places for most of the linens and decorations. A box of fragrant soaps, molded into bars, was next. After removing one, the remainder joined the candles in the pantry. Her favourite books, bound in leather were the last to come out of the trunk. These she placed on the large mantle. There were four of them. A copy of Jules Verne's 20,000 Leagues Under the Sea, Charles Dickens's book, Oliver Twist, the Poems and Songs of Robert Burns, lastly was a leather bound book of Aesop's Fables. There was one more book, a small family Bible that would be placed next to her bed. Pausing she opened it. In the centre was a record of her family tree. The Stockton ancestry was a long one and she wondered what they had been like. Were they all as unhappy as her family? She was the last of this branch of the Stockton line. There were probably distant relatives somewhere, but she didn't know any of them. Closing the black leather bound book, she took it to the bedroom and then returned to the living room.

The empty trunks were in the way. She looked into the pantry and saw that she could store them side by side just under the shelves on one wall. As she started to drag the empty trunks across the floor she noticed a trap door that they had been hiding. Curious she lifted the door and saw a set of steps disappearing into the darkness. She finished putting the trunks away, lit the lantern and held it up in front of her she carefully descended the stairwell. It was steep, but someone had thoughtfully put a handrail on one side. She found herself in a small cellar. It was cool and damp and had an earthy smell. The walls were made of dirt. Shelves on one side held quite a few more jars of preserves. Bins, holding potatoes and carrots were under the shelves. It was cool down here. She shivered, quickly returning upstairs.

She was overwhelmed at the generosity of her new community. Most of her winter supplies were already in place, she would only need to get in fresh food, on a regular basis.

She decided she had better go do her shopping. Jenny blew the borrowed lantern out taking it with her as she headed for the store. She realized that courtesy required she bypass the direct path to the store. It was part of Janet and Ray's private home. She rounded the hedge, following the grassy lane to Main Street. There was a boardwalk in front of the store, but it was the only one. The rest of the town shops could only be accessed by the dusty road. She wanted to explore the town some more, but Jenny decided to shop first.

There was one wagon with a team tied up across the street and the pleasant buzz of voices, told Jenny that Ray and Janet already had customers. Jenny entered the store, to be greeted enthusiastically by both. Janet introduced their customers as Donald and Betty Burns. Their male customer was a tall man, with homespun trousers held up by suspenders on a cotton shirt. He had a beard and a booming voice. The lady was dressed in cotton gingham, with an apron which prevented it from getting dirty and a she wore a bonnet, which protected her from the sun. They had both turned to her in curiosity, at the Brown's enthusiastic greeting. Their two children had their noses glued against the glass window of the counter. Stick candy and other goodies were kept there.

After greeting Jenny pleasantly, Betty called her children over and introduced them as Ronald and Jessica. Ronald was eight and called Ronnie. He was the image of his father, without the beard. Jessica, fondly called Jessie, was six. She looked adorable in her pink gingham frock, with a white linen bonnet and apron. Both children were in bare feet, which was common for most country children in summer. Shoes were expensive and saved for the cold winters. Jack and Betty lived on a homestead about five miles down the valley, on the other side of the bridge.

Ray told Jenny that the residents in the district of Water Valley were being told of her arrival. It was cause for celebration and a big picnic was being planned for the next day after church, to introduce her to everyone. In the meantime, James Borland had sent word to gather as many men as possible for a work crew to build the boardwalk. It was something he had promised to do the previous spring but had not found the opportunity to do as of yet. Janet and Ray expected to be extremely busy that afternoon. Jenny's heart gave a little leap at James' name. Her face flushed. Embarrassed she turned quickly away, pretending to look at some supplies on the numerous shelves in the store. Jack was needed to help with the project, so he wanted to get Betty and the children back home quickly. They waved goodbye and hurried away.

Janet came over to Jenny to see if she could help find what was needed. Jenny spent over an hour, purchasing various things. All her staples had been provided, so she needed only to get other small necessities. She purchased lard and a pound of oatmeal. She picked out three new lanterns, each of a different design. She also bought a jug of Coal Oil, to fill them. Her home had been provided with a couple of small pots, but she added to her inventory with a caste iron frying pan and a larger cooking pot. She needed some cooking utensils as well. A huge wheel of Cheese sat on a special table and Ray cut her a generous wedge. Jenny spotted some apples sitting in a barrel. She indulged herself by buying six of them. Although she was not accustomed to baking, Jenny thought she may like to try so she bought some baking tins for bread and cakes. She purchased some coco and a small bottle of vanilla. She tried to think of what else she might need and added molasses, currents and raisins to her growing pile of supplies. Ray carefully wrote her purchases onto his books. Jenny could have paid cash, but thought she may do it on a monthly basis. Most homesteaders bought on credit, paying their bills once a year after harvest. Jenny shied away from calling attention to the fact that she was wealthy. She didn't know how it might affect her newly made friends.

She asked if they had any bread, eggs, milk and perhaps even butter. Ray told her that fresh goods were usually arranged for in person from the homesteaders that raised cows and chickens for their own use. Extra income from selling what the family didn't require was always a welcome way to supplement their income. In fact the Burn's would be a good choice if they had more than their family could use. Jenny nodded, and decided to find them if they hadn't left town already. Jenny asked Ray to hang on to her purchases for the moment, while she hurried out of the store to look for Jack. The family had disappeared, but Jenny knew she would see Jack later this very afternoon if he was coming to help build the boardwalk.

Returning to the store, Jenny looked with astonishment at the gigantic stack of wrapped parcels sitting by the door. Most of them were sitting in the middle of Jenny's new tin bathtub. When Jenny had tentatively inquired for a tub, Ray had answered in the affirmative. He took Jenny outside to the east side of the store. An open shed housed most of the larger items that could never fit in the store. He told her David Olson, the blacksmith made many of the implements. There had been several tubs stacked together, along with some larger farm implements, barrels, boilers and even some pot bellied stoves. Janet and Ray had finished wrapping her purchases and were not beyond teasing her about her mound of supplies. She grinned and began to laugh. She joined Ray and Janet in their teasing and light hearted banter.

She eyed the pile and gauged that it would take her several trips to get everything home. She was especially looking forward to having a good bath. She hated the feeling of not being clean. She had a bath every other day when she lived in Boston. She had no intention of doing without one here if she could possibly help it.

At the moment Jenny was Ray and Janet's only customer, so Jenny felt bold enough to ask, "Can you tell me about some of the other residents in Water Valley?" She blushed a little, because what she was asking might be construed as gossip.

Janet laughed and said, "That will take time! Would you like to come in the back to our living area for a cup of tea? Your parcels will be fine right where they are for the moment. "

Ray spoke up then, "Jenny, you'll likely be in there for a week, as Janet is the village information expert!"

In other words she was the town gossip. Janet scowled at Ray, but he didn't back down an inch. He grinned until her mouth started to twitch, then a grin started to force its way back on her face.

"Oh you!" she sputtered, and turned her back on him. "Come on Jenny lets go!"

Jenny followed her. She had read the warmth between Janet and her husband. It was obvious the couple loved each other very much. Jenny followed Janet into the kitchen where the delicious stew had been prepared the night before. The walls were bright and cheerful in the daylight. The walls had been painted yellow and the cupboards white.

"Oh Janet, I love your kitchen so much, you've worked hard to make it cozy and nice."

Janet thanked her and poured out some tea for the both of them. A plate of cookies joined the cups on a tray and Janet took Jenny into the sitting room. Two comfortable chairs were there that had the look of much use. A serviceable horsehair rug had been dyed a bright red and placed in front of the chairs. A small table stood between the chairs. Janet placed the tray on it. Jenny sat down and Janet handed her a cup, then seated herself. Both of them took a cookie and sat back. Janet had been working steadily all morning and was glad of the break. Jenny sat back to listen.

"Well," she said. "I guess I'll start at this end of town and work down the street."

"The livery barn is first. David Olson, I am sure you have heard about him already, but he is both our Blacksmith and Liveryman. You'll like him. He is a bachelor with the size and strength of a small bull. Oh, but wait until you hear his voice. He can sing like an angel. He has the deepest bass voice I've ever heard. He sings solo's for the church service quite often." Janet commented enthusiastically.

"The next building is the flourmill. Pops McIntosh runs it once a week, His main livelihood though is carpentry. He's the one who built the furniture for your school and home. He used to live with his daughter, but found himself constantly working in his shop." Janet laughed. "He finally gave up the walk between buildings and built himself a room right in the mill. That way he can work or sleep without venturing outside his shop."

Janet continued "Pops is the father of the widow Louise Jones. She lives in the house next to the mill. Louise has three children to support. Her husband was lost last year in an avalanche. Charles is fifteen and helps out with whatever odd job he can do. Lucy is a timid girl, just turned thirteen. Barbara is a mischievous nine year old. The girls help Louise with her work. Louise makes a living by taking in laundry. She also bakes the most wonderful breads and cakes. Bachelors and others that don't care for laundry or are not handy with baking adore her."

Jenny's eyes lit up at that. She confided, "Oh that sounds wonderful, I can't bake and I also hate laundry at any time. Do you think she might do those chores for me?"

Janet laughed. "Well, I'm sure she would be happy to have your business. All you can do is ask her."

"Now the next building is still under construction. The plan for it is to be a doctor's office, with his home in the back. Plans are in the works for a Town Hall, with a sheriff's office and so forth.

"Well that is it for the one side of the street, now we come to this side."

She said musingly. "First off we have the church and rectory. Reverend Art Chase and his wife Nellie lived there. I have no doubt that they will be over to see you soon. They are a very nice young couple. They have no children yet."

Voices heard through the curtains separating the living quarters from the business, told them that customers had arrived. Janet got up and went to help her husband. Jenny rose also realizing that an hour had passed while they were chatting. Her stomach was telling her in no uncertain terms that cookie and tea were no substitute for a proper lunch. She followed Janet deciding to take all her purchases home so she could prepare something to eat. The visitors to the store turned out to be the Reverend and his wife. They had first gone to Jenny's home and finding her not there decided to try the store.

They quickly volunteered to help Jenny with her packages although they grinned when they saw how much she had bought. Rather embarrassed, Jenny agreed. That pile seemed enormous.

Ray left Janet to run the counter while he helped the Reverend, Nellie and Jenny hoist the packages and head for her cabin. They managed to get all but the tub in the one load. Jenny led the way thanking them profusely for their aid. The bathtub would be brought over later in the day.

There were two packages on the veranda that had not been there when she left. Nellie retrieved them with a smile and said. "These are a welcoming present for you." She produced a loaf of bread from one with a flourish. A small ceramic pot of butter and a jar of chokecherry jam was conjured from the other. Jenny looked at the jam dubiously. "What on earth was a chokecherry?" She thought. The name caused her to be a bit apprehensive, but not wanting to appear ignorant she set the jam aside.

"What a treat!" Jenny enthused. "Would you join me for lunch?" Ray declined stating he had to get back to the store, as Saturday was his busiest day. Nellie and Art however agreed with pleasure.

"I can see that having only two chairs for the table is going to be a problem especially if I have company often," she thought.

The three of them sat and began a delicious lunch. After observing the pleasure which Art and Nellie tackled the jam, Jenny tried it. After one bite, she became an avid lover of the humble chokecherry.

Reverend suggested, "Why don't you ask Pops McIntosh to make a bench that can seat at least two people. I could ask him for you if you like."

Jenny smiled, "Thank you for your offer but I was going around to meet everyone anyway. I will ask him. Your bench idea would make an ideal solution. If it is sturdy enough, I can use it to stand on as well if I need to get to the higher shelves in the pantry. These chairs could break under my weight."

Jenny became aware of noise out in the street. Politeness was the only reason she never raced out to see what the commotion was.

"That will be the men working on the boardwalk" Nellie said. "James Borland promised last spring that he would put one in as soon as he could.

The trio chatted easily, getting to know each other over the next hour.

Art and Nellie prepared to leave Jenny's company. She escorted them over to her veranda. At that moment she had another visitor. James Borland opened her gate to come in passing the Reverend and his wife as they left.

James looked up at Jenny startled. "It's you!" he exclaimed in delight. "Why didn't you tell me you were our new teacher?"

Jenny blushed. Her heart was beating fast as she answered him. "I didn't know you had anything to do with Water Valley until Dora told me."

"I received a letter from Ben Moss, stating that a teacher had been arranged for us. I thought it would be a man coming," James stated bluntly.

"Are you disappointed, with my being a woman at all?" Jenny asked apprehensively.

James smiled. "Not at all," he said softly. "Ray told me that the new school teacher had arrived and I came to welcome you. As you can tell by all the noise we are making a boardwalk. I have been promising the settlement one since last spring. A branch will come down your lane as well, I won't have you walking in mud where you need to go.

"Mud!" she exclaimed. "I was beginning to think it never rained here!"

James laughed and said. "This has been an unusually dry year, but there's always lots of snow in winter here in the mountains. There's usually no shortage of rain during the spring and summers either, normally."

James sobered. "Miss Stockton, do you have everything you need? We did our best to stock this cabin with most of the staples. The school was different. We could provide the material things, but none of us had a good idea about what supplies you may require. I need to get a list of your needs as soon as possible, before the school session begins."

"Please call me Jenny," she said shyly. "I have brought a lot of things with me, I'll let you know if I need anything else. I was going over to the school to empty the trunks this afternoon. I can give you a list tomorrow if you like. I think you have built a beautiful school and the people I have met are very nice. Everyone so far has made me feel at home and I am not sure how I was so lucky to find this position. My house is very nice as well," Jenny told James sincerely. "May I offer you a cup of tea on my new veranda?" She asked smiling.

James was rather dazzled by Jenny's beauty and ingenuity. He found himself rather disconcerted at seeing her again. After all it was only this morning he had been thinking about her. The color on his face heightened a little. He suddenly felt unsure of himself. He declined her tea invitations a bit abruptly, saying he had to go help the men with some hammering. He excused himself and quickly left the yard, waving at her from the gate.

Jenny was disappointed wondering what she had done to chase him away so fast. "Was he angry with me that I never told him I was a teacher in Big Rock? He could have spent a few more minutes with me," she thought forlornly. Her heart was still beating faster than normal. She finally admitted to herself, that after seeing him again, she was definitely attracted to him.

James's mind was in turmoil. He knew he had acted the dolt and was upset with himself. He was not sure why his hands were shaking and his face hot. He slowed down his pace. He was usually so calm and in control of situations, he wondered why he was reacting like this. The noise of the construction around him didn't lend itself to thought. Brutally he closed his mind on the problem for the moment. This was not the right time to think. He grabbed a nearby hammer and started hitting nails with a studied concentration. The men nearby noticed and wondered but never commented.

Chapter 6

After James had disappeared up the street Jenny slowly went in and tidied up her kitchen. She decided it was time to organize her school room. She got the iron key from the peg by the door and exited the back way. The grass was a little long, but Jenny knew that constant travel over it would soon create a smooth path. She crossed over to the schoolhouse. She noticed a brass bell bolted to the exterior wall. This bell would call children to classes. The entry way, was designed to keep anyone standing inside dry if it happened to be raining. A set of shelves on one wall would be fine for holding wet or snowy boots. She unlocked the door and entered. The two trunks of supplies were right in the middle of the room. Where was she going to put everything?

The back wall on one side of the door had two rows of pegs to hold coats and winter wear for the students. The double shelf under the pegs would hold the children's personal supplies, that wouldn't fit in the desks. The shelf above would hold the children's lunch boxes or bags. Her desk had three drawers on either side. Her chair had wheels. Jenny was thrilled. It would be easy to roll her chair where ever it was needed. When she examined the students' desks, she realized that the lid of each lifted up to allow books and slates to be stored. A table, with a basin, and a pail for water stood in one corner at the back of the room. Two water dippers hung on a nail above the pail. Students would use these dippers to both drink or to fill the basin for washing hands. A bucket underneath would be used for wastewater. She discovered the three windows to either side of the room could be opened. "That will be nice during the warmer days of school," she mused.   Jenny decided to stack all the supplies neatly in one corner, until some more shelves could be made. The trunks would fit one on top of the other in the front corner near her desk. Surplus supplies could be stored there.

She was just starting to get herself organized when a knock on the schoolhouse door made her pause.

A boy in his mid teens stood at the entry. "Good afternoon Ma'am, Mr. Borland sent me to help you get settled in.," he said cheerfully.

"Thank-you…!" Jenny said looking at the tall muscular boy. He had black hair and deep blue eyes. His smile was open and friendly. A plain leather belt with a silver buckle held up homespun trousers. He had a green checked shirt on. The sleeves were rolled up past his elbows. His face and callused hands were tanned. "Here was a boy used to hard work outdoors," Jenny thought. The boy was looking around the room with keen interest.

"I'm Bill Storm," he said eagerly. "What would you like me to do?"

Thankful for his help the two of them worked to empty the trunks of all the books and supplies. Bill's eyes were wide with wonder. He handled the books with careful reverence. "Wow!" he said "You have so many books here!"

Jenny could tell the boy was longing to delve into the treasures he had carefully stacked. "Are you attending school here?" she asked.

"When I can, I will," he stated. "Harvest time I have to help my dad."

"Come winter though, nothing can keep me away, unless I am lucky enough to get a job in the sawmill," he said with conviction.

Jenny smiled at his enthusiasm. "Are all the children as eager as you?"

Bill looked startled for a moment. "Well, most are," he stated diplomatically. "But there are some who don't take school seriously," he shrugged.

Jenny laughed telling him that she was finished here for the day and that he could go. Taking a last glance at the books, Bill left the school whistling as he disappeared.

Jenny left the schoolhouse, carefully locking the door. She turned around. She was amazed at the progress the sweating workers had made. The log base for the walk was already in place. It stopped a couple of feet past her gate. The boards were complete half way across the school property. The teams of men were nailing the boards in almost as fast as they were placed in position. It would not be long before her walk was complete.

Jenny decided to explore around the area of the schoolhouse. Someone had thoughtfully made a playground at the back of the schoolyard. Ropes with wood boards, hung from every available tree limb. The swings were a wonderful idea; there was even a couple of Teeter Totters, their smoothed wooden boards tapered at the ends to accommodate small legs. She found a double outhouse out back. It had a screen of pine trees. A red girl painted on one of them and a blue boy on the other. She looked to her right noting her pump house. That was when realized that her pump and the schools were the same. Cords of wood were stacked under the windows of the school. Seeing all of them, she shivered. Winter was obviously long and hard here.

She decided that it was still early enough in the afternoon that she would visit Pops McIntosh. She made use of the new boardwalk to the corner. Jenny took a good look around. The Main Street stretched east and west from the store. Jenny gazed at the huge church just across her lane from the store. It boasted a tower with a large bronze bell hanging from the belfry and six stained glass windows along the wall. The new boardwalk crossed in front of the church and westward down the hill to the river. There were other buildings next to the church on the other side, but Jenny couldn't make out what they were from her position in front of the store. Janet had been interrupted before she could tell Jenny about them. She could see a bridge, crossing the river at that point. Part of the lumber mill was visible on the other side of the bridge. It was an industrious area. Horses, mules and oxen working with at least a dozen men were bustling with activity.

Across the dusty main street was a park like area dotted by a few scattered trees. The underbrush had all been cleared. This was where people would park their buggies and wagons when they came to town. There were a number of horses tied to the hitching posts and a few buckboards neatly lined against the fence. These were undoubtedly the stock used by the folks making the boardwalk. Shade from the sporadic poplar trees was keeping the patiently waiting horses cool. They stood at ease, swishing their tails at persistent flies. The bank of the stream was low at one point where they could be watered. The other side of the stream was a solid mass of underbrush and trees. However for their convenience there was also a pump connected to a watering trough for the animals. A water dipper for people hung over the iron handle.

Looking east, Jenny noticed there were no other buildings right beside the store, the edge of the Brown property was marked by a wooden fence. Natural woods remained on the other side. This part of the forest, Jenny knew stretched back behind the school and her home. There was lots of room for expansion if anyone desired too. North east across the street was the livery stable. Seeing it in the daylight gave Jenny an appreciation for its size. The barn itself was easily as large as the one in Big Rock. The surrounding area covered at least three acres. Fences divided the corral several times. Many horses could be accommodated outdoors. A large shed just on this side of the barn contained many different vehicles. She noticed that there were a few small fenced in areas butting up against the park. If families or other came for any great length of time, their horses could be turned loose in them. It was obvious that people here cared greatly about the comfort of their animals.

Directly across from the church was her destination, the flourmill. Its huge water wheel was being turned merrily by the fast flowing stream. Her eyes followed the creek and noticed it joined the large river a short ways north of the bridge.

Mayor bounded up to her, his tail wagging in delight. He followed her as she crossed the street to the flourmill. Pops was there grinding some grain. He ceased this activity when she entered.

He smiled, step forward hand outstretched to shake her hand. "Miss Stockton, isn't it?" he asked.

Jenny was surprised, obviously word travelled fast in this little community. "Why yes," she said taking Pops hand. His warm handshake was firm.

"I'm known as Pops, please come over here into my workshop," he said pointing to a large room on one side of the mill. Jenny entered a room filled with wooden projects, finished and unfinished. He continued. "Please have a seat."

Jenny saw a highly polished rocking chair. She sat gingerly into it and found it amazingly comfortable. Jenny said. "Pops, I'll not take up much of your valuable time, but I do need some more furniture when you have the chance. First of all I need a sturdy bench about five feet long. I would like it to serve two purposes. Extra seating and yet sturdy enough to stand on if I need to reach up high for something. Also I need at least three sets of portable cases, with four shelves in each for the school supplies and books I have brought."

"Figured you would," he said. "I thought there was no use making something that might not have been what you wanted."

Jenny smiled. "You do wonderful work, I love everything you made me very much. Thank you."

She was standing up to leave when a young woman, who looked to be in her thirties entered the mill. Pops stood up and introduced Jenny to his daughter Louise. She was a plump lady, with a friendly open smile. A wisp of hair hung down, having escaped from the severe bun that held up her mouse brown hair. Jenny notice Louise's hands were rough, probably from hard physical labor.

"Welcome to Water Valley," she said. "Barbara and Lucy are looking forward to the first day of school. I am not sure about Charles," she laughed.

Jenny said, "Mrs Jones, Janet told me you do wonderful baking and you've taken in laundry, is this true?"

Louise smiled and said. "How nice of Janet to say so, yes I like to bake breads and cakes, as you can see by my figure. Please call me Louise," she added.

Jenny asked, "May I buy bread and other goodies from you on a regular basis?"

Louise was delighted. "My breads are second to none. My specialty though is chocolate cake with fudge icing. Does that sound good to you?"

"That sounds marvellous, chocolate cake is one of my favourites." she confessed. "I truly dislike doing laundry and was wondering if you would take in mine?"

"Most certainly I can. I do laundry once a week on Mondays. Baking I do on Tuesdays and Fridays."

They made agreeable financial arrangements, and Jenny bid both of them farewell and exited the mill.

She was returning to the store when she spotted a familiar face. Donald Burns was down on his hands and knees pounding in nails for the boardwalk. Jenny walked over tapping him on the shoulder to catch his attention

"Mr. Burns?" she shouted over the sound of the construction.

Donald turned and looked up at Jenny. Smiling he stood up and she drew him away from the rest of the workers, so they could hear each other better.

"Is there a possibility of purchasing milk, butter and eggs from you?" she asked.

Donald slid the hat off his head, wiping his sweating forehead on his sleeve. "I would be most happy to," he said, "but I only have two cows and that provides mainly what my family needs." He stated apologetically. "We can however provide you with eggs. Some of our income is made by selling them."

Jenny pondered for a few seconds. She had an idea. "Do you have time to milk an extra cow if you had one?" she asked.

"Yes" he said very puzzled by her query, "but they are very expensive and I can't afford one."

"If I buy one would you stable it for me and milk it? I would be happy to pay you for the trouble." she asked hopefully.

Donald was rather taken aback at the request but didn't take long to answer. "Sure I could, but it would probably provide much more milk and cream than you would really need."

"That is no problem," Jenny said. "Anything I do not need is yours. Perhaps you could sell some to other people like you will be doing for me."

Jenny and Don, as he requested she call him, agreed on a price for his services.

"Can you get a cow from the ranch?" she asked.

Don shook his head. "No, the ranch raises longhorn's and they don't make good milk cows. They do have a few cows for their use but none extra. In fact James buys his from the same farmer that I have in mind," he said. "Frank O'Leary brought a small herd of Jersey cows all the way from the east. As far as I know he is the only one with that breed in the whole state. They're known for their wonderful milk, with a high cream content. I looked into getting one. They were frightfully expensive, so I dropped the notion. In fact he has a cow along with her heifer calf up for sale at the moment but he wants fifteen dollars for the pair.

Jenny reached into her reticule and gave Don the money to buy them. Don eyes widened when he saw the cash. However he happily agreed saying he would talk to the farmer on Monday morning. Don then went back to helping with the boardwalk.

Jenny was pleased with her days work. She made her way home using the new walkway. She noticed that the workers had made a step between the boardwalk and her gate. This was nice because the walkway was at least a foot and a half higher than the ground.

She was tired with her day's activities, so she sat in on the veranda, picked up her bag of embroidery and worked deftly stitching the design with beautiful colored cotton. Ray arrived with David Olson bringing Jenny's new tub. Ray introduced her to the huge man. He was easily the tallest man Jenny had ever seen. He had to duck under the doorway so not to bump his head. The door frame barely let him through. Jenny thought he must not be more than twenty-five or thirty years old. He had a big smile and spoke with a deep bass voice. They did not linger as both of them were busy. Jenny called her thanks after them, as they hurried down her walk. She examined her bathtub, looking forward to later that evening when she could indulge in a good soaking.

Time was passing quickly, and before she realized it, the afternoon was gone. Jenny decided to see how far the workers had gotten with the boardwalk. She walked to the corner It was almost complete. It benefited all the shops and residences right down to the river. Jenny could see the gang of them finishing up the last of it, joining it to the bridge. Jenny was impressed with the industry of these wonderful people. It was no accident that the school and her home looked so nice. It was obvious they worked together well.

Jenny was startled when her stomach growled. She looked at her watch to confirm that it was indeed suppertime. She returned to her home to prepare supper. She built up the fire, placing the copper boiler filled with water onto boil. She ate some bread and cheese, and some of her precious jam. An apple topped off her simple meal. She wondered what she could do about getting some meat. Where could she keep something like that? She would have to ask Janet. Meat would spoil quickly in the summer heat. Maybe she should learn to fish. Jenny laughed. She would have no idea how to even begin that task.

Noticing that her water was steaming, she wrestled the tub close to the stove. She ladled the water from the boiler into it. She could not lift the heavy boiler until at least half the water was removed. The water was too hot, so she had to make a couple of extra trips to the pump to get water to cool it a bit. When it was finally ready, Jenny made sure all her curtains were closed and the door latched for privacy. It was wonderful to step into the clear soft water. After luxuriating in the bath, she combed her waist length hair until it was dry. She day dreamed, with her mind flitting from one subject to another. She thought about James, ending up with a wee bit of homesickness for her adopted family back in Boston. The sun had set long before so Jenny roused herself to light the lanterns. She made use of the bath water to wash out some undergarments with the yellow bar of soap, Janet had recommended for that purpose. She took them into the bedroom and hung them on a rope, strung across the room. She was pleased with her ingenuity in making an indoor clothes line. Returning to the kitchen, she emptied the tub, by making several trips outside the back door with the "slop" pail.

She prepared for bed, crawling under the warm quilt. She was well satisfied with her start in this community. Not even the pervasive chirp of crickets could keep her eyes from closing. With thoughts of her friend Frances and how much she missed her, Jenny fell asleep.

Chapter 7

Jenny awoke with a start. Her heart gave a quick flip-flop of panic. A glance out her window assured her that it was only a little past dawn. She was not late. Her nerves were getting the better of her. She had slept rather fitfully during the night.

Jenny snuggled down again into the soft feather bed. She closed her eyes in a futile attempt to go back to sleep. The light from the window did not let her. She did doze a bit, but her nerves for today's events wouldn't let her rest. Reluctantly she got up. It was cold in the room, so she hastily put on her dressing gown. It was made of warm chenille in a deep green color. She put her sheepskin slippers on, enjoying the immediate warmth created by them.

She quickly built up the fire in the big iron stove. It seemed she had learned the trick of banking the coals, so that the fire never completely went out. There was a definite chill in the air, indicating that fall was approaching. The leaves on the huge maple tree in her front yard were starting to turn red. A grey squirrel chattered at her from the safety of the long branches. Calling a hasty greeting to the squirrel, Jenny hurried to the outhouse. She refilled her pails with water and retreated gratefully into the warm kitchen.

Jenny put some fresh water in her kettle. The water in the stove's reservoir had been a little warm from the coals, but would take an hour to heat up enough to be useful. What a modern convenience that was. She admired the new stove. The black cast iron top was still shiny. There was a beeswax container, on the side of the warming oven. She would need to rub the wax on the stovetop to keep the black pristine and shiny. This stove boasted a warming oven situated above the main part of the stove. Its purpose was to keep food warm, but Jenny used it to store her pots and pans. The ceramic door was a cream color that pulled down on springs. The fire only burned on the one side of the stove. Heat was conveyed to the oven and reservoir on the far side by heated air. Ashes were gathered just underneath the fire section. Ashes had to be dumped at least once a week. In spite of the warmth from the stove, Jenny shivered a little. It was obvious that she was going to have to start using the fireplace soon.

"It is a good thing this house is small," she thought to herself. "It will be a chore come winter to keep this place warm." Jenny returned to the bedroom. She took out her Sunday dress. It was royal blue muslin. She took out one of her fancy tatted collars. This one was a dazzling white. Jill Paton, the Stockton's former housekeeper had given her several in varying colors. Jill had worked hard making those collars "to remind Jenny of her." There was little chance Jenny would ever forget any of her 'family'. Seeing that beautiful collar brought on another wave of homesickness, together with doubt about her ability to cope in this new land. Life here was so different from what she was used to and Boston was so very far away.

Jenny donned her dress. "Thank goodness it has buttons down the front," she thought. "I can at least put it on without help." She wished Frances was here to help her. Oh how she missed her friend.

Crossing to the mirror, Jenny picked up her tortoiseshell comb and brushed and did her hair. Swinging it up on top of her head, the natural curls formed a halo effect. Using combs she fastened the hair into place. She put on a small round hat that matched the color of her dress. It had a small white feather on one side of it.

She frowned when she saw that her freckles had become more distinct with the sun. "I'll have to start wearing a larger sunhat," Jenny resolved." Either that or use lemon juice to fade them." She had done that faithfully in her youth. The results on whether it worked was still debateable as the summer sun always brought them back again in their horrible splendour. She smiled at the memory, displaying perfect teeth.

Throwing her shoulders back in determination, she took stock of herself in the mirror. "Yes this life is new and a bit strange, but I'm strong. I'll make it just fine," she told herself firmly.

Today was a very special occasion. A picnic after church in her honour would be an introduction to prospective students and their parents. Ray and Janet told her that everyone had been very excited about the new school and her pending arrival. The whole community had worked together to build this house and school. Granted, they had no idea she was a woman until she arrived, but the house had been appropriate for either. The few people she had met so far hadn't seemed upset over the fact that she was a woman.

Jenny could understand their surprise at her gender, because of the tremendous odds favouring the men. Her classes in New York, there were seventy-five men and only three women taking up school teaching. Many times she had been sneered, taunted and laughed at. Mainly by men, but even some women were of the opinion she didn't know her place.

Perhaps that was why she was so nervous, "Will everyone accept me?" she thought to herself.

Jenny returned to the main room. It was warm now. She poured herself a cup of tea and ate some bread, with cheese for breakfast. She tidied the house. Since it would be at least another three hours before church, she sat down at her table and started a letter to Frances. In spite of the fact that she had only been here two days, she had lots to tell her. When she finished, she curled up in her chair and attempted to read her book.

She couldn't seem to concentrate on her book. Her mind was busy on the wonderful people she had met so far. One man in particular dominated her thoughts, James. She went over all the facts that she knew about him. He owned the largest ranch in the area. It had been his family's idea to start a small settlement here. He had brought in independent business people from all walks of life helping them build their homes and shops. The entire village of Water Valley still had that new look. The oldest building was the year old General Store. It had been James's idea to build a school because of the children coming to the area. His own ranch had many workers with families.

"Yes, he was certainly handsome, in his own way," she thought as she reviewed her impression of James. He was tall, well over six feet with a dusty blonde hair. His hands were calloused from hard work but it was his eyes and mouth that had attracted her attention. The vivid blue eyes, sparkling with good humour, had small laugh lines extending from the corners. His grin was wide and charming. Yet there was something sensual about his mouth too.

Jenny realized this man was attracting her as no other had done. She blushed and told herself again that she was out of her mind, just as she had the first time she met him. They had only met a couple of times after all!

Jenny must have dozed off, because the ringing of the church bell caused her to jump. She quickly got up and checked herself in the mirror. She straightened the hat that had gone askew while she dozed. She slipped on her white gloves, took her bible and made her way outside. The sun was already making itself felt. Fortunately she only had to walk to the corner and cross the street to the church. Dozens of people were already there. Some were filing into the church, but most stood chatting outside. Buggies and wagons crowded the park across the road. The horses tied in the shade, stood with one hind leg taking the weight, the other relaxed. She grinned at the lopsided rear views this caused.

The group outside the church had been exchanging lively greetings and banter, but their voices broke off when they saw Jenny coming. However for Jenny's peace of mind, the looks she received were ones of curiosity. There was no hostility for her being a woman, that she could see. The Reverend stepped away from the front doors and began to shoo his flock into the church.

A smiling Ray stepped forward to greet her, "Janet and I would love your company in our pew, we've saved you a seat."

Jenny smiled and said, "Good Morning Ray, I would love to sit with you and Janet." She then turned to the Reverend and the rest of the bystanders. With a radiant smile, "Good Morning everyone," she said. Ray then escorted her proudly into the church.

"Introductions will come later," the Reverend said to the rest of the congregation. Everyone hurried to take his or her place. Ray and Jenny joined Janet in the second row pew. The church was packed with area residents. Many were forced to stand at the back. Jenny took a quick look around. The sun shining through the stained glass made one feel in the middle of a rainbow. Walnut pews had been polished to a high sheen. The pulpit, also of walnut stood on a raised platform. It had been crafted by a master. The front had a carved panel depicting Christ holding a small child on his lap. Other children sat around him gazing up at his serene face. It took Jenny's breath away.

Janet, noticing where Jenny's attention had been drawn whispered to her. "Good Morning, isn't that a beautiful scene. Pops carved it," she continued, "What a lovely day! There are many more people in church today than usual. I suspect they have come to meet you Jenny."

Jenny blushed, but said nothing. She had spotted James among those standing at the back of the room. She could feel his eyes focusing on her.

After the interesting service was over, the Reverend called Jenny up to the front of the church. He introduced her to the congregation. Rather embarrassed at being singled out, Jenny recovered quickly.

"Thank you for welcoming me to your wonderful community. I have met a few of you and look forward to becoming acquainted with the rest of you. It may take me a little time to learn who is who but I will do so as quickly as I can," she said with a warm smile.

The Reverend invited everyone to the grassy area behind the church. Tables, consisting of boards over sawhorses were waiting for them. Ladies quickly set out the main courses. The tables groaned under the weight of the good food. Beautiful oak trees were scattered around the churchyard, their dense foliage creating welcome shade. The lawn had recently been cut, leaving a soft carpet for parishioners to lay their blankets on. When the food was all laid out they stepped back. Reverend Chase held his hands in the air to get people's attention. He said grace, then beckoned

Jenny up to get her plateful of food first. It was the greatest honour these folks could give her.

Jenny was very self conscious as she moved forward to take a plate. She made sure she took a spoonful of every dish. It was not hard to fill her plate to overflowing. When she reached the end of the table she looked around to find a place to sit. James was there. He escorted her to a blue and white checked blanket. He held her plate while she made herself comfortable.

He smiled. "May I have the pleasure of sitting with you?

"Yes, that would be nice," she said flushing.

"Thank you," he said. He hurried to join the line waiting to get their food.

Everyone wanted to greet Jenny right away, of course, but courtesy kept them from surrounding her with their curiosity. They leisurely ate their lunches knowing that the time to meet her would come.

Mayor was making himself to home as well, happily greeting everyone and begging handouts. He loved picnics. James returned and balancing the plate, utensils, napkin and drink, it was a wonder he didn't lose everything in a heap as he folded his tall body onto the blanket. He managed to splash coffee on his shirt. Laughing lightly, Jenny helped him wipe it off. Slightly embarrassed they dug into the delicious meal.

James was inwardly berating himself. "Why do I have to get so awkward around women! I can't even keep myself from spilling things."

Jenny in turn, was a bundle of mixed emotions. A veteran of high society she could cope with just about any situation with coolness and decorum. Yet here with one man, she felt uncomfortable and ill at ease.

The silence between them grew. James had to break the ice. "How do you like your house?"

Jenny looked up from her plate. She quickly swallowed the mouthful of food she had just taken. "The house is just beautiful and the school is wonderful. Whoever designed both is a master artisan."

It was precisely what James needed to hear. He beamed with pleasure. The ice was broken. Their uneasiness died away as they chatted gaily about Water Valley and how all the different inhabitants were working together to build this settlement.

Jenny was a good listener. James found himself explaining about the problems he had with getting supplies and attracting workers for his ranch. Big Rock was thirty miles in one direction and Butte was forty miles in the other. If they happened to need anything in a hurry they were just plain out of luck. He was an ambitious man, and spoke to her of his family's decision to make this settlement. The Water Valley site was chosen as being close to midway between cities. The river crossing had been a popular overnighting area for many years. He found himself talking about his future ideas for Water Valley expansion. At the moment his one main concern was to attract a doctor to this remote area.

Jenny listened to James talk. She found him and his ideas fascinating. She made comments and suggestions here and there. When James finished talking he was shocked to see that over an hour had passed. While talking about his favourite subject he had confided to Jenny as if he had known her all his life. Knowing his awkwardness and uneasiness around most women, he was amazed. James was impressed by Jenny's perception and understanding of what he was trying to accomplish. Her comments had been realistic and intuitive. Realizing that he was monopolizing her, he reluctantly closed down their conversation.

The good-natured folks, who had politely waited until Jenny and James finished eating and talking, started to come by introducing themselves and their families. James was loathe to give up his place by Jenny, but did not want to interfere. He reluctantly excused himself and went to talk to other friends.

The first family was Bill Storm's, the boy who helped her organize the school. He smiled at her and introduced his father Adam and his mother Susan. They chatted a minute. Susan handed Jenny a jar of strawberry jam. Jenny thanked the Storm's and they stepped aside for the next family. Rudolph and Emma Summers had two school age daughters, Irene who was fifteen and her sister Evelyn, aged nine. Irene handed Jenny some cinnamon buns. Evelyn and Irene had made them especially for Jenny.

Jenny said, "Oh my goodness, thank you, I love cinnamon buns."

A group of men shuffled toward them. First came David Olson, the blacksmith along with Joe Walters, the leather crafter. David brought a wrought iron weathervane. It had a running horse that would swing easily whenever the wind blew. Joe brought a leather bellows, just right for getting fires started in the fireplace or stove. The bachelor contingent from the Rocking B came forward with their hats clutched in nervous hands. Morgan Landsdowne, the wagon driver for the ranch's school children, introduced himself, and the five others to Jenny.

The Burns family came to renew their acquaintance, bringing her some peach preserves. Jenny was delighted. It seemed to Jenny that she was just meeting altogether too many people. Some of them came from the ranch, some from the rural farms and homesteads. The afternoon wore on, faces became a blur. Small homemade gifts started to cover the blanket. She would never remember them all.

Jenny was sure she had met everyone now. She started to relax. Everyone had been friendly. It seemed that it didn't matter in the least about her being a woman teacher. They seemed to welcome her with open arms to their community.

The afternoon was very pleasant, but the mood was shattered when a new family arrived at the picnic. A large man in faded coveralls strode aggressively into the picnic area. The congregation went silent. Hands on his hips, he stared at everyone until his eyes rested on Jenny. James immediately moved forward to stand in front of Jenny in instinctive, protecting manner. Mayor, sensing the danger bounded in to confront the belligerent man with his hackles raised.

"So you're the new School Marm aye!" His voice boomed. Then addressing James he taunted. "Trust you to get a woman in here!" Then staring at Jenny he said. "Why don't you go back to makin' babies and let real men have the job?" he snarled. With his view expressed and satisfied he had made his opinion known, he kicked out at the dog, turned to the table and grabbed some food.

Jenny was stunned at the swiftness of the attack. James started forward to confront the man, his face showing anger and embarrassment. Jenny swiftly stood and grabbed James's arm before he had taken two steps. James was sputtering his outrage almost incoherently.

"It's all right. There's no harm done. James, look at me! It really is all right. I am not offended. The attitude of the man is not unusual. The fact that the majority of the people here accepted me is a miracle of no small order in my mind." She finally persuaded him to rejoin her on the blanket.

"That," he said cuttingly, "is Gus Appleby, his wife May and their son Jake." he continued more softly. "I feel sorry for May and Jake, it can't be easy living with that man."

Jenny observed the family. A lean woman with a sad face had followed Gus Appleby and a sullen youth into the churchyard. Her son was a morose young man, who looked to perhaps fourteen or fifteen. May Appleby was dressed in a faded green gingham dress that had several patches, covering numerous holes. She wore a full bonnet, in a vane attempt to hide a bruise covering the side of her face. She spoke to no one. It was as if she didn't dare. May flung a quick look of apology in Jenny's direction before scurrying after Gus. The boy too, looked unhappy. He stared defiantly at Jenny. She saw the challenge in Jake's eyes. In her whole life Jenny had never seen behaviour like this. If this boy were coming to school, Jenny would certainly have her work cut out for her. In her observation, Jenny noticed something. Jake always stood between his father and his mother. Was he protecting her? She wondered. All these impressions came in the blink of an eye.

Jenny could not put her finger on it, but there was something intriguing about Jake. Jenny frowned thoughtfully. James looked at her, noticing the frown. He sympathized silently with her, thinking it would not be easy having Jake in the classroom. Jenny was thinking the same thing.

Gus rudely dumped scoop after scoop of food onto his overloaded plate, then stood near the table shovelling the mass into his mouth. Crumbs dropped into his beard and down his shirt. He wiped them away with dirty hands. In the meantime, May and Jake tried to find some food in the mess Gus had left on the table. They managed to find a few pickings, quickly sitting down on the ground eating almost as quickly as Gus. They ate with the hurried intensity of the starving. After he had inhaled his first plate full Gus went back to the table again. Disgusted that he couldn't find much left he threw his empty plate on the ground and stared contemptuously at everyone. He headed toward the street, growling at his wife and boy. "Git a move on!" They hurried after the miserable man.

A cloud seemed to have descended on the picnic. Most families started to pack up to go home. No one had wanted to confront the Appleby family. Jenny suspected violence within that family. It was not an uncommon occurrence and based on the bruise on May's face, it was not that hard of a conclusion to come too.

She fumed a little to herself. "This is 1896 for goodness sakes, why couldn't this modern, enlightened government put down a law to protect wives and children from being slaves to the man of the family. The law protects him as head of the home and supposed breadwinner of the family and allows them no protection what so ever."

James said, "Gus is a trapper. They own a cabin in the mountains, just a few miles north along the river. The Appleby family has lived there for many years. eking out a scant living from hunting and trapping. It seems that Gus resents the building of the community in what he considers his territory."

As the pleasant mood of the day was already broken, Jenny decided it was time for her to head home as well. It had been a wonderful afternoon and she hated for it to end in this sobering manner. She slowly gathered together her many gifts from the generous congregation. Janet joined James in helping her. Everyone said goodbye to Jenny as she crossed over to the Reverend and Nellie giving them both hugs of appreciation for their thoughtfulness. James and Janet, loaded with Jenny's many treasures, led her across the street to her house. To her surprise several boxes and sacks were piled high on the veranda. They proved to be more supplies for Jenny's larder.

"Would you allow me to help you put all these supplies away?" he asked.

"Yes, thank you James," she said. "There is so much here, I believe I could use both of you, please come in."

They worked together in perfect harmony, putting away all the food. Someone had even brought a ham. James took her outside, and showed her something she had not noticed before. On the north side of the house, where the shade would remain all day, there was a wooden box with a tight fitting lid buried even with the ground. Inside Jenny found a block of ice with a package of beef steaks and jar of milk. It was cold inside the box. Jenny was sure she had not seen it before and said so. James laughed and said one of his men had dug the hole while they were at the picnic.

James told her that fresh meat would come from the ranch every week until winter set in. Fish and meat could then be kept in a frozen state. Perishable food lasted longer in the winter.

"When your ice melts, you can get more from David Olson. He has an icehouse down near the mill. In winter we fill the building with ice from the River. It's covered with sawdust that acts like insulation and the ice remains there all summer, without melting.

When they were finished putting everything in place, James found himself reluctant to leave. He had enjoyed her company immensely. Somehow Jenny had stopped his nervousness. With the exception of the first few minutes, he had felt at ease with her. Jenny put the kettle on and invited them both for tea. They accepted instantly. Jenny used some of her unique tea for this very special occasion. When it was all prepared, they went out into the warm late afternoon sunshine and sat on the veranda to enjoy the tea.

James said, "This is wonderful tea, I've never tasted the like of it before."

"I got it just before I left Boston. There is the nicest little shop that has many different blends of coffee and teas. I have tried them all but this Rose Pearl tea is by far my favourite," Jenny smiled.

"I agree, it is wonderful," James said and then proceeded to tell her of his final surprise. "I have a horse for you to use while you stay here. She's gentle and used to both riding and driving. She's waiting for you at the livery barn along with a spare buggy. When the snow comes I'll make sure you have a sleigh."

"Thank you James!" Jenny was overwhelmed. She didn't know what to say. A simple thank you didn't seem like enough. Yet, it was all she could give.

It was close to suppertime before James took his leave. "Goodbye Janet, Jenny. I had a lovely afternoon. Thank you for the tea."

Janet and Jenny stood on her front porch till he disappeared from view. Jenny clasped her hands together, hardly daring to hope. She was beginning to like James Borland, very much indeed.

Janet looked at Jenny's face and smiled. "I must be getting along too, you have a nice evening." She kept silent on her private thoughts about James and Jenny.

Her new life here was going to prove very interesting. If she had counted right this afternoon, it looked like she would have at least sixteen students in her first class. That was if she had met them all, but it was likely she hadn't. She was quite sure not all people had made it to the picnic. In the meantime, she would continue to get settled and get to know everyone.

This interest in James needed to be pursued. Jenny grinned. The children, especially Jake Appleby, would be a challenge. But that is what she wanted. Wasn't it?

Chapter 8

S he was starting to fully enjoy herself and her independence. The squirrel that lived in her maple tree stopped being scared of her. Jenny always talked to him. Jenny thought he was adorable and wanted to make friends. She bought peanuts and sunflower seeds, placing them on the veranda railing. "Squeaker" as she named him soon learned where these special treats were. She would sit on the chair watching him eat a seed. At first he would chatter at her if she remained too close, but soon got used to her.

Monday morning, Jenny was up early. She was anxious to go see her new horse.

She took a carrot with her hoping to bribe the horse into liking her. David Olson was hard at work in the blacksmiths shop. She had met David when he helped Ray bring her bathtub over. He had been at the picnic as well.

David was a gentle man, knowing that his size intimidated many people. He greeted Jenny cordially. He showed her to the large box stall where the pretty little mare stared back at them David took a hold of her halter, leading the animal out into the sunlight. She was as black as Jenny's cook stove top and just as shiny. A white star was partially hidden under her forelock. She had a broad forehead that tapered down to a fine velvety nose that eagerly reached out to sniff Jenny's proffered hand. She snorted and shook her head. Her small pointed ears flicked forward in interest, as Jenny held the carrot.

The mare's tail swished back and forth with nervous energy, as she carefully examined the offering. She took it and crunched happily as Jenny stepped back to look at her more closely. She had four white socks, to match the star on her forehead. Jenny eyes grew large, a memory flooded into her mind. She recalled the stooped figure of the old Osler in Boston. One of his favorite old sayings had stuck in Jenny's mind about horse buying. She had never understood it, but seeing this pretty little mare made her uneasy.

"David, are you familiar with this saying and can you tell me what it means?"

"One white foot buy him,

 Two white feet try him,

 Three white feet, be on the sly,

Four white feet pass him by.

Four white feet and white on nose

This horse will be trouble where ever he goes!"

"Oh," he laughed. "Yes that saying has been around horse people for generations. Essentially, what it means is that the white hoof is softer than the black feet. They will go lame more often. You are not to worry though, James gave her to me, because I know how to make a special shoe to protect the hoof. You'll never have a bit of trouble with her."

Jenny smiled, her spirit lifted, "Thank you, does she have a name?"

David shook his head, "James told me you could name her anything you want. This horse is not a purebred Morgan. She's half Morgan and half mountain pony. In my opinion, if she is the result of cross breeding, it sure is a pretty combination."

Jenny had heard of the Morgan. It was a fairly new breed, developed in the eastern States. They were known for their beauty and strength. She was impressed.

Jenny pondered for a few minutes. She wanted a simple name that the horse would come to know. "Soot" she said. "That's what I'll name her."

Mayor came in and the two animals eyed each other. Soot stretched her head out to touch noses with him. She threw her head up snorting, then reached out again. Soot's ears flicked forward and Mayor's tail was wagging. They had become friends. David and Jenny laughed at them.

David smiled and said. "Soot it is. It suits her well. I haven't had the chance to shoe her yet, were you planning on taking her out today?"

"No," Jenny said blushing, "To tell the truth, I haven't learned to ride astride like the people here. Also I need to learn to drive horses properly, as I have always been a passenger before," she confessed. Jenny blushed even redder at the astonished look David gave her. "Not knowing how to drive is definitely going to be a disadvantage to me," she thought to herself.

"Oh...! Alright, I don't have a side saddle. I don't rightly know anyone who has the time to teach you to drive, but I'll inquire," he said scratching his head in wonder. Being born and bred in the west it was hard for him to feature anyone her age not knowing how to ride and drive.

She gave Soot a pat and left the stable. She saw the buggy that James had given her over in the carriage shelter. Jenny detoured over to look at it. It was in very good condition. The green leather upholstery on the seat was a little worn in places, but it certainly was not falling apart. It was nicely laid out. The black body work was still glossy. A short box behind the seat could be used for carrying supplies. It had a leather flap to repel rain. The canopy also in black leather could be raised or lowered as one wished. Two small lanterns were fixed to the front of the buggy to give light in the evening.

The buggy was not alone in the shed. There were several buckboards, and wagons of varying sizes. The largest one was steel. It was a bright red Fire Wagon. It had a huge tank filled with water. It was ready to go at a moments notice. Fire was an ever-present danger in the fall. Grass and trees turned brown from lack of rain. There had been no rain for over two months. Dust clouds were common making the vegetation tinder dry. Farmers and homesteaders were losing their crops due to the arid conditions. Eyes would scan the skyline constantly. People didn't realize they were doing it. Instinct seemed to take over.

As Jenny sauntered along the road back to the store, she smiled. James was a very thoughtful man. Every time she thought about him, she found her heart beating just a little bit faster. She would have to learn to drive horses soon and get a proper riding dress made. It was the one item she had never thought of when she was preparing for her trip here. Actually she wanted to go back to Big Rock, as there were a few items she needed that she could not get in Ray's store.

She decided to explore the rest of town. She made her way down the boardwalk passing the church and the rectory. Mayor had really taken a liking to Jenny. He was following her everywhere. She enjoyed his company as well.

She came to the next shop, a small sign out front saying Joe Waters' Leather Works. She remembered meeting Joe at the picnic as well. She saw a couple of western style saddles hanging on specially made wood frames, shelves of leather boots, shoes, coats and other items. Joe greeted her. He was sitting in a chair taking advantage of the bright light near the window stitching carefully at a pair of boots. Seeing them reminded Jenny that she needed a pair of riding boots. She would need heels to prevent her foot from slipping through the stirrup of a saddle. If a person were thrown from the horse, their foot caught in the stirrup they could easily be dragged to their death. Many a person had died in just such a manner.

Jenny asked. "Joe, I am going to need a pair of riding boots. Can you recommend something for me?"

"Of course, let me take your measure first," he said. Joe quickly made concise measurements of Jenny's foot and leg. Joe then showed her some fine leathers in black, dark brown and a rust color.

Jenny felt the leather, her mind thinking ahead about what she wanted in a riding habit. She chose the black color in soft calf hide.

He asked, "Will next week be satisfactory for you Miss Jenny?"

Jenny nodded "That will be fine, I doubt I'll need them before then." That settled, she looked at the other goods Joe had on hand.

He noticed her gazing doubtfully at the saddles. There were two and Joe hastened assist her. He swiftly realized Jenny was not familiar with the styles.

Joe pointed to the smaller of the two saddles saying, "I made this saddle for a lady. It has a smaller cantle than the ones used by the men. I tooled this myself thinking a lady may like the flower pattern."

"It is indeed beautiful. You do wonderful work. As long as it fits Soot, I would love this saddle." Jenny said.

"Hmmm, if Soot is that little black mare up at David's, yes it will," he assured her. "I would like to show you the bridle and breast collar I designed to go with the saddle." Jenny followed him and he showed her the flower designed tack. The bridle had silver conches holding the Brow Band to the Head Stall. The reins were leather braids six feet long. There was a silver bit attached.

"Yes, that is Soot. Alright Joe, I'll buy this saddle and the matching tack," Jenny said. "Can you deliver this to the Livery stable for me when you have time?" she asked.

"With every purchase of a saddle I give a free saddle pad," Joe said. "Come over here to the corner." Jenny followed him curiously. In the back corner of the store there was a stack of varying colored blankets. Most were solid colors but Jenny was attracted to a multicolored one. Geometric designs in reds, yellows and blues crossed the material. "This is a Navaho blanket," Joe said. I got a couple of these with my last shipment from Texas."

Jenny chose the Navajo blanket. Jenny paid for her purchases and left the leather shop. Joe followed her to the boardwalk. She was looking across the street at the building under construction. It looked like it would be fairly large when completed.

Joe noticed her looking at the building, and said. "That will be the doctor's office and home. We haven't had any luck yet with finding a doctor to come out here. He went on to tell her about the other huge building, being built just past his next door neighbours the Vanderhoffen's.

"It will be a boarding house and café." Joe had told her, "Single men 'round here need a place to eat. Most of us are only tolerable cooks," he stated brightly, obviously looking forward to its opening. "Hilda Perkins is a lady from Butte. She's waiting until the building is finished before coming out here to run it." Joe said.

"We're hoping that tremendous event will not be long in coming," he sighed in anticipation.

Jenny turned and smiled at Joe, "Thank you for telling me. I'm not fond of my own cooking either, so I understand." Joe returned her smile.

Jenny jauntily proceeded on her exploration. At the next shop she renewed her acquaintance with Karen Vanderhoffen. Jenny had met the couple at the picnic.

"My husband," she said, "is out working at the big forge at the back of our property. Sven is a metal worker and does beautiful gold and silver work. As you can see, I am the potter." She was sitting at a potter's wheel, with her hands covered in wet clay when Jenny came in. Three year old Susie was playing quietly in the corner with clay figures, probably made by Karen. Jenny looked in the display case. Exquisite jewellery covered half of the shelves. Many fine works of pottery were on the other half.

"Sven and Karen do beautiful work" Jenny thought. Jenny saw ceramic pitcher perfect for cream. The design and color were exquisite. She bought it and bid Karen and Susie farewell.

Jenny continued on down toward the river. The boarding house exterior was complete. Jenny entered it. Much work still needed to be done. There was only the basic framework in place. She noticed a definite resemblance to Dora's place, in Big Rock. Jenny figured the idea was probably based on Dora's home. If James was the designer, she could understand. James was a frequent visitor to Dora's boarding house.

The area on the other side of the street was cleared of brush and trees. It was the future site of the town offices, according to Janet. Jenny eyes look toward the only other inhabited area left to explore. A bridge crossed the river, with the huge lumber mill on the other side. It was the part of town that had the most activity going on. Even from here she could hear the sound of the huge saws, the roar of the donkey engine and shouts of the workers trying to be heard over the din. She started for the bridge.

A gust of wind almost blew her over. She looked at the sky startled. Dark clouds had come over the mountains. The air had a moist feel to it and Jenny knew it was about to rain. The sudden flash of lightning follow by a deafening thunderclap, told her the storm was just about on her.

Chapter 9

Jenny quickly turned around and headed for home. She was just passing the church when huge drops of water started to hit the dusty road and boardwalk at random. She started to run, but by the time she reached her veranda the rain was coming down hard. Jenny was soaked. She paused to look behind her and could hardly see across the street it was coming down so hard. Jenny got herself inside and noticed the chill in the house. She hurriedly rebuilt the fire and then went to the bedroom to change. Jenny was not expecting any company, so she decided to put her warm nightgown and robe on. She hung her dress and undergarments up to dry. Then the note of the storm changed. The huge deafening sound of the next thunderclap almost set Jenny into a panic. The whole cabin shook. Jenny couldn't hear anything but the noise of hail hitting the roof of her cabin. She made her way to the window, and saw huge hailstones bouncing off the grass and wood of the boardwalk. Branches were being torn off the trees, and the leaves stripped away. Jenny went and sat close to the stove. There had been a drastic temperature drop from the heat of the last few days.

The pounding of hail only lasted ten minutes, and the rain stopped soon after. Jenny opened the front door and out to the veranda. Hail a foot deep covered the yard and street. She looked at the size and saw hailstones ranging in size from one to two inches in diameter. The damage was alarming. Steam was rising from the fast melting hail. Her beautiful trees were stripped of their foliage. Her first thought was of her neighbours, and if everyone was all right. The veranda had protected her kitchen window, and the bush in front of her bedroom window had prevented damage to it. She was very lucky. It could have easily broken. Deciding to see if everyone was all right, Jenny hurried into the bedroom to change. She put on an oiled cloak and her rain boots. The storm had passed however, and blue sky and sunshine were back.

Jenny checked the school first, and found no real damage to anything. It was lucky the windows had faced north and south, and not west. Branches from denuded trees were laying everywhere. Thankfully she continued. Jenny waded through the slush, until she got to the store. Janet and Ray's windows on the west side were gaping holes. They were busy putting up tin sheets, which would do until new glass could come in.

Ray asked, "Is your home and the school in one piece?"

"Yes, I seem to have come through this unscathed. I see the two of you have everything under control here, I am going to see if anyone else needs help," Jenny said.

Jenny crossed the street to the church. One of the church windows was gone, and the Reverend was looking forlornly at the mess inside the church. Jenny helped Nellie clean it up while the Reverend looked for some boards to cover the opening. They worked swiftly and it was soon clean.

Nellie and Jenny then teamed up and both went to see if any other neighbours needed help. Joe was not in his shop, and they found him in the back yard. He was trying to get into the corral to rescue one of his baby goats. A hailstone must have hit the kid just right. Joe was so proud of his small herd, but he had to be wary of the Billy Goat. The male goat, which went by the auspicious name of Billy, had a mean streak, and watched his three Nanny's and three kids with a furious temper. He was well known in the neighbourhood. He was bleating in anger over the humans' intrusion of his yard. The mother nanny was silently standing over her motionless kid. Joe timed his move carefully, raced in and picked the baby up. He ran for the fence and vaulted over just as Billy charged him. He examined the kid, and saw that it was truly dead, not just knocked out. Joe had tears in his eyes, when he faced the women. Nellie and Jenny sympathized with him, and silently left Joe to mourn in private. Luckily his shop was next to the Vanderhoffen's. Hail coming from the west had no windows to hit.

Karen and her husband were none the worse for the storm so Nellie and Jenny crossed the street to Louise's house. Windows were broken on the west side of their house as well. Pops had just finished boarding up the windows with Louise and the kids help. Jenny and Nellie joined them in cleaning up the inside of the house. No one spoke very much over the loss. They were a stoic people. By the time they arrived at David's livery barn, rivers of water were gushing down the street to the river. Everything was fine at the stables, and although Soot and all the other horses were a little wide-eyed with fright everything else seemed to have come through unscathed. Jenny and Nellie had just returned to the store's boardwalk when a horrendous noise was heard. They looked toward the river, and saw an amazing sight. A flash flood originating up stream had swollen the river to almost twice its normal depth. The Bridge was just high enough not to be washed away. Although the full sized trees racing downstream hit the bridge supports in a very scary manner, the bridge survived the deluge.

Jenny had never seen anything like that. Her face must have mirrored her astonishment because Nellie explained to her that the storm must have caused the small streams high in the mountains to overflow and when they combined to join the river it created the flash floods. Nellie went on to say she hoped no one was caught in it.

Jenny eyed the river with a greater respect. She vowed to be very careful crossing rivers or streams just after a storm. Jenny was tired so she said goodbye to her friend and started to return home. The pounding of hooves on the bridge alerted the town, and everyone turned to see a farmer on an old plough horse galloping up the hill. It was Homer Bowie.

"Fire!" he yelled.

For just a second time froze, then everything happened at once. The Reverend ran to the church bell and pulled furiously on it. Men from the town raced toward the livery barn where, David was already hurrying the team to the Fire Wagon. Jenny was astonished at the speed David had the horses hitched. She later learned that a team was harnessed in readiness every minute of the day.

Jenny stood uncertain of what to do.

Janet yelled. "Jenny, come help me."

Jenny didn't hesitate, she rushed after Janet who was heading into the store. The next few minutes they carried shovels, blankets and buckets onto the boardwalk in front of the store. Other ladies, no doubt prepared in advance to know their duties, rushed to help.

It only took a minute, and several men hanging onto the fire wagon rushed down the hill and across the bridge. The man on the horse that had alerted them was in the lead. His horse was doing his best to imitate a thoroughbred

Three teams of horses hitched to wagons, halted in front of the store. Everyone threw the blankets, buckets and containers into the wagons.

It took no more than two minutes and just about everyone piled into the wagons. Jenny did too, although she had no idea what she was going to do.

"I'll help where I can," she thought to herself.

The ladies in the wagon were doing a very strange thing, but Jenny caught on quickly. Dresses were being removed, as Janet handed everyone a pair of overalls. Men discreetly looked away as every woman put the trousers on. It was obvious in this emergency modesty was being ignored.

Jenny followed suit. It was awkward changing in the racing-bouncing wagon. Louise explained. "If we are helping fight a fire, it is best not to have loose clothes around you." Although Jenny was a little embarrassed she was in total agreement with the plan.

The Bowie homestead was a mile and a half south on the Ranch Road. As the racing teams flew around a hill, faces filled with apprehension. Smoke was billowing down the steep hillside. The wind was blowing down the mountainside driving the fire toward the Bowie home. The fire crew was helpless to stop the main conflagration. It was too large. They aimed the hose at the roof of the cabin, arms frantically pumping in the attempt to keep the hoses filled. The house was closest building to the fire.

When they arrived they had found Martha Bowie frantically carrying heavy pails of water to splash on the house. She was at least six or seven months pregnant. The men took over from the exhausted lady. Fortunately the buildings were close to the river. It would halt the progress of the blaze. Their main goal was to save the farm buildings. The wagons carrying the helpers careened to a halt close to the river. Everyone grabbed the first thing that came to hand. Those with pails hastily filled them and formed a long line toward the cabin. They passed the pails from one to the other keeping a steady supply of water dousing the dry wood of the cabin. The roof was already smouldering.

The people that received the blankets soaked them in the river. They began to beat at the flames. Stronger men and women used the shovels to throw dirt on the fire.

The purpose of the large church bell became apparent to Jenny. It's loud sound echoed around the valley bouncing off canyons and mountain. It could be heard for miles. No one ignored that alarm. On any day but Sunday at the expected times people would know something was amiss and hurry to find out the cause.

The bell had been heard as far as the ranch because thirty men including James arrived in the wake of their Fire Wagon. Their help was welcome as the earlier fighters were tiring. Exhausted fighters would be replaced by fresher workers. More and more people from the surrounding area were arriving. They joined the battle lines.

No sooner had the ranch crew arrived that the cabin burst into flame. Nothing would save the house now. The soot and ash covered people made the decision to try and save the barn. They formed a determined semi circle around the building. The tired grim people managed to keep the flames away from the last remaining building. The rest of the forest fire reached the river and gradually died down. The barn and a short area surrounding it was saved. No one left until the fire was completely out.

Jenny wiped her sleeve across her face. She was surprised to see the sun coming up over the horizon. They had worked continuously all night. James traced the start of the fire to a dead tree that had been struck by lightning. The fire left nothing but smoking skeletons of ravaged trees in its wake. It was later estimated that the area burned was confined to about ten acres. It was actually a blessing that it hadn't started further up the slope than it did.

The Bowie couple were helped into one of the ranch wagons. The horse and Homers two cows were tied to the back of the wagon. James would find accommodation for them at the ranch until a new home could be built. The whole procession prepared to leave.

Jenny wearily climbed back into the wagon. Everyone else was in a similar condition. No one spoke on the way back to town. The tragedy had been only partially averted this time. Once they got back to Water Valley, Jenny stumbled her way home.

She was dirty and her overalls were ruined. She grabbed an apple to stave off her hunger. Jenny wearily put on the boiler to heat water for a bath. She forced down some bread and cheese. She was really too tired to eat but knew it was necessary. When the water was barely warmed she washed up and fell into bed. She had no trouble sleeping through the rest of that day.

James had slept a few hours but responsibility roused him late that afternoon. He came to Water Valley to get an idea of the devastation. Jenny did see him for a few minutes. The hailstorm had caused enormous damage to everything and everyone. The worst casualty was to the Bowies. He gathered everyone from the town and had an impromptu meeting. He told them that workers would come in from the ranch to help where they could after they had finished clean up at the ranch. He wanted word passed that a"house raising" would be organized for a week Saturday to rebuild the Bowie cabin.

James needed figures on what the townsfolk needed in the way of window glass. He was sending to Butte for replacement windows the following morning. This was welcome news to everyone. He detained Jenny after the meeting to see if she was alright. He knew this had been her first community crisis. Jenny was grateful for his concern, reassuring him that she was fine.

Over the next few days, reports from out lying areas came in. It was not good news. Crops and gardens that had survived the drought were destroyed by the hail. Jenny joined the rest of Water Valley cleaning up the worst of the mess left behind. It was a big job. Jenny heaved a sigh of relief when the next Saturday rolled around and the bulk of the work was finished. She was exhausted with the unaccustomed manual labor, but exhilarated with her accomplishments as well.

"I truly belong here now, I feel like I have become a part of the everyday workings of this beautiful little village," she said to Mayor, who was sitting on her front porch. He wagged his tail in agreement.

She decided to go for a brisk walk. It was a lovely day. She walked down toward the river. There were still signs of the flood. Debris littered the banks showing where the water had risen. The level of the river had receded to its normal height.

As Jenny was crossing the bridge, she stopped to look down at the rushing water. The water had almost a hypnotizing effect. She leaned on the rail enjoying the relaxation of the moment.

Her dream was broken by hoof beats on the bridge coming toward her. She looked up at a young cowboy, who stopped his horse and took his hat off. "Are you Miss Stockton?" he asked. Jenny nodded. "I'm from the Rocking B", he stated. "The boss heard I was coming in for some supplies and asked me to give you this message."

He handed a small paper to Jenny. The man bid her farewell and continued up Main Street to the General Store.

Jenny opened the letter and saw the Rocking B Brand in one corner.

Dear Jenny,

I'm sorry I didn't get time to come in and tell you myself, but things are a little busy here at the moment. I wanted to let you know that a few wagons will be passing Water Valley early Monday morning. We are getting supplies in for winter from Big Rock. I thought you might like a chance to get to the big city before winter. Bart Humphries, one of my hands said he would be happy to give you a lift into town and back to Water Valley Wednesday morning. I am sure Dora can put you up for a couple of nights. I imagine you have found some things you'll need, that can only be found in Big Rock. There had not been a year, in the last twenty that an avalanche hasn't closed 'The Pass'. It may be the last opportunity you have to go before spring.

If you buy anything for the school, just give the bill to Daniel Rowley in Big Rock, he will take care of it.

Sincerely,

James Borland

Jenny refolded the letter and looked toward the huge sawmill. This was twice now she had been thwarted from getting across the river. She was rather excited at the prospect of going into Big Rock. She would finish her walk another day.

On the way home Jenny debated on whether to go or not. She sure would like some items. As she was passing the General Store, she made her decision. She hurried into the store and told the cowboy that she would to Big Rock. She would be waiting for Bart that morning if he would be so kind as to stop for her. Jenny then continued home and sat down at her kitchen table to make a list of supplies.

The school and her cottage needed a clock. Her small pocket watch was just not big enough. She wanted large ones with big numbers. Her biggest desire was to visit Samantha and order a proper riding habit. It needed to be split in the middle allowing her to ride astride. She wished Water Valley had a seamstress but although there were some good sewers, Jenny wanted the best. There was a multitude of other items to be added to the list as well. Jenny spent the rest of the day pondering and adding to it.

Chapter 10

Monday morning Jenny was up bright and early waiting for the wagons to come by. She did not have long to wait. Her watch told her it was six-thirty when the wagons made their way up the street from the river. Bart, a big pleasant man, doffed a sombrero and bid her to climb up on the box seat beside him. To Jenny's delight the seat was padded. No sore behind today. Bart was a very talkative fellow and the two of them chatted constantly on their way to Big Rock. They did not stop for lunch, but ate sandwiches that Bart conjured up from under the seat. There were six wagons altogether going to the town.

They reached Big Rock about four o'clock in the afternoon, Jenny hurried to Dora's Boarding House. Upon being reassured by Dora that the same room she had before was available, Jenny thanked her. She hastily bid Dora goodbye because she had to see Jean Drummond and Samantha Riggs immediately. Jenny hurried along the street until she came to their dress and hat shop.

"Good afternoon Miss Stockton", Jean and Samantha said in unison. "What a surprise. We didn't expect you back so soon. What can we do for you?"

Jenny smiled and said, "I need a riding habit designed for riding astride. It is imperative that I get it before tomorrow night because I have to return home the next morning. There is a good possibility that I may not be able to return before spring if the usual avalanche closes the pass. I would be happy to pay for the extra help you may need to complete it on time."

Jean was rather overwhelmed by this request, but wasted no time taking Jenny to the back of the shop to view fabrics. They spent the next hour looking over materials and designs. Jenny chose an emerald green linen fabric. She then chose some braided material in a cream color to accent the dress. Just as Jenny completed her order, Samantha re-joined them. Showing her the chosen material, Jenny asked if she could have matching gloves and a suitable hat made. Samantha took Jenny to her work room. There were several completed hats on a shelf. Jenny delighted in looking at each of them. They discussed ideas for her riding outfit. They chose a straw hat and only needed the correct color of ribbon and a small cream feather to be complete. It was rather a severe style, but somehow it suited Jenny. The gloves would have to be made however. Samantha and Jean both assure Jenny they would try very hard to have her order completed by the next evening. Jenny bid them both a cheerful goodbye.

Well satisfied, Jenny returned to the boarding house and spent a lively and vivacious evening visiting with Dora and the other tenants. A chance comment by one of them regarding plans for a town Christmas party caused Jenny to sit up and take note. It was unlikely she would be able to attend especially if snow isolated them. She needed Christmas gifts. She could possibly make some but it would probably be a good idea to get what she needed now. Thankful to the lady that had jogged her memory, Jenny sat up late deciding what to purchase.

After breakfast, Jenny hurried out to Main Street. She had a long list of items now to purchase. She was elated about her day of shopping. It was one of her favorite pastimes.

She visited the bank, and withdrew more money. She wanted a tidy sum on hand. Jenny happily visited every store making her purchases. She bought a beautifully carved mantle clock for her home and a wall mounted one for the school.

She was having a wonderful time. Even with no worries about finances, Jenny was careful with her money. She kept to her shopping list spending the time looking over the quality and workmanship of each purchase. Still, by the end of the afternoon she realized just how much she had bought. There was no way she could get all of this home on Bart's buckboard. After all, he had his own load of supplies to take for the ranch. Jenny's face turned red. Deciding quickly what she should do, Jenny hurried to find John Frost the liveryman. She asked if Benny or someone was available to take her purchases back to Water Valley the next morning. John however was dubious. Benny was out on another job and wouldn't be back until Monday. He had no one else that could go.

He frowned deep in thought. He looked up and snapped his fingers. "I know just the person if he's available." A man was heading past Water Valley in the next day or two on his way back to Butte where he lived. He had made some deliveries here and would be empty on his return trip. It was possible that he would be glad of some extra income to deliver her goods. John then sent one of his stable boys to get the freight driver.

They chatted as they waited. The man arrived shortly and John introduced him to Jenny. "Jenny, this is Hank Scott." Turning to Hank, John explained what Jenny needed.

Hank, a medium sized man with a receding hairline, grinned at Jenny. "Certainly I can take your things. It'll mean a slight change of plan for me as I was going to wait until Saturday to return. There's no problem for tomorrow however. How much do you have to load?"

Jenny frowned slightly in thought. "I'm not sure, is it alright if I have everything delivered here this evening? I don't think it will fill your wagon. None of it is too heavy either. I do have two clocks that will take careful handling," she said.

Hank replied, "Clocks will be no problem, I can protect them with my blankets. I often have delicate trade goods to deliver. My wagon is just over there," he said pointing. "Have the delivery folks ask John which wagon is mine and we'll get your goods loaded."

Jenny said farewell and hurried back to the various stores and arranged to have her purchases delivered. She then went back to the dress shop, to see the progress on her riding habit. It was almost complete. Jean had Jenny try it on. It fit beautifully. The braid still needed to be attached and a few other minor adjustments. It would be finished by later in the evening. Jean would deliver it to Dora's boarding-house. "I really appreciate your hard work. It is beautiful."

Samantha brought in the completed hat. It was nestled in a green and gold hat box. Samantha showed Jenny the gloves and a lovely cream silk scarf that would finish off the ensemble. The gloves and scarf would be kept with the habit. Jenny was thrilled. She took the hat box with her when she left the shop.

There were only a few items left to purchase. Jenny went to the Goldsmith's Shop. Since she would not be back before Christmas, Jenny wanted to get Dora something. She saw a lovely necklace, with a fine gold chain. The pendant was a circle of gold, with a Tiger's Eye stone set in the middle. She knew Dora would love it. The man serving her placed it in a small box for protection.

In the corner of the shop Jenny saw some pretty paper. She went closer to have a look at it. The delighted clerk told her the boss's wife, had learned the art of making paper. Jenny looked through the stack. Each one was different. Jenny was delighted with them and bought them all. They would be perfect for wrapping her gifts. She needed ribbon to fasten them on her gifts, so she hurried back to Jean and Samantha's shop. They laughed when they saw her, but were pleased to help her buy a variety of different color ribbons.

Jenny went to the dry goods store and thoughtfully looked through all the shelved items. She was thinking of Martha and Homer, the fire victims. She purchased a trunk and filled it with items the family would need to start up a home again. She bought two ready-made dresses, which she thought would suit Martha and a couple of shirts and trousers that would fit Homer. She added undergarments for both of them and a cute little baby outfit also went into the trunk. She bought a soft baby's blanket, a tablecloth, towel and some linen for the bed. Satisfied that she had done everything she could for the devastated family she arranged for the trunk to be delivered to her wagon.

She took all her smaller items back to the boarding house. It was just about suppertime. In her room she carefully wrapped the tiny box that held Dora's gift. Well pleased with her day's activities she lay down for a short rest before the supper bell.

Later when everyone else had retired for the night, Jenny presented Dora with her gift. Dora was rather overwhelmed that Jenny had given her anything. She carefully stored the box in the China Cabinet until Christmas. The clock was just striking ten o'clock when a knock on the door proved to be a weary Jean with Jenny's completed riding dress. Jenny gave Jean a generous gratuity for her diligence.

Jenny turned around to speak to Dora, but the lady had disappeared. When Dora did not reappear right away, she took the packages up to her room. There was a knock at the door very shortly after she reached the room. It proved to be Dora.

Dora entered with a basket in her hand. A tea towel hid something in the basket. "This is for you Jenny, you're a wonderful friend. I hope you enjoy these small gifts. Merry Christmas Jenny!"

Jenny was surprised and pleased. She hugged Dora and said, "Thank you Dora. This will be the first gift I open on Christmas Morning!" She carefully took the dainty basket and put it next to her new hat box.

The next morning she gathered her precious packages. Tommy, Dora's assistant walked beside her carrying the two picnic baskets full of food for the trip. They hurried to the livery barn. The wagons were in the last stages of loading. Jenny took a quick look at Hanks wagon. Everything seemed to be there. She gave the smaller basket of food to Hank, much to his delight. The bigger one was to be shared by Jenny and Bart. She had debated which man to ride with, but the decision was not a hard one. She rode with Bart on the comfortable seat as she had noted the plain boards that Hank was sitting on, and didn't relish a bruised bottom again. The day was passed with chatting and good natured banter, between Bart and herself.

The heavily loaded wagons made the return trip much slower. It was late evening when they arrived back in Water Valley. Bart and Hank helped unload all of Jenny's supplies. Jenny paid both of the men generously for their trouble. Jenny was exhausted. She ate a couple of cakes bought from the bakery in Big Rock. She tumbled gratefully into bed. Tomorrow was soon enough to unpack all her goodies.

Chapter 11

The rest of the week flew by. Jenny spent most of her days in the school preparing for her first day. Pops had brought over the new shelving units and bench. They were very nice and she was thrilled. Once all the books and supplies had been neatly arranged, Jenny felt she was ready for anything.

Saturday was a beautiful day, just perfect for the house raising. Jenny had baked a chocolate cake complete with icing for the event. She was going to travel with Ray and Janet to the Bowie property. People were converging toward the construction site. Several buckboards contained the tools and supplies needed.

When they arrived, everyone noticed the hard work Homer had put in to clear the old rubble away. There was still more to be done, so the men pitched in. Burned trees and stumps were removed and piled to one side. When the area was ready, the contest began. They divided into teams, with the winning team being allowed to eat first, at lunch time.

At the starting yell, the teams worked furiously on the foundation and floor. It would be built very similar to Jenny's home. It was basically a rectangle with a wall to divide bedroom from the main room. The ladies cheered them on. Once their part of the foundation was complete each team started on the wall. They built the framework on the ground. Then they raised it into place using ropes and long poles. Once that was nailed into place, the boards were put on. The contest closed at that point. James had urged his team to victory. The cheers and applause from the avid watchers of the event gave all the workers heart. The tired men looked forward to a much needed lunch. The enthusiastic winners did indeed get to grab up the sandwiches and coffee first. Everyone sat on the ground to eat. For the next part of the construction the teams were dissolved. They all worked together on varying assignments. Some built the roof and a few worked on the fireplace. Jenny thought the process was amazingly quick. It was late afternoon when the men started to shingle the roof.

The ladies were not idle. They gathered in a circle near the river, far enough away from the construction so that it was not dusty. They worked diligently on a quilt. It was to be donated to the Bowie's. It had been started months ago at the weekly quilting bee. It was almost complete by the time the table needed to be set for supper. When they saw the men finishing up, they laid out the huge supper. Everyone had contributed to the pot luck. It was nearly dark when the last shingle was in place. The men went to the creek and washed up. Everyone ate a hearty meal. Jenny was pleased to note that not one crumb of her cake was left.

Jock and Jim (the Frederick brothers) dug out their fiddle and banjo, tuning them up. A bonfire was lit not to far from the house. The newly laid floor was excellent for the dancing. The wall to partition the bedroom from the living room had not been put in yet, so they had plenty of room for ten couples. The rest of the people found seats around the campfire.

James came over. "Would you dance with me?"

Jenny hesitated,"I don't know how to square dance."

"I'll teach you as we go," he said with a grin. He pulled her up from the blanket.

Jenny was breathless by the time she had finished a couple of sets. The twists of the dance were difficult to learn, but she was having fun. Every time James touched her hand or swung her around, she found her heart beating faster. She was a bit puzzled by her body's reaction to him.

Many men, especially the single ones, wanted to dance with her. Unbeknownst to her the ladies (eyes twinkling in mischief) watched the men out-manoeuvre each other to reach Jenny first, or to fill her glass. It was a source of great amusement to them. The men never let her have any peace and Jenny revelled in the attention. Her eyes were sparkling. She was having the time of her life.

James danced with other ladies but his eyes kept straying to where Jenny was whirling about. He was conscious of where she was at all times. Strangely, he felt his heart race, whenever she laughed. It was a pretty laugh and she seemed so nice. He was fascinated.

James got in his share of dances with her, he made sure of that. He was unaware that he was being glared at by thwarted men when he did so. He didn't even realize that he often stepped right in front of someone, to take her hand.

All of the young bachelors were attracted to Jenny. She would be quite a catch for some young man. Most lost heart when they saw the expression on James's face. If ever a man was entranced, he was. Jenny enjoyed herself and was totally blind to the competition for her attention.

Half way through the festivities everyone sat down, and all the surprises were presented to the awestruck couple. Homer and Martha received their gifts from everyone with sincere tear filled thanks.

Pops McIntosh had made a table for the couple. David Olson produced a metal bed frame. The homesteaders had got together and made two chairs and a highchair for the new baby. James had a stove brought in from one of the wagons. The ranch women had banded together and made a goose-feather mattress and two pillows. One of the neighbour ladies gave Martha a braided rug. Ray, Janet and the other Water Valley residents donated plates, utensils, pots, pans, along with a washtub and washboard. Everyone brought whatever food they could afford. The mill of course had supplied all the lumber at no charge.

Nellie, the reverends wife stood up to say, "All ladies are invited to a party honouring Martha and her expected baby next Saturday evening. It will be held in the rectory."

The formalities finished, the whole place erupted into more dancing. Jenny's feet were getting sore from all the activity. No one wanted the evening to end but the dance wound down around one o'clock. Everyone headed home. Some men would return the next day after church to help finish off the house. There was a cellar to be dug, a pantry to be put in and a few other things essential for living. Martha and Homer, their faces wreathed in smiles headed back to their temporary home at the ranch. It would still take a few days before the couple could actually move back in, but there was no doubt they would be ensconced in their new home before the first snow.

Chapter 12

Butterflies invaded Jenny's stomach when she awoke Monday morning. She was understandably excited, and nervous. Imagine, it was her first day of teaching. The day she had worked for was here. She glanced at her clock on the mantle. It read seven-thirty. School would begin at nine o'clock.

Jenny cooked some oatmeal. She poured some cream into it, then sprinkled some brown sugar on. It tasted really good too. "This will give me strength to get though the day on," she said to herself.

By eight-thirty, Jenny could hear the sound of children. Her stomach gave a huge flip flop. She hurried to look in her mirror. She redid her hair and tried to settle her nerves.

Precisely at eight forty-five, Jenny went out her front door, onto the boardwalk toward the school. The girls were in a tight little knot to one side whispering to each other. The boys were racing around chasing each other and yelling with excitement. Some parents were standing uncertainly on the boardwalk. Jenny smiled. It was like the parents were not sure whether to stay, or leave. She solved their problem, by greeting them as she walked toward them.

She said, "Good morning, isn't it a lovely day? If you would like, please come into the school for the first little while. It may make you feel better about letting your children stay with me. You can leave whenever you feel like it."

The parents were reassured but still a bit hesitant and slightly embarrassed.

Jenny continued. "I really don't mind. The first day will be spent getting organized and figuring out where the children are in their studies. So it will be a casual day altogether."

She mentally counted all the children she could see. There were fourteen. A couple more were walking toward them from the store.

Seeing her helper's familiar face, she called, "Bill Storm, can you and a couple of other strong fellows come assist me?" she asked.

"Yes ma'am" Bill said immediately. Turning to a couple of other classmates, "Charles, Greg, come on."

Telling them to follow her, she again smiled at the parents and said, "Just a minute, and I'll be right back."

She hurried back to her house, the boys following. "Boys, please take these over to the school," she said pointing to the chairs on her veranda. She added to Bill. "Come inside. We will take my kitchen bench and chair for the parents to sit on."

The boys cheerfully did as Jenny asked. They all quickly returned to the school and Jenny unlocked the door. Directing the laden boys as to where to set the chairs, she went outside to ring her new bell.

The children and parents filed in. There was much chattering and bustling around while everyone took seats. Jenny walked to the front of the class and took a new piece of chalk from the ledge of the blackboard.

Jenny wrote her name on the board. When she finished, she turned toward all the smiling and happy faces. Some of them had been very freshly scrubbed judging from their red cheeks. She pointed to her name on the board. She said, "I am Miss Jenny

Stockton." Some of the children could read she knew, but some couldn't. "You may call me either Miss Stockton, or Miss Jenny."

"We will start class, by singing the Star Spangled Banner. Then we will all place our hands over our hearts and give the 'Pledge of Allegiance' to the Flag. She pointed out one small boy and asked him to hold the flag. Proudly he did so. She found that some knew the song, but most did not. Very few knew the 'Pledge of Allegiance.' They would learn over time, as it would be a daily ritual.

Having completed that, she said. "Most of you may stay in the seats you are in until tomorrow. I will then know what grades you will be in and I will assign you desks at that time. Today, I'll be asking you questions to see where you'll fit in." Because there were a couple of extra seats in the front, she did ask the smallest children to move in there. That made it less crowded toward the back of the room. She said, "There will be chores list posted. Everyone will take turns performing them. The boys will be responsible for the heavier chores, like bringing in a fresh pail of water each morning, filling the woodbox, or emptying the slop pail. In winter they will shovel snow, making a path to the school and to the outhouse. The girls will be responsible for sweeping or washing the school room floor as needed. They will clear the blackboard, clean the water dipper and tidy the shelves." The desks were the responsibility of each of them. Lunches were to be put on the shelf at the back of the room. Food in the desks was not allowed. They also had to share their desks equally with their partner.

She then handed out a brand new slate and piece of chalk. She asked each of them to write their names on the slate and if they didn't know how, to wait and she would help them.

In this way Jenny learned what level the children were in writing. They were just getting well started when the door slammed open and Jake Appleby sauntered in. There was total silence by the other students. Jenny moved forward to greet him. She smiled at him and asked him to put his lunch on the shelf and to take one of the empty seats. Jake stood there belligerently for a minute. Jenny held his eyes not giving in. Jake returned the stare. The tension was tangible. Jake's eye dropped first and he did as she requested. The whole room took a collective breath.

Before they knew it, recess time came. Jenny dismissed them for fifteen minutes. They filed out and were soon talking and playing in the yard at the back of the school. The parents decided that their children were safe enough to leave with Jenny but waited to talk to her before they left. They were apprehensive about the Appleby boy.

Jenny told them, "I would like you to give me a chance to work with Jake. If after two weeks we have not been able to work together, I will call for a parental meeting and your concerns will be aired." The parents were not happy, but were willing to give her a bit of time. They left the school grounds.

Recess was just about over when the commotion started. Yells and screams caused Jenny to race outside. Bill Storm and Jake Appleby were rolling around on the ground. Both were trying to get in punches. The other children were shouting taunts and encouragement to the fighters. Jenny yelled at the two combatants. When they did not stop, Jenny ran inside and grabbed the water bucket. She came out and threw the entire bucket of water on the battling boys. Both came up sputtering with indignation. One of the girls was crying.

"Into the classroom immediately, all of you!" Jenny demanded loudly. .

The student's, young and old scurried to do her bidding. Jake and Bill dripped water all the way into their seats. Jenny got two of the towels, from the stack that was beside the washbasin. She handed one to Bill and one to Jake. She then went to the front of the room and faced them. The faces that looked back at her were mostly frightened, but both Jake and Bill were defiant. Lucy Jones was crying. Jenny decided to settle her down first.

Telling the children to carry on with their assignments, she approached Lucy. Jenny knelt down to Lucy's level, asking her quietly "What's wrong Lucy." The girl didn't want to say anything at first, but Jenny's soft sympathetic voice finally broke Lucy's reluctance.

"My slate, my slate is broken and I can't afford a new one!" she wailed.

"How did your slate break?" Jenny asked. "Did it fall?"

"No, Jake grabbed it and threw it at a tree," Lucy sobbed.

"Lucy," Jenny coaxed, "Lucy, it's all right, we'll think of something. Stop crying now, it's not that terrible."

"But it was new!" Lucy said, lifting tear drowned eyes to her teacher, "And you gave it to me."

"Here," Jenny said, handing her a handkerchief.

Jenny had a policy of not punishing students in front of their peers. Punishments were going to be dealt with at the end of the day. She stood up and faced the two boys. "You two will stay in here when class is dismissed, after school today." Her voice intoned dire consequences to the two boys.

The class carried on. When the noon hour came, the children got their lunches from the shelf and went outside to eat. It was nice to be able to eat outdoors while the weather was nice. All too soon winter would come. Jenny returned home and made her lunch. At five minutes to one o'clock Jenny went back to the school and rang the bell. The students had behaved themselves for the most part, she observed. At least there were no more fights. However Lucy just about dissolved into tears again when the students were asked to do a lesson on their slates. Jenny hastily gave her a new one saying she could use it until the end of the year. Lucy spontaneously hugged Jenny in thanks.

At three o'clock Jenny dismissed the classes. Jake and Bill remained in their seats. Jenny deliberately ignored the two troublemakers. When they started to squirm uncomfortably, Jenny relented. "Jake, Bill come up to the front desk and take a seat."

Jake and Bill both expected to be strapped. They felt foolish sitting in the front seats, made smaller for the younger children. They watched with trepidation as Jenny came around the teacher's desk. Their knees hit the top desks and made them feel six years old. She stood in front of them, giving her a psychological advantage of height. She had learned at teaching course that when she needed to do any disciplining it was always better to be taller than her adversary.

"Bill," she stated, "I will not tolerate fighting in my school, even if the reason seems to be a good one at the time!"

"But," Bill said.

"No buts" Jenny said. "Bill you will be responsible for the next month for filling the water pail every morning and if it gets colder you will also fill the school's wood box. Do you understand me?"

"Yes, Ma'am." Bill said. It was clear he felt badly used.

"You may go now, but be sure to be here on time to do your chores," Jenny said.

Bill untangled his legs and left the school, leaving Jenny with Jake. Jenny had thought hard about what to do with Jake. She paused while she figured out what to say first. Jake stared morosely back at her.

"Why did you break Lucy's slate?" Jenny asked.

"Cause I felt like it!" he said belligerently.

"I see," Jenny said. "Why are you in school if you don't want to be?"

Startled at that question, Jake stammered, "Ma made me come!"

"Why do you think your mother wants you to come here?" Jenny asked.

"She wants me to get schoolin' so I can do what I want with my life! But I don't need school!" Jake practically yelled.

"Oh!" Jenny said, "What does your father say?"

"He said I don't need book learnin', he never had any and thinks it's a waste of time!" Jake said.

Jenny ignored those comments for the moment.

"Jake, what would you really like to do if you got the opportunity?" Jenny asked.

Stunned, Jake just stared at her. "I... I guess I'll be a trapper and hunter like my old man."

"I see," Jenny said. "Is that what you really want to do?"

"That's what Pa wants me to do!" Jake insisted.

"Yes but if your father or mother had no say in what you wanted to do with your life, what would you really want to do?" Jenny persisted.

"No ones ever asked what I want to do before," Jake said looking up at Jenny for the first time. "But I don't need schoolin' anyway!" he quickly added.

Jenny didn't comment but looked straight into Jake's eyes. Jake felt compelled to answer her. "I think I'd like to train horses," he stated almost defiantly. "I'm good with animals."

"I think that is a wonderful idea," Jenny stated. "You like animals?"

"I got a deer and a squirrel up at the cabin. They were hurt and I fixed them up. They like me," he said.

"I have a squirrel too!" She exclaimed in delight. "I named him Squeaker."

Jake looked at her in astonishment. "Really?" he asked.

"Pa hates 'em. Says he'll shoot 'em one of these days!" Jake spat.

Jenny had a brainstorm. "Jake," she said, "Do you ride and drive horses really well?"

Jake stared at her warily, like she had suddenly grown horns. He didn't answer right away.

"Yeah," he said finally, "I love riding and driving, but we only got one old horse. Pa don't let me do it that much." Jake paused and looked at Jenny with fear on his face. "Are you booting me out of school, Pa said you would the first day!"

"Should I?" Jenny asked, "Is that what you want me to do?"

"Sort of," Jake said, "but Ma, she wants me to read n' write and cipher!"

"You know," Jenny said, "Your mother is right. If you learn to read, write and do your arithmetic, then you would know if someone that hires you to do horse training or whatever, is cheating you. If someone were to pay you for a job, how will you know if it is what he or she agreed to pay you or not? If someone writes an agreement for you to sign, how do you know it is one you want to put your name too, if you can't read? You would have to depend on others to do it for you. What if they don't tell you what the paper really says?"

Jake didn't answer, but Jenny could tell he was at least thinking about what she said.

"Never thought about that before," Jake said thoughtfully. "Not even Ma 'splained it like you just did. It kinda makes sense."

Then Jake stiffened up again, "So you kickin' me out or what?"

"No Jake, I am not." Jenny took a deep breath,"Your punishment will be to teach me to drive a horse and buggy and to ride well!"

Jake stared. He couldn't believe what he was hearing. "You want me to what!" It was plain that he thought Jenny was crazy.

Jenny agreed with him a little. But there was something, just something behind all his bravado that seemed to indicate vulnerability. His attitude told Jenny that he hated his father. He also knew that was wrong. He seemed to love his mother, but thought her weak. He was one bundle of confused emotions.

This could very well be a turning point in his life. Jenny was determined to help him if she could.

"I do not know how to drive a buggy, hitch the horse, or ride very well. I need to learn! Your assignment for breaking Lucy's slate will be to teach me to do all of this, after school and on weekends until you think I am capable of doing it myself."

"That my punishment?" he asked amazed. "You really don't know how!" he exclaimed.

"No, I don't," she stated firmly. She did not add that she was really too embarrassed to ask any of the adult population in Water Valley. Jake didn't need to know that. To everyone at school it would be a punishment. But just knowing that Jake secretly would love the project and that it would help Jenny as well gilded the lily. Just maybe, Jake would find the assignment as a positive in his life.

Only time would tell. Jenny told Jake to go home and tell his folks that he would be late getting home after school for the next while. His punishment would start tomorrow. Jenny in turn had qualms about this decision. How would Gus, Jake's father, react to her punishment? She hoped he would not turn violent.

Chapter 13

J ake left, but his attitude was one of extreme puzzlement. He trudged home kicking up clouds of dust as he shuffled along. By all rights, blisters should be covering his hands from the strap right now and just the thought of it made his palm tingle. It was a four-mile walk uphill to his home. As he neared the yard, he listened hard for the sound of his father's voice. He was late because of staying after school. His stomach started to twist itself into a bundle of knots. If his father were home he'd get a beating for being late. He crept up on the house and looked around from behind a nearby tree. He studied the homestead trying to sense where his father was. His mother came out of the house and stared down the road, no doubt looking for him. Jake came out from behind the tree, and his mother spotted him.

"He's not here," she said. "Give me your excuses later, you had best get your chores done quick though, 'cause he will no doubt be home soon."

Jake never said a word but hurried to get the chores done. He milked their one cow, that he affectionately named Aggie. He then raced to feed the chickens and the old brown horse, Prince. He pumped fresh water for all the animals.

He had just one more thing to do, and he ran up a vague path to the west of the house. He came to a tiny clearing, and started a chirring noise in his throat. His call was answered and soon he saw movement in a spruce tree. It was a huge grey squirrel. It scampered toward him with no fear whatsoever. It grabbed hold of his pant leg and crawled up to his shoulder. It immediately explored Jake's pocket for a nut that was always hidden there.

He raised his voice and called out "Jasper, Jasper." His summons was answered by a shy brown form, amazingly camouflaged in the bush. It was a mule deer. Jake coaxed him out and fed him some fresh grass from the valley he had picked. Both of these animals he had rescued from certain death. Their injuries had been life threatening and he had nursed them back to health. He gave them both a last petting and hurried back to his house. He breathed a sigh of relief when he was finished.

He got back just in time to see his father coming down the path from his hidden still. He was weaving, a sure sign that he had been drinking his deadly brew. Jake headed for the house in a hurry. If past experience had taught May and Jake anything, it was to stick together when his father had been drinking.

May was putting the food on the table as fast as she could set it. Jake helped her. Gus slammed the door open and stomped in. He grabbed a chair, and sat at the table dumping most of the stew onto his plate. He grabbed a couple of biscuits and started to shovel it into his mouth. Then he looked up and glared at Jake.

"Whatya standin' there for, sit and eat," he mumbled with a full mouth. He ignored his wife.

Jake hurried to sit down. Jake carefully divided what was left of the stew between himself and his mother. There was not much. Both kept a cautious eye on Gus, while he ate. It was the same, day after day it seemed. Gus turned violent when he drank, which was most of the time. Even when he was sober he had a nasty short temper.

Jake had never known a time when he had been completely bruise free, nor as far as he remembered had his mother. She had been beaten into complete submission. A spark of bravery would show up every once in a while, but never in Gus's presence. Jake knew that soon his body would fill out. He was getting taller all the time. The day would come when he was strong enough to take his mother away from all this.

To make the dream a reality he needed time and money before they could defy Gus. If only he could get a good job. Both May and him would be glad when winter came and Gus would be gone for three or four days out of every week. He would tend his trap lines. It used to be a real good living, fur trapping, but the area Gus worked had been pretty well tapped out.

This also made Gus the harder to get along with. The fewer furs Gus brought home the less money they made and the poorer the family became. This also made Gus harder to get along with. The beatings in turn became more frequent.

Jake helped his mother clean up the dishes and went straight to bed. He woke up later that night, hearing the cries of his mother, and the slap of Gus's hand on her flesh. It was hard to say what she had done this time. Gus needed no excuse to abuse. Jake rolled over, put his pillow over his head, and tried to drown the sound out.

It was early the next morning when Jake awoke. His father's snoring was shaking the house. In winter and cold mornings he would wake up to frost on the inside of the roof. He hated the thought of winter for this reason. It wasn't too bad this morning though. It would be a nice day from the look of the blue sky. He had no window in his loft. All of this information came through the cracks in the roof boards. He quietly got up and tiptoed downstairs to the outhouse. Re-entering the house he grabbed the biscuit his mom had hidden away for his lunch. He started his long walk down the mountain to school.

This trip would be horrible in winter, but by that time he probably wouldn't be in school anyway. He would surely be expelled by then. This new teacher was a real mystery. She was very pretty though. He didn't know what to think about her methods of punishment.

"She may call it punishment," he grinned, "but for me, it'll be great." Jake started to think of all the tricks he could pull on her while teaching. He sobered then and tried to think of why the teacher couldn't ride or drive. Even the youngest of his classmates could do both. He scratched his head. It was a real poser. During his walk he contemplated about Lucy. Why had he broken her slate? It was a dumb thing to do, he admitted to himself. He would be furious if some one had taken his and broke it. He had felt no desire to break any of the other kid's slates. Why Lucy's?

The sun was full up when he crossed the bridge into town. The children from rural areas and the town were converging on the school as well. The shopkeepers were sweeping the boardwalks and yelling greetings to one and all. All of them seemed to avoid him like he was diseased. It made him angry, and hurt his feelings as well.

"They were all cowards. They deserved what they got. I'll back down from no one. Those babies will see me getting revenge. Just see if they won't!" he stewed.

Stomping up the incline to the lane in front of the school he found he was actually on time. Bill was just entering the door of the school with a full bucket of water in his hand. The teacher was talking with the younger children. Jake hesitated. He wished everyone would just leave him alone today. Deep down he really didn't want any more trouble. His mother told him one day that "Blood flows deep." It was an archaic saying that meant the blood of the father runs in the son. He would likely become just like his father. He saw the way his father was. He just knew he didn't want to become like that. In fact he didn't like the way he was behaving at all. But he couldn't seem to stop himself. He saw Miss Stockton check her watch and start toward the school doorway. Jake made his way toward her.

Chapter 14

Jenny watched everyone file into the school. She noticed that Bill had fulfilled his duty with filling the water bucket. The firebox was stuffed to the hilt.

Jenny smiled at Jake. "Good morning Jake." Still, she eyed Jake just a little warily. He still seemed sullen and angry.

After the Anthem and Pledge, Jenny started off with a roll call. She had the list of everyone's grade level, and where they would sit for the remainder of the year.

She sat down behind her desk and said. "Everyone please stand up and move to either side of the room." She watched as the students did so. When they had quietened down she continued. As I call your name take the seats assigned to you. You will have time after I am finished to move your belongings.

"Now for the first graders, Annie Breckinridge and Jessie Burns you will share the first desk on my right," Jenny said pointing at the correct spot. The girls dutifully went to the designated desk. "Jamie Burns and Henry Potts, you will take the first desk to my left, both of you are in the second grade.

Evelyn Summers and Barbara Jones, you are in the third grade. Johnny Breckinridge, you are also in the third, and will be partnered with Jason Greeves of the fourth grade. Grace Tyson, forth grade will sit with Lucy Jones, who is in the sixth grade. Now Dick Redmond and Greg Wilson you are both in fourth grade and will sit together there," Jenny said pointing. "Mary Barnes and Irene Summers you will take your places next. You are in the ninth grade. Irene, you are the eldest girl here and will be the spokesman for all the girls," Jenny said. "George Payson you will be sitting with Charles Jones, both of you are in the eighth grade."

"We have two desks left, and they will be given to our biggest boys. Jake Appleby you are in the sixth grade, you will take the next seat. Last of all Bill Storm, ninth grade will take the final seat. Bill, you are the eldest of all the boys and will be their spokes person," Jenny said smiling at all the children. "Alright, take your belongings to your new desks and get yourselves settled."

There were some grumbling and complaining, but the situation played itself out like Jenny had planned. She told them that their assignments would be placed under their Grade number, on the chalkboard. She did so, and when the class was busy following her assignment, she took her chair to sit between the first and second graders. She started the first graders learning the alphabet. The second graders she helped with their readers. Before long, a reminder from Charles had Jenny looking up at the clock. It was indeed noon. She dismissed the class for lunch. All of the students took their lunches outside to eat. Jenny again cleared her desk and left the school. She was just in time to hear Jake telling an interested crowd that his punishment was to help the teacher after school, "forever".

Jenny laughed to herself and hurried home for lunch. Amazingly enough there were no fights all day and Jenny sent everyone home in a relatively good mood. Jenny fully expected to have to deal with some more fighting between students.

Jake was waiting outside for Jenny to finish up the last minute details of a schoolteacher. She told him she needed to change her clothes to something that could get dirty. Her light blue dress was just not appropriate. Jake agreed, so Jenny hurried to change into a dark brown cotton dress, she had especially made for working around the house and outdoors.

Jenny and Jake walked to the livery barn. Jenny introduced Jake to Soot.

Jake's attitude was totally transformed. Jenny could hardly believe her eyes as he portrayed gentleness very uncharacteristic to his usual attitude. He petted Soot's nose and talked softly to her. Jenny looked at Soot's enchanted behaviour, it was just as if she was trying to understand his words. It was a good thing Jenny had changed her dress because Jake taught her how to look after the animal He had her currying the horse, cleaning the feet and making Soot's shiny coat gleam. Jake then taught Jenny how to harness Soot up. Jake was in his element. He laughed uproariously when Jenny made mistakes. When Jenny started to laugh with him, the ice was really broken. They both started to enjoy the day. Soot was one very confused animal, when her harness was put on, taken off and put on again and again.

David Olsen would look out from the blacksmith's shop, at first to make sure Jenny was all right and his astonishment grew, that this useless boy was in his glory. He couldn't believe what he saw happening in his barn.

David was a very discreet man, but he couldn't help watching the progress of the two of them. He never did tell anyone although he was aching to. He watched as Jake's attitude toward Jenny changed and he was amazed at the knowledge Jake showed with regard to the animals.

"Well, isn't this an interesting situation," he said to himself.

The week seemed to fly by. Jenny was extremely busy. Jenny loved her work, and she grew to love the children almost instantly. They in turn worked their hearts out for her and soon she became their adored "Miss Jenny" to all of them.

Saturday night the ladies got together at the rectory and had a party for Martha Bowie. Her baby was due very soon. She also told them that the house was nearly finished and that they would be moving into it the following weekend. Martha's face mirrored her delight. They had a lovely luncheon and sat Martha down to open all her gifts. Some had names of the person who was giving the present, but most were anonymous. The overwhelmed lady had a mound of items that had been wrapped in brown paper or hidden in boxes. The first thing that was given to her was the completed quilt, which the ladies had been working on the day of the house raising.

It was a patchwork of, red, blue, green and white squares, in a pretty design.

She folded it and set it aside with shining eyes. There were blankets, tablecloths, tea towels, washcloths, and sheets. Pops came over for a couple of minutes, and brought in a cradle, lovingly done in birch bark. He left as quickly as he came, not even letting Martha thank him. Jenny's trunk was opened and Martha's eyes grew wide at the various items inside. No one told her that Jenny had brought it. In fact Jenny had gone out of her way so no one would even know who donated it. By the time the party was finished, Martha had need of an entire buckboard to carry her acquisitions home.

Jenny was happy to be able to help someone in need. After all what was the use of money if she couldn't do something nice for deserving people?

Jenny continued to enjoy the lessons on riding and driving. On one of their drives, Jake headed Jenny west across the bridge. It was Jenny's first test, as Jake called it. He sat behind her, saying nothing and letting Jenny handle Soot alone. Jenny didn't do too badly, Jake had admitted. On the way back to town, they were passing the Burns farm.

"Oh," Jenny said. "Let's stop here for a few minutes. I want to see my new cow and her calf." Jake was willing so Jenny turned into the driveway.

Don and Betty both came out of the house, at the sound of the horse and buggy. Jenny and Jake both were greeted enthusiastically. Don took them both out to a field just past the barn. There were three cows and a calf nearby. Donald called to them and the four animals sauntered towards the fence.

Jenny's cow was a lovely Jersey. Her soft brown eyes and beautiful head leaned over the fence to be petted. Jenny asked Don if she had a name and he shook his head. "Daisy," Jenny said. "That name seems to suit her."

Daisy's calf was five months old and was frisking about. She was the image of her mother. "Buttercup" Jenny added, "will be the name of that little cutie." Donald and Jake both laughed and agreed with the names.

When they got back to the livery barn, Jenny unharnessed and groomed Soot herself. Jake was very proud of her.

Chapter 15

Jake had lots of time to think on his journeys back and forth to school. He wished he could use their horse Prince, but his father refused. Gus said it served him right to walk seeing that he couldn't get himself expelled. Gus wanted him at home and out trapping with him. School was a bunch of nonsense.

Jake had always agreed with Gus on that point, until now. Miss Jenny was really nice treating him like an adult. It was kind of fun to teach her how to ride and drive. He knew the lessons would soon be over and he regretted the thought of that. However his work with Jenny had not gone unnoticed.

Jake remembered that exciting moment when David Olson the livery man had said. "Jake, I've watched you teach Jenny. I can tell by your actions around animals that you like them. I respect that. I could use some help around here once in a while. Would you like to work for me a bit?"

Jake recalled how the invitation had stunned him. He was excited about helping David haul and stack hay the next weekend. David would need a lot of hay for the coming winter.

He debated whether to tell his father about the job, then decided against it. The money he earned was his. His father would take it if he knew about it. Besides, he wanted to replace Lucy's slate. Lucy was using the slate Miss Jenny gave her, but Jake felt it was important to replace what he broke. They cost twenty-five cents and that would take him a day to earn.

He thought about Lucy, more and more. He liked her. She was really a pretty girl. She had long blonde hair, usually done up in braids. She was a bit shy and scared of him. That's why he had grabbed her slate. Her fearful reaction angered him, which was why he smashed it. Everyone was scared of him. He laughed confidently, then the laughter turned sour. He wanted Lucy to be his friend not to be scared of him. The other kids too.

"Really," he thought, "They think I am just like my father. It's no wonder I don't have any friends." A solitary tear of frustration surprised him, as it leaked down his cheek. He brushed it away impatiently.

Jake pondered the problem for another mile, on his walk to school. Jake made up his mind then that he would try to be nicer to everyone. He hated his father's mean and belligerent attitude. He hated the abuse Gus laid on his Ma and him. He vowed he would change everyone's opinion about him if he could. "Miss Jenny likes me. Just look at how she treats me. Maybe others would do the same," he thought.

Gus wasn't home when Jake got there. He hurried through his chores. It was not quite suppertime, so he ran up the hill to visit with the deer and squirrel. The shy creatures were not afraid of him. Supper was waiting when he got to the house. His mother and him sat down together, and had a sparse but nice meal.

He had never really talked to his mother about much, but somehow that night seemed ideal for confidences.

"Ma, can I tell you a secret?" Jake asked.

May looked at her son. His voice was so soft and gentle that she was startled. "Of course you can."

"I like school. Miss Jenny is wonderful and I like teaching her to ride and drive. It has been a rather nice feeling to be liked and not have her scared of me."

"Oh!" May was rather taken aback. Was this really her son talking?

"Ma, David Olson asked me to work for him this weekend, but I don't want Pa to know." He looked at this mother pleadingly.

Pride in her son, swelled May's heart. "I won't tell, Jake. You don't know how long I have wished for this. I'm very very proud of you." Tears of joy were running down her cheeks. "I believe you're doing the right thing. It will be hard for you to change but I know you'll succeed." His mother sobered. "I don't think we should tell Gus about this. Any change won't sit well with him." Jake nodded agreement.

The next day, Jake put his plan into action. Asking Miss Jenny's permission he stood up and came to the front of the mystified class. Turning around to face the other children, he became tongue-tied. He shifted from one foot to the other. Finally he got a hold of himself and began.

"I wanted to apologize to everyone for my bad behaviour, especially you Lucy." Jake said. "I'm working this weekend. I'll buy you a new slate with my earnings. I know I've been awful to you all and I'll try my best to be a better person," Jake added.

He hurried and sat down at his desk. The stunned class and Jenny were silent for a moment. Then Jenny started to clap. The rest of the class joined her. She gave Jake a big smile. But Jake's biggest reward was seeing a shy smile come from Lucy.

When lunchtime came, he was asked by the older boys to join them over in the spruce grove. This had become a favourite haunt. It was a treat to all the children to pry off the hardened spruce gum and chew it. It had a sappy sweet taste and they loved it. It was the first time they had included Jake in their pursuits.

True to his word, Jake handed a blushing Lucy a new slate that next Monday morning.

That afternoon after Lucy received her new slate from Jake, her mind was a bundle of confusion. She walked slowly toward her home. On one hand, she was sure she hated Jake. It seemed like he was always teasing her, and after he broke the slate, Lucy had tried hard to avoid him. Now she was not sure what she felt. Here was a brand new slate in her hands, and she had gotten a public apology. It must have been very hard for Jake to do that. She would have been petrified. Lucy was a pretty girl, with freckles covering her nose and cheeks. She had beautiful blonde hair that hung down past her waist when it was not in braids. She was shy, and avoided confrontations with anyone if she could. She dutifully tried hard to help her mother with the housework and chores. Life was difficult without her father. He had been killed in an avalanche. She missed him very much. Today for example she had to help mother with the laundry. It brought in money for necessities. It was fortunate that Water Valley had their share of bachelors, who delighted in bringing their laundry to them. Even Miss Jenny had started sending her laundry to her mother Louise. Lucy sped up and hurried into the house. She put her books away and went outside. Sure enough her mother had several washtubs full of water, soaking the clothes. Charles was busy refilling boilers with water. Once they were hot he would replace the water in various tubs as needed. Lucy rolled up her sleeves, picked up a washboard, soap and started to clean the clothes in one of the tubs. After fifteen minutes of this vigorous activity, she realized why her arms were so strong. She often surprised her classmates by winning some of the arm wrestling tournaments that kids were fond of playing. She had even beaten some of the older boys.

Lucy wrung the sopping clothes out by hand. She then put them in the rinse water, waiting in another tub. There were two tubs, one with clear rinse water and one with "bluing" in it. Bluing was a deep blue powder that mixed with water to create a light dye. When white clothes were put in it they took on a faint blue tinge. In bright sunlight this caused white clothes to become even more white and pristine than if rinsed in the clear water. Lucy's sister Barbara, a bright eyed precocious nine year old was stirring the clothes in the rinse water with a huge paddle rather than with her hands. Bluing had a tendency to turn your skin blue after a while. The two worked together wringing the excess water out of them. Both of them took them to the multiple clothes lines crossing the back yard. With wooden clothes pegs, they hung the clothes to dry in the sun and wind. They all kept a close eye on the weather while the clothes were drying. If a sudden storm overtook them, the blowing dirt and heavy winds could cause them to have to redo the entire batch.

Lucy's mind was not idle during her participation in the Wash Day. Her mind spun around and around with one burning question. What did she truly think of Jake Appleby? In her heart she knew the answer. Her brown eyes softened in the knowledge that Jake was rather cute. It was a beautiful apology that had been delivered direct to her. He had been talking to everyone but his eyes had focus on her. He was apologizing to her. She sighed; knowing deep down strange feelings were welling up. When the laundry was complete and hung out to dry, Lucy went into the house. She sat at the table to do her homework. However today her mind was on other things. She daydreamed a little; her head propped up with her hands, elbows on the table. Lucy's eyes followed her mothers every move as she made supper. Barbara sat on the other side of the table busy doing her assignment. Charles had his own desk up in the attic. A Dormer window on either side of the roof let light into the single room. Louise had divided it into two rooms with a curtain. Charles on one side, Lucy and Barbara on the other. Louise had a cot on the main floor near the stove. As small as it was, the home was comfortable and filled with love. Louise turned away from the stove where a stew was simmering and noticed Lucy's distraction from her task.

She smiled at Lucy and asked, "Day dreaming?"

Lucy blushed a bright red, and furiously shook her head.

Barbara giggled. "Lucy has a boyfriend!" Barbara sang in a lilting voice. Upstairs, Charles's deep-throated laughter joined Barbara's in their light teasing of the embarrassed girl. Louise's eyes begged the question but, when none of them were forthcoming with the name of Lucy's young man, she smiled and turned back to her work. She knew it would not be long before she found out anyway.

All of the family went to bed early. Tuesday was baking day. Before school all the children would be busy. Charles would get the fire going in the huge stone ovens. Pops had made them when Louise decided to start her baking project. These huge ovens baked the best bread in the country. Louise had need of the extra income to support her family. Lucy and Barbara would help knead the dough for the first part of the bread making. However by the time the dough had risen to the next stage they would already be in school.

So it was with a great surprise that Louise, dropping off to sleep felt a soft hand on her arm. She turned over and saw that Lucy was there. With lowered voices, Lucy talked to her mother about her confusion over Jake's behaviour, and his apology. She needed the advice that only a mother could give. Louise was rather taken aback by whom it was that Lucy was talking about. She had only heard of Jake's bullying side. She listened to Lucy's story and wondered at the change being wrought in the boy's life. She couldn't let her self believe in this change, so she cautioned Lucy to stand back a little and observe the situation. Watch Jake's behaviour in the future. Maybe he had changed and if so the young schoolteacher would have performed a major miracle. Satisfied Lucy returned to her bed.

One day in late September, on their lunch hour, all the class was behind the school in a spruce grove harvesting spruce gum. Most of the lower gum had already been removed, so the girls would sit on the shoulders of the boys and reach up for the higher snacks. Lucy had been hoisted up on her brother Charles's shoulders and she was reaching high above her head for an extra special tidbit, when Charles foot turned a bit on a small rock. He overbalanced and fell. Lucy tumbled off and with a small yelp of surprise she went head first into a nearby tree. She lay in a crumpled heap. Jake was there in an instant. He was aware of Lucy's every minute. He gathered her gently up and started toward the school. He hurried as fast as he could go in safety and breathed a sigh of relief when he saw Miss Jenny crossing the yard back to the school after her lunch. Jenny saw them coming and hurried to open the door. The younger girls were wailing in near hysteria, thinking that Lucy may have been killed. Lucy however, was only dazed and had soon realized she was in Jake's arms. Her bump on the head was nearly forgotten in her shock of being held by him. Jake set Lucy down on a bench near the water bucket. Lucy's head was aching, but she didn't cry. She did bit down hard on her lip as Jenny took a towel and dipped it in the cold water. She carefully cleaned the dirt and blood away from her forehead. There were only a couple of scratches, but there was a definite lump on it. Jenny asked Charles to take Lucy home. She advised her to stay in bed for the rest of the day. Lucy was a bit wobbly when she stood up, but otherwise seemed just fine.

The feud however was over between the students. To Jake's amazement, the older boys started to talk easily to him. He had friends for the first time in his entire life. He was embarrassed to be in the sixth grade at his age so he found himself discouraged easily. He didn't really put much effort into his work so his grades remained mediocre. Miss Jenny had told him school was important and kept encouraging him. In spite of his complacency he was learning. When he managed seventy-five percent on his arithmetic exam, he was shocked. Jenny's smile of pride spurred him to try harder. He started reading more and studying. His transformation was complete and his heart took over. Jenny's patience and tact had won this battle.

Chapter 16

The end of September came with frost and a definite chill in the air. The older boys were all out helping with the threshing and harvest of whatever was left from the hailstorm. It was a discouraging project at best. The girls and the small boys still came to school. Jenny been so used to Bill getting the water, she failed to notice the empty bucket. Irene mentioned it, and chagrined Jenny asked if Irene and Mary could go get the water. The girls were happy to oblige, but when they came out of the pump house after filling the bucket, they got a dreadful surprise. Joe Walter's billy goat must have escaped his enclosure and gone in search of trouble. He hated humans and barely tolerated Joe. He bleated and lowered his head. Irene and Mary screamed, dropped the bucket and ran for the safety of the schoolroom.

Billy charged after them and the girls raced inside. The goat was on their heels. All the girls started screaming and laughing nervously. All the children scrambled onto the tops of the desks. The goat started butting at the desks trying to get at the terrified students. Jenny was in a panic herself. Goats were dangerous. She didn't want anyone to get hurt. She too wanted to climb on the desk but it was her responsibility to get rid of the goat. Those horns were sharp too. Jenny spotted the school broom and retrieved it. Poking it in front of her Jenny advanced toward the furious Billy. The straw ends of the broom were sharp, and he started to retreat from the pointed bristles. Mayor, who was never far from the school, arrived to the rescue. Between Mayor's barking and nose biting and Jenny's prodding with the broom the irate goat made a slow retreat. Once they had him out the door with Mayor following, Jenny slammed the door shut and leaned against it in relief. Mayor could be heard chasing the goat back to his pen. The kids and Jenny started to laugh. A small crisis was averted. No one wanted to venture outside. They heard Mayor's barking and Joe's voice rising in impatience, as they attempted to round up the recalcitrant goat. The children happily did without water until they were sure the goat was corralled.

October seventh, the dry spell broke. It started to rain. As James had predicted the mud soon became ankle high and more in places. Jenny and Jake still had their lessons, every afternoon. When it was not raining, Jake had Jenny out driving. When Jenny practiced her riding, Jake rode David's horse, named Roan. It was a strawberry roan, with a big roman nose. It had a rough gait, but was reasonably obedient.

On the wet miserable days, they worked side by side cleaning stalls and grooming all the horses. David was fast becoming a part of the fun and as the two learned more about each other a mutual respect formed. David asked Jake to work for him more and more. Jake was thrilled.

Jenny and Jake practiced constantly. The lessons after school and on the weekends continued, until Jenny's driving and riding improved to the point where Jake and David both could not fault her. She was a natural in the saddle.

Jenny and Jake both agreed that he had more than completed his "Punishment." With the lessons finished Jake said, "Miss Jenny, you have done really well. You'll be an expert driver before long at this rate. Soot is a really nice horse, I wish I had one like her," he said softly. "My Prince is a nice horse too but he's very old now." He laughed. "Prince has a sway back and is fat. I gather grass for him and Aggie the cow as much as I can. The hay Pa brings home for the stock is sometimes mouldy. She is old too and Pa will probably butcher her mid winter for food." He sobered at the thought. "Well good night, Miss Jenny," he said and started on his walk home.

"Good night Jake, thank-you for your lessons, I enjoyed them immensely," Jenny called after him.

Jenny's students' grew to love her as well. She taught them using her sense of humor and wit to keep them interested. Corporal punishment was never a part of her plan. It would have horrified her New York professors.

"How will you maintain discipline? The children will not learn anything! Spare the rod, spoil the child!" they had said. The cliché's had burned their way into her brain, but Jenny was a gentle person. She tried hard to figure out why a child was behaving in a certain way and then tried to help the situation.

Her idea of punishment was usually a physical task, especially one that the student disliked the most. One of her favorites was making the troublemaker clean the outhouses. It was a nasty task, but was not really hard. Lime needed to be put down the hole to break up the waste. The bench with the hole needed to be washed at least weekly, more often in warm weather. The walls and ceiling were constantly swept of cobwebs and insects. The worst part was the stench created by the chemical reaction of the lime to the waste. Eyes often watered if you went in too soon after introducing the lime. This punishment worked extremely well. It proved a great deterrent.

Each of her charges personalities was becoming clear. She had two young boys whose mischievous nature would often get them into trouble. Practical jokes and teasing was normal for them. They ranged from being hellions to angels. Johnny Breckinridge and Jason Greeves were fast friends and Jenny was often their target. The two boys were usually disappointed that their efforts gained them little satisfaction. One day they placed a garter snake in her drawer. They waited in giggling anticipation of Jenny's horror at the discovery. The boys were totally disappointed when Jenny picked it up and had an impromptu class on reptiles. The boy tried to frighten her with mice, toads, worms and once a spider. They almost succeeded with the latter. Jenny had a phobia of the creatures. She steeled herself and placed it in a jar. Each critter she was given turned into a nature lesson. The boys gradually gave up. In fact the two had been fairly quiet recently. Jenny knew she was in for some trouble. Jenny relished the boy's challenges and wondered what would be next.

Chapter 17

On October twenty-third, the students were industriously applying themselves to their studies, when a squeal from Greg Wilson startled everyone. They looked up to see him pointing out the window. It was snowing. The huge fluffy flakes were drifting gently down to the ground. It had been chilly all morning and Jenny had the fire in the stove going. There was little wind and the beautiful crystals were keeping their shape for a while. The spontaneous cheers of the students lifted all their spirits.

It was almost noon anyway so Jenny took the class outside. To get everyone settled down again for the remaining ten minutes would have been useless. The first snowfall was always exciting. Tongues came out as everyone tried to catch the snowflakes on them. Jenny called their attention to the individual flakes as they landed on their clothes.

She had brought out her magnifying glass and showed the fascinated students the structure of each flake. She told them that each snowflake was formed differently. When she said it was a good possibility that no two were identical, they were amazed and not a little sceptical. When Henry asked how the delicate little crystals formed, they listened to Jenny as she talked about the way frost developed on the windows when the children's' cold breath blew on a frozen pane of glass, and how way up in the sky tiny rain droplets froze in frigid high levels and the combination of wind and cold formed the fragile flakes.

The students ate their lunch then. Part of the afternoon was spent talking about weather, condensation and how snow came into being. Some of Jenny's precious paper was given to each student, along with a pair of scissors. She showed them how to make paper snowflakes. Afterwards, she had them compare one another's flakes. She showed them that every one was different. They hung them from the roof beams with strings and small nails. It was this kind of teaching that had the children learning, but having fun at the same time.

While the class continued, the snow became heavier and came down faster. The snow stopped just before school was complete. It had accumulated around five inches. The excited students were soon rolling and playing in the snow.

Bill and Jake had disappeared just after the bell rang. They returned in triumph. Not too far into the woods near Jenny's home, was a grove of huge Birch trees. Jake and Bill had cut several huge sheets of bark from them. All the children yelled in anticipation. Jenny was curious. Irene and Mary enthusiastically grabbed Jenny's arm and drew her to the main street. The hill down toward the river was perfect for sledding. There was much laughter and general all round good fun, which everyone in town became a part of. Everyone, adults included, joined the children taking turns to slide down the hill on the birch bark sleds. Due to the snow, the ranch wagon was delayed. Even the settler's children stayed a while for the fun as well. Mayor was everywhere, barking and playing with the children. He avoided getting run over by a whisker.

Jenny had never been on a sled and was just as excited as the children. She sat between Bill and Gracie on the flimsy projectile. She felt exhilarated by the race down the hill. Mayor was there racing beside them. His tail never stopped wagging. At the bottom all three were tumbled into a heap and Jenny sat up gasping from the surprise of a face full of snow. The children roared with delight. Mayor jumped on top of her and gave her a good licking. Her hair was askew and her dress soaked. She thought, "I don't think I look like a prim and proper school teacher at the moment."

She was startled to be confronted by the chestnut colored legs of a horse and when she looked up she flushed in embarrassment. James sat there looking down at her, grinning. She hastily got up, and tried to straighten her dress. James laughingly dismounted and helped her back up the hill. Although she had fun sledding she declined the begging of the children to go again. James however went down a few times himself much to the delight of the students.

She was about to go home and change, when a deep bass voice caught everyone's attention. David and Pops came out of the woodworking shop with two beautiful sleds. The two of them collaborated when they saw the snow. David had gotten busy at the forge making the runners and brackets and Pops hastily made the wooden platform. The children gathered around them with their eyes full of wonder. The littlest ones had the privilege of sliding down on them for the first time. They played a while, until the wagon from the ranch arrived to take the children home. The party broke up. The two new sleds would stay at Pops workshop. Anyone could borrow them and the class would often sled on the lunch hour or after school.

James had noted a possible danger to the children. The river was still running and the new steel runners of the sled often had the kids flying close to the bridge. James had a rope net made and strung along the river banks for safely. This would stop any children from landing in the freezing water. The children knew the rules about not sledding when horses were using the roadway. There was always an adult keeping an eye on the playing youngsters anyway. Mayor had made himself personal guardian of them as well.

Chapter 18

Halloween was fast approaching. Jenny was not sure of what people in the west did. She went to talk to Janet, who filled her in on the country traditions. All children were brought to the town at five o'clock. Several volunteer drivers would bring a hay layered wagons to carry the children to all the rural and ranch areas. The lady of the various household would go all out to create goodies to give to the children. Children delighted in dressing up in costumes. Once the children had gathered up all the treats, the wagons would bring them back for the bonfire. In the parking area of the town just across from the general store, various people would tend a blaze starting around seven o'clock. The wagons full of excited children would return around eight-thirty. Everyone who wished to come could take part in the corn roast.

Jenny thought this tradition was wonderful and decided to plan special treats for the children. A bout of warm weather had melted all the snow, leaving a muddy street again. It was nice during the daytimes but was chilly during the evening. She bought a pumpkin from Ray, as he had a few come in for sale. She chose the largest one she could. Halloween night landed on a Saturday this year, so Jenny had all day Saturday to prepare. She scraped the pumpkin out carved a scary face. "The Jack-O-Lantern is perfect!" Jenny thought. She put a huge candle in it. She set it on the table, to wait for evening. She got apples, candy and decided to try and make some popcorn balls. Her housekeeper in Boston had made them the previous year and Jenny loved them. She had brought the recipe along with her from the city. Popcorn balls had only come into existence just a few years before, so she was pretty sure the children here would never have had them. It was hard work, but Jenny was thrilled with the results. She could hardly wait for the children to try them.

She decided that she would dress up in costume as well and perused her closet for costume ideas. She had one black dress and got the idea of a witch. She hurried to the store and bought some black material. At home she sewed busily. She wanted a pointed hat. Once the form was done it hung limp in her hand. She needed something to make it stand upright. Material stuffed into it, supported by a wooden spoon in the middle did the trick.

Jenny then went out into the woods and cut some willow branches. These she put around her broom and it took on the appearance of a witch's broom. It was dark out when she finished her task. The clock read six-thirty. She put her costume on and decided she looked rather scary. She heightened this effect by mixing up a little flour and water. She took bits of the resulting paste and dotted it all over her face. When it dried it looked like she had scars and warts. Jenny lit the huge candle inside the carved pumpkin. She blew out all the lanterns and set the pumpkin on the veranda. When she looked back on it from the gate, she was pleased.

She could hear the townsfolk laughing as they made the bonfire and prepared the corn for roasting. Janet was brewing a cauldron of hot chocolate in the middle of the fire. Their mouths dropped open as they caught Jenny's transformation. Joe Walters had already taken the town children out to make the community rounds. All would end up back in town by around eight-thirty.

James was busy putting more wood on the fire, when Jenny appeared. He was amazed by her transformation, but was soon laughing at the costume like the rest of them. The town's folk were delighted. None of them had thought to dress up. They chatted while the kettle brewed. The corn was just being taken from the fire when the sounds of excited children were heard coming over the bridge. All the hosts and hostesses, including Jenny hurried home. The children piled out of the wagons and started to race around the village, making sure not to miss a house. When they reached Jenny place, the children were awed by her candle lit Jack-o-Lantern. Their mouths dropped open in astonishment when they saw Jenny's costume. Eyes grew round when they saw all the treats. All of them took a bite from their popcorn ball. Jenny couldn't have been more pleased by their enthusiastic response. After they left, Jenny returned to the bonfire. The children soon joined them. Butter and salt were slathered on the hot corn. It was delicious. Hot chocolate hit the spot for the chilly children and adults alike.   Everyone was allowed to eat as much corn as they wanted. Leftover corn was handed to the children so they could take them home. Parents gathered their sleepy children to take them to their beds.

James and Jenny sat by the bonfire and chatted for a while longer before he walked her home. He cheerfully said goodbye and left Jenny alone. As Jenny closed the door, she leaned back against it. She was delighted that her relationship with James seemed to be going so well. She went into the bedroom and lit the lantern there. She slowly got ready for bed, with her mind weaving daydreams. When she finally blew the lantern out, it took her a while to fall asleep.

Noise woke her just before dawn. She sat straight up in bed wondering what the commotion was all about. It sounded like it was coming from the schoolhouse. She lit the lantern slipped her shoes on and threw a cloak over her nightgown. Carrying the light she rushed out the back door. Ray, Janet, the Reverend and Nellie were hurrying toward the tumult.

The bawling of a distressed animal greeted them at the door of the school. The door was closed but the lock was broken. Ray gingerly opened the door and staggered back as an irate cow dashed by. Jenny hurried in to find total chaos and destruction. She stopped in horror and looked around. Desks were overturned and some broken. Children's personal books and belongings had spilled out. Items were stepped on, broken or torn. Much of the school supplies were ruined for any further use. The blackboard was overturned and broken where the upset cow had landed on it. Nothing had escaped the attention of the bovine.

That was not the worst however. The stove was lying on it side. The stovepipes were hanging. Soot was everywhere. Luckily there had been no live coals in the stove or the school might have burned. The cow had diarrhoea. She had soiled everything in her frenzy to escape. Jenny could not say a word. She stretched her hand out helplessly, tears welling up in her eyes. What a disaster. Who could have done this wicked thing?

Jenny moved forward to try and salvage anything. All of them moved silently through the mess. They picked up very little that wasn't ruined. They stacked what they found on the shelf. Janet and Nellie persuaded Jenny that there was really not much more they could do at the moment. The cleanup would be a project not a small job. Finally Jenny nodded and the five of them walked slowly out of the school.   Ray held the lantern up to the door frame. The door was splintered where it had been forced by some object. Art and Nellie, Janet and Ray returned to their homes. Later that day would be time enough to think about cleaning the mess up.

Jenny returned home. She was agitated and upset. Thinking a bath might calm her down, she built up the fire and put some water on to heat. She lay down but could not sleep. Her beautiful school, her pride and joy would never be the same. Desks could be repaired the school could be cleaned, but the atmosphere had been violated. She cried herself into oblivion.

When she awoke later that morning, her head was throbbing. Her eyes were swollen and red. She looked in the mirror and turned away. She felt horrible. She was wondering where to start on the clean up. She cooked herself some oatmeal and poured cream and brown sugar on it. It was one of her favourite breakfasts. When she finished she filled her tub and soaked in the hot water. She let it relax her stress-tensioned body. Once she was out of the tub, she started to shiver. She hurried into the bedroom to dress. Jenny had just finished brushing her hair into place, when a knock sounded on the door. Jenny hurried to answer it. James had come to get her for church. He was grim faced, having heard of the fiasco from the Reverend, when he arrived in town.   Jenny looked into his eyes and felt the telltale signs of tears wanting to come. She fought this feeling off but her voice cracked, when she asked him to wait a moment while she donned her winter coat. It was very cold this morning. They walked quietly to church just as the bell started ringing. Jenny could not look at the school.

In the mysterious ways of the small town, word of the Halloween damage brought everyone out to church that morning. Reverend Art looked over the congregation. A family from the ranch arrived during the hymn. He did not pay much attention at the time. His sermon was short and to the point. He talked about sins and the guilt one has when they have done something wrong. He orated on how the sinner needs to confess and own up to what he has done. Otherwise the guilt would fester and grow. The sermon was very short.

The traditional time for announcement and meetings was after the service. When the Reverend was finished, James stood up and called for attention. James spoke of the damage to the school. Others stood up and talked. It seemed that the school was not the only target of the mischief makers. Everyone was upset and agitated. Joe's goats had been turned loose from their pen. Just about everyone's outhouses had been turned over. James called for a discussion to see if his perpetrators could be found.

There was a call from the back of the church. The Greeves family pushed a white faced youngster toward the pulpit. "Here is one of your culprits," said Sam Greeves.

The Breckinridge family was all there. Johnny's face had been a picture of innocence. When he saw Jason his complexion visibly paled. The dejected Jason shuffled face down to stand in front of the people. Sam went on to say that Jason had been caught coming into the house that morning, naked. It seemed that after he left his friend he decided to tip over just one more outhouse. Without his friends help he had lost his balance and had fallen in. Snickers and guffaws were heard at that. Anyway, Jason's mother and father had forced a confession from him. As for his friend, Jason would not say who he was.

Johnny Breckinridge, having been fretting since the sermon, stood shakily up and said, "It was me, I helped Jason."

Johnny's mother and father were looking at their son in horror. They were under the impression Johnny had been with the other revellers who were in the wagons. Johnny was sent up to the front to join Jason. The petrified boys grabbed each others hand for comfort. Sam Greeves rejoined his family, leaving the boys, James and the Reverend to themselves up front.

The chastened boys finally told the congregation that their pranks had not been intended to harm. It was a spur of the moment idea for the cow in the school incident. They had found her wandering the road. Apparently she had broken down the fence to her field.

Johnny said, "We took Jock Fredericks ol' black and white cow and got the idea to put it in the school house. We thought it would be funny to add some Epsom salts to a bit of oats and feed it to her. I am really sorry Miss Stockton. We didn't mean any harm."

"Neither did I, Miss Jenny," Jason said tearfully.

James and Jenny both knew that the boys were only ten years old and would probably not have thought their plan through to the dastardly conclusion it had come to. Between eating the salts and being trapped, the cow had panicked. Jenny didn't blame her, she must have been extremely uncomfortable. Once the cow had exited the school, she had calmed down and was found down by the river eating some grass. Ray made sure the displaced cow had got back to the Frederick brothers' farm.

The only thing that remained was what punishment could be dealt these boys. The boys were told to stay put while the congregation had a meeting. Both the Breckinridge and Greeves family volunteered to clean up the school because it was their sons' mess. The debate and ideas kept the discussion going for more than half an hour. Finally someone came up with a brilliant suggestion. The congregation approved.

James returned to the pulpit. He held up his hands for silence. Everyone including the terrified boys glued their eyes on him. "It is our decision," he said facing the boys, "that your punishment will be in three parts. First it is write an apology to Miss Jenny and every other family you have wronged with your pranks. Second is to clean up the school all by yourselves. No one will be allowed to help you. Pops McIntosh, will assist with the repair of the broken desks and other broken equipment. This is however after you have removed all of the broken, but cleaned items to outside of the school. If something is beyond your strength, you will then approach an adult and politely ask for their assistance. You will continue to clean until the school is as spotless as you can get it. Thirdly you will be responsible for shovelling the walks and a path to the school from Main Street including Miss Jenny's house after snowfalls until further notice. Do you understand?" James asked the cringing boys. They nodded despondently. James continued. "School will be dismissed until all repairs are complete. Since we are not sure how long this clean up will take, school children will be notified when school can begin again."

The congregation conversed with each other. The general clamour got louder. For the most part people agreed with the punishment, including the reluctant families of the boys. The boys were to start work in the morning. The whole congregation including the boys were taken over to observe the sorry condition of the schoolroom. From the wide eyes of the boys they had no idea of the total destruction the cow caused. Then and there the boys turned manfully to Miss Jenny and they apologized again. Jenny accepted their apology with a hug. They vowed they would be good forever more, and Jenny just smiled. At least they were good for the moment.

It took the boys three days to clean the school completely. It still had a foul odour for many days even with Jenny's fragranced candles and hot vinegar. The classes resumed on Thursday. Everyone sat on the floor because it would take Pops days to repair and build new desks.

Chapter 19

During the second week of November the blizzards came. Most people stayed home in front of the fire. School was sporadic in-between storms. It was a rather lonely time for Jenny. She did visit Janet quite a bit and she joined the quilting bee. All the ladies that lived in town gathered on Mondays, Wednesdays and Fridays when the weather was bad. Jenny had a wonderful time and soon learned the tricks of hand sewing the detailed patterns.

James also became a regular visitor to town. He and Jenny spent many hours' playing cards with Janet and Ray. You could count on him coming in every Saturday evening. It became a routine enjoyed by all four of them.

James found himself enthralled with Jenny and the feeling seemed to be mutual. Janet and Ray would look at each other and smile. They loved both of the young people.

An avalanche on November twenty-third closed off Water Valley from Big Rock. Fortunately no one was caught in it this time. The road to Butte was flatter. Even though it could get blocked by huge drifts of snow, steady shovelling could get a person through if it was necessary. James kept the road to the ranch open at all times.

They ingeniously made a snow plough that was hitched in a reverse pattern from the usual pulling movement. Four heavy horses would push the plough in front of them. The wedge shape would push the snow to either side. It was slow tiring work, but effective.

Temperatures varied from freezing to deadly. Jenny was amazed how everyone adjusted to the low temperatures and managed to do just as much work in twenty-below temperatures as they did when it was above freezing. Stock still had to be fed and chores completed. It was funny to see laundry out on the clothesline stiff with ice. If there were a wind it would stand straight out with no flopping.

"One becomes accustomed to the cold eventually," she realized, as she made her way to Janet's house for the quilting bee. "Mind you I wouldn't want to be out in it for very long. It's fortunate that the clothes and underwear they have in these modern times keep you warm a lot better that they did in my parents day," she said to herself.

The laughter of children playing outside on the river caused her to pause and watch them for a few minutes. They had cleared a section of snow leaving the slippery ice. They were chasing a ball around the area. Some of the boys had curved sticks made from branches, they were playing hockey with a ball. Most of them looked like balls themselves because they wore so many clothes.

A couple of them even had ice skates and raced around their slower companions in glee. There was a fire built of willows on the shore where the children could get warm.

Jake was just coming out of the Store, his face wreathed in smiles. He proudly showed her his new ice skates.

"These cost me all of my wages since September," he said solemnly.

"Oh, Jake they're wonderful. Are you going down to play with the others?" she asked.

"No," he sighed, "I have to get home for now, but tomorrow morning Charles said he would go with me, to try them out." He smiled in anticipation and waved goodbye to Jenny.

Jenny entered the store and she had a wonderful evening with Janet, Nellie Karen, Louise, Lucy and Barbara. The quilt they were working on had every color in the rainbow. The sheep's wool Janet acquired to stuff the quilt would be very warm and nice too. The ladies finished the evening out with coffee and dainty sandwiches. Jenny enjoyed herself thoroughly and went home well pleased.

Jake however could hardly sleep. His skates were hidden under his bed. He swore when he saw the snow was lightly falling that night. Too much snow would prevent an early morning skate. He was relieved when it had only accumulated about three inches. He hoped nothing would deter him from trying out his new skates.

Charles had just finished up his chores when Jake arrived on his doorstep.

With a smile he hurried to get his own skates and they ran down to the River. The first thing they did was to build up a fire, using the dry willows along the river bank. It blazed up merrily. Jake and Charles put their skates near the fire to warm up. It was nice to be able to change from their boots to the warmed skates. They cleared the ice of snow with shovels and a broom. It took them ten minutes to complete the task. They hurried back to the bonfire.

Halting in horror, Jake saw his skates, blackened and shrivelled. Their shiny silver blades seemed to mock him. Charles and Jake never said a word about this disaster. Jake sat down in torment.

"I will not cry, I will not cry!" he said over and over to himself. Charles put the fire out, and the two of them walked slowly back to Charles' home. School would start in an hour. They talked about anything except skating. Charles felt so bad for Jake. He did not know what to say or do. Charles had picked up the blades and an idea started to form. He did not tell Jake his plan, and the two of them went to school

Jenny saw the depression on Jake's face, but the boy would not talk to her.

At lunch Charles quietly told Jenny what had happened.

"Miss Jenny, I need your help," Charles said softly. "I was wondering if I could exchange chores or anything for a dollar? I want to do something special for Jake."

They agreed to terms and Jenny handed Charles one dollar. It would take Charles a long time to pay it off, but he was proud to do something for his friend. After school he hurried to Joe Walters Shop.

"Can new boots be attached to these blades?" he asked Joe. Charles then told Joe what happened to Jake's new skates. Joe examined them with interest and assured him he could.

Joe put aside the jobs he had and started on the new skates for Jake. Fortunately the burnt sole was still attached. Joe used that as a measure for Jake's new boots. He worked for a whole day on them.

On the Friday before school, Charles hurried over to Joe's. The skates were ready and looked even more beautiful than the originals. Charles pulled out his money and asked how much it would cost. He braced himself to hear the total and was floored, when Joe said twenty-five cents. Charles stared at him and stuttered. "But that can't be right..."

Joe grabbed Charles hand and shook it binding the bargain. "Now git!" he said to the speechless boy. Charles stumbled out of the shop. Joe smiled to himself as the observed Charles race toward the school. Miss Jenny was just ringing the bell for class.

"Miss Jenny, Miss Jenny" he yelled in excitement. "Look, look! Aren't these great skates? Joe only charged me twenty-five cents too," he said with a puzzled frown.

Jenny turned to the young man and smiled at the beautiful skates in his hand. Jake had not arrived yet, he was often late because of the morning chores he had to do.

Jenny smiled at Charles and said "Why don't you go meet him, he should be along any minute."

Charles smiled and turned to hurry back the way he had come. Charles met Jake just outside of the leather store, and unbeknownst to them, Joe saw the whole transaction.

Jake's legs failed him as Charles handed him the precious skates. He shook his head in wonder, tears welling up in his eyes. He took them with shaking hands and stroked the soft leather.

When strength returned to his legs he stood up and formally shook Charles hand in thanks. He couldn't speak. Suddenly that just wasn't enough he grabbed Charles in a bear hug.

Joe who was watching had tears running down his cheeks. They flowed unnoticed in his observation of the touching scene. He felt very satisfied with his part in the secret.

The two boys made plans to skate as soon as school let out. Jake was the happiest person alive that day, except maybe for Charles who was well compensated for his thoughtfulness.

Chapter 20

When the first snow stayed on the ground, Cyrus Hatfield, the owner of the Hatfield Lumber Company hired workers. Winter time was logging time. The farmers and homesteaders looked forward to supplementing their income by working for the growing lumber mill. Winter was the perfect time to do the logging because the heavy draft horses could easily haul the heavy logs across the snow. Cyrus was a strong man rivalling David Olson in size. Jenny had only met him once. He happened to be in the General Store one Saturday when she was there. He stayed in a cabin at the back of his mill. He was rather reclusive, but worked very hard. He also paid his workers a fair wage which was almost unheard in these modern days. A man could get five dollars a week and if he used his own horse or horses, they would get one dollar a week for each horse.

Water Valley itself was never used for logging. Cyrus liked the way the valley looked and didn't want it spoiled. He and his men would drive over to the next valley west and he was very picky about what trees were cut. He had a large piece of white chalk that he would mark the tree to be harvested. He was wise enough to take only medium sized trees. With his part time helpers more used to farming than logging, it would have been next to impossible to do the larger trees. Cyrus dreamed of one day having a large full time business, with skids and logging roads. He wanted professional loggers to come in from the East or maybe even Canada. Right now though he had enough work to keep him busy for the next year just using this part time help. He had six full time men in the mill. These men had been homesteaders who couldn't make a go of it. They were happy to have a full time job. They didn't have families and lived in a bunkhouse not too far from the boss's house.

Logging was hard work and Cyrus judged the men and gave them the jobs he felt they could handle. Men doing jobs unsuited for their capabilities got hurt. He never wanted anyone to be hurt.

Bill came into the school one winter morning, with his face a wreath of smiles. "Miss Jenny, I've been hired for the logging team as a 'Yarder'." He told Jenny proudly. Bill had passed the age and size limits Cyrus set as a standard hiring guide. Bill felt duty bound to help his family. The harvest had been a poor one and the bill at the store was increasing rapidly.

Jenny asked, "What about your school work, Bill?"

"That's what I come to talk to you about. With your help I would like to study at home if you give me the assignments. I do the logging every day but I'll study at night. I don't want to get behind if I can help it," Bill replied.

Jenny said"Of course I'll help you. Perhaps you could bring your completed works to me on Sundays after church. I can give you the next week's assignments at that time." Jenny was very curious and asked Bill to explain what a 'Yarder' was and tell her about logging in general.

Happily, Bill told her what the main jobs of the Logger were. "Men work as teams. There are various sized trees of course and some of them take longer to cut through than others. Choppers use sharp double handled saws that are very long. Once the tree is brought down, the Choppers use axes to cut all the branches off. Depending on the size of the tree, it would then be cut in reasonable sized pieces. Then comes my job as the Yarder. Huge logging chains are attached and my horse will haul it out of the bush that the Swampers have cleared to the nearest main trail down the mountain. I walk beside the log guiding the horse. This was the most dangerous part of the trip because the rounded log could slide or roll sideways. We have to be alert at all times. Logs are loaded by the Teamsters onto unusual sleds. The ones used here, are two bobsleds one behind the other with a double chain fastening them together. Horses mules, or oxen use a block and tackle to either lift the logs onto the sleds, or the sled would get as close to an embankment as they could and the logs rolled onto the sled. The most logs that can be put on one wagon were three unless they are very small. Even then the horses strain to pull the wagon back to the mill. Several men will unload the wagon and stack the logs up in a huge area prepared for this purpose. The process was repeated over and over again. I feel very lucky to be a part of the crew."

Jenny later learned that logging never stopped until the snow melted toward spring. Then the work at the mill started. They would start the huge round saws up and start cutting the logs into boards. A Donkey Engine would assist the regular crew to haul the logs to the saw. Cyrus boasted one of the few machine driven saws in this part of the country. A huge steam run tractor, made a canvas belt turn the huge steel saw with sharp jagged teeth. Perspiring men and lathered horses would put the log on a metal conveyor belt and steel clamps would hold the wood in place, sending it through the saw. Depending on where the clamps were set, the thickness of the board would be determined. By the end of the day men would be covered in sawdust and sweat. Exhausted men and horses would go home, to repeat the process the next day. Sundays and bad weather were the only deterrents to this routine.

Jenny saw very little of Bill in school for the next few months. In fact Jenny was amazed that Bill's schoolwork hardly suffered with doing the job and the homework. Jenny was very proud of the young man and missed his cheery smile in the classroom. She worried that the young man was taking on too much but there was really nothing she could do about the situation. Bill was so proud of helping his families financially.

Chapter 21

Irene and Evelyn came in one morning all excited holding a blanket covered box. "Miss Jenny!" Evelyn said, "We have a present for you!"

"That is if you want it," Irene added mysteriously. They then uncovered the box, to show Jenny the cutest little kitten all curled up in a furry ball. It had big splotches of orange, black and white.

Jenny melted at the sight and picked up the tiny kitten. "She is adorable," Jenny said looking at the blue eyes of a six-week-old kitten.

"Dad said that this one is too small to survive out in the barn. He said it would probably die," Irene said. "We thought you might like her."

Jenny laughed and said "I would love to keep her."

At noon Jenny took the kitten home and debated on what to do with her. The ground was frozen, but she had an idea. Taking a little used cake pan, Jenny descended into the cellar and scraped some of the soil up from the dirt floor for a litter box. Jenny named the kitten Kally-cat. She was a smart little animal and instinctively knew what the box was for. The kitten proved to be a delightful companion for Jenny. The affectionate animal loved to curl up with Jenny when she sat on her chair or next to Jenny on the bed. Kally made Jenny very happy.

Days were passing quickly. Children began to get excited over the upcoming Christmas season.

Things were not at all well in the Appleby household. Jake started coming to school with blackened eyes and huge bruises. When Jenny saw May her situation looked even worse.

Jenny tried to talk to Jake. At first he refused to say anything, but Jenny persisted. "Jake is there anything I can do? I want you to know I am here if you ever want to talk."

Jake relented one afternoon after school. "Miss Jenny, I want to warn you. My Pa hates you. I think I know why. I haven't been careful enough to hide my changed attitude toward the people of Water Valley and you. He's blaming you 'specially 'cause I won't quit school and you won't kick me out. Please be careful Miss Jenny!" he blurted.

The situation proved true. If Jenny came anywhere near Gus he would glare at her in pure hatred. The town's people could feel the tension between them and were concerned. They kept a close eye on the situation.

The Saturday before Thanksgiving the blow up came. Gus had come to the store to get some supplies. Jenny just happened to be there chatting with friends.

When Gus saw her, his face turned red. He pushed his way toward her and Jenny bravely stood to face him. Gus started yelling obscenities and told her to let his son alone.

"I don't want no Mama's Boy in my house," he yelled. Jake's changed attitude toward the towns people did not sit well with Gus. He was losing control of the boy and the stupid brat was defying his authority more and more. Now here was this "good for nothing" teacher, standing before him totally without fear.

Gus's temper broke. This woman unnerved him and this would have to change. A defiant woman had to be put in her place. Gus swung his ham like fist at her face. This would teach her to look at him like that. The blow never landed. He found his arms held by four strong angry men. He struggled, fighting dirty by kicking with his hard leather boots. Ray ended the fight when he cocked his rifle. The sound stopped Gus in his tracks.

"Get out of my store and don't come back or I'll shoot you on sight!" yelled the angry Ray. More men joined in and Gus was forced out of the store. "If you need something from town send either Jake or May. Your presence in this community is no longer tolerated!" Ray told Gus.

After Gus left, Jenny sat down again. She felt light headed and she found her hands trembling. Janet led Jenny into the kitchen where she handed her a glass of wine. It helped and she tried to put the incident out of her mind. She instead concentrated that day making sure people knew about the Thanksgiving Supper on the coming Thursday, and that everyone was invited.

That Sunday Jenny took a mental note that Jake was not in Church. He had started attending regularly since the beginning of October. However when Monday morning arrived, Jake's absence was very notable. It was a nice day, and Jake rarely missed school. Jenny was uncomfortable and prickles started going up and down her neck. There was little she could do however, so she dutifully taught the children their lessons.

Alarm bells rang in her mind when Jake did not come to school on Tuesday either. She anxiously chatted to Ray and Janet and couldn't help but wring her hands in nervousness. They told her that Jake was likely with his father on a trap line run.

Wednesday came and she saw Jake coming toward the school she breathed a sigh of relief. That was until he got close. His face was one massive bruise. He was limping.

"Jake, what happened!" Jenny burst out. She never gave him the chance to answer but turned to the wide eyed students. "Go ahead and play! School will be delayed a bit." She steered Jake over to her home. Once inside she started wiping Jake's cuts. Jake winced every time she touched him.

"Tell me what happened, Jake," she insisted.

Jake did not want to tell her, but didn't really have the courage to ignore her query. "When Pa got home from town Saturday, he was extremely angry. He took his belt off and beat me 'til I blacked out. Ma tried to stop Pa. She was beaten even worse. I was out for over six hours. I crawled to Ma and lifted her into the bed. Pa was gone for the moment. I stayed with Ma until she woke up. That was twelve hours after I did. This morning was the first time I felt I could make it to town. Ma is still in bad shape." Jake was relieved to have the story into the open.

Jenny wished they had a Sheriff here in the Valley. She talked to Ray and Janet, and even James. She was told the same thing by all of them. There was no law to protect wives or children in this so-called modern age. Jenny was depressed, so much so that she delved into the Thanksgiving feast with unusual intensity.

Just about all the community turned out for Jenny's Thanksgiving supper. It was held in the church as that was the only building big enough to hold everyone. All the ladies pitched in to help and they had a beautiful dinner. The meal consisted of turkey, potatoes, vegetables and pumpkin pies for dessert. Jenny was acting hostess and she kept her self busy, serving and chatting with everyone. When she got the chance to sit down and eat herself she saw a letter sitting up against her glass. Puzzled she opened the missive. It was an invitation. The mauve paper had a lilac scent to it. She read.

Dear Miss Stockton:

I would like to extend you an invitation to join James and myself here at the ranch for Christmas. I have heard lots about you from James and am looking forward to finally meeting you in person. I hope I may be privileged to call you by your first name Jenny as James does now. You would have your own room. It would be our pleasure to have you come as soon as school lets out for the holidays and for you to stay as long as you wish.

Sincerely,

Alice Borland

Jenny was astonished. Her heart skipped a beat and she was thrilled. What a wonderful invitation it was.

When James asked to escort her home after the festivities, Jenny consented, but first she needed to ask him some questions. She asked him to sit down at one of the tables in the church with her.

"James, I have some questions about this invitation if you don't mind," Jenny said. At James affirmative nod, she continued. "This was unexpected, but to my embarrassment I would like to know who Alice is. Is she your mother?"

It was James's turn to be embarrassed. "Oh I am sorry, I had gotten to know you so well lately, I forgot I may not have mentioned her. Alice is my Grandmother. My Mother, Father and Grandfather have passed away. She is my only living relative. She's anxious to meet you and I want you to come very much. Please?" James asked.

Jenny smiled at his plea. "Give me a minute to collect my thoughts, James. Why don't we walk to the house?" James escorted her home. Jenny opened the door to enter. She turned to James to bid him good night.

Kally the kitten took that moment to rub against James's trouser leg. He laughed. "I think she is so cute and I like her. She'd come with you wouldn't she?" James coaxed.

Looking into his begging eyes, Jenny relented. "I would be delighted. But are you sure Kally should come?" Jenny asked.

"Of course Kally can come. She'll love having the whole house to roam. I am so happy you'll come," he said as he stared into the beautiful green eyes and drew her close. "I have found great pleasure in your company," he said intensely. He bent his head down and their lips met, tentatively at first and then more firmly. Jenny was breathless.

"Goodbye for now," James said softly and left.

Jenny was in a complete state of euphoria. She picked Kally up in an embrace of enthusiasm and swung her around. Together they danced around the room.

Then Jenny laughed. "It's a good thing no one was watching us Kally!" she said. "They would think I was not dignified enough to be a school teacher!" She laughed in delight.

Chapter 22

S nowstorms averaged about two a week. Snow piled up and many classes at the school had to be cancelled. When school did go ahead, Jenny started her class on ideas for a Christmas Concert. By the beginning of December the students, were getting excited. They had singing, dancing and skits planned for the big occasion.

Jenny still saw James quite often. Jenny was fast developing a deep friendship with him. She was looking forward to spending the Christmas holiday with he and his grandmother. She arranged to arrive at the ranch on the twenty-third of December. Tentative plans were for her to stay at least until the twenty-ninth or perhaps even the third of January if she felt like it.

It was an extremely happy time for everyone. Smiles were plastered on faces and shouts of Merry Christmas were ringing through the chilly air. Excited children's voices kept the season truly merry. Once Jenny had found out about her vacation at the ranch, she was determined to give every man woman and child a gift. Her lack of knowledge about how many people resided at the Rocking B worried her. She enlisted the aid of the Ranch School wagon driver, by the name of Morgan Landsdowne. He provided her with a list of everyone that lived on the ranch. Other than her students, the list told her which ones were children with their ages and gender included. Jenny was very grateful.

One gift worried her. Alice, James's grandmother, needed a special present. Jenny fretted over it until she noticed the unopened box on the top shelf of her wardrobe. In it was a black crocheted shawl. It was exquisite. Jenny smiled. This would make a lovely gift. She wrapped it with some of her special paper.

Jenny worked hard making some of the gifts for people in the Valley. Most of her gifts were commissioned from Karen and Sven Vanderhoffen and Joe Walters as well. They worked laboriously on Jenny's gifts, crafting them to perfection.

On Thursday December seventeenth, the children went on a field trip to get a Christmas tree. The concert was to be held in the church. The children had worked hard the week before on paper decorations, popcorn strings, cranberry ropes, and a multitude of other home made trinkets. The children spent Friday the eighteenth their last afternoon before Christmas Holidays, decorating the tree. Their eyes got huge, when Jenny brought out stick candy with ribbons to hang in the tree. Seeing their faces brought great joy to Jenny's heart. These country children were so happy with the simplest of things.

That Sunday after the service, the concert was performed. The church was packed. Everyone was happy and having wonderful time. The entire class sang "God Rest Ye Merry Gentleman." Bill, Charles and Jake donning colorful cloaks and sang, "We Three Kings of Orient Are." Jessie and Annie held a doll, and sang "Away in a Manger." The entire class took part in a Water Valley version of "A Christmas Carol." When the concert was finished the applause was thunderous. Jenny stood up after the last performance and stated she had some special awards to give. She called her students up one at a time, giving them a stick of candy and a paper rolled in red and green ribbon. She had written up the awards, honouring the children for what they did best in school. She spoke of each award to the crowd packed into the church. Bill got an award for reading as he had read fifteen books so far that year.

Then Jenny said, "I have one very special award. It goes to a student who has improved his marks over the last few months by a fifty percent average. So for most improved student, I call up Jake Appleby." Red faced with embarrassment and pride, Jake came up to accept his award. It was a book bound in red leather. Jake's eyes shone with happiness. He looked out where his mother was sitting. She was crying with joy. It was only much later that Jenny found out May had dared to come only because Gus was away attending trap lines. Seeing the pride that May had for her son was a revelation to all that had come to the concert. Word had spread about Jake's change of attitude. The whole church burst into a clapping and a backslapping free for all.

When everyone had quietened down, Jenny asked "Bill, Jake could you please remove all the candy from the tree and give a piece to everyone here."

Bill and Jake whose faces were still animated with excitement did as Jenny requested. The concert had been a wonderful success. Jenny closed out the event by saying. "Thank you for coming to our concert, I wish you all a Merry Christmas and a Wonderful New Year. School will resume on January fifth. Have a happy holiday."

Enthusiastic applause greeted this last announcement. It was a jubilant crowd that made their way home.

The next day Jenny took some of her parcels, and hitched Soot to the small sleigh James had given her. The snow was two feet deep in most places and much more than that where it drifted in. There was a narrow track for the horse to follow, while the light sleigh rode on top of the snow. She was quite a proficient driver now. She felt confident enough in her abilities to deliver all her parcels in person. It was a nice day, just right for the drive. Every family got the same parcel. It contained a ham, butter, bread and a jar of jam. The only differences in the packages were the children's gifts. She delivered the parcels to the townsfolk first, then proceeded to every farm and homestead. Toward the end of the afternoon, there was only one package to deliver.

Jenny started up the narrow path toward the Appleby residence. It was rough, but Jenny took the road slowly and made it safely to the cabin. Jake and May met her at the door and their eyes got huge when she handed them her Christmas present.

"I've got something for you too," Jake said, "wait here a minute." It was not long before he returned. He had a huge stack of furs. "These are muskrat skins, that I trapped myself. There should be enough here to make you a beautiful coat," Jake stated proudly.

"Thank you Jake," Jenny said. She knew that this would have been a whole year's work for the young man. She was overwhelmed. By the surprise and horror on May's face, this act of Jake's was not expected.

In fact May was terrified. These furs came from the shed and she knew Gus was aware of every pelt in there. It wouldn't matter to him that Jake had been the one trapping them. They all belonged to Gus. May felt faint with worry. How could they possibly explain their disappearance? She wrung her hands.

At the worry in May's eyes Jenny knew Jake was in trouble. She thought quickly.

"These furs will make a beautiful coat," Jenny said.

Jake beamed with pride.

"Mrs. Appleby, I find I have need of someone to help me out on weekends doing odd jobs. May I hire Jake?"

"Up to him, I guess," May, said wearily, almost hopelessly.

"Sure I will," Jake stated.

"I'll pay you your first month in advance," Jenny said.

She got out her bag and handed Jake ten dollars. It was probably more than the furs were worth, but just looking around, Jenny could see the family needed the money. Hiring Jake was a way of giving them what they needed without their losing face. Jenny was fearful for Jake. She was pretty sure of what Gus's reaction would be to him giving Jenny the pelts.

"You best be getting!" May said, her eyes furtively looking toward the woods. "Gus don't like you none, and he is due home soon!"

"I couldn't agree more!" Jenny said under her breath.

Bidding the family, a Merry Christmas, Jenny turned Soot around and started back down the steep road to town. Soot was a very gentle horse, but when she slipped on an ice patch things got very interesting in a hurry!

Soot scrambled back onto her feet, with a snort. Soot was terrified. She bolted, and there was nothing Jenny could do but hang on. It was a series of slips, slides and careening around bends. Jenny's heart was pounding and she felt like screaming with fear. She dared not in case it further distressed the mare. All she could do was hang on and hope that she could keep to the road. They finally reached level ground and Jenny managed to stop the horse. Soot was white with lather and sweat. Both of them were trembling. Jenny got out of the sleigh and struggled through the deep snow to the horse's head. She hugged Soot, petting her while she soothed the frightened mare with gentle words. They stayed this way for fifteen minutes, both too weary to carry on. Finally, the terror left Soot's eyes and she snuffled Jenny's coat with her nose. Jenny always kept a carrot in her pocket. Grateful to Soot for getting her this far safely, she happily fed the carrot to her.

Jenny's breathing too had settled down back to normal. She got back in the sleigh. Encouraging Soot to start, they made the rest of the journey back to the town with no more incidences.

David had been on the lookout for her and saw Jenny's flushed face. He knew that something had occurred. His eyes spoke with inquiry. Jenny told him what happened. David was thankful that Soot and Jenny were all right. Both of them rubbed the little mare down. David went and made the horse's favorite treat, a hot mash. When she was dry, and comfortable, Jenny returned home. Her body was aching already from the bruises she knew she had received on her wild ride. Jenny took a hot bath and went to bed. Nightmares of tumbling off of cliffs and banks didn't give her a restful sleep.

She spent a quiet day, packing her trunks. She wanted to look her best out at the ranch. She had two of her trunks already full of gifts and now a third with her clothes and toiletries. Jenny had never been to the ranch, because school had started soon after she had arrived. Jake, in their driving lessons, had always taken other routes. Jenny was excited to be going to see the home of the man that was fast becoming the love of her life. She wondered if the ranch would be like she envisioned. She hoped so.

That afternoon Jenny went to have tea with Janet and Ray. The sunlight on the snow was nearly blinding. The whole town looked beautiful. Hoar frost covered every tree. Windows were also covered in frost. Jenny was concerned over her house because she did not want her food to freeze while she was gone. The cellar protected her root vegetables, but she wondered about the canned goods she had in the pantry. Ray assured her it would be just fine. He said he would go over and make sure a fire was burning for the next few days. .

"It will be nice to come home to a warm house as well," she thought. Jenny gave them their Christmas presents. They had a small decorated spruce tree in their front room and they carefully put her packages under it. They too handed her a small parcel from the both of them. Jenny thanked them, giving them both a hug. They had become very dear friends of hers. Then she slipped away, to say goodbye to all her other friends in the town. When Jenny returned to her house, she was chilled right through. The temperature was dropping fast. The next morning there was frost on the walls of the house, and the stove seemed to give off no heat at all. Jenny shivered and prepared to leave. The cold hit her making her gasp. Her breath created clouds of mist. She could not recall a time when her lungs felt like they were freezing. She quickly tied the scarf over her nose and mouth. Breathing through the cloth warmed the air a tiny bit.

Jenny bundled up in so many clothes that you could hardly tell there was a person under all the garments. When she ventured outside, the snow crackled under her feet. A hard crust had formed during the night. When she got to the stables, Jenny was surprised to see Soot already harnessed and waiting for her. David stood beside his stove in the blacksmiths shop. He too was bundled for the cold weather. Jenny thanked him profusely, and David blushed. Jenny asked him if he would help her load the heavy trunks onto the sleigh. He said he was happy to do so and accompanied her in the sleigh to her cottage. The loading went swiftly. Hot bricks were put on the floor of the sleigh and covered with a huge quilt. Jenny was quite comfortable once she climbed under it.

He handed her the valise and special box holding Kally. She tucked them safely under the quilt and prepared to leave.

David said he would walk home and volunteered to take the key from Jenny's house to Ray at the Store. Jenny thanked him and wished him a Merry Christmas. Kally meowed plaintively in the box, but Jenny did not let her out.

Chapter 23

Jenny drove down toward the frozen river. She crossed the bridge, turning south along the road toward the Rocking B ranch. Her freezing breath had turned her scarf to a stiff cloth that was rubbing her chin raw where it touched her. Soot's nose and muzzle was also covered in icicles. Jenny huddled down under the quilt as much as she could.

Jenny plans were to reach the ranch that morning so the Borland's knew approximately when she would arrive. Still, she hardly expected James to brave the cold to meet her. She was only two miles from the town when he rode up on his horse. He was bundled up as well to keep warm. He told her in muffled tones, that he wanted to make sure she got to the ranch all right. She quickly invited him to join her under the warm blanket and he gratefully took her up on the offer. He tied his horse to the rear of the sleigh and climbed in beside her. James said the ranch thermometer was reading thirty-below Fahrenheit. Fortunately there was no wind or it would feel even colder.

James had taken note of the three trunks and teased her. "I see your thinking of moving in with us, Jenny."

Jenny laughed. "I decided to make you work at carrying them all into the house. It would give you something to do."

James looked at her in consternation. "You just want me to break my back, that's all. Just see if I invite you out here again," he threatened.

Jenny just grinned. She looked around. They were passing the Bowie's new home. "The mountain here is sure bare because of that fire. I think it will take a long time to grow back," Jenny said. James nodded agreement. They sat in companionable silence until they topped a hill a couple of miles later. Jenny stood up to look at her destination. The ranch spread out below them. The river they had followed wound around like a silver snake through the middle. Large Oak trees surrounded most of the main ranch. In the summer it would provide a leafy shade from the oppressing sun. Now with the leaves gone, she could see a multitude of buildings, and corrals.

Her eyes focused on the main ranch house. From here it looked huge. The building had a vaguely U Shape, with the middle part having a second story. It was built mainly of red brick, with the columns in white marble. It was very beautiful against the snowy backdrop. Jenny could hardly wait to get a little closer. There were many small cottages down near the river. Smoke rising from every building created spiralling clouds in an otherwise clear blue sky.

James noticing the direction of her gaze said "Those are the homes of the staff that are married." "That large long one is the bunkhouse for single men. The larger cabin over there right beside the river is for the single ladies."

Jenny was impressed. There were at least three barns visible but there may be even more. There were many smaller buildings and sheds that gave Jenny no clue to their use. White board fences formed corrals and pastures. In the winter these fences disappeared into the landscape of snow. "I bet the white against the green of summer grass will be beautiful. I hope to be able to see this in the spring or summer months," she thought to herself.

"It is all very beautiful," Jenny said.

Her simple comment couldn't have pleased James more. He was proud of his home.

Jenny was very cold by the time they got down to the ranch house. The attentive staff had spotted them descending the hill and were waiting. A couple of young men came out to take her trunks up to her room. James stepped out of the sleigh, then took Jenny's hand to help her out. He took her valise and the box carrying Kally. Jenny proceeded up the steps to the front door. A boy was hurrying from the side of the house to take Soot and James's horse around to the stable.

Jenny noticed that the wide veranda extended the full length of the house. A young girl in a white apron and cap opened the double oak doors. Closing the door behind them, she took Jenny's wraps and another girl came from the back of the house to aid her. James handed his coat and hat to the girls. The house was warm and Jenny felt her body starting to thaw.

Jenny looked around at the wide bright and cheerful hallway. She was surprised at the elegance, as this whole house could have been transplanted right out of the Boston high society district. The central hallway stretched all the way to the back of the building, broken only by a huge staircase. There was a parlour to the right. The smell of warm cookies, wafted from the room. James escorted her into the sitting area where morning tea awaited them.

Jenny looked around. The parlour was elegant in warm tones of celadon and cream. Jenny never thought she would see this kind of luxury again after leaving Boston. There was no fireplace in the salon and Jenny was puzzled at the warmth of the room.

"James it is lovely and warm in here."

James noted her look and told her with pride. I use a central boiler and cast iron radiators throughout the house."

Jenny turned to him in surprise. Central heating was fairly new and she certainly had never expected this out on a remote ranch.

An elderly lady leaning heavily on a silver topped black cane came into the room to join them for tea. Jenny turned to face her.

"Jenny, I would like you to meet my grandmother, Alice," he said.

Jenny curtsied hiding her confusion. "I'm pleased to meet you, ma'am."

"Please call me Alice." The silver haired, proud lady said kindly. "I am thrilled to meet you at last," she added. "May I call you Jenny?" she asked.

Jenny nodded, "Please do," she said. "Thank-you for inviting me into your home for the holidays."

The three of them sat down and they chatted merrily over tea and fresh made cookies. After tea, Alice called in a young Spanish girl. "Jenny this is Lola, she has been assigned to you while you are with us. She will show you to your room. Come down after you're settled. I will be in the living room."

Lola Alvarez curtsied then escorted Jenny upstairs to her room.

A disoriented and scared Kally greeted her as she entered. The kitten was happy to see a familiar face. Jenny knew she would soon feel at home. Jenny looked around. It was palatial in comparison to her place at home, in fact her cabin would probably fit nicely inside this room. A white four-poster bed was covered in a yellow silk quilt. It looked very soft and comfortable, like all feather beds did. Matching yellow drapes covered numerous large windows and the double doors to the balcony. The table, vanity chairs and the huge wardrobe were all white. Accents of yellow silk brought the ambiance of sunshine into the room.

Jenny was especially delighted when Lola showed the door that allowed her private entry to the water closet and bathing room. A ceramic tub that could be filled hot water from specially made taps thrilled Jenny.

"The water comes from heated cisterns located on the roof." Lola said. "You're the only guest here at the moment so the doorway to the hall will be locked. This will be your own private room unless more guests arrive. Then this room would be a shared with them."

"What about James? Does he not use this room as well?" Jenny asked curiously.

"No, Ma'am, he has his own private bath located within the Master bedroom," Lola told her.

There was a large radiator in the room, giving pleasant even warmth. Jenny was impressed, she knew of places in Boston that did not have as many modern conveniences.

"This is a very nice room, Lola. Also, please call me Miss Jenny," she said.

"Thank you Miss Jenny. This room used to belong to Senora Alice. She has difficulty in climbing stairs now so she has a suite on the main floor."

Lola helped Jenny unpack the one trunk. Her curiosity about the other two remained unsatisfied. Jenny did not allow her to touch them except to move them to an unused corner. Once everything had been stowed away, Lola left to perform her other chores.

Jenny sat down at the dainty vanity table as Kally jumped on her lap. The kitten was getting used to her new residence. Jenny looked at herself in the mirror. Her eyes took on a dreamy look. James had a beautiful home. Jenny liked Grandma Alice too. She could get used to this place very easily.

Jenny changed from her travelling dress to an afternoon gown. It was a soft amber color, with butter yellow ribbons and accessories. Jenny had a knack of choosing shades that went well with her complexion. She giggled when she realized that she blended right in with the room's décor.

She gave Kally, who had made herself at home on Jenny's bed a pat. She took a small bag containing her embroidery and her book Oliver Twist from the valise and returned to the main floor.

James rose from a comfortable chair to greet her when she entered the living room. Alice lay in a chaise lounge, resting her aching legs.

"My room is just beautiful, I feel like it has captured the sunshine," Jenny enthused.

Alice smiled. "I am glad you like it. I know I always loved it myself."

James grinned in pleasure. "Would you like to see the rest of the house?"

"I'd love too," Jenny responded.

"We'll go to the west wing first," James said escorting her toward the hall. There were two doors on Jenny's left, one right in the corner of the living room.

"That's the water closet and the other door is the entrance to my grandmother's suite. They entered the brightly lit hall with lanterns all along the walls.

On Jenny's right there was a doorway and James opened it to reveal his office. Jenny realized there must be a lot of work to running a ranch like this one. Returning to the hall they continued to the next set of double doors again to the right. It was the entrance to the library.

Jenny was in awe. "Oh, wonderful!" she exclaimed. The shelves were full of books. James was obviously an avid collector. There were comfortable chairs and low tables set up near a fireplace on the end. A fire had not been lit in it.

James said, "This room is usually warm, but if you want to come in here let one of the staff know and they will light the fire.

"I will," Jenny said silently vowing to do so very soon.

There was only one set of doors left and that was straight ahead of them at the end of the hall.

Glass doors let the beautiful sunlight in. James threw the doors open and. Jenny gasped in wonder. It was a lush green conservatory. Hundreds of plants thrived in the warm humid atmosphere. Marble walkways meandered through the gardens. Ponds and small waterfalls flowed amongst the greenery. She spotted some multicolored fish swimming freely in the ponds.

James said. "Those fish are called Japanese Koi. These were raised in Japan and imported to San Francisco. It was a real trick getting them here in safety. They have thrived. In fact do you see those small ones over there?" He said pointing to a dark pool further on.

"Yes, I see them," she said moving closer

"These were born here. They're about a year old now," James said. The fish were congregating near the surface close to the small stone bridge.

"They're hungry. Here Jenny, take these and throw them to the Koi," he said handing her some pellets from a box hidden in a tree.

Jenny was elated as she watched the fish inhale the pellets into their huge mouths. She knelt and put her hand in the water. The fish allowed her to touch them. Jenny was amazed at their lack of fear. Jenny stood up and slowly continued her tour of the gardens. In one corner there was a lovely table made of marble with chairs made of wrought iron. It would make lovely cozy setting to have tea or lunch.

"I can't begin to tell you how much I like this room," Jenny said softly to James.

James smiled, happy that this lady he had grown to love over the last few months approved of his home.

Reluctantly Jenny returned to the hall with James. He was obviously delighted at his surprise. They re-crossed the living room heading east toward the Main Hall. On Jenny's left was the parlor where they had morning tea. There were huge oak doors standing open to her right, revealing a formal dining room.

James said, "The family uses this for special occasions. We usually eat in the breakfast nook or the conservatory. I have a tendency to keep things here at the ranch as informal as Alice will allow. My grandmother prefers a more formal setting." He then stuck a pose and quoted Alice. "You can be as bourgeois as you want outside the house, but inside the house is my domain," James laughed. It was obvious that he loved his grandmother very much.

They crossed the main hall and passed the stairs that ascended to the second floor. The east wing was a hall that followed the south exterior wall of the house. Sunlight poured through the windows. A rug covered the polished marble floors. Wall sconces held lanterns although they were not needed in the bright light of day. The first two doors on the left were his and hers water closets. These could be used by guests or staff. "We entertain here quite a bit," James said. "It only makes sense to make sure both men and women are equally accommodated," he grinned. Jenny smiled back at him.

The hall had a smaller branch on the left. James said. "This leads to the laundry and housekeeping areas." They did not walk down this hall but carried on east.

Two large swinging doors opened into the huge kitchen. Wonderful smells were wafting out of the room.

Jenny's stomach growled. "It must almost be lunchtime," she thought. As if her thought triggered it, the lunch bell rang. They took a quick look into the kitchen but did not disturb the cooks or their helpers. The cook's helpers were hurrying into the next room loaded down with trays of food. It was a huge dining hall, which covered the rest of the house to the end. This was one of the largest rooms Jenny had ever seen. There were noises of the hands coming in for their lunch. Two huge long tables were set with plates and food. There were four swinging doors direct from the kitchen to the dining hall. Two fireplaces burned merrily on the wall.

"Radiant heating doesn't entirely work in this large room. That's why we have the fireplace burning at all times in here," James said. He then pointed at an office in one corner. "My foreman, Bruce McMillen's office, it is where the running of the ranch really begins," James said. "We won't go in and disturb the meal. Ours will be ready by now and Grandma Alice will be waiting for us."

Jenny and James returned to the living room. The breakfast nook was in one corner and was raised up from the main floor by at least a foot. Two steps gained you access to it. They joined Alice at the round table and ate a wonderful lunch. Afterwards they went to sit by the fireplace, while staff cleared the dishes.

James said, "I hope you'll excuse me but I have work to do. I'll see you both at supper."

"Thank you for the wonderful tour, I enjoyed it very much," Jenny said, taking out her embroidery.

Alice admired the work. "This is beautiful needlework Jenny, but I hope you will forgive me. I need to rest. It seems that age is catching up with me. Will you be alright on your own this afternoon?"

"Of course I will," Jenny assured her. "You go right ahead and rest, I'll be just fine."

Alice added. "Make yourself at home. Go anywhere and do as you please. I am so glad you have come." She then made her way leaning heavily on her cane, to her suite.

Chapter 24

Alice slowly made her way to the door of her suite. She glanced back at the lady concentrating on her embroidery. Time would tell if Jenny was being herself, or putting on a good show. Alice frowned slightly. A school teacher was not really the type of person she thought James would go for. Her first impression of Jenny was good though. Alice was finding it easy to like her.

She leaned heavily on her cane. She winced as a sharp pain shot through her knee. Her maid Sylvia Turner was waiting to help her get ready for her nap. Sylvia helped Alice remove her dress so it would not get creased. She settled Alice into her bed. Alice grimaced. There was a time when no one was able to beat her in athleticism. As a young lady and bride, she could ride with the best of them. She had been an avid horsewoman when she lived in Richmond Virginia. She was the daughter of a wealthy old southern family. She had been Christened Alice Marie Sherborne seventy-four years ago in 1822. She had grown up in the lap of luxury and had the proper upbringing and schooling. She was seventeen when a chance encounter at a neighbour's picnic, introduced her to James William Borland, or Will as he was called. He was a guest of the host. The dashing tall man dressed in sober black, fascinated Alice. If fact, Will quickly swept all of Alice's beaus away, and became her favourite. It was a whirlwind courtship based on love. Her father was dubious, because this man wanted to take Alice to a distant territory, Montana. True, this Will was a landowner, which had impressed him but he didn't seem to have much in the way of savings.

Alice always could wind her father around her finger, and with much persuasion, he had consented to the marriage. Alice smiled. It had been a grand wedding and a memory that Alice would never forget. June fourteenth, 1839 would always remain in her heart. How naive she had been. Living in a small house on a huge ranch, that covered over one hundred square miles, life was much different from what she expected. The nearest town was about forty miles away. Alice had been used to getting waited on hand and foot. Here she had to rely on herself. Alice learned quickly and soon became a good cook and helpmate to her devoted husband. The personal tragedies that followed only made their love stronger. She miscarried three children before the tiny baby boy had been born October seventeenth, 1845. Will had named him James Benjamin Borland Jr. or JB for short. JB was a good lad and loved the land as much as her husband did.

When JB was sixteen, the Civil War erupted. Alice was beside herself, with worry. Her family was fighting for their political lives in Virginia. JB wanted to go and it was with great reluctance that Alice and Will had finally given permission for him to join the Southern Army. JB had traveled to his grandparent's home and joined with his cousins to fight for the preservation of the southern ways. Many of Alice's nephews were killed in the various battles. She was heart broken and tense with fear for JB. JB was wounded and mustered out of the army. He returned home in 1864. It took him over a year to fully recover from his injuries. Alice loved and cared for him while he regained his health.

As JB grew older, he married a lovely girl. She was a delicate lady and so thin that it seemed a strong wind could blow her away. Her name was Emma Beatrice Young, a girl from a poor family in Butte. They had a beautiful wedding in the Butte church and the loving couple honeymooned in Kansas City. Nine months later Alice's first grandson was born on September twelfth, 1870. Emma never recovered from the birth of her beloved son, but withered away before all their sad eyes. James Edward Borland lost his mother when he was just two weeks old. A determined Alice stepped in to save the baby. She found a young Mexican lady who had given birth to stillborn baby two days previously. The young mother was willing to nurse and care for the boy.

Will Borland had just started work on the beautiful ranch house. He had always wanted Alice to have a nice home. He could afford it now because the ranch had become very prosperous. All the Borland men were devoted to its welfare.

The ranch went through many troubled times, but it was rather worrisome when James was six years old. The Indian Wars were raging. However Will had made friends with the tribes that lived on his southern border. The harmony and respect between the two cultures never wavered in spite of what was occurring in the rest of the territories.

When James was just a teenager, Will developed tuberculosis. Knowing the contagious nature of this disease, he still refused to go to the State Sanatorium. He did however isolate himself in the conservatory. This room was chosen because of its glass walls. Sunlight would pour in to aid the man. Being on one end of the house it was easily isolated. No one was allowed to enter, even Alice. Food was left outside the door for him He grew too weak to walk. When he fell beside his bed, Alice who had up to this moment reluctantly done exactly as she had been instructed, ignored the orders and ran into the room. Enough was enough. In spite of his panicked pleading, she had helped him back to his cot.

Weeping she held him. He finally returned her hug and whispered how much he loved her. She stayed with him, isolating herself just to be near him. Their respite was short and he died a few days later. The memory caused her to cry again, as it did every time she thought about him. She always held her tears until she was alone like now. Oh, how she missed Will. April twenty-ninth, 1883, was when part of her heart had died. She could see the Borland family cemetery from her window. She often gazed out at it in the winter and kept fresh flowers on it in the summer.

She had thrown herself into helping her son and grandson as much as she could. There were many good times, but the winter of 1886 and 1887 saw their good fortune crumble. Thousands of their cattle died in worst winter Montana had ever seen. It had taken years to rebuild the ranch to its former glory. Her son and grandson had worked ceaselessly to revive it to what it was now.

Lately, she ruefully admitted, she hadn't been able to do too much. Her knees wrenched badly in a fall when her horse slipped on ice had started to ache. It got worse every year. She tried not to complain but the old injury would not allow her to ride at all. Even carriage trips were to be avoided if she could. Instead she threw herself into landscaping the large yard around the house. She had a green thumb, and loved mucking about in the dirt. JB and James consulted her on every aspect of the new community of Water Valley. She was a skilled planner and much of the towns design was based on her ideas.

Everything was going well, until that spring two years ago. JB had tried to save a pregnant Morgan mare, who had escaped her stall. The foolish horse had tried to cross the rotten spring ice. She predictably had fallen through and JB never hesitated. He had grabbed a lariat and crossed the ice. One end was held by a group of men on shore. He got the rope around the horse's head and they had tried turning the frantic mare. In her thrashing she caved in some more ice. JB had gone completely under. The horrified men watch as the hand holding the rope let go. It was assumed that the mare might have knocked him out with her slashing hooves. The horse was saved and an intensive search conducted for several miles along the river never produced JB's body. A stone for him was also raised in the family plot.

No stranger to loss, Alice coped by keeping as busy as she could. Her knees were now swollen to twice their normal size. That's why she liked her maid Sylvia so much. She had a knack of massaging the knees that made them feel better for a while.

Alice took a guilty look around. Here she was supposedly having a nap. Sylvia would scold her if she found out. Alice smiled, "That's what I get for reminiscing instead of sleeping. However, James is the only family I have left. Naturally I'm worried about this girl he's interested in," she thought to herself. "Time would tell as to how it'll work out."

Chapter 25

After working on her embroidery for over an hour, Jenny got restless and decided to go explore the library. She poured over the titles like a child in a candy shop. The afternoon sped by and before she realized it was five o'clock. She returned upstairs to change her dress for dinner. It proved to be a delicious meal, with a pleasant camaraderie between the three of them. As with most evening meals it was held in the formal dining room. After dinner they played a quiet game of cards and then Alice bid them good night. Jenny and James played a few more games, chatting amiably. It was ten o'clock when Jenny too, said goodnight and went upstairs to bed.

Jenny hadn't realized how much she missed luxury. Lola had heated Jenny's bed with a bed warmer and Jenny revelled in the warm sheets. She knew things would be back to normal when she returned home, but she decided to enjoy herself while she was here. "What a hypocrite I am!" she giggled.

The morning of the twenty-fourth arrived with a lovely surprise. A Chinook had blown in during the night. It was positively balmy outside, with a temperature of thirty-six degrees above Fahrenheit. The temperature change from the thirty-below to above freezing was cause for a real celebration. This was wonderful.

After breakfast, James asked"Jenny, are you up for some fun outside?"

"I sure am!" She said and hurried upstairs for her warm clothing.

When she was ready James led her outside where a team of horses stood. They were hitched to a huge hay lined wagon. The children of the ranch and a few merry cowhands were already ensconced in the hay. They cheerfully made room for Jenny and James. The team headed across the river toward a pine forest not too far away. When they got there, an impromptu contest was made up, to find the nicest Christmas tree. They finally chose one that was about ten feet tall. The branches were heavy with needles and looked beautiful. The tree was cut, attached to the back of the sleigh and dragged back to the ranch in triumph. They all sang Christmas Carols at the top of their lungs, to pass the time.

After lunch the tree was set up between the two hall fireplaces. The fallen branches were swept away. The ranch children, ranch hands not on duty, James and Jenny spent hours making decorations for the tree.

Grandma Alice came in mid afternoon "Rob and Chuck!" she said, "Go out to the storage shed and bring in the blue trunk with brass bindings," she ordered.

The two men designated hurried out to do what she asked. When they returned, Grandma Alice took her special brass key and opened a treasure chest. Children gathered around with wide eyes. It contained gold Christmas ornaments all carefully wrapped in protective cloths. The ornaments had been handed down from generation to generation in both the Borland and Sherborne families. As Alice carefully removed each one, the children held their breath. The room was filled with their exclamations of delight in the delicately crafted decorations. There were many sets of gold filigree candle holders. Great care was needed by the ones placing them on the tree so the candle would not catch the tree on fire. When the last of the decorations were in place, Alice reverently took out the last and largest decoration. It was a multifaceted gold star. It would reflect any light in the room, creating rainbows of color. It was breathtaking.

"James," she said softly. "Would you put this star in place?"

James climbed the ladder and proudly placed it on the top of the tree. Everyone present promptly started to cheer. The happy group finished just as the cooks brought out the supper.

Jenny went upstairs to freshen up. She then joined Alice and James for the evening meal. There was an air of excitement in the whole house. Grandma Alice was beaming.

At eight o'clock the entire ranch came into the hall for the Christmas Eve celebration. When everyone was seated and comfortable, mulled wine was served. Bruce McMillen the foreman had the honour of lighting the Christmas tree candles. He held a taper and started at the top of the tree. He worked his way down to the floor and when he was finished, all the lanterns were extinguished. The only other light in the room besides the tree were the fireplaces. The candlelights gave the tree an awe-inspiring ethereal look. A piano was uncovered in the corner. One of the wives sat down at the keyboard and filled the hall with Christmas music. Everyone joined in singing when a favorite carol was played.

At nine o'clock the cook came out with snacks and more mulled wine. There were bowls of popcorn and sugar plums. James had the children play some lively games at one end of the hall. They were so excited that they couldn't stay still. By ten o'clock the children were taken home to bed. The adults too, retired. Tomorrow would be a most special day.

Chapter 26

Christmas morning was beautiful. After breakfast, Jenny had a couple of men help her take the trunks of gifts down to the tree. She waited until the room was empty, then took each gift out of the trunk. She made sure each one still had the label of the person it was going too. She carefully placed each one evenly under the tree. When she was finished Jenny recalled the men to take the trunks back upstairs.

She then left for the living room, to join Alice in having a cup of tea. At eleven o'clock Jenny went upstairs to put on her green velvet gown. It was trimmed in white rabbit fur and looked very festive. When the dinner bell rang, Jenny descended the stairs and walked toward the dining hall. Everyone was there waiting politely for James to invite them to sit. Christmas dinner was never missed if one could help it. Two long tables had been moved to make room for a third table at one end. It was to be the head table. Jenny was invited to sit there. She glanced at the tree and noted a huge mound of presents, had joined her gifts under the tree.

There were lots of banter and good-natured shouts of Merry Christmas as people crowded in.

James held Jenny's chair until she sat. He had previously done the same for his grandmother. Bruce McMillen the foreman was also to be seated at the head table.

Once both of the ladies were seated, James said. "Merry Christmas everyone, please take your seats." Then Bruce and James sat down.

Jenny watched the ranch personnel hurry find their places and was sure they would not all fit at the tables. The deed was accomplished in record time. The kitchen helpers began putting out steaming bowls of mashed potatoes, gravy, carrots and a multitude of other dishes. It was a regular banquet. Every person there held their breath as the cook and two of his helpers marched into the room. Each held a platter with a huge turkey on it. They were golden brown, and cooked to perfection. People sighed with anticipation. A special table had been set aside and it became loaded down with these huge birds.

James stood and offered grace. He then as tradition dictated he carved one of the turkeys. It didn't take James long, it was obvious he had plenty of practice.

Returning to the head table, James lifted his glass. "I welcome you to this feast and I wish everyone a very Merry Christmas!" Everyone burst into spontaneous applause, raised their glasses and returned the toast. It shortly became amazingly quiet as they delved into their scrumptious dinner. Throughout the afternoon Jenny noticed that many people took turns clearing or serving. All of the workers had a chance to sit and enjoy the meal. Jenny was vastly impressed.

When everyone was sated, a young ranch woman stood up and beckoned all the children up to the front. She asked everyone to bear with her as she got all the children into costumes. Then Bruce stood up and with a soft baritone voice, which carried to every part of the room, started the ages old Christmas Story. Various children acted out the parts of the story very well. When the birth of the baby was announced the youngest of the ranch residents, just three weeks old was laid in the manger. When the play was complete everyone cheered the actors and beaming they went to join their parents again.

James assumed a listening pose. "What's that," he exclaimed. From out in the hall, there was the sound of sleigh bells. The children screamed excitedly.

"It's St. Nick! St. Nick!" They shouted. A white bearded old man entered the room. He had a red suit on and black boots. He had a red hat trimmed with ermine. "Ho, Ho, Ho!" he shouted. Everyone clapped and welcomed him. The children became even more wide-eyed with excitement, if that were possible.

St. Nick sat next to the tree, in a huge easy chair. Tradition dictated that children could not receive their present until they sat on his knee. James became St. Nick's assistant by handing him the children's presents. The children were quick to oblige.

James opened a box of oranges and he passed them out to everyone. The men received new grey, black or brown felt hats, and the ladies received a brooch. Each one was different. The children each received a toy. The girls were given little china dolls and the boys, a train or soldiers. Babies received wooden toys easy for their tiny hands to hold.

James presented his Grandmother with a large cameo brooch. James kissed her proud wrinkled face. Alice with love lighting up her eyes looked up at her grandson and hugged him. Jenny held her breath, it was a very intimate moment, and Jenny was in awe. James then turned to Jenny and handed her a small box. Jenny opened it and gasped with pleasure. It was a gold filigree locket. It too sported a cameo carved out of Mother of Pearl. A delicate gold chain was attached.

Jenny was trembling, "Thank you James." He helped her put it on.

Jenny then assisted St. Nick to give out her gifts. The men of the ranch all received hand-tooled leather belts. The silver buckles were all different, each containing a polished stone of various colors and shapes. The ladies were given a set of tortoiseshell combs for their hair. The children were delighted to receive a bag of assorted candies and toys appropriate for their ages. Soft cloth animals were given to the babies and toddlers. The older children received storybooks.

Jenny then handed Alice her present. Alice's eyes watered a little, as she caressed the beautiful shawl. She put it on immediately and pinned her new broach on it to hold the wrap closed. Alice handed Jenny a shiny black Jewellery box lined with black velvet. The outside of the box was inlaid with Mother of Pearl. Jenny loved it.

James opened his gift with delighted grin. He found a hand-tooled belt, with a silver buckle. It had gold "B" in the centre surrounded by tiny Turquoise stones. Intricate designs were etched into the rest of the buckle.

He too put his on immediately. "I'll wear this with pride," he said.

Jenny opened her gifts from Ray and Janet. It was a hand knitted set of dishcloths and towels. They were bright red and blue. Jenny loved them.

She also uncovered the presents hidden in the wicker basket that Dora had given her. There was a bar of soap, with a matching lavender scented candle. Next to it was a box of lavender talcum powder. There was a lilac colored soft washcloth, and a bottle of a light lavender scented perfume. Jenny thought her gifts were just wonderful.

Cards and various other interesting games were played. The children went outside to play in the snow with their new toys. Jenny and Alice joined the other ladies in the easy chairs beside one of the fireplaces, they chatted gaily. There was never a shortage of punch and by evening some of the revellers were just a slight bit tipsy.

Sandwiches were put out around seven o'clock, but the cooks knew from previous years that the large mid day meal caused small appetites for an evening meal. Eight o'clock seemed a signal for more active festivities. A couple of fiddles were produced, along with the piano. Tables were pulled to the sides of the room clearing the center of the floor for dancing. An impromptu concert was given. Some people told tales, others sang, or told jokes. Between these efforts, dances were held. There were fewer women than men, so Jenny never lacked for a partner. James too danced with all the ladies. There were Irish Jigs and Square dancing. Toward the end of the evening there was a waltz.

James came over to Jenny and asked softly. "Dance with me Jenny?"

Jenny nodded. Her heart was beating faster. She went into his arms. They began the dance and Jenny's body automatically conformed to his. The whole feeling of being with him felt right. Somehow, Jenny's feet felt like she was dancing on air. She loved being so close to him. She kept her eyes demurely down.

"Jenny?" he whispered softly. She raised her eyes to his and both of them were transported away into a world of their own. She was definitely in love with this wonderful gentle man. She almost stopped breathing altogether when she saw the love was being returned right back. She tore gaze away and took a deep breath.

The party wound down, and the families with children took their tired charges home. The men and ladies gradually drifted off to their beds as well.

James sat near Jenny at the fire. She was reluctant to call this wonderful evening to an end. She stared mesmerized at the flickering flames. A blazing branch exploded bringing her back to reality. James and Jenny were alone in the hall. She decided reluctantly that it was time to go to bed so she rose. James came up to her and took both hands in his.

"I had a wonderful time today," he said.

Jenny nodded agreement, but her tongue was numb. She couldn't think of anything to say. Her eyes met his and they were transported away again.

James pulled her closer, and he gently kissed her. She was not prepared for the fire that roared through her breast. She couldn't breath and her lips tingled. The kiss became much more. Jenny was panting when they came up for air. James was breathing hard too.

Jenny almost stopped breathing altogether when she saw the caring look in his eyes.

He asked her to come for a walk with him and the two of them made their way to the hall. With a twinkle in his eye, James stopped her at the kitchen. He beckoned her to come in with him. The kitchen stoves were always hot and it didn't take long for James to find the ingredients for a couple of cups of cocoa. He put a teaspoon of cocoa powder into cups and added 2 teaspoons of sugar. He went to the cold room and retrieved cream. He added enough to moisten the cocoa and sugar mix. Then he added the hot water. He put the cream back in the cold room and the two of them carried their drinks, down the hall and to the conservatory. It was beautiful with the moon shining down through the glass. They walked over the tiny stone bridge to the wrought iron chairs and table. Jenny was quietly enjoying the romantic atmosphere of the conservatory. She looked up and the stars seemed to cover the sky. There was plenty of light with the moon shining brightly. Jenny relaxed and sipped her hot cocoa. James pulled his chair around, so he could be close to her. Both were wrapped up in their own thoughts.

"I'll always be grateful to my grandfather for building this room," he said softly. "It's one of my favourite places to relax."

Jenny nodded. "I love it. No matter how cold it gets outside this room would always be warm."

"Yes, he said. "If something happened to our main boiler, this room has its own small boiler. It is hidden over their just under those plants." He pointed to where a few plants seemed to cover a decorative hill.

"This room could also be used in an emergency if the main boilers failed," he continued. Small talk was not one of James's finer accomplishments and he decided perhaps that home heating was not the most romantic of topics.

He fell silent, the two of them enjoying the ambiance of the beautiful room.

They slowly finished their chocolate drink. Simultaneously they rose from the chairs, deciding it was time to call it a night.

As they crossed the tiny stone bridge, he stopped her and gave her a kiss. This was just so romantic, that tears came unbidden to Jenny's eyes. However neither of them wanted to dip too far into their emotions. Neither was prepared to declare deeper feelings at this time.

He then escorted her upstairs. At her bedroom door, he kissed her again and bid her sweet dreams. Jenny entered her room trembling a bit. She sat in her chair, and clasped her hands together. Could this really be happening to her? She raised her hands up to her face covering her mouth. She was falling in love. This was a completely new experience for her. "Goodness me!" she cried as she picked up Kally. She held the kitten close as her heart finally stopped beating so hard. She got up and took her dress off. As she slowly changed into her nightgown her thoughts tried to find some peace. She had to write a letter to Frances. "Wouldn't Frances laugh, Kally?" Jenny said. "My icy heart toward most men is melting." Jenny hugged Kally one last time and crawled into the huge bed. This was the best Christmas Jenny had ever experienced. Kally cuddled down close to her beloved mistress. It was just possible her bridges were not quite as burned as she thought. She giggled and composed herself for sleep. With Kally purring in her ear, she finally did.

Chapter 27

The next morning Jenny awoke slowly. Kally yawned and started her morning purring. Jenny stroked her beloved pet and decided she had better get up and moving. She crawled out of bed and dressed in a morning gown of dusty rose silk. She descended the stairs and entered the living room. James rose to meet her. He had been waiting for her and reading. He led her back to the conservatory where a delicious breakfast had been laid out in an alcove near a huge window. Surrounded by beautiful shrubbery, James and Jenny chatted gaily about ranch activities.

As Alice usually stayed in her room until later in the morning, James asked Jenny if she would like to go for a ride around the ranch. Elated, Jenny excused herself and hurried to put her riding dress on. The Chinook was still in full force; in fact the temperature was even warmer than the day before. Jenny still dressed warmly and was soon ready.

As she came down the stairs, she was a vision of loveliness. Her green riding habit and straw hat set off her beautiful hair and eyes. It was partially hidden by a fur coat, hat and woollen gloves. But

James still seemed to appreciate it! They went outside and Soot was saddled and ready for her. A beautiful sorrel was waiting for James. His name was Twister and James mounted him after helping Jenny to get on Soot. She gave her a tour of the Ranch's main area and then they crossed the river on the same wooden bridge the wagon had used when they went Christmas tree hunting. They followed a well-used trail. Cowboys were seen in the distance doing whatever jobs had been given to them.

They rode at a walk. The air was refreshing and by the time they started home. Jenny felt completely at ease in James's presence. Jenny's cheeks had become rosy with the cold. She could not remember such a wonderful holiday season.

It was nearing lunchtime, when they crossed the river again. They could see a commotion near the house. Several people were radiating their agitation. This to James meant there was trouble. They kicked their horses into a lope, and soon reached the scene. The activity centred on a team and wagon just pulling in from Water Valley. Ray Brown, drove the team, and was accompanied by David Olsen and the Reverend Chase on horseback. The Reverend had raced ahead to alert the Ranch's Doctor. In the back of the wagon was Nellie Chase. She was holding the head of a bloody body not immediately recognizable. Jenny was horrified at the sight. What on earth had happened, she wondered?

Doc Murphy, the ranch Veterinarian, was the closest to a doctor the community had, and he was on his way at a run from the staff cottages. He had his bag with him and he arrived almost breathless. His wife was right behind him. James took control of the emergency situation, and ordered the patient to be taken to the dining room. Doctor Ed, didn't hesitate, but started his examination as soon as they got inside. Jenny hurried inside after them. When Jenny got a look at the patients face, she went white. It was young Jake Appleby. James sent the servants scurrying for blankets and hot water.

Jake's clothes were removed, and everyone was shocked. He had been beaten unmercifully. His clothes were soaked in blood. And when Doc Murphy turned him over a bullet hole was found in his left shoulder. Most of the blood had come from there. Jenny stood with James ready to assist if she was needed, but was relieved that the two ladies, Nellie and Lilly took over. Both had experience with being medical assistants. Nellie had started a nursing career when she was younger. She had not completed the course because of financial difficulties, and by then she had met the young Theology Student. They had married when Art finished his schooling. Lilly, Dr. Ed's wife, was a trained mid-wife. She had worked so often with Ed she seemed to know what he wanted instinctively. Jenny clung to James, shaking with anxiety.

Doc prepared to probe for the bullet, as there had been no exit wound. Jake remained unconscious, which was probably a very good thing. Doc was a very efficient fellow, and soon found the bullet. Jenny was physically ill. She had never been around anything like this before, but she forced herself to hold together.

Once the bullet was out, they bandaged him. They then washed the rest of him up. He had deep bruises, and cuts on him. Doc examined Jake very carefully and discovered he had probable broken ribs. One arm was definitely broken. James helped Doc straighten the bone, and then they splinted it and taped up the ribs. Then under the careful instructions of James, the boy was carried upstairs to the spare bedroom. It was two doors down from Jenny's room. Jenny had every intention of staying with young Jake and after seeing him made comfortable, she sat in a chair next to the table. Nellie also pulled up a chair to sit and wait.

James left the room to speak to the Reverend, Ray and David. These worthy men told him that Jake had stumbled up the road toward the Store, leaving a trail of blood. Mayor had alerted everyone with his frantic barking. James decided it was prudent to do some investigation. Jake had not regained consciousness so he couldn't answer any questions. Jenny looked out the window just in time to see James leading a group of men. Ray, driving the team, was accompanied by several of James cowhands, mounted on their horses heading up the road toward Water Valley. David Olsen and the Reverend were also with them.

When they disappeared Jenny turned and went over to look at Jake's bruised face. She was overwrought. She broke down and wept.

Nellie came over and hugged her. "I think he'll be all right," she said.

"I hope so." Jenny said teary eyed. "But he is so young, and his injuries are so bad!" she added.

"He's tough, like all young men his age, and he will live," Nellie said encouragingly.

Alice came into the room. She was leaning heavily on her cane. A maid was helping to support her. Jenny quickly got her a chair.

"My, my," she puffed. "That was quite a climb. I haven't been up here for over two years," she stated. She then turned and instructed the maid to have lunch for the three of them brought upstairs. The maid left to do her bidding.

Alice looked over at the boy, and inquired as to whom he was. Jenny haltingly told her Jake's story, while they waited for the promised lunch. Jenny was standing, nervously wringing her hands together.

"He is more my friend and protégée, than my student," she finished.

Alice nodded understandingly. Then trying to think of something to take Jenny's mind off of Jake, she said "Your riding habit is beautiful Jenny, did you enjoy your tour of the ranch?"

Jenny turned away from the forlorn figure in the bed, with a start. "Oh yes, the ranch is just beautiful. You live in such a pretty area here. It has the best of all the different countrysides. Flat lands, hills, mountains, forests combine to make one of the nicest places I have ever seen," she said.

Alice beamed. "I am so glad you like it. I've always loved this ranch and am not happy leaving it for any length of time. Of course all my memories live here with me," she laughed.

The lunch arrived and the three ladies chatted quietly. There was a groan from the bed and Jenny was beside Jake in an instant. Jake wonderingly, gazed up at Jenny's face and obviously didn't know where he was. Jenny told him, and then held his hand as memory and reality sunk into his befuddled mind.

The first words he said were, "Are you alright Miss Jenny, he's coming for you!" then as his awareness grew he continued. "Oh no, oh no, no, no, no!" he choked out hoarsely. "She's gone, Miss Jenny, my Ma's gone." He turned his face away from them. When the pain of his wounds started to become apparent, combined with the anguish of his mind Jake passed out again. Jenny had tears welling up in her eyes. Her eyes met those of Nellie and Alice. What in the world had happened in that far off cabin?

Jenny guessed that May might be dead, and suspected that Gus had gone off the deep end. They would have to wait until James got back to find out the rest of the story. Doc had left some medicine for pain, and would also cause the boy to sleep. While it was not needed now, Jenny knew that it soon would be.

Nellie said that she would be staying to help nurse Jake, and Jenny said she would also. Jenny had no intentions of leaving Jake until he was up and around no matter how long it took.

Jake woke up, every once in a while, and Nellie would dispense the medicine. He never spoke another word that day, and the medicine put him to sleep very quickly.

Nellie, Jenny, Lily, and Sandra another efficient lady from the ranch staff decided to divide Jake's care into four equal shifts. Since Jenny was an early riser, she would take the early morning shift. Lilly would take the afternoon shift and Nellie would take the evening one. Sandra would take the night shift. A comfortable chair, and table, were part of the room, and got a lot of use in the next few days.

Chapter 28

James and seven of his men toiled up the mountain toward the Appleby residence. David Olsen, driving the two horse buckboard picked his way up the snow covered rough path.

Not knowing what they would find, everyone rode alertly, eyes scanning either side of the road. Everyone could see smoke rising slowly into the air. They had grimly been following the bloody trail Jake had left behind him on his journey to the town.

As they topped the rise, James steeled himself for the sight he figured they would find. However it was the acrid stench, of smoke and death that greeted them first. Noses stopped breathing in and for the rest of their stay at the farm, everyone breathed through open mouths.

Firearms were drawn, and the men looked warily around. The whole farm was eerily quiet. Instinctively the men spread out. The cabin was nothing but a burnt shell. Smoke was rising from the huge timber that had been the roof support. The only part that still stood was the stone fireplace. The fire had been hot and the snow around it was melted. Soot mixed with the melted ice to form black pools, now refrozen. The men were careful because it was very slippery.

James headed straight for the cabin and pushed some blackened timbers out of the way. The sun was setting over the western part of the mountain but it dyed the remaining snow blood red. James shivered apprehensively. He found May's body. It lay stretched out between what was left of the table and the fireplace. James holstered his gun and picked his way through the mess.

"Men, get the tarp from the wagon. We'll take May down to the church, until funeral arrangements can be made." There was nothing to be salvaged here.

A strangled cry from one of the men brought James out of the cabin in a hurry. Other men were converging on the barn where the cry had come from. One of the men was folded over being violently sick.

James arrived at the barn to see why. His gorge rose at the sight of the bloody barn yard. Blood spattered the barn and in front of the broken door, a cow and horse lay sprawled in a mangled heap. They had been beaten with a bloody post that lay near them in the snow. Their misery had been ended by a shot in the head.

"The man is insane!" James choked.

Angry muttering of his men hung in the air. There was no sign of Gus, but the looks on their faces, bode no good for him if he had been found. They spread out again, with James telling them to look for anything that could be salvaged. Jake was going to need all the things that could be found.

Anger blacked every visage, as the necessary duties were carried out. A dilapidated old shed held some furs. These were gathered and put into the wagon. A couple of hungry chickens were found. They squawked in outrage as they were caught and loaded onto the flatbed.

James followed a shallow trail westward up the mountain. There was not much to see at the end of his search. Deer tracks crossed the small area. A squirrel chattered at him from one of the trees. James retraced his steps.

One of the men adept at tracking, found the path up to the still. Gus was not there. The still was destroyed with malice. Men breaking it apart took some of their pent up anger, on the smelly equipment. They then set the whole thing on fire. The path continued past the still and on up the mountain. It seemed to be the trail into the back country that contained the Appleby trap lines. James and the others followed it for over a mile, but reluctantly turned back due to the lateness of the hour. Gus had many places that he could hide in that wilderness. He would have the advantage of knowing the land if he decided to ambush them.

With heavy hearts they returned to the farm and proceeded to get ready for the ride back down the mountain.

James knew he would never forget the stench of the farm that still caused him to breathe through is mouth not his nose. Neither would his men.

The procession including May Appleby's body made their way back to the town. Her body was put in a wooden coffin. Pops always had a couple on hand at the back of his workshop. The lid was sealed. She would be buried the next day.

It was decided that a town meeting would take place the following day to figure out what to do in regards to Gus. Having arranged everything he could, James and his men left wearily and silently for the ranch.

Jenny and Alice were waiting up for James when he got home. Tight lipped, he told them that May was dead and Gus had disappeared, but he refused to give them any more details.

Jenny and Alice did not press him, but they both knew it was bad, just from the look on his pinched white face. James refused a cup of tea and soon excused himself and headed toward his bedroom. For James the night was not over, he had a bath drawn and tried to relax, but the nightmare of the afternoon's horror keep replaying in his tortured mind. He broke out a glass of whiskey in the hopes it would help him get to sleep.

The ladies had watched him make his way toward the bedroom. Alice looked at Jenny and they quietly said good night. There was nothing much more to say. Jenny slowly made her way up the stairs. She looked in on Jake, he was sleeping so she left for her bedroom. She said a prayer for both Jake and May. She crawled into bed. Kally joined her. Jenny was grateful for the kittens company. It took her a long time before she managed to fall asleep.

Chapter 29

Jake took a turn for the worse during the night. When Jenny came to take her shift the next morning, she found Sandra, dipping cold compresses and placing them against Jake's forehead. He was awake but his eyes were glazed and he was unaware of his surroundings. His breathing was raspy, and he started to have bouts of coughing. Pneumonia was setting in. His arduous journey into Water Valley during the night with little winter clothing on was catching up with him. Doc was in to visit several times during that long day. He mixed up several potions, which only he knew the ingredients of. Fresh snow was brought up every half hour, so that she could keep wiping Jake down. By the time Lilly came in for her shift, Jenny was exhausted. Nightmares were disturbing Jake's sleep. He would toss and turn about.

Jenny went downstairs and begged for a bite of lunch. Lola had brought her some tea and sandwiches earlier, but with Jake so restless, she had not eaten. James was back in town, and the townspeople were having a meeting to decide what to do about Gus Appleby. It was full winter, and with Gus's knowledge of the backcountry he could probably hide out indefinitely, but James felt they would have to try.

When James came home it was just in time for supper. Alice, James and Jenny sat down to a casual meal in the Breakfast nook. James told them that it had been decided to wait until Jake could give them more information before taking off on a manhunt. The Chinook winds had blown snow into any tracks left by Gus. The three of them attended the church services, and when they returned to the house, all Jenny wanted to do was go to bed, but when James and another young man went up to help Nellie get Jake into a cooling bath, she dutifully offered to help.

James told Jenny, in no uncertain terms, to get some sleep, herself. She was rather relieved. She was not cut out to do nursing, but in Jake's case, she felt she was obligated too. He was her friend.

The next morning, Jake still had the raspy cough, but his fever had broken.

He was still hurting a great deal, and the coughing usually left him spent and shaking. They spoke quietly together, and when James joined them Jake turned a little whiter, if that was possible. He did not want to talk about that fateful Christmas Day. James was gentle, but firm, and slowly the horrid story came out.

Christmas morning had arrived, and Gus had gone out. Jake had helped his mother with the Christmas dinner. It was to be the lovely ham that Jenny had given them. Neither of them had considered the price that ham had cost them. It was nearing dinnertime, when Gus returned, drunk. As soon as he had arrived in the house, he knew that there was ham in the oven. You could not mistake the smell. He demanded to know where May had gotten it.

Gus was particularly stingy with his money and knew that May could not have afforded to buy one. He leaped to the correct conclusion that Jenny, that horrid good for nothin' teacher was responsible. First she dared take his son's affection away from him, now she was givin' them food. Jenny was Gus's obsession at the moment.

He threw open the oven door and grabbed the ham with his bare hands. He sent the ham flying against the wall. Yelling in pain from his burnt hand, he looked around for a scapegoat. Jake tried to get between his mother and Gus but he was too late. Gus's eyes had landed on the iron poker. Grabbing it he swung, hitting May a bone-crunching blow on the side of her head. She went down without a sound. Gus then lunged for Jake, and the boy fled. Unluckily he tripped on the drippings from the ruined ham. The first blow from the poker landed on Jake's arm. Dizzy with pain, Jake scrambled up and made for the door. Several more blows to his ribs and other places, disoriented him for a minute. Fortunately for Jake, Gus left him to kick his wife repeatedly, yelling at her to get up.

Jake finally found the door. Gus's befuddled brain finally realized his wife was dead. Screaming with rage, he grabbed the hunting rifle. Jake was out into the snow now, running for his life. The last thing that he remembered was Gus yelling about making that damn teacher regret she ever came here, and the agonizing pain that lanced through his shoulder, sending him into a snow bank.

It was dark when he regained consciousness. The house had pretty well disappeared, although the fire was still burning. He did not know how the fire had started. He fought his way up to a kneeling position. He looked warily around. He wondered where his father was. From here he could see the fenced area where their single horse was kept. Prince was not standing anyplace that Jake could see, so he figured Gus had taken him and left. Jake was now on foot. The searing words that his father had yelled, gave him the courage to start down the long cold road to town. He had to warn his beloved teacher, and he hoped the town's folks would help him as well.

While Jake continued his tale, James glanced anxiously at Jenny. The woman he was fast falling in love with was in danger, until Gus could be apprehended. Mentally vowing that capture would not be long in coming, he focused back on what Jake was telling them.

Jake had walked as best he could most of the way, but a lot the progress down the mountain had been crawling. His shoulder and arm hurt, and every bone seemed to ache. He passed out a couple of times. His winter clothes had been burnt in the house, but luckily he still had his boots on when all the trouble started. He had been out doing the chores, and had just come into the cabin. He had taken his coat and hat off, and when his mother had asked him to refill the firebox he had done so. The Chinook had raised the temperature outside, so Jake did not bother to put his coat on again. Now the warm wind was a blessing as well, because he would have frozen to death if the temperature had dropped too much that night.

The trip had been a nightmare, and he never even realized he made it to the bridge crossing into Water Valley. He just remembered Mayor licking his face, and then the rest of the tale was pretty hazy, just vague recollections of concerned faces standing over him. When he realized he had made it to his destination, he let himself fall into oblivion.

James thanked him, and Jenny gave him some more medicine. He soon fell asleep again. James took Jenny out into the hall, and said to her.

"I would like you to stay here longer, Jenny. Until Gus is caught I would not like to risk your safety," he told her. "That man hates you."

Jenny looked up into those gorgeous blue, but troubled eyes and smiled. "Thank-you for caring James, and maybe it would be a good idea to stay. Can you send someone to let Ray Brown know that I am staying on here for a while?"

James nodded. "I'll tell him myself." He was only too happy, for the occasion, horrendous as it was, that let her stay near him a little longer. He gave her a quick kiss and went off to do some long delayed chores. Jenny went back to sit with Jake. It was not long until Lilly came to relieve her.

Chapter 30

Jenny went back to her room. She knew at this time of the afternoon that Alice would be having her rest. James had gone out so she was free to do as she wished. She glanced outside, and it seemed to be very nice out.

Jenny decided to go outside for a walk, she had been given a general tour, but she thought she would like to see what she might have missed. Donning her coat, and fur hat she examined herself in the mirror. Woollen gloves would make sure she didn't get too chilled. Felt lined boots impervious to snow and wet completed her outfit.

Lola had been faithfully waiting on Jenny since she arrived at the ranch. She smiled shyly at Jenny and said "You look beautiful, Miss Jenny, Mr. James will have no eyes for anyone but you!" Lola had developed an unswerving loyalty to Jenny.

Jenny returned the smile. "Thank-you Lola, and I hope you're right!" she laughed. She descended the stairs and around to the back door. The veranda had been swept clean, and a path all around the gardens gave Jenny a good opportunity to wander around. A pretty gazebo in the centre of the garden stood white and empty. Bushes covered with snow created beautiful sculptures, with very diverse designs. Using her imagination Jenny could see animals or people in their unusual shapes. From the bare branches climbing the sides of the gazebo, Jenny could envision the leaves and vines, which would shade and give privacy in the hot days of summer. The garden even boasted a maze with a formal layout like the pictures she had seen of English Castles. It looked desolate at this time of year with the hedges covered in snow. Jenny did not go into it at this time because the snow had not been shovelled out and looked quite deep. It would be nice to explore it when summer came.

She hoped she would have opportunity to see it in the summer time. Toward the back of the garden, there was a flat shiny surface of an ice-covered pond. The snow had been shovelled off the surface, and Jenny watched the ranch children playing on the smooth plane. Some of them had skates, and were racing around. Branches were being used as hockey sticks, to chase a ball around the pond. Stones placed at either end were considered goals. Spotting her they waved and then carried on playing. Jenny left them and continued her travels. The chapel was on the southwest end of the yard.

She had already been to it for the Sunday Service, but she wanted to see it in the daylight. She opened the door, and quietly went in. The first thing she did was go to the front of the chapel and kneel. She said a little prayer for Jake. When she rose up she turned to examine the beautiful building. It was not a large chapel, but it did boast a small stained glass window on the back wall, above the pulpit. It had dark mahogany pews, and woodwork. The pulpit was also of richly carved mahogany. There were arched windows on each side letting in the sunshine. There was no need for lanterns or candles at this time of day. It was altogether a lovely site. Reverend Chase came out to the ranch Sunday evenings to hold services for the ranch residents. He would travel here when the weather allowed. He had a permanent room with a private entrance attached to the Foreman's home. He often spent Sunday night at the ranch before heading home to Water Valley the next day. Nellie would often accompany him on his duties to the Rocking B. At the moment Nellie was making use of this room to sleep when she was not nursing Jake. At the back of the church was an enclosed area, with a wrought iron fence and gate. There were three headstones there. Jenny bowed her head in silent prayer. She left the cemetery quickly.

Jenny followed the path to the far end of the garden area. A hole in the hedge revealed another wrought iron gate, which opened easily to allow access to the barns and other ranch buildings. She crossed the lane and went into the closest barn. The barn consisted mainly of huge box stalls, housing numerous horses that were special to the Borland Family. A man immediately came out of the tack room near the front of the barn.

"Well, well, Good Day to you Miss Stockton," he greeted cheerfully. "My name is Toby Wells, I look after the barns here. Is there anything I can do for you on such a lovely day?" he asked with a wide grin.

"No, Toby, I was just wandering around. However I was hoping to find Soot, and give her a scratching around the ears," Jenny laughed. "I was also kind of wondering if you knew where James was," Jenny continued.

"Well now, Soot is just down at the end of this aisle and Mr. James is out in the pasture, just behind the Carriage shed, with a couple of hands, fixing some damaged fences. If you follow the road just past the shed you should come upon them. I am not sure how far away they are though," he said doubtfully.

"Thank you Toby, please do not let me disturb you further, I'll find my own way," she said with a smile.

"Ok, ma'am, just make yourself at home," and Toby turned and went back to the tack room where he was polishing some bright work on a harness.

Jenny slowly walked through the barn, stopping at each stall to admire the beautiful horses. Each stall was raised a few inches from the main barn floor, with wooden walls that were about five feet high on each side and the front. From the top of these walls round iron bars, created a vertical fence up to the roof. It gave the stall air circulation, yet the bars were close enough together that the horses were not able to reach his or her next door neighbour, even though they could easily see each other. The front of each stall was also five foot high, with bars, including the wide door, which was divided into a top and bottom so that it could be fully closed, or the top half opened to allow the horses to look over into the aisle.

On the lower part of the door, was an oak board with the horse's name, on it. The letters had been carefully burnt out, and then, beautifully oiled, to give it a lovely shine. The back of the stall also had a door. The upper part had a glass window, protected from damage by bars. This allowed the resident animal to go out in good weather to enjoy his or her own private corral and have a small run. A shutter on the outside could also be close fully to keep the cold weather at bay. Today though the shutters were open wide to let the sunlight pour in. Every wall and stall was painted a gleaming white. Jenny smiled and thought that it must be a full time job for someone to keep the stall walls so clean.

The horses were indeed beautiful. From what James had told her, the Morgan was fairly new to Montana. The originals had been developed in the eastern States. James himself had travelled east to purchase his starting stock. He was proud to say that the horses' pedigrees could be traced back to Justin Morgan's horse "Figure."

Soot had Morgan blood in her, but her mother had been a ranch bred mare. Her horse had taken on many of the same qualities as her sire, Miracle. He was a bay, with a zigzag blaze across his face. Miracle was James's premier stud and the purebred offspring were raised to sell to lucky people for small fortunes.

Horses were James's hobby and first love, but cattle were his main business. The Borland ranch covered one hundred and fifty thousand acres of prime land that included mountains, valleys, flat country and rich pastureland. Rivers and creeks abounded throughout the ranch. Jenny found Soot in the end box stall, and the mare nickered a welcome, stretching her neck over the stall door begging for a scratch and her carrot.

Jenny laughed and obliged her, sending the mare into ecstasy. Soot's eyes closed in total relaxation as Jenny scratched behind her ears. She looked reproachfully at Jenny, when the scratching stopped, and the expected carrot was not forthcoming.

"So sorry, Soot. I forgot all about going to the kitchen to get you a carrot. I promise I'll come back later with the largest one I can find!" she told her.

Jenny exited the barn at the back, and admired the view to the south. The snow-covered fields almost blinded her in the sunlight.

Turning to her left she walked toward the carriage shed. All the ranch's vehicles were housed there out of the weather. Jenny took note of the different buggies and road wagons there. It was obvious that James collected carriages the way Greg Wilson collected bugs. She slowly walked around them all taking note of what James had. The shed also contained the fire wagon, which had helped put Homer and Martha's fire out. Leaving the building Jenny walked back to the main road that travelled further into the pastures. It was still early, so Jenny decided to walk along the road for a while. She hadn't gone more than three hundred yards when she topped a small rise. Ahead of her was a bridge, and a little further on she saw a small group of men. Shading her eyes against the bright sunlight, Jenny saw James and a couple of hands fixing the rails of a white washed fence. Smiling in pleasure, Jenny continued forward, and was soon upon them.

They greeted her with enthusiasm, but never stopped doing their task. Jenny stayed out of the way and watched. When the last rail was fixed, James walked back to the house with her. The chill in the air had made her cheeks turn a pretty rose color. James was bewitched and thought she was the most beautiful girl in the world. He couldn't believe his luck in finding this lady. They went inside and took off their wraps. Lola was there to take Jenny's coat up to her room. Jenny thanked her.

They entered the living room, to find Alice relaxing on her chaise lounge. She put her book down, observed their glowing faces and was well satisfied. She had come to like Jenny very much and the look of adoration on James face told her that he was smitten, beyond words. This gave her the courage to pursue her curiosity. Still she wanted to know about Jenny's family, her antecedents. James would not thank her for this, but her patience had run out.

Gently so she didn't alarm Jenny, Alice asked, "Jenny, I would like to know more about you, James doesn't tell me anything. What brought you out to Montana?"

Jenny smiled understandingly. Jenny had been expecting this conversation. She told them her story. She ended with the arrival at the train station where she had met James for the first time. Both of the Borland's were amazed that Jenny was an heiress. It had been obvious from the start that Jenny was not poor, but it definitely eased Alice's mind from the notion that Jenny might be a fortune hunter. James had given Alice the "I'll get you later, look." Now that her curiosity was satisfied, Alice didn't care; about the lecture her grandson would likely give her. This young lady was definitely suitable as a possible consort to her grandson.

The tea she had ordered soon arrived. The three of them talked about everyday occurrences on the ranch. It was a very pleasant meal.

Jenny excused herself to go up and check on Jake. James climbed the stairs with her and they went into Jake's room together. He was sitting up in bed, a little shaky but said he felt much better. Jenny smiled at him. James said he had more questions for Jake, so Jenny excused herself saying she had some things to do and left them together.

Jenny went into her room and closed the door. Her conversation between Alice, James and herself had caused her whole body to shake in uneasiness.

It had been obvious that Alice had been looking for assurances that Jenny was marriageable material. Jenny had worked so hard to gain her independence. Marriage for her at this time was out of the question. She did not want to be tied down. James was wonderful and she loved being with him. She didn't know which way to turn. She decided to try and keep James at a bit more distance if she could. The debate raged in her mind and time passed. She had come to no clear decision by suppertime. Gathering her scattered wits about her, Jenny descended the stairs for supper.

After supper James and Jenny sat close to the fire. The temperature outside was dropping rapidly again. Alice had excused herself early stating she had some letters to write.

Jenny stared into the flames, almost hypnotized. James was in much the same state and sat in silence gazing into the fire.

James broke the mood of the evening by telling her that the next day he and several of his hands were going after Gus Appleby. Jake had told them where he would likely be holed up. There was a small cabin at the far end of the trap lines, about fifteen miles up river from their house. After Gus's threat to Jenny, James was taking no chances with that crazed man.

These thoughts agitated Jenny and she begged James to be careful. She did not want anything happening to him. Vowing he would do so, he gave Jenny a peck on the cheek and bid her good night. He then retired to his room. Jenny sat near the fire for a little longer trying to bring back the quiet camaraderie of a few minutes before. It was useless. Soberly she too went to her room.

Chapter 31

The morning of New Years Eve, Jenny came in to relieve Sandra. The lady was ecstatic. Jake had gotten himself out of bed, to the privy and back again with no help. Jenny, Lily, Nellie and Sandra decided with Jake's agreement that a night nurse would not be needed. Stairs would still be a bit much for him to navigate for another day or so maybe, but Jenny said that she would stay with him to keep him company, so would Lily.

Nellie was lonesome, missing her husband. She decided she would go home after the dance that night. He was coming out for the New Years Eve Dance, and would be bringing Nellie's party dress. The Reverend wouldn't be the only one coming out to the ranch. Everyone was invited. This New Year's Eve Party had become an annual occasion for everyone in the community and few missed attending it.

Jake was in a very good mood. The arm didn't hurt very much and his shoulder was healing. The worst problem he had was the itch his wound was giving him. Other than that he felt one hundred percent better. He was a bit agitated from the confinement but Charles came out to the ranch early just to entertain him. They would spend hours hunched over the chess board. He said he would like to walk the hall, as he was tired of the bed and the four walls surrounding him. James had loaned Jake a robe and Charles and Jenny fought to get it over the huge plaster cast on Jake's arm. Jake then spent the next while pacing up and down the hallway with Charles keeping him company.

Jenny had the maids change the linens again. They just finished making the bed up neatly, when Jake got tired. Jake sat in the easy chair and Jenny arranged the pillows comfortably for him. He still had the occasional coughing spell, which would drain him of energy. Still it was obvious that he was on the mend. The three of them spent the morning playing cards. James joined them at noon. He brought up a tray of sandwiches and drinks for them all. They ate and talked about nothing of importance, just enjoying each other's company.

James said that he would be up for Jake, at around nine o'clock if he wanted to join the New Years Eve Party. By this time Jake was so tired of seeing the same old room and hallway that he jumped at the chance. Lilly arrived and advised Jake to have a sleep before the party or he would get too tired.

Jenny returned to her room, and looked in her closet to see if she had anything to wear for the party. She chose a light purple velvet dress with deep purple braiding. She checked it to make sure it was unwrinkled, and when a few were found, she rang for Lola, and the girl reassured Jenny it would be ready by evening.

She spent the rest of the afternoon in the library, reading. Kally now had run of the house, and followed Jenny everywhere. She curled up on Jenny's lap while she read.

At supper Jenny joined Alice and James in the dining room. They had a lovely meal. Jenny asked "James, will there be dancing this evening?"

"I've asked the Frederick brothers to provide the music." He laughed. "I hope you have left me at least one dance," he teased.

Alice chimed in. "I hope your card is full up, Jenny. This lad is too full of self confidence. You need to teach him a lesson," she spoke with a wicked grin.

"Yes he is. Isn't he! Well I am sorry James, you are out of luck. I'm booked solid." She replied with a haughty face. She couldn't keep the look for long and joined Alice in laughter at the mock horrified expression on James's face.

When the laughter subsided Jenny said softly. "I didn't say who booked my card solid, now did I?" Her soft luminescent eyes bore deep into his own.

James caught his breath. "No, you didn't come to think of it," he whispered.

Alice looked at the two of them. She was touched at their obvious devotion to each other.

With the meal completed they went to the hall. The cowhands had been busy. The tables were stacked to one side, and their benches were placed around the hall for easy use. It would be an old fashioned barn dance. The cooks again outdid them self with treats of all sorts. People had been arriving all afternoon. Winter driving was hazardous at best. No one wanted to travel after dark if it could be helped. The people arrived in carriages, sleighs or cutters.

The official party would not start until nine o'clock. At eight o'clock two old gentlemen from one of the homesteads, the Frederick brothers, arrived. One was a wonderful fiddle player and the other a banjo player and caller for the square dances. At nine o'clock James and another fellow went upstairs and brought Jake down for the fun. He was ensconced in an easy chair and Lilly followed, bringing a blanket in case Jake needed it. Kally was a bit scared at all the noise and spotted the one person who was not constantly on the move. She jumped on Jake's lap, much to his delight and settled there for the evening.

Jake's face was flushed with excitement. This was his first dance. He knew he couldn't do any dancing, but the thrill of being there made up for his shakiness. Jenny made sure he had some punch beside him and all kinds of goodies.

Everyone seemed in good spirits and not one of the families failed to drop by Jake's chair to give him their good wishes. Jenny watched Jake's face as the look of amazement grew every time someone wished him good luck. That lonely love starved boy could hardly believe that people really cared about him. The concept was almost beyond his comprehension.

Jenny was asked to dance by every man in the room. Even Charles square danced with her, although he spent most of his time near Jake. Jenny was sure her slippers would be worn out completely before the end of the evening.

A few minutes to midnight, James asked everyone to refill glasses with their favourite beverages. At a minute to midnight, James started a countdown and people waited with baited breath the final stroke. Shouts and laughter burst out as everyone tried to get his or her Happy New Year in before everyone else's. It was bedlam, it was chaos and it was wonderful.

James stood on the raised hearth and held his hands up for attention. When he had everyone's eyes focus on him, he said "Happy New Year. I hope that 1897 will bring you all good fortune. God bless each and every one of you."

Everyone cheered and raised their glasses in total agreement with his feelings.

Jake was starting to droop, so James and Charles helped him up to his room. James gave him a huge cowbell, which he was to use if he needed any help during the night. Kally had followed him and jumped on the bed beside him. This was to be his first night without someone being right there with him.

"I'll be just fine," Jake assured them. "See, Kally will keep me company," he laughed.

James and Charles rejoined the revellers. No one wanted to leave. It had been a wonderful party.

Gradually, the party wound down. James and Jenny bid everyone good night. The ranch folk returned to their homes, but the ones that lived a fair distance away, curled up in blankets near the fire. They would travel home in the morning.

James escorted Jenny up to her room. They walked arm in arm, slowly up the stairs. They stopped at Jenny's bedroom door. Jenny looked up into the blue pools of James eyes. James bent his head and kissed her gently. Jenny's blood raced, her breathing became faster. James raised his head a bit, and looked deep into Jenny's eyes.

James hugged her close and kissed her passionately. Jenny's knees grew weak. A fire seemed to consume her. She became light headed and dizzy. Jenny never wanted the kiss to stop. James pulled himself back to reality. He had to keep control of himself. Never had he wanted any lady so much.

James groaned, forcing his emotions to stop pushing him deeper. He broke away from Jenny, startling her with abrupt disengagement. She thought she had done something wrong, until she caught the look in his eyes. There was naked emotion there. It was James respect for her that stopped his advances. She noticed his trembling hands as he pulled away from her. Jenny turned slowly to open her door.

"Good night James," she whispered. "1897 will be a very good year. Happy New Year."

She left him standing there and closed her door. Jenny heard him say good night through the door. Jenny stood with her back against that door until his footsteps retreated down the hallway to his own room. When the distant door clicked shut, Jenny continued into her bedroom. Never had her emotions been so roused. It was an ache that had not been satisfied. Her body felt cheated. She wanted him. She needed him.

She smiled and took a deep breath. As she slowly changed into her nightgown her thoughts raced with various exciting day dreams.

Jenny hugged herself and danced around the room. This was the best Christmas and New Years that Jenny had ever experienced. Gradually her excitement toned down, and she crawled into the comfortable bed.

It took her a while to actually close her eyes and composed herself for sleep.

Chapter 32

New Year's Day commenced with a bright sunny sky. It was not warm out, but it was not the searing cold of previous days. The temperature hovered around twenty degrees Fahrenheit. Lola came in to open the curtains. She brought a message from James.

Jenny now wide-awake read the short missive. It asked if she could dress warm and come out to the carriage house after breakfast. She was very curious. She quickly dressed and downed a quick cup of tea and piece of toast. Jenny hastily donned a warm coat and boots. She put a warm scarf over her ears to protect them. Taking her gloves, she glanced and the mirror. She felt ready for anything. She hurried out the door and across the yard. When she arrived at the carriage house James had a sleigh pulled by two of his horses ready.

Jenny and James climbed in under the buffalo robe blanket. They then headed toward the river and crossed the bridge. He drove about a half a mile to an area between two hills. He got out and asked her to come with him. He tied the horses to a tree and to her surprise he took out a gun from under the seat. He got a box of shells and at her look of wonder, explained.

"Gus Appleby has threatened you and I'll not let you go back to your house without protection. I positively do not want to lose you even by accident if a lesson I can teach could mean the difference between your safety and your being helpless to combat him," he said doggedly.

Jenny looked at him and could read the love there and also his fear. Determination in the set of his mouth told Jenny he was not going to be swayed. Jenny did not like guns, but could see the sense in his reasoning.

She reluctantly said "I understand James and I'll learn to shoot because you want me too, but I also want you to know I dislike guns and am very afraid of them."

James and Jenny walked about a hundred yards into the hills. James set up a target, and showed her the workings of the tiny gun. It was a Derringer, with a coal black shiny barrel. The handle had pearl grips. He taught her to load it, and then, with trepidation, Jenny pointed the gun at the target. It was a stump, with a log standing up on it. Jenny tried to aim, but when she squeezed the trigger, she shut both of her eyes. Of course she missed by a mile. James laughed, and assisted her. By the time noon came around she could hit the target five times out of ten. James was pleased with her progress.

In perfect harmony with each other they headed back for the house. After lunch, James went out to look after ranch affairs, and Alice and Jenny had some fun chatting about women's fashions of the day. Alice was very knowledgeable about the newest and modern styles. A little while later Alice retired to her room for a nap. Jenny went to the conservatory, and studied all the exotic plants and trees living there.

She went to the library, and got a book, and returned to this restful area. She daydreamed more, than read. She was totally happy. Jenny hugged herself, and sent a small prayer of thankfulness up to God.

At three o'clock Jenny guiltily went upstairs to see how Jake was doing. He was not in his room. A bit alarmed Jenny ran downstairs to inquire as to his whereabouts. As she got to the big hall she found him playing cards with Charles and the cook. The cook was on his break, but would soon have to start supper.

Tucked in beside Jake was a dozing Kally. Jenny laughed, she had forgotten all about her kitten.

When Jenny didn't come in that morning, Jake had made his way slowly downstairs, accompanied by Kally and had been enjoying himself in the lounge area of the dining room. Charles had come in from the bunkhouse and joined him. Various staff had come in to keep him company on their breaks. He was having the time of his life. The doctor came by a few minutes later, and removed the tape wrapping Jake's ribs. Double-checking the gunshot wound, he said that a bandage was no longer needed on it either. He was to take it easy, but there was no reason that he couldn't do what he wanted within reason. The arm cast would have to stay on for another two weeks at least. Jenny stayed with them until suppertime. Jake decided that he did not want to return to his room so he was going to eat with the rest of the cowhands.

Jenny excused herself and went back to the living room. She waited along with Alice for James to come in. When he did, he had a visitor with him.

James said. "This is Sheriff Mike Sutton from Butte. Mike this is my grandmother Alice Borland and my friend Jennifer Stockton."

"Pleased to meet you," he said with a small bow.

Alice said "Would you join us for supper, Mr. Sutton?"

"Delighted," he said.

Alice had a place for the Sheriff set very quickly. The four of them sat down.

The Sheriff, Mike Sutton from Butte had arrived to do some investigations of the crime. He had spent the day up at the Appleby cabin and in Water Valley questioning the residents there.

After the meal was finished Jenny hurried to the hall to prepare Jake for the Sheriff's visit. Jake gulped and started to shake. James brought the sheriff in, but to Jenny's surprise, the man was very gentle in talking to Jake. It was obvious that Jake was upset. Within a few minutes of the encounter, Mike had calmed Jake down enough to stop his shaking.

Jake retold his story, and Mike took notes. It was obvious he was a skilled interrogator, because he managed to get more details of the crime, out of the boy than even Jake thought he remembered. He was also a skilled artist, because he drew a good likeness of Gus's face, with all their help and criticism to the details.

He accepted the invitation to spend the night at the ranch and told them he was leaving for Butte in the morning. He would put wanted posters up everywhere before the week was out. He was confident that Gus would be apprehended very soon.

In spite of this confidence, Jake, James and Jenny felt uneasy. They had their doubts. James noticed that Jake was still anxious about something.

"Jake is there something wrong?" James asked quietly.

"Umm, my home is burned up right?" he said slowly. At James's nod, Jake continued. "I feel guilty staying here at the house, umm… I wonder if I can move out to the barn or hayloft until my cabin can be rebuilt. I won't be any bother, I promise," he said earnestly.

"You're not a bother Jake," James said soberly. "But I do understand your dilemma about a place to live. It will be spring before we can help you rebuild your house, if you decide you want to." James smiled and continued. "There is a spare bed out in the bunkhouse, unless of course you would really rather sleep in the hayloft."

Jake stared at him then smiled a bit when he realized James was teasing him.

James continued. "You can stay here as long as you like, and when you're well enough, I want to hire you to help Mel Stang work and train young colts. I have watched you with Soot, and David Olson told me you're a natural with horses. You're just the kind of person I'm looking for to assist Mel. I'll hire you at the same wages any new workers would get."

James said, "There is one stipulation however." Jake grew apprehensive again. "You are to continue going to school, you can travel with the other students in the school wagon."

Jake was totally overwhelmed by the offer. He stammered his thanks to James. It was more than he had ever dreamed of. Jake's eyes shone, then suddenly their light dimmed.

"I can't take you up on your wonderful offer, sir," he said sadly. "I already have a job working for Miss Jenny! She gave me money before Christmas to do various things for her," he glanced almost hopelessly at Jenny.

Jake was startled when Jenny laughed, "There is no problem. I have an idea about what you can do for me! It's winter," she said, "and I've discovered that in spite of your wonderful teaching, I am still rather nervous driving a horse in snow. Soot needs loving care and exercise. Otherwise she will just be eating her head off for nothing in David's barn."

"There are times I may need Soot but in the meantime we can share her. I would like you to ride her everyday," Jenny said thoughtfully. "It is my suggestion that you ride her from the ranch to school, and that way if I need you to do something, you'll have Soot to take you back home rather than walking. I can't imagine any chores I have lasting more than an hour after school. You can work for James all other times, like evenings and week-ends."

Jenny glanced sideways to James for approval of her solution. James just grinned, "That sounds fine with me. What about you Jake, what do you say?"

Jake just stared at them both, stupefied. Then gathering his scattered wits together he grabbed James hand and shook it. He then spontaneously hugged Jenny.

James laughed and bid Jake goodnight and went to his office. He had gotten behind on his paperwork. Jenny also tendered Jake a good night and retired to her room. It was still early, but Jenny was a bit tired. She soaked in the bath for an hour while a curious Kally batted at the soap bubbles and walked along the edge of the tub. The inevitable happened and Kally slipped. She gave a yowl of fright as she landed in the water. Jenny laughing helped the soaked kitten out and onto the floor. The indignant cat, shook herself, and then shook each leg separately. It was hilarious to watch. Kally then sat down to thoroughly wash herself, with her pink tongue working furiously. Jenny climbed out of the tub, dried herself and put her nightclothes on. She happily curled up in bed with her book. She soon fell asleep.

Chapter 33

The next day dawned beautifully. Once again James took Jenny out for a couple of hours of target practice. They did not go back to the house for lunch, however, but drove further into the hilly countryside. Jenny was thrilled when she saw a small herd of White-tailed Deer picking their way through the deep snow. James said this time of year was hard on them, because deep snow forced them to eat the bark on trees.

They moved on. With the magic of a conjurer, James provided a snow picnic for them. He spread it out on a small foldable table right in the sleigh. It was a joyous meal.

Both were surprised when a mounted party hailed them. As the riders drew closer, Jenny was even more surprised to see they were Indians. James glanced apprehensively toward Jenny. To his delight Jenny's face only registered curiosity, not abhorrence. The Indian Wars left most people disliking the Natives.

James got down from the sleigh with a big smile on his face. "Thorn!" he shouted. "It's great to see you."

Thorn dismounted and came toward James and Jenny.

"Thorn my friend, I want you to meet Jenny. She is staying with us for our holidays."

Turning to Jenny, James continued, "Jenny I would like you to meet Thorn, Medicine Man and Spirit Guide to his people."

Jenny stepped out of the sleigh and greeted Thorn with a bright smile. "I am very pleased to make your acquaintance, Thorn."

She glanced at the other riders with Thorn. They we bundled in furs and buckskin leather garments. Each had a spear in a special holder on their mounts. She turned back to hear Thorn addressing James.

"We are hunting for more food for our village. It has been a hard winter so far and supplies are running low," he said.

James nodded and told Thorn that there was a deer herd not too far away. "However, Thorn I have a great idea, just a mile or so from your village is a bull with a broken horn. He is situated up in Dead Valley. He has collected a few ragged cows for his herd, but with his nasty temper, ends up hurting anything that comes close. I wouldn't mind him being taken as food for your people. Just take care he doesn't gore someone. It will save me a lot of trouble. I was going to kill him come spring anyway. I doubt a cougar will have got him."

Thorn studied James face. Seeing he was sincere in his offer, Thorn thanked him. "Beef would be a welcome change from wild game," he grinned.

Remounting his horse Thorn raised his arm in the air, in salute to James and Jenny. They filed passed the sleigh heading for where James told them the deer herd were holed up.

Resuming their seat in the sleigh, James drove the horses in a wide circle, coming into the ranch area from a different direction. They stopped on a hill overlooking the ranch, and Jenny started to feel edgy. Sensing this James put his arm around her and held her close. The conversation lagged. Tomorrow was Sunday and time for her to go back to Water Valley. Jenny did not want to go, but she had her duties to get back to.

James also did not want her to go, but could find no real excuse for her to stay.

Jenny told him, "I'll be fine James. I wish I could stay here too, but I know I can't. I know you're worried, but I should be fine right in the middle of town. I'll make sure my doors are locked when I'm in the house and my students or friends will be with me when I'm not."

They returned to the house and Jenny reluctantly ascended to her room to pack. Jake had been moved out to his new home so the upstairs was lonely.

It was so quiet Jenny talked to Kally to create some noise. When Jenny descended downstairs for supper, it proved to be a strange meal. Everyone was sad at Jenny's imminent departure, but tried to put a good face on it. The laughter was a little forced, too loud and a bit too sharp. Jenny decided to stay up as long as possible, just to be with James.

Alice retired early, and James and Jenny just sat together holding hands, in front of the roaring fire. It was late when James escorted Jenny up to her room. He kissed her, but neither of them said very much. It was a long time before Jenny managed to get to sleep.

Sunday morning Soot was waiting with the sleigh. Her trunks were brought down, and piled in it. Alice was up early, and the three of them ate breakfast together.

Jenny dressed in her warmest clothes. The Borland matriarch gave Jenny a warm hug. "I hope you come to visit often Jenny," Alice said. "It's not that far out here, and I get lonely."

Jenny hugged Alice again and told her, "I will try and come out as often as I can," she promised.

Jenny then made herself comfortable under the blanket in the sleigh. James rode up on his favourite horse. He was going with her to Water Valley where they would attend church together.

Jenny drove slowly, because she wanted this drive with James to last forever. When they crossed the bridge into town they noticed many sleighs hitched in the parking area. The town's folk and homesteaders greeted them both with enthusiasm.

The church bell began to ring and all went inside for the services. It was a lovely sermon, but at the end the Reverend reminded everyone about the memorial services for May Appleby at one o'clock.

Most of the people stayed after church to attend the sad service. They chatted on the boardwalk until it was time. At twelve-thirty a whole contingent from the ranch, accompanied by Jake arrived. One of the men had given him a black suit that was much too big for him and he had his hair slicked down. No one had ever gotten close enough to the Appleby family to know May very well, but all of them knew and had come to like Jake.

Reverend Chase said prayers and gave the eulogy. Afterwards they all went out to the gravesite where the Reverend prayed over May's grave. James had given Jake a bouquet of flowers from the conservatory. Jake knelt and placed the blooms on the grave. Jake was silent in his grief. The service completed, everyone came around and offered him their condolences. Jake accompanied James and Jenny to her house.

They had a small luncheon. Jake and James brought Jenny's trunks into the cottage. Jake then took Soot to the livery barn. He brushed and curried her more than was necessary, it kept his hands busy. He was alone and his stoicism had failed. Soot got rather wet in the next few minutes. This was the first time he felt truly alone and it felt good to let his emotions run without interference.

"Soot, I'm feeling so low right now. I wish I would've taken Ma away last month when I had earned some money. I wish, I wish I had been stronger, you know. Maybe I could have stopped Pa." He hugged Soot. "Everyone's been so nice. I can hardly believe it. Miss Jenny said I can ride or drive you, at least for the rest of the winter. It supposed to be how I am working for her. It's not work, not for me anyway." Jake felt a little better. Soot sensed something wrong, with him. She turned her head around, and nuzzled Jake's chest. He hugged Soot hard. Once he regained his composure, he went over to the water trough and splashed icy water on his face so no tears would show. He then made his way back to the church entrance, where the Ranch residents were getting prepared to head home. Jenny was there to see them off.

Jenny could see traces of Jake's emotions, but said nothing. She hugged him and told him that she would see him in the morning unless the pending blizzard arrived. The clouds in the Northwest were indeed looking ominous.

The whole outfit then set of at a trot for the ranch, hoping they would make it home before the storm. Jenny hurried home. The wind was picking up, and seemed to go right through her clothes.

It did come, not an hour later snow started falling. Jenny decided she had better get in more firewood. It was hard to predict how long the snow would last. She opened her back door with difficulty. The snow was already piling up. She made several frigid trips to bring in the firewood. Instinct caused her to keep working until she was completely exhausted. She fought with the snow to get the pantry door closed again. The wood was stacked all along the wall of the living room. The temperature was falling fast. Night fell making the howling wind sound like shrieking animals. It was eerie and frightening. The cottage was cold. Jenny dragged her blankets out and placed them in front of the stove. Her bedroom was too cold and the heat would never reach it. She could not believe the howls and moans of the trees and wind. She knew that unless it stopped soon there would be no school.

She stayed awake most of the night, taking only quick cat naps. She had to keep the fires stoked. She ranged from the stove to fireplace desperate to keep them going. The blizzard never abated. The next morning she woke up to frost on the walls of her house. Where the nails poked through the wall frost formed shiny white marbles.

Both fires didn't seem to give off any heat. The water in her bucket over on the counter had a layer of ice on top. Her bread and the jam on her counter were stiff with ice crystals. Her butter was rock hard. She put a pan on the stove to cook some bread and eggs. She laughed rather grimly at the eggs retrieved from the pantry. The frozen hard white balls thawed in the pan. Still it gave her something to eat. She thawed more water for tea. She was constantly stuffing the stove with wood and stayed mostly covered up in her blankets cuddling Kally.

A crash from the bedroom caused Jenny to scream in fright. Visions of Gus coming to get her. She panicked, searching frantically for the gun James had given her. She was shaking so hard that the rolling pin she grabbed was vibrating. She waited horror stricken for Gus to come through the bedroom door. When nothing happened, Jenny fearfully started toward the bedroom curtain. Her heart was beating frantically. No further sound had come from the bedroom so she gingerly peaked around the door. The bedroom was empty. The windows were not broken. Heaving a sigh of relief she went right in. Her ceramic pitcher lay broken inside the basin. Ice formed in the shape of the pitcher lay in the basin. Expanding ice had caused the heavy ceramic pitcher to crack and break.

Jenny felt a little foolish at her panic. It did however make her realize how much Gus really scared her. The day passed with horrible slowness. Jenny used the slop pail for a toilet because there was no way she was going outside. She tried to sleep a great deal. The sound and fury of the blizzard became muted and Jenny realized that her house was being covered completely in snow. It became dark in the cabin even in the middle of the day. By the next day, Jenny was looking in fear at her pile of wood. It seemed to be diminishing, way too quickly. Once the cabin was covered in snow the heat seemed to stay in a bit more. It was a natural insulation.

The second night Jenny woke from her fitful sleep by another horrendous crash. Jenny was not sure what it was, but surmised that one of the huge trees near her home had fallen victim to the storm. She felt so alone and she was scared. As close as her neighbours were they might as well have been miles away. She was truly isolated at the moment.

She never dreamed that the weather could be so harsh. The snowstorms they had to this point were mere babies compared to this one. Three days the storm raged on.

Wednesday morning, the silence was incredible. The storm had stopped. Jenny's ears used to the roaring of the wind were ringing in the quiet aftermath of the blizzard. She crawled out of her makeshift bed and got dressed. She remade her bed and put her coat and warm boots on. When she opened the front door, a wall of heavy snow covered the door. Jenny sighed and tried to remain patient. The other residents of Water Valley would dig her out in time.

It was afternoon before she heard the sounds of shovels on her walk. "Why is it taking them so long?" she wondered. It was another half hour before they reached her porch and cleared the doorway.

She had put her coat on again and greeted the men of the town with enthusiasm. The feeling was mutual, as they had been worried about her too. Jenny went outside, and was awestruck. The landscape, what she could see of it was totally transformed. The snow was at least five feet deep in all areas, but had huge drifts measuring at least twice Jenny's height. All she could see of her house was the smoke rising from her stove. She glanced at her wood supply, and saw only three pieces left. If the blizzard had lasted any longer she would have had to burn her furniture.

No wonder it had taken so long to reach her. Jenny said,"Thank you for rescuing me. Is everyone all right?"

"Yes," David said. "Everyone made it through. Even the animals managed to keep from freezing."

The whole group including Jenny headed for the general store. The clearing of the roads and sidewalks would take a long time. The men carried on working and Jenny, happy to be free, joined Janet in helping where she could.

It took the rest of Wednesday and Thursday for the town to fully dig itself out. On Friday, Jenny had the school open, but only the few children who lived in town made it to class. Jenny gave them time to clean their desks and draw pictures. Without the majority of her students, she elected to make it a very light study. At recess and noon hour the kids went outside to build snow forts and tunnels under the snow. The heavy dense snow was wonderful for digging, but Jenny had to keep a close eye on the students so a cave in wouldn't trap them. Jenny remembered her terror when the pitcher had broken. Now that it was nice, Gus Appleby may show up any time. She shivered and vowed to be vigilant.

She dismissed school early, as the temperature took another plunge. It was a long cold snap this time. The walls of snow and the crust became thick. People were able to walk on top of the snow, with no danger of falling through. On Sunday Jenny ventured to the top of a bank and stood in wonder. Only the tops of houses and trees could be seen, with the exception of tunnels to front doorways. It was truly a wondrous sight.

School resumed on Monday with most of the students attending. Jenny with her gun in a special holster strapped to her thigh, remained uneasy. But as day after day came and went with no incidents, she started to relax. Maybe Gus would not return. Maybe!

Chapter 34

The long cold days of January seemed interminable. The kids worked hard, or at least most of them did. Squabbles broke out between the various children, but were patched up again as quickly.

Jenny hardly ever saw Bill anymore; he had come for his month's assignments just after the blizzard, and she hadn't seen him since. All the men were working hard sawing the logs and hauling them to the lumber mill. From the top of the hill near the General Store you could see a huge mound of logs growing rapidly.

Bill loved the work he was doing, he was proud to be a Yarder. Cyrus had let the younger men work as Yarders because the agility and swiftness of the young people. They could move faster to get out of the way in a hurry if something went wrong. There were always accidents, but this year had been lucky so far. One broken arm from a man falling off the log he was denuding of branches. Of course there were always the cuts and bruises from ordinary wear and tear of the job.

"A chaw of terbaccer could cure anything from, cuts, and bruises to toothaches," Bill laughed to himself. Sore muscles, were cured by a concoction kept hot over a bonfire. It was called "Cyrus's Cure All." A dose was a tablespoon of black pepper mixed with a tablespoon of liniment. It was put in a pint of boiling water, and molasses added to sweeten the drink. Men would down this as hot as they could take it. Bill had tried it once, and vowed to never use it again. It was an unforgettable brew.

However Bill was tired. He had promised Miss Jenny he would keep up with his schoolwork, and yet, with the crop failure last fall, his family needed all the income they could get. He was proud to help his family.

His father was a Chopper, and Bill would haul the prepared logs down to the waiting teamsters. Bill found himself yawning, and his father looked anxiously at him.

"Are you alright son?" he asked. "Perhaps you had better go home and get some sleep."

"I'm alright, Dad," Bill said, and finished attaching the chain to the end of the log. It was a big one this time. Mark, Bill's dark brown Clydesdale would have a hard time getting this down the mountain. The nose of the log had been tapered so it wouldn't catch on the ground so badly.

Bill clicked his tongue and the tired horse moved forward. He strained to start the log, but once it was moving, it was not too bad. When the horse finally hauled the log onto the main logging trail, it was much easier to pull. Or rather it was too easy. The snow packed from so much use, was extremely slippery. The log started to slip a little faster. Bill called for the horse to increase his speed a little. Bill was hurrying beside the horse. The log started to slip sideways. Then the unthinkable happened. The front of the log caught on a rut. The log swung around, and the horse was pulled off his feet. Bill yelled in fright as he tripped over the now slack reins. And the log kept coming. Bill scrambled up and ran for his life.

Bill didn't remember much else. Men came racing toward him when they heard him yell, but it was too late. They saw the log roll right over him.

It had missed the horse by scant inches. The log had dragged the horse several feet before the horse's dead weight had stopped it. The horse had stood up, shaking with fright, and white with lather.

One of the men ran to the horse, to unhitch him and make sure there were no other injuries. All the rest ran to Bill, who lay unconscious in the snow. It was the deep snow that probably saved his life, because it cushioned him when the log rolled over him. He was a mass of scratches and had deep bruised areas that were already turning blue. The worst was his leg; it was doubled up beside him. The blood was flowing from a deep cut, and the broken bones were showing through his overalls. While the boy was still unconscious, the men straightened his leg, splinted it and got him onto a sled. His father white faced was right beside him holding a tourniquet to stop the bleeding, as the team and sled headed for the town. The racing team never stopped at the town but headed straight for the ranch. Doc Murphy was already waiting. A young man had reached him about ten minutes before, sent by Cyrus to make the doctor aware of the situation. James was with him as well as a few other men. The speeding sled had come to a halt as near the new infirmary, as they could get. The men unloaded Bill and took him inside to a table that had been prepared by Lily, Doc's wife. They cut the overalls off, the boy, and Doc blanched at the extent of the injury. Muscles and tendons were torn. Doc grimly, just rolled up his sleeves and started to patch the tendons and muscles as best he could. He then made up a half cast. The leg needed to be kept straight but with the wound, it could not be enclosed. They would need to get at it for cleaning and to see how it progressed. Adam sat near the operations in a state of shock. Tears were running unheeded down his face. James brought him some whiskey, and the man downed it without knowing what he had taken.

Since Jake's illness, James had been busy. He had built an addition onto Doc Murphy's house. It was meant to be an infirmary. It was this building that was being used now. It was handy for Doc and his wife to look after him there. There were a few women, wives of the ranchmen that would take turns looking after patients as necessary.

Doc approached James later that afternoon, and shook his head at James's mute inquiry. "It is not good, James," he said. "Infection, which is inevitable, could cause us to have to amputate the leg. He needs a hospital with knowledgeable doctors that know how to handle the delicate work this needs. Butte has such a hospital. Bill needs to go there as soon as possible," Ed said firmly.

James nodded in agreement. He assured Ed that the trip to Butte would commence the next morning. James then went over to speak to Adam.

"Adam?" he said, and waited until his inquiry registered on the distraught man. "Adam, Bill needs to go to the Butte hospital."

Frantic denials formed on Adam's face, as he took in what James was saying. "No, we can't afford to have Bill go there. The expense would be phenomenal. Doctor Murphy can do what's needed, can't he?" Adams eyes pleaded.

Ed joined them, and he put his case before the father. "Adam, I know it would be expensive, but Bill could lose his leg to gangrene if it is not properly taken care of by surgeons that know what they are doing. Please believe me!" He added.

"Lose his leg? Oh my god, No!" Despair seized Adam, and he collapsed back into the chair he had risen out of.

Susan arrived on horseback, accompanied by Cyrus, who had gone to get her. Cyrus was extremely worried. Susan rushed into the infirmary to look at her son. The three other men, James, Ed, and Adam, joined her and Susan, sobbing hysterically, came into her husband's arms for comfort.

Cyrus, James and Ed, left the couple to themselves, until they could regain their composure. Cyrus, asked Doc to update him of the situation, and when told about the necessity of taking Bill to Butte, said that he could help defray some of the costs, but knew he couldn't handle the whole thing. James said that a fund would be set up both here on the ranch and in town. If everyone contributed something it would certainly help the Storm family out. The community pulled together and raised enough to pay the entire hospital bill. It came in by pennies, dimes, quarters and in a very few cases dollars. However this generosity did not get relayed to the affected family. James planned it to be a surprise when Bill recovered. So the family remained ignorant of the melding of the charitable community.

Adam and Susan would take Bill to Butte. A buckboard was filled by a feather mattress, and covered with a dozen quilts. Bill was loaded into it early the next morning. Susan dressed as warm as could be managed climbed onto the seat. Adam would drive the wagon. They were surprised when Doc Ed came out dressed as warm as he could and silently climbed in to the back of the wagon with Bill. He had been very worried when Bill had not regained consciousness. The couple smiled gratefully at him. They started back to Water Valley and the road to Butte. Adam and the Doctor both would leave Susan in Butte and return home when Bill was settled.

Jenny met the wagon just on the other side of the river. She handed a huge picnic basket to Adam and a small one to Susan. "The big one is filled with food for your journey. The small one is to be used by your family in Butte."

Thanking Jenny, the mystified couple kept the wagon moving. Jenny had hurried back up the street toward home. Adam gave Ed the picnic basket, which was settled, under the seat. The curious couple opened the small basket. Inside were two books that Bill might like to read when he was feeling better. A note, addressed to Bill, stated that he was not to worry about school or his assignments. Jenny said with Bill enthusiasm toward study and reading he could probably take and pass the examinations now, and do well. He had several months to recover without worrying. Adam and Susan knew that Bill would be pleased over this note. There were a few sticks of candy, and a final surprise. Lying on the bottom of the basket hidden by the books was a ten-dollar bill. A small note pinned to it stated that this was to be used for living expenses while they had to stay in Butte. It would pay for accommodations and food while Susan was there.

Susan and Adam were speechless. A warm feeling came over them when then thought of the wonderful generosity of Miss Jenny. Adam kept the horses moving at a steady pace. Bill was not doing well. He remained in a coma due to a huge bump on the side of his head. That alone could have killed him, but his situation was now critical. Doc Ed sat in the wagon beside Bill and watched him closely.

The long cold trip seemed interminable. The only stop they made was to rest the tired horses, and it was late that night when the lights of Butte came into view. The hospital was near the centre of town, on a small hill. Adam pulled up at the main entrance and halted. Doc went in first to find someone in charge. A nurse hurried out with him and she gave instructions to have Bill brought in immediately. They put him on a bed with wheels and put him in an examination room. A Doctor hurried in from a side door, and told the family to wait outside. He questioned Ed while he exposed the wound. Ed told him all they knew about the accident. The doctor then told Ed to leave and stay with the family. This would probably take a while.

Ed left the family for a few minutes while he took the exhausted horses to the livery barn that was not too far away. The man there assured Ed the horses would be swiftly taken care of, and that he was not to worry. Thanking the man Ed hurried back to the hospital.

He was just on time, as Dr. Swift, the Head Surgeon, came out of the examination room to talk to the family.

"Infection has started in the wound, and it is going to be touch and go as to whether we can save the leg," Dr. Swift said. "I need your permission to perform some necessary surgery. We will try to save that leg."

Adam and Susan were clinging to each other. The news was devastating to them. They looked in each other's eyes, and in unison said. "Please do all you can to save our son's legs. No matter what the cost, we will pay you and your hospital back somehow."

"The surgery will likely last all night, and it will be even longer before you will be allowed to see him," Dr. Swift told them. "Why don't you go to the Townsend Hotel, just down the block? It is reasonably priced, and maybe you can get some rest. Come back around nine o'clock tomorrow morning. We should know more by that time."

"But…" Susan started to object, only to be silenced by her husband.

The doctor smiled reassuringly to her. "We will do our best for him, Mrs Storm. Bill is young and that can only help him get better the faster. You will be of no use to your son until tomorrow, and it makes sense to rest yourself and get prepared to help your son when he does need you," Dr. Swift said softly.

Susan reluctantly nodded agreement and the three of them left to find a place to stay. They all went down the hill to the Main Street and got rooms at the recommended Townsend Hotel. It seemed expensive but they had plenty of funds, thanks to Jenny. The three of them had a late supper and discussed plans for tomorrow. Adam, although he wanted to stay, knew that he had to get back to work. This was even more important now that there would be a huge bill to pay. He would return to Water Valley the next day, and Doc would ride with him. Doc Ed said he would like to see how Bill was the next morning first, and Adam agreed. They would return home after that important interview. They then retired to their rooms for the night.

The next morning on the dot of nine o'clock, they were all back anxious for the results. Doctor Swift, true to his word met them with a smile on his face.

"I am very pleased," he said. "The surgery went better than I expected. I'm pretty sure he won't lose his leg now, and with time we'll know how much use he will have in it." He turned to Ed, with a smile. "For country doctoring, you did a marvellous job on putting those ligaments and muscles together. Normally the ends would have died by the time he got here, and there would have been nothing we could do."

Ed had not known that his work was that important, and he breathed a sigh of relief. Adam and Susan both hugged him.

"Now," said Dr. Swift. "If you'll come with me, I'll show you where we have set Bill up. He regained consciousness at six o'clock this morning, and he's awake for the moment. We've drugged him so he is not feeling any pain, but he may drop off to sleep on you at any given moment."

With sounds of delight, Susan and Adam entered the ward. Bill was at the end of a big room. There were five beds on each side of the aisle. They had him right next to the Nurse's Desk. The nurse was wearing a Nun's habit, and it was completely white. She came toward them as they entered and introduced her self as Sister Agatha, the Day Nurse for this ward. She smiled encouragingly to them as they rushed to Bill's side.

Bill grinned, wanly when he saw his parents. His face was as white as the sheets he was on, but he looked much better. His head was bound in a tight bandage, and the rest of him that they could see looked covered in bandages.

Pillows placed underneath Bill's leg supported it and raised it up above the rest of his body. A light sheet covered the cast up.

Susan kissed him on the forehead, and broke down and cried. Bill tried to comfort his mother, and looked up at his father. "The doctors wouldn't tell me what happened, and I don't remember. They say it's because of this bump on my head."

His father told him what happened, and Bill's eyes widened in horror. "I'm so sorry, Dad," he said, "I should have listened to you when you asked if I was alright. I was just plain stupid to try and do that job as tired as I was. I'm paying for that now," he whispered despondently.

Adam sat beside his son, and smiled. "All of us are foolish every now and then, it's just that most of us get away lightly with it. It is too bad that you're hurt more than you deserve for a moments foolishness. Foresight would be kind of nice, but that's not in our power."

Bill sighed and tried to wriggle into a more comfortable position as Doc Ed came into the room. "Good luck Bill and come home to us soon. This Dr. Swift is a good man, and if anyone can get you up and moving he can. I'm hopeful you will make a complete recovery," he said.

Bill flushed and said, "I'll do my very best, and thank you. Dr. Swift told me what you did for me. I'll always be in your debt," he added softly.

Then Ed said "Goodbye Bill, I hope to see you soon back home." He shook Bill's outstretched hand, and left his parents alone with him.

"Thank-you again, Doc," Bill called after him, "Say hi to everyone, and tell them I'll be back soon."

"I too have to go," his father said, "I have to get back to work. Your mother will remain here until you come home"

"But Dad," Bill said with worry on his face. "This will cost a lot won't it?"

"Son, you are not to worry about it, all right? Your mother will tell you about some of our luck, and the rest will come in time. Now…" Adam hugged his son and said, "I'll try and come back as often as I can. Hopefully every weekend or at least every other one." Susan stood to receive the farewell hug, Adam gave her, and he hurried to catch up to Ed.

Susan sat in the chair next to the bed, as Bill looked questioningly at her. Susan made herself comfortable, and handed the precious basket Jenny gave them to Bill.

With eyes full of wonder, Bill read the notes and looked at the books in the basket. He looked questioningly at his mother when he read the note about help for living expenses.

"Miss Jenny gave us ten-dollars, for my stay here and anything else we need," she said.

Bill was impressed, but his eyes were starting to cloud over and he held his mother's hand and fell asleep. Susan removed the basket, and put it under the bed. She remained there for the rest of the day taking short breaks for lunch and tea.

The nursing staff was wonderful, and they did their best to keep Bill comfortable. It was hard for the active young man to stay still, however, but it was necessary for the horrendous wound to heal properly. Gradually his bruises faded away, and he stopped most of the drugs that had gotten him pain free to this point. He felt like the drugs were making him sleep all the time and he didn't like it. However it was not long until he changed his mind because the pain was terrible. His mom played cards with him and checkers. Bill taught his mother to play chess, but his mother always lost. She just could never figure out the right moves to make.

Four weeks passed and the wound finally closed, without any sign of infection. The pink healthy skin would leave a permanent scar, but it was better than the alternate consequences. Once the wound was completely healed, Dr Swift had a heavy cast put on his leg. A thrilled Bill was allowed to get out of bed and move around with crutches. He was weak and wobbly from lying in bed for so long. The nurses worked with him to get his strength back. This took another two weeks.

That weekend, Dr. Swift told the happy family that Bill could go home but that he was to return in four weeks to have the cast removed. He was not to get it wet, and he was not to roam around in the dirt either. He laughed at Bill's dismayed expression. He was to use his crutches at all times, and not try and walk without them yet. At this stage the newly healed break could be forced out of alignment with very little provocation.

This was on March sixth, and the family hurried to comply, not wanting the doctor to change his mind. Dr Swift smiled at the families delight and handed them some medicine.

"Take this only when the pain gets too bad Bill. It is very strong, and will likely put you to sleep," he said.

Bill nodded and thanked the doctor. As they were getting ready to leave the hospital, the three of them went to the Accounting office, with trepidation. The accountant asked them to be seated while he looked up their bill. He got it out and perused the paper thoughtfully.

"Your bill comes to two hundred and forty five dollars and twenty-five cents," he said. The Storms looked at one another in despair. However your payment for two-hundred and fifty dollars leaves us owing you four dollars and seventy-five cents. The family sat there in shock as the elderly man took out the cash box and counted out the money. He gave it to Adam, who stared at it in amazement.

"But," he said in bewilderment, "I never gave you any money! Who?"

The accountant looked down at his records and said. "It's all right here, paid in full!" he said, pointing at the offending book. "Have a nice day." He bowed, effectively dismissing them.

The family left the hospital in a daze. They had expected to be paying off the hospital bill for the next couple of years. They never did find out who paid the bill, although they had their suspicions. No amount of inquiry would gain them the information.

Chapter 35

In the meantime, Water Valley struggled along in the miserable weather. It was a great relief when February introduced a change. The storms stopped, and the sun seemed warmer. Chinook winds blew, and the masses of snow started to melt. Children took coats off and played in the melting drifts. The veterans of the community advised Jenny that this was only a calm before the inevitable restart of winter. It was still very cold at night.

Coughs and fevers abounded within the ranks of student. Jenny tried to tell them to stay out of the wet snow. But they didn't listen too well. One morning Jenny was sitting with the older students, helping with a science project, when she heard a small cry. She whirled around and saw Jessie Burns fall to the floor. Jenny was horrified. She knew that the girl had a cold, but had no idea it had gone so far. She knelt beside the six year old, and noticed her flushed face. A hand to her brow told Jenny that this little one was burning up with fever. She berated herself on not noticing before this.

Looking up at the anxious faces of the other students, she spotted Jake.

"Jake, head to the ranch for the Doctor, and have him come to my house. Charles, please carefully pick up Jessie and follow me to the house," she said giving her orders quietly and quickly she organized the frightened children, to keep them busy in the next few minutes.

"Irene," Jenny said, "It is almost noon, you have the children eat their lunches and take them out to play. Watch them for me and make sure no one gets in too much trouble. I'll be back as soon as I can."

"Greg, did you ride your horse here today?" Jenny asked.

Greg nodded, and Jenny asked, "Please ride out to the Burns farm, and have Jessie's mother and father come in to my house.

"Jamie you can come with me if you like," Jenny said to Jessie's terrified brother. Jenny then hurried to her house followed closely by Charles carrying the little girl.

Charles laid her on Jenny's bed, and waited for further orders. Jenny had him fill the boiler with snow. In the meantime Jenny undressed Jessie and put a light nightgown on her. "Jamie, find me the towels in the pantry," she said, and the boy ran to do her bidding.

Jenny filled the towels with snow, and placed them around the burning hot girl. One she made into a compress and placed it on her head. Jessie's eyes were glazed, and her breathing was getting raspy. Jenny covered her lightly, and sat beside her to wait for the doctor. Jamie was sitting as close to the bed as he could. Tears were dripping down his face. Jenny felt like crying herself, but she tried to give the boy some encouragement.

When it neared one o'clock, Jenny made a decision. Putting her coat on she hurried back to the school. All the children playing outside had raced toward her. They were all talking at once.

Jenny called for order and when they fell silent she told them. "Jessie is quite sick." She looked at the worried children, and continued, "I want you all to be brave for the next little while. I am putting Irene and Charles in charge of you all. You older students that have projects to work on, do so. Irene, look after the younger ones, would you? Read them a story, and give them each a piece of paper, and have them draw a picture about it." Jenny then asked "Irene and Mary, could you make sure the schoolroom is neat and tidy, then lock up and bring me the key?" The children hurried to do as Miss Jenny asked.

Jenny then ran back to the house. "It shouldn't be long now until Doc arrives," she thought, but her patience was running thin. Her mind felt trapped in a circle of self-reproach for not seeing how sick Jessie was. It was not long before voices were heard outside her house. She ran to the door, and found Jake, with Doc and James, hurrying up her walk.

Doc went straight to the ailing child. While he was making his examination, James held a very worried Jenny close to him. Doc came out after a few minutes. He was very sober. Jenny caught her breath in fear. Doc looked at James and shrugged his shoulders.

"Her cold is developing into pneumonia," he said. "But I am hoping her fever goes down. It is terribly high. We need to cool her down more and the snow in towels is only doing part of the job. Jenny do you have a bath tub?"

"Yes Doc. Help me please, Jake," she said. "We'll bring it into the bedroom." Then she added "Take my pails, and fill the bathtub with cold well water. We will have to warm it a little, because the shock could hurt her." The boiler was then emptied of snow, and the first pails from the well were put on the stove to heat. Then Jake half filled the tub with the cold water. He dutifully kept at the task until it was done.

In the meantime, Jenny re-joined James and Doc. The later with lowered voice was telling James, "I am not a human doctor, no matter how much I try. There are some things that are cut and dried between humans and animals, this is not one of them. His shoulders drooped in defeat. "James, Jenny if this develops into something worse, I'm not sure I can handle it," he said bluntly. "Do you realize that hardly a day goes by when I'm not needed somewhere by the human population? Water Valley is growing, we need a proper doctor here. I am a vet remember, I am supposed to only treat animals. What if something comes up that I have no knowledge of?" he said pointing in the direction of the bedroom. "There is a very good example right in that room."

James was in shock. He had never heard Doc talk this way before. James looked at the upset doctor. "I am sending to Butte for a doctor," he said. Doc looked at him in relief.

"I hoped you would," he said gratefully. "You realize that Jessie could have complications with her high fever and pneumonia.

That is why we need to cool her down quickly." James left the house immediately.

Jenny swallowed the lump that had appeared in her throat. She looked at the boiler on the stove, it seemed to be taking forever to warm up. She heard a team and wagon pull up outside. The doc went to his bag of medicines to try and figure out the best for Jessie. Donald and Betty raced in the door breathlessly. Jamie, started wailing about Jessie dying, ran to his mother for comfort. At the startled frantic look on Betty's face, Jenny smiled faintly in reassurance. They hurried to have a look at Jessie and Doc went in with them. Jenny distracted Jamie with a stick of candy. Jenny could hear the voices softly talking in the bedroom. Jenny had put the kettle on for tea, and Donald and Doc came out to the living room, while Betty stayed with the little girl. They accepted the cups of tea. Donald was rather pale with apprehension. James came back in and told them David Olson was on his way to Butte to get the doctor there, but it would be the next day before he could possibly get here. In the meantime Doc vowed to do his best.

The boiler finally heated up enough, and they poured it into the bathtub. Donald help Doc lower Jessie into the Luke-warm water. As the tiny girl acclimatized to the water they added snow to cool it further. Gradually Jessie internal temperature started to come down. When she started to shiver they hurried her into a bed warmed with heated bricks. They covered her well.

When Donald and Betty mentioned bundling her up and taking her home, he said it might not be a good idea. He had been honest as he could with them in regards as to what was wrong, and felt the pressure of uncertainty. Don and Betty wanted their baby with them, and looked helplessly at the doctor.

"Betty, Don, don't worry you can all stay here. I'll stay with Janet and Ray in their spare room if they will let me. We will fix up a bed for the three of you." Jenny told them.

Betty threw a grateful look at Jenny, "That is very kind of you, Jenny, I am sorry for this inconvenience to you, but it seems we have little choice."

Don was torn with indecision, and said, "I can't stay here because I have stock to feed and cows to milk."

Just then Jake spoke up, he had sat near the fireplace, and they had forgotten he was there. "Mr Burns, sir, I'll be happy to look after your place for you, and will do all the chores. I'll have my friend Charles help me, if his parents let him. You're needed here and don't need the extra worry of your farm."

Donald and Betty studied the young man standing in front of them. They could hardly believe the change in this former delinquent. Don took a deep breath, coming to a decision. He nodded in agreement of the plan. "There's not much to be done, bein' winter" he said. "Just the stock to be fed and cows milked. If the weather turns they need to be brought into the barn."

"That will be no problem sir, don't worry about anything. If we have any trouble we'll contact you. I hope Jessie gets well soon, Mr. and Mrs. Burns. She's a really cute little kid. I hate to see her so sick. Well I had better go get Charles. Can I take your horse and buggy to the livery barn, or should I take it back to the farm for you?" Jake asked.

Donald said, "Please take 'Sally' home, and give her a good rubdown. You may use her to travel back and forth to school, as long as you're staying at our place. Help yourself to anything in the house to eat, but please keep the cabin neat for Betty," he grinned, as Betty gave him a dirty look.

"Don't have any worries on that account. We are neat fellows," Jake returned Donald's grin. "You take care now." He left the house and headed for the school to get Charles.

Doc said, "James, I would also like to stay here at Jenny's place too. I would not feel at ease leaving Jessie at this critical point."

"Of course Doc, please stay, I'm going to find extra bedding for you all. You'll sleep better with good bedding," James said and hurried out the door. He soon came back with extra blankets for the Burns' to use and some for Doc as well. The Burns moved the big chairs and laid the bed out there for the three of them. Doc put his in the bedroom.

Irene arrived with the school key. It was after three o'clock and the students had gone home. Jenny thanked her, and Irene left. Jenny volunteered to stay and cook supper for the distraught family, but Betty politely declined. She said she needed something to keep her hands busy or she would go crazy.

Jenny looked at her to see if she was sincere. Seeing that Betty was determined, Jenny went to the bedroom to pack a few things.

When she was ready to leave she said. "I am sure Jessie will be fine, try not to worry and get some sleep tonight. If you need me or anyone else send Jamie to the store for us. Help yourself to whatever you find in my larder for supper, and make yourself completely at home, alright?"

There were tears in Betty's eyes, as she hugged Jenny. "I'll try, and thank you so much for what you are doing for us."

Don spontaneously grabbed Jenny in a big bear hug as well. Jenny was rather startled, but saw how grateful he was, and smiled. Bidding them farewell, she left for Ray and Janet's house.

James walked with her, and noticed the set of her shoulders, and her silence.

"What's wrong, Jenny?" he asked softly.

Jenny did not answer at first; she just pressed her lips firmly together and shook her head at him.

Alarmed James stopped her, and turned her to face him. When she refused to look up at him, he gently raised her chin with his hand. When she finally did look him eye to eye, he could see tears hovering in the corner of her eyes, and the tension there.

"We are not going a step further until you tell me." He stated. "Come on, 'fess up!"
"Well, I feel so bad; I should have realized how sick Jessie was. I feel so guilty, and blame myself for the lack of attention." Jenny was wringing her hands in agony of self-loathing. "I am supposed to keep an eye on all my students. Jessie should not have fainted."

James just hugged her close, and said "You did your best Jenny, I believe you would have noticed, but I think she got worse very quickly. Not even Annie sitting beside her saw anything wrong until she fell, did she?"

"I don't know, I don't think so." Jenny said reflectively.

"Well then, there you are, you are not infallible," he said teasingly, trying to shake her out of this negative mood.

Jenny looked up at James still troubled but could not help but be buoyed up by his confidence in her. She smiled a little. James grinned back. "You have a way of making me feel better," she said. The two of them continued the short walk to the Store.

Bad news travelled like lightning and so of course Ray and Janet knew all about Jessie. Janet gave Jenny a hug, and led her into the back, and escorted her to the spare room. Jenny put her valise down, and went back to the store with Janet.

The four of them chatted about the Burns child, and Ray and Janet agreed with James about Jenny having done all she could. Jenny was still a little doubtful, but smiled and put on a brave front to them all.

Janet invited James to stay for supper, but he politely declined saying he had to get back to the ranch. He then gave Jenny a hug and bid farewell to all of them.

When he was gone Janet left Ray to look after the store and took Jenny into her spotless kitchen, and started to make supper. Jenny helped peel potatoes and carrots for the roast of beef Janet put in the oven. When everything was prepared, they went and sat in the living room chatting, and worked on various projects, that were invariably laying around the Brown's living room. Jenny actually started to relax. Her mind though still seethed with self-doubt and guilt.

The meal was lovely, and afterwards they played some games, and Jenny retired early. She was tired but could not sleep. Her frantic mind would not let her settle down one bit. It was late and only when she was totally exhausted did she drop off into a nightmare filled sleep.

The next morning, Jenny ate a quick breakfast and excused herself. Janet told her to never mind about the dishes, just to go.

Jenny hurried to her home, and found all of the inhabitant's wide-awake, including Jessie. She had a horrible deep cough, but her eyes were focusing and lucid for the moment. Jenny knelt down beside her, and took Jessie's hand.

"I am so sorry I didn't see how sick you were Jessie," she told the girl.

The tiny girl smiled at Jenny and said. "It wasn't your fault Miss Jenny, I hid the fact I wasn't feeling well from you, and Mom and Father too. I didn't want to miss the Arithmetic Test. I was trying to surprise my parents with a one hundred percent mark. I like school, and want to be a teacher like you," Jessie said.

Jenny hugged her and went back to join the others in the main room. Doc said that Jessie's clear state usually only lasted a few minutes. The fever was persistent, and her cough was getting worse. Jenny had come at just the right time. In fact, they could hear Jessie starting to thrash about again, and Doc and Betty hurried back into the bedroom. Jenny peeked through the curtains, and saw that the lucidity was gone. Her fever was growing again.

Jenny said goodbye to the worried family, and crossed over to the school. She kept busy marking papers and preparing for the day's classes. At nine o'clock she called all the students in. After the morning ritual was over, Jenny told them that Jessie was still very sick. Jamie had come to school too, and Charles and Jake were there as well. They obviously had enjoyed being the caretakers of the Burns farm. There were justifiably proud of themselves.

This was Friday the fifth of February, and Jenny decided to lift the spirits of the children, by having them do a play about Lincoln, for that man's birthday the following Friday. She then announced, "Boys and girls Valentines Day is coming soon. We are going to have a contest for the most original Valentines box. These boxes will have your name on them so your friends can put their cards for you in them. The box can be any size shape or theme. The only rules are that it has to have a lid, and it has to fit easily through the school room door!"

The students all laughed at this and began to plan their special boxes. They would have a small party for Valentines Day, and the children would make Valentines to give their friends and parents, for Valentine Sunday. This excited the children and took their minds off of Jessie.

Jake put his hand up and when Jenny acknowledged him, he said. "What about Jessie and Bill, they're not here to make themselves boxes. Maybe the boys could get together to make Bill one, and the girls could make Jessie one."

"What a wonderful, thoughtful idea, Jake! Jenny said. "Do I have some volunteers to do it?" Every hand in the room went up, and a very proud Jenny allowed them to make the two special boxes, that very afternoon.

It was just about ten o'clock when Jenny heard the sound of a buggy arriving down her lane. She looked out the window and saw a tall sober looking man in a black suit arrive at the house. David was with him, and Jenny knew it was the Butte doctor.

She kept the children at work until noon, and left them eating their lunches while she hurried over to the house.

Doctor Alfred Morton was busy at the stove brewing up some concoction to help Jenny. Doc Ed introduced Jenny to the busy man. He acknowledged her with a brief nod, and went back to work. Jenny found him just a bit rude, but forgave him and she watched him efficiently work. He had created red sticky looking syrup that seemed to sooth the cough. He had made up poultices and they covered the little girl. She was obviously breathing easier and was asleep.

When the doctor from Butte finally decided to say something, he was pointedly blunt. "She just about died thanks to your country mucking about. She'll be fine now that I'm here!"

Jenny saw the ranch doctor cringe. He was so depressed you could see the agony in his face. That made Jenny angry. James walked into the house just as Jenny laid into the City Physician. She told him exactly what she thought of his bedside manner.

"Of all the nerve, you rude arrogant man, Jessie was still here for you to treat because of this man here. I do not care how efficient or knowledgeable you are, that's no excuse in this community for your deplorable manners, you miserable cruel snobbish beast. We all did our best for her," Jenny ranted.

The whole room was dead silent. They all looked at Jenny like they had never seen her before. Jenny stood in front of them all like a protective hen.

The Butte doctor merely raised his eyebrows at her, and turned his back. He uttered not a word, but continued his work.

Jenny was seething. James came to her and gave her a hug. "It's ok," he whispered trying to calm her down, "Let him do his magic, and leave." Jenny glared at him. She turned her back on James, indignant.

Doc Ed was sitting in a corner. She crossed to him and knelt down beside him. "Ed," she said. "Please don't let that horrid man upset you. You did a wonderful job. Ed shook his head in denial.

Betty and Don both came over and added their words of comfort to their beloved Doctor Ed.

Doc Ed sighed and looked up at his loyal friends. "It's okay, I'll be just fine. I'll stick to animals, which is what I know best," he said.

James frowned. He glanced at the Butte doctor's back, in distaste. "Ed, you *are* a good doctor. I want you to know that. It is my intention to get a doctor here in this village as fast as I can. I just haven't found anyone appropriate yet." Throwing a glance at Doctor Morton, he continued. "We know what kind we don't want."

Ed looked up then at James. He smiled faintly, and looked at all of them. "Thank-you for your support," he said. "But I do know my limitations."

He stood up then, and said "You're in good hands, and I'll go back to the ranch now." Stiff with pride the old man took his bag, and left. James was very troubled.

"I just have to find a doctor now," he said. "This jack-ass just tore one of the best men I know down to a nubbin. It could balk him at a critical moment if he lacks confidence. I'll be back later," James said then he hurried after Ed.

At one o'clock Jenny hurried back to the school. She told the class that the Butte Doctor said Jessie would be just fine. The students all broke out in a spontaneous cheer. Everyone loved Jessie a lot. Jenny gave them all a paper, and had them draw a get-well card for her. Then students happily went to work on the cards and on Bill and Jessie's Valentine Boxes.

After school was finished, Jenny took all their cards over to the house. The family was chatting quietly at the kitchen table. Dr. Morton was in the bedroom with Jessie.

The worried look on Betty's face was gone. She looked up at Jenny, with a vague smile. "Jessie is going to be all right. The doctor will give us all the medicines we need, instructions on their use, and he will be leaving for Butte in the morning."

Jenny glanced toward the bedroom, and smiled back at Betty. "I think you should still stay here for a while longer, until Jessie is stronger."

Don thanked Jenny again, and Betty just hugged her. With a smile Jenny said she would leave them alone. She rejoined Janet and Ray, and spent a much nicer evening with less worry.

Five more days passed before Jessie was well enough to transfer back to her own home. Jenny told them that she would send readers home for Jessie to look at. She hoped Jessie could come back to school soon.

The weather was still mild, and the trees were starting to bud. The older settlers were biting their lips in apprehension. When cold weather hit again the trees could die in some cases, as the buds would freeze off.

On Tuesday, Jenny had all the children paint pictures to send to Bill, who was still in the hospital. When they were finished she gathered them up and went for a ride on Soot to the Storm's farm. The sun was setting and Adam had just come home from work. Jenny asked for a progress report on Bill and was delighted that he was doing fairly well. She handed the packet of papers to Adam, and that worthy promised to deliver them the next weekend when he rode to Butte. Jenny thanked him and wished the family well, and left for home. It was full dark by the time she crossed the bridge and up the street.

David had been watching for her, and helped her rub Soot down.

On Wednesday, Jake came to Jenny. It was obvious he had something on his mind. She looked up at him in surprise, because he seemed so nervous about something. She smiled at him encouragingly. Jake was shuffling his feet from one to the other, and he ran his finger around his collar, a sure sign of agitation in him. Jenny waited for him to speak his mind very patiently.

Finally he burst out, "Please, Miss Jenny could I have a piece of your white paper, and could I borrow your special box of paints? I won't use them during school, but could I stay after everyone has gone?"

Jenny looked at Jake's flushed face, and was hoping Jake would tell her what he wanted them for. "Of course you may," she said, restraining her curiosity about the project. She hoped she would eventually find out.

Friday February twelfth came, and the promised party, play and Valentine Box contest. The afternoon had the children laughing and having a wonderful time. Louise had sent over some heart shaped sugar cookies. There were eaten to the last crumb.

The time for the judging of the Boxes had everyone on the edge of their seats. There were some big ones and small ones, painted or covered with scraps of cloth. Jenny, who was judging, examined each one with care.

Out of all of them there was one that stood out. Dick Redmond, a twelve year old from the ranch had been criticized and laughed at constantly for his entry. Of all of the entries, his was the most commented on and made everyone laugh.

Dick was a red haired, freckle-faced boy; who's hand at carpentry was already shining out with his entry. He had a constant sense of humour, and liked nothing better than to make people laugh. For his Valentine box he had carefully taken apart an apple crate, and using saw and hammer made a perfect outhouse, right down to the miniature seats inside. The only difference from a real one other than the size was that the usual moon cut in the door, was in this case a heart. Mail was put in through the door. The roof was covered in shingles, cut out of birch bark. It was exquisitely done.

Jenny pronounced Dick's entry the winner, and he received a small bag of candy that he promptly shared with everyone. They all opened their boxes and enjoyed the mounds of handmade cards.

Lucy was carefully going through all of hers, like she was searching for one in particular. Jenny saw disappointment cross her features, but the teen said nothing to anyone. Jenny kept an eye on her in concern. The rest of the excited children exchanged cookies, and treats, wishing everyone a Happy Valentines Day. Since Jenny was keeping a special eye on Lucy, she was probably the only one that saw Jake, with a very red face hand his precious paper to Lucy.

He had worked very hard, and painted a beautiful mountain scene, with a big red heart in one corner. Lucy blushed shyly, taking the paper from Jake. Jenny couldn't resist taking a closer look at the card. It was beautiful. Jake obviously had a hidden talent. The watercolor had captured the mountain just beautifully.

She dismissed class at the usual time and asked Dick to stay behind for a moment. When he came to the desk, Jenny asked, "Dick, your little wooden outhouse is just beautiful, and I'm sure you want to keep it, but I wonder, can you make me one like it? I'll pay you well, for it. I have an idea to put it in my tree at home, and maybe a bird will want to nest in it this spring."

Dick was wide-eyed in astonishment. "Why Miss Jenny I would love to make you one, but you can have this one if you want it. I would likely just throw it away anyway!"

"You did a wonderful job, have you ever thought of helping Pops with some of his woodworking projects?" Jenny asked. "I believe you have a real talent for carpentry."

Dick blushed, and said. "Awww Miss Jenny, I just do it for fun. I love working with wood though. I likely would just get in Pops' way."

Jenny said nothing more but vowed to talk to Pops about apprenticing the boy. She went outside just on time to see Jake carrying Lucy's books, as the two of them walked home. Smiling in delight, she locked the school door and turned looking at the sky. The sunshine had disappeared. Clouds were gathering and they looked ominous.

The temperature was also dropping, and she hurried home. She was making her supper when the wind rattled her shutters. In anticipation of the upcoming storm, Jenny had brought in lots of wood, so she was prepared. By six o'clock snow was falling steadily. Jenny started the fireplace and then curled up in front of it. Things were going well, and Jenny was quite content.

Chapter 36

At the beginning of March the snow was deep and the temperature cold. The children had had enough of the snow. They were tired of learning. They were restless and moody. Jenny had a hard time keeping their minds on work. One Thursday she announced a skating party for the following afternoon. The children's eyes sparked with delight. They would sled, skate and play a game of team hockey. Snow fell lightly that night and the next morning the older boys were out clearing a patch of ice for the party. The children worked with a will to finish the day's lessons. When lunchtime came they hurried to eat their lunch. Jenny went with them to the river. They built ice slides down the banks of the river so the kids could sit and slide onto the ice. Between sledding, skating and sliding, the children were having a ball.

The usual bonfire was kept going, with all the children taking turns feeding it. Jenny brought a huge black caldron down and placed it in the middle of the fire. With excitement the children watched her put some kernels of corn into the pot. Soon the crackle and pop of bursting corn filled the air. When it was done,

Jenny poured melted butter over the steaming kernels. Everyone got a few handfuls. Ray and Janet brought hot chocolate and cups to the ecstatic students. The children enjoyed their afternoon and went home with a fresh outlook. Jenny knew they would come to school ready to learn again.

David came to the school one Friday. With hat in hand he asked, "Miss Jenny? May I speak to your students?"

Jenny smiled at him and invited him up front.

"Hi," he said smiling at the school children. "I have come to ask all the older boys to work for me tomorrow. Spring is on its way and I need ice cut and hauled to the ice house. I would request all to ask your fathers to help if they would. One day should be all it takes to fill the shed to the brim."

Enthusiastic boys agreed to the day of work. Jenny wanted to observe this yearly ritual and decided to watch the proceedings.

The next day was cold but sunny. Groups of energetic boys and men gathered in front of the livery barn. Jenny saddled Soot and followed the procession down to the river. She was informed that the best place to cut the ice was where the river widened just south of the island. This was about a mile downstream. The horses and sled made their way down the embankment and onto the river. It was faster going on the ice itself. Jenny's heart was in her mouth a couple of times when Soot slipped on the ice.

The older men used oddly shaped saws with blades on the end to cut the ice. They had long handles so they didn't have to bend over to far while sawing. They had a horse harnessed to a plough like instrument. It only had one blade and it was vertical. To make the first vertical cuts the horse went back and forth drawing the sharp blade against the ice. Every trip it went deeper and deeper. Some of the men had long pikes with curved end on it. When the vertical saw cut through to the running water. The horse would make a second cut parallel to the first. Then the men with the hand saws took over. The horse was too heavy to make any of the cross cuts. Once that had been done the pikes were used to pull the ice block out. The first one was the hardest. After that it was easier because they had room to manoeuvre the stubborn blocks of ice. This year the blocks were around eight inches deep. Some years if it were colder the ice could reach twenty or thirty inches deep. The thaw earlier had made the ice thinner. It was fascinating to watch the whole process. The blocks were loaded onto one of the buckboards and hauled to the ice house near the lumber mill. Sawdust was spread over the mound of blocks to keep them frozen all summer. It was strange to see the huge rectangular hole left in the river when the men were done. Black rushing water made a picturesque backdrop to the white area around it. It was a wonder someone didn't fall into it.

March progressed. Gradually the sun got warmer and the blizzards stopped. The snow melted little by little. Children were cautioned by Jenny not to go out on the river any more. Although the ice looked solid, it was getting soft.

Everyone knew and understood the danger, but as so often happens, circumstances made little ones forget. Henry Potts was one of these children. Henry had missed the wagon, taking the Ranch children to school.

When Henry didn't show up Morgan Lansdowne the school driver thought he might be sick and didn't worry too much about him. He took the rest of the children and hurried to school. Henry's mother and father had left home early to get some needed work done. They had awakened Henry before they left, but the precocious child had fallen asleep again.

It was close to eight o'clock when Henry came awake with a start. He was late. He hurried into his clothes and grabbing a piece of bread hurried for the wagon. The wagon was just disappearing over the hill. His heart froze and he panicked. He had a History test today and he had hoped to do well on it. He started out running after the wagon. If he ran hard he might catch up, if not it should still only take him an hour to reach the school. Henry got a stitch in his side. He was soon puffing and sweating in his heavy coat, but in determination kept going.

In due time he arrived close to town. He saw the wagon coming back toward him and he hid in the brush. He didn't want Morgan to see him. Henry then hurried even faster, his breath coming in gasps. As he neared the bridge he heard the faint sound of the school bell. He had to go faster.

He saw one of the old ice slides and got an idea. He never thought twice but slid down the bank and started across the river. He was half way when Miss Jenny's warning came back to him.

He stopped and froze. He moved forward slowly. The ice cracked. Henry started to run but only got three steps when the ice gave way. He shrieked in terror as he fell through the ice. His heavy winter clothes were buoyant with air. This was the only thing that prevented him from sliding under the ice with the current. He grabbed for the edge of the ice, trying to climb out.

Mayor had spotted Henry a few minutes before. His curiosity was peaked when Henry hid out in the bush. He started to follow Henry. When the boy fell through the ice Mayor knew Henry was in trouble. His frantic barking alerted the town's folk. They came when they heard his barking alarm. They headed for the river at a run. Mayor dug his claws into the ice and grabbed Henry's collar. The stubborn dog would not let go. Henrys clothes started to soak through, weighing him down. The frigid water was making it hard for Henry to keep moving. He was cold and tired. Mayor hung on and would not let him go. His paws were braced, trying desperately not get pulled into the water himself. Slowly, ever so slowly, Mayor was being pulled forward toward the open water, as Harry weight became heavier and heavier. Still the determined dog did not let the terrified boy go.

In the meantime men from the other side of the river at the sawmill had grabbed boards and were slowly making their way to the drowning boy. Men from town made a human chain by lying on the ice to spread their weight and were working their way to Henry. Both rescue parties made it there at the same time. Boards were put across the broken ice and the two nearest men grabbed Henry and hauled him onto the boards. The men from town pulled him toward shore never once doing anything but lie flat and spreading their weight so the ice would not give.

Once on shore the half drowned boy was pounded back to awareness. He was covered with a blanket and hurried to the nearest home. Karen had Susie's bed all ready. They stripped Henry and got him under the blankets. He could not stop shivering. Sven gave poor Henry a swig of whiskey, which to him was to the world's best cure for most ailments. Henry choked, and his eyes watered. The flaming liquid settled in his tummy like molten lava. Gradually the warmth spread, and the boy stopped shaking. Miss Jenny came in, and Henry burst into tears. He was so ashamed of himself. Jenny hugged him and told him it was going to be all right.

It turned out that Henry never even caught a cold from his dunking. Miss Jenny allowed him to take his test later that week. He was totally embarrassed and took some kidding from his classmates, but otherwise, he knew he had gotten off easily.

To his parents though, God had performed a miracle, and Mayor received a blue leather collar, with a silver tag, stating the family's thanks. He also received a bone every week for the next year.

Chapter 37

Jenny never ventured far from the boardwalks. The mud was deep, and the crust of the snow was gone. Jenny heard that Bill was home now and she wanted to go visit him. She was busy and never found the time to go out to the Storm farm.

Sunday March twenty-first was a lovely day. Jenny attended the church service and to her delight the Storm's arrived. Bill came in using his crutches with extreme care. Everyone was thrilled to see him and started trying to talk to him all at once.

The Reverend raised his arms. "Good morning everyone!" He waited for the conversation to quiet down. "There will be a special lunch meeting after the service today. All are invited to attend."

Jenny was puzzled. She could not figure out why she hadn't heard about it. James was sitting beside her and noticed her bewilderment. He just smiled and listened to the sermon.

Jenny sighed and fidgeted a little in curiosity. When the church service was over, the pews were pushed aside and tables set up. It seemed everyone had given something toward the luncheon.

Jenny was embarrassed and whispered to James, "Why did no one tell me of this luncheon? I would've brought something. Maybe I should hurry home and bring some cheese, or fruit." Jenny started toward the door.

James stopped her and said. "Wait Jenny, there's plenty of food. Please don't worry about it. See, just look at those loaded down tables."

Jenny was rather annoyed at James. He just didn't understand her embarrassment. Jenny was fairly agitated until the reason for the meeting was announced.

Nellie, the Reverend's wife came through the door with a gigantic cake. She started singing "Happy Birthday," and everyone joined in. Jenny was in total shock. She had no idea anyone even knew of her birthday. If fact she had forgotten it herself. She blushed very prettily and thanked everyone.

After lunch the school children put on a play honouring Jenny. It was hilarious and all the people, Jenny included, laughed until tears were running down their cheeks. Several of the older students read passages from various books, or recited poetry for the audience's enjoyment.

It was a wonderful afternoon and Jenny was overwhelmed with the love these people were showing her. She belonged here.

That evening as James sat beside her on the veranda, he handed her a small parcel. When she opened it, she found a gorgeous rope of pearls with a silver clasp. They were lustrous and had a faint pinkish tinge. She gasped with pleasure. He gently placed them around her throat. Jenny looked up into James's sparking eyes. He bent his head and gave her a quick kiss on the cheek. "Happy Birthday, Jenny," he whispered.

Jenny allowed the kiss but blushed. "How did you know it was my birthday, James? I thought I would die of mortification, when all the food came out and I didn't have anything to give."

James laughed, "It was meant to be a surprise. All of us were so scared you would get wind of it, that we were the nervous ones. As to how I found out your birth date, well it was on the School Registration Papers. I had to sign them in order for you to get paid."

She smiled and gave him a hug of thanks. Then more soberly he stated, "Jenny, I am going to be gone for a couple of weeks. I have to go to San Francisco on business."

Jenny was a bit sad, but she accepted his departure. James kissed her hand in farewell and left for home. He was well pleased with his surprise party.

Chapter 38

By late March a great majority of the snow was gone in the valley. Rocky slopes were beginning to show through the snow on the mountaintops. The shady places under trees and northern exposures of the buildings still had snow. It was not long after, however even that was gone. The streets dried up. Spring was here; the trees developed their leaves.

Jenny surprised her students with a bat and ball. She told them that there were enough students to form two teams. Jenny had sewn up some bags, stuffed with straw to use as bases. A broken board was the pitchers mound and another formed the home base. The children were thrilled and Jenny divided the class into two teams. After school they all hurried to the area down by the river. It was the flattest place in town. They set up the bases and started on their first game. It was hilarious, because none of them had played before. They were fine at throwing the ball, but the batting took some time to learn. They decided to have a game on Wednesday's after school and on Saturday afternoons. It was very popular, and soon everyone was watching them play. Bill, unable to play, because of his huge heavy cast, sat behind home plate and became the umpire. Ray volunteered to be first base umpire and Jenny was the coach.

Everyone wanted in on the games and soon teams of adults were formed. They had a wonderful time. Jenny's class practiced all the time. They earned a reputation for being hard to beat. Everyone got together and built a ball diamond south of the lumber mill. It had a large flat area. It was the perfect size for it. Cyrus had some unused poles, so they set up a backstop. Chicken wire was stretched out from pole to pole. As time passed they even built some seats for the audience, behind the protective screen.

The warm weather was causing the snow high in the mountains to melt quickly. The ice in the river broke up with a crash one afternoon in early April. Jenny hurried out of the school to see what caused the noise. Ray was outside his store viewing the river.

"The river just broke up Jenny," he said. "I have a feeling there will be flooding. The snow was deeper this year than usual. We're lucky to be on a hill. The building I worry about however is the boarding house. It's on the lowest level."

Jenny said, "It looks to be fairly high on the bank. Surely it will be safe!"

Doubt was creeping into her voice, because now that the ice was gone the fast rushing river was rising.

James had been wise and had them build above the high water mark. This year however it was different. The river passed the high water. Everyone watched the water creep up toward the building's floor. The flood stopped just six inches from the foot of the building. The citizens of Water Valley breathed a sigh of relief. That is, until the bridge was hit by some floating trees. They swept down from the high mountains and crashed into the central piling. The pillar gave way. The town's people watched it crash and swirl its way down the gorge.

The children in her class who lived across the river had no way to get home. That included the children from the ranch. There were fifteen of them that needed a temporary home. Hastily dismissing class, the ladies of the town met at the church to decide what to do. Some thought it would be better if the girls stayed together in the school and the boys in the church. Some figured it would be easier to divide them up between all of them. It was voted to keep the kids together, with the girls bedding down in the school and the boys finding shelter in the church. Food would be cooked by the ladies and brought to the school or church.

The store was raided to get blankets and other necessities for the children.

Some of the younger ones were terribly upset that they couldn't get home, but the older ones took them in hand and comforted them. Once the kids got used to the situation, it became a true camp. They played games and had an all round good time. The ladies made sure they had plenty to eat, so the few days that passed before the bridge could be rebuilt was a great treat for them, a regular holiday. Of course on weekdays they still had classes. Bill was happy to have rejoined the lessons for he had genuinely missed them when he was working and injured. The only bad thing for Bill was that the coming weekend he had been due to have his cast removed. This obviously would have to be postponed a week or so until Dr. Ed could get across the river.

The town had unexpected visitors one day. The river was still high, and Greg came rushing onto the school grounds before classes early one morning to say there were bears walking down Main Street. The children screamed in excitement and Jenny could not stop them from racing over to the store. Jenny hurried after them. They all stood along the boardwalk watching the mother bear and her two cubs being confronted by Mayor. He was trying to protect his town by barking up a storm. The bear was roaring in return.

Joe came out with a shotgun and fired it above the bears back. Mama bear retreated in confusion. The two cubs started to wail in fear. The mother bear got angry. It charged the dog. Mayor retreated, coming right back barking harder than ever.

Janet came out with pots and pans handing them to everyone. "Bang these she said, "Maybe we can scare her back to the bush."

Everyone shouted or banged the pans. Joe fired another shot over the Mother bear's head. It started her toward the creek. The cute cubs followed her faithfully. She crossed the swollen creek with no problem, the cubs swimming after her. The dog followed still barking. The bear soon disappeared into the heavy brush. Mayor pranced back up toward the people with his tongue lolling in pride for vanquishing the foe. The children hugged him and told him how brave he was. Mayor accepted their hugs and rolled over so they could scratch his belly.

It was doubtful the mother bear would return, so Jenny gathered her students up and ordered them back to the school.

The weekend was spent helping the town where they could. It seemed like forever before the Grange River receded. Once it did, James, his cowhands, and the town's men worked together to rebuild the bridge. It was a relief to everyone when it was finished. There was a joyous reunion between the families of the stranded students.

Jenny was just as anxious to see James and the two of them met enthusiastically. He had been the first one across the new bridge. He clasped her hands in excitement. He had wonderful news. He called for everyone's attention.

"There is a young man, a newly graduated doctor, coming to Water Valley. He will be here in just a few days," James said.

Everyone cheered. Jenny was so happy for James. She knew how much the lack of a proper doctor had worried him.

"We need to get straight to work on the clinic and residence." He stated. "I'll come with my men tomorrow morning to start the project. I would appreciate any extra help the rest of you can give."

Jenny finally knew why James had gone to San Francisco. The city had a teaching hospital and he had been hoping to find a young doctor willing to start a practice in Water Valley. Ecstatic with his success James arrived back in town just in time to help rebuild the bridge.

Chapter 39

On Saturday April tenth, Dr. Reuben Chalmers arrived in front of the general store. He drove a buggy, with a pretty chestnut mare. Ray greeted him with enthusiasm. There were several families about, including the busy workers who were finishing up the boarding house. Janet ran to get Jenny and James. They had been planning on a picnic together but hadn't left yet. They both hurried to meet the new doctor.

James beaming with pride said to the group gathered in front of the store. "This is Dr. Reuben Chalmers."

"Pleased to meet you all, I would like you to call me Ben or if you must, Dr. Ben," the tall black haired man said with a grin. He then swept off his black top hat and bowed. He wore a black suit and there were two trunks on the back of his buggy.

James led him down to the newly completed doctor's office. James proudly showed him around his new place. Reuben was thrilled. He carefully looked over his office, examination and surgery room.

"Your surgery has no windows and has been sanded and varnished to a smooth finish. It'll be easy to keep sterile, I believe," James said.

A larger room in the back had two beds in it for patients. They went out the back door and across the yard to the cabin in the back. It was almost identical to Jenny's home, just done in the reverse style. A couple of men brought Reuben's trunks to the small house. Reuben shook James' hand.

"I love my new place, James. Thank you." Ben said.

"There will be a get-to-know you picnic after church tomorrow," James said. "We are so happy to have you come here."

One of Dr. Ben's first patients came in barely before he was settled. It was Bill, he wanted to get the burdensome cast removed.

Dr. Chalmers was very happy to do that honour. Ben had Bill soak his leg in a tub of water. The plaster came away in bits and pieces. With scissors he cut the protecting cloth away from Bills white leg. Bill coughed at the smell that came along with the removed cast. This of course was due to the lack of air able to get at the leg.

Ben examined the leg thoroughly and felt it all over. There was no pain and Ben was finally satisfied that the leg had healed well. As well as being white from being out of the sun, the leg was smaller from the lack of muscle tone.

"Bill, I still want you to use your crutches while you're out and about, however when you're sitting down I want you to exercise this leg by bending it and generally getting it back into condition. Do this for the next few days and then come back, say, Wednesday and I'll see if you can proceed to walk on it. I'll also write a letter to Dr. Swift in Butte and tell him of your progress," Dr Reuben said.

Dr. Reuben had a wonderful personality and Jenny liked him immensely. For lack of patients, Reuben helped with the various activities that were being done to repair winter's damage.

Palm Sunday was the day of the picnic to welcome Dr. Ben with their accustomed friendliness. Everyone was light hearted and gay, looking forward to the usual springtime activities. The ploughing and planting season was almost upon them but the fields were still a bit wet.

Chapter 40

Most men at the ranch were busy. It was calving time. Everywhere tiny adorable additions were being brought into the world. Men would carry rifles with them, because this time of year was bad for wolves, coyotes and even some of the big cats, like Lynx, Bobcats and the odd Cougar. The spring roundup was in full swing. They had to bring the bovine mothers and their babies closer to the ranch for safety.

Farmers and settlers were glad of something to keep them busy and give them extra income. Logging was finished for the season and fieldwork yet to come. They helped complete the boarding house. Since the flood had not damaged the foundation, the progress moved along steadily.

With everyone working together, it was finished in no time. Hilda Perkins, the new proprietor of the boarding house arrived on the Monday in the late afternoon, with a house full of furniture piled high in no less than eight wagons. It was a regular caravan that drove across the bridge to stop in front of the new building. She got out and looked around. People from all over town came to welcome her.

"Hi y'all, now this here is real perty," she said. She cocked her head at all the crowd and grinned. "Now the faster I get settled, the faster I can start serving you starving bachelors your meals."

A clapping, roar of approval swept over the observers. Everyone, the wagon drivers included pitched in to get Hilda settled as quickly as possible. Hilda seemed to know precisely where she wanted everything and stood on the porch and gave orders of where each box or item was to be placed.

The ladies including Hilda put their heads together and arranged for a fast barbeque to be set up for all the workers, Hilda included.

The weary movers welcomed the sound of "Supper's ready". They trudged up the hill, and grabbed a plate and served themselves. They then dropped on the nearest piece of grass and inhaled their supper.

Hilda was not one to stand on ceremony, but came around to everyone introducing herself and getting to know each person. Jenny's first impression was that Hilda would very rarely forget a face or name.

It only took Hilda two days to straighten everything out where she wanted it, and then she was then open for business. The café opened to lip smacking reviews of the cooking. Joe couldn't get enough of the meals. David, Joe, Ben, Pops, Cyrus and the other men that worked at the mill all became Hilda's regular clientele.

James took Jenny there for Saturday supper. Hilda made a special table for two, for them out on the veranda. It gave them some privacy and Hilda was tickled about the romance of the situation. Other couples used it too when Jenny and James were not around.

James realized just how much his fast growing community needed modern conveniences. He started making plans for the area on the other side of the bridge across from the sawmill. Expansion with streets, houses and a few more shops would be wonderful.

The single men had come to him earlier in the year with the request for a saloon. James had sighed at the inevitable. He sent out word in Butte and Big Rock that new businesses were welcome but that they had to apply in person to himself. He vowed that unsavoury business people or practices would not spoil all the work he had put in making this village a pleasure to live in. He might be a trifle naive and idealistic, but he was sure going to try his best for Water Valley. He could certainly designate where these businesses were to settle. After all, he owned the land for miles in either direction, except for what he had sold to the individual settlers.

Chapter 41

April started out a miserable, wet month. It rained constantly. The grass and trees were lovely in their green finery. But the flowers drooped in despair as water dripped off their petals and leaves. The boardwalk was indeed a blessing, as the mud in the streets grew deep. The mill workers brought some boards, which were useless for sale, because of some flaw, to make a path across the streets. It certainly did make a difference, as the Boardwalks only covered the front of buildings not the street crossings. David forged some sharp iron bars from old horseshoes, and imbedded them with the sharp edges upward in front of every business. Jenny was puzzled as to what they were for until she saw Pops, make a shortcut to Joe Walter's place without bothering to go to the corner where the boards were laid down. Jenny watched him slop through the mud. Pop then scraped his boots very carefully on the metal bars. Jenny thought it was an ingenious idea.

Jenny dropped in every day to Joe Walters' leather shop. He was making special red leather harnesses for a team of horses. The metal work was made from silver plated steel. They were beautiful.

The second week of April came, and the weather turned gorgeous, sunshine lit up the valley, and the flowers were out in all their splendour. Buffalo beans and crocuses covered the pastures. Indian Paintbrushes grew in the mountainous hillsides.

The leaves of all the trees had the light green of spring. They would turn darker as the summer came on. The earlier rain had assured the growth of vegetation. The farmers had finished their planting, and were taking in hay.

The gorgeous weather brought a surprise to all of Water Valley. The boarding house was doing good business especially in the café. Her rooms had not been rented out yet, when a well-dressed stranger arrived at her front door.

He doffed his top hat, and asked, "Ma'am, my name is Howard Whipley, how many rooms do you have available for tomorrow night?"

"My goodness," Hilda said in surprise. "I do not have any boarders at the moment. I have eight rooms prepared, but what on earth do you want so many rooms for?" She asked curiously.

"I am preparing the way, for Sir Russell Aimsley. He is due here tomorrow evening with his entourage." He frowned at Hilda's rather blank look.

"You know! The candidate for the leadership of the Republican Party and the next Gov'ner of this here State!" he stated impatiently.

It was suppertime when the man had arrived and Hilda's regular customers from the village were seated in the dining room watching this interchange with great interest. Noticing the audience, the man felt he could impress these locals with the superiority of his candidate.

"He is on a campaign tour, and sure to obtain the leadership of the Republican Party. He will become the next Governor of this beautiful state. He is sure to win over the present governor, John E Rickards. He is on an extensive journey visiting quaint villages like yours. Tomorrow he will leave Butte and will need to overnight here in your fine establishment before he heads for Big Rock." He spoke, waving his hands about rather pompously and condescendingly.

"Oh!" Hilda said faintly. "How many people are coming?"

"We'll need all of your rooms! How many can accommodate at least two people?" He asked.

"All of them have a double bed," she said proudly.

"Good!" The man said. "I want to take a look at them and choose which one is suitable for Sir Aimsley. Of course you will need to provide meals for everyone. I believe there is a total of twenty dignitaries and their aides."

Hilda escorted the man up the stairs to her pristine bedrooms. She frowned in displeasure, as the annoying man sniffed disparagingly at the size of the bedrooms. He chose the biggest one at the front of the house for Sir Aimsley.

"If this man is anything like that there candidate, I sure hope he don't get elected," she thought silently.

The man seemed horrified that his leader would have to use the outhouse like all the other tenants.

"I insist we have an indoor privy set up! Sir Aimsley can't use the outhouse. Please make those arrangements immediately!" Howard said. "There are twelve dignitaries plus myself. We will use these rooms. Of course there are the drivers, aides and other menial staff. They will have to find their own accommodations in the barn or where ever, I refuse to worry about them." He said officiously. He took one of the rooms himself for the night. The next day he was out covering the town with posters and talking to the people. He handed out flags, encouraging people to come out to greet the carriages when Sir Aimsley arrived. He strung banners between trees and generally made a nuisance of himself. He brazenly joined Joe Walters, David Olson and Ray Brown as they stood chatting beside the general store.

Joe had been mentioning some escapade of Mayor when Howard joined them.

"Mayor! You have a mayor in this community! Why didn't you say so! He must be present to greet the candidate!"

Ray and David fell silent. Joe turned to face Howard, annoyed at the intrusion. Then he grinned. "Why yes, Mr. Whipley, we do have a Mayor in town. I am sure he would be delighted to greet and inspect our future governor." He spoke facetiously.

Howard then trotted off happily content that he had done well to ferret out the leader of this community.

In the meantime the Mayor in question was following the impulsive man everywhere. He was highly suspicious of him. Howard in turn was infuriated at the dog's constant attention. There was little he could do about it as none of the Water Valley residents came to claim the canine.

Howard burst into the school, handed every child a flag, asking them to come see the next governor and bring their Fathers. Jenny tolerated him for only so long and then politely asked him to leave. It was probably a good thing he did leave because the children had been holding in their laughter, at the snobbish gentleman. Since the opportunity had presented itself, Jenny taught the children about the government and the elections that would come up in the fall. The older boys were interested, but the girls were questioning why the boys and men should be the only ones to vote.

"I am every bit as smart as Bill, or Charles, why should they get to vote when they are of age, and I won't!" Irene asked in irritation.

This was one of Jenny's sore points too, but she tried hard to explain the injustice to the girls. The boys realizing their superiority in this particular situation, all vowed to go to the meeting the candidate would likely have sometime during his visit.

The children were playing in the Schoolyard after the classes were dismissed. They were all primed and ready, when the church bell rang announcing the arrival of the celebrities. Jenny hurried to join the flag waving children, who were rushing toward Main Street. All the townsfolk were curious and came out to see the parade coming across the bridge. It was quite a caravan coming up the street. The three main carriages came first with one gentleman waving his top hat in greeting. The horses were bedecked with ribbons and flags. Banners and bunting covered the carriage. A huge poster on the back of each one read, 'Vote for me', and a picture of Russell Aimsley his finger pointed outward.

The first three carriages were followed by heavily loaded baggage wagons.

Several people were in these wagons and were obviously the harried staff. The carriage containing the candidate pulled to a stop in front of the church.

A couple of footman raced to the side of the carriage with a wooden set of steps. Russell Aimsley carefully stepped on the ladder and descended to the sidewalk. He was a huge man and had a smiled plastered on his rotund face. His moustache was impossibly curled; his iron-grey hair was slicked down.

Mayor, who rarely left Jenny's side started to growl, his hackles were raised in annoyance. The low growl never totally subsided until the candidate disappeared into the buildings. It just as quickly returned when the Russell put in an appearance. Mayor obviously did not like and did not trust the lordly candidate. Jenny knew that the man would not be able to make a move without Mayor knowing it.

"Greetings, Ladies and Gentlemen, boys and girls." He began. "I do hope I can count on your votes, Men." He frowned faintly, as the crowd remained quiet listening politely. He started to orate. "I will make the best leader of the Republican Party. I will make a better governor for this state than my opponent. He has proved over the last four years that he is unworthy to lead this great country into the new century. Progress, gentlemen, progress, that's what we need in the coming future. More roads, more railroads and more modern conveniences that's what we need; Ladies encourage your men to vote for me and I promise you that you will not be sorry." He said.

Mayor's low growl became an audible rumble. Jenny shushed him. Mayor lowered his voice but the growl was still there. Faint clapping followed Russell's speech and he bowed. He sailed forward to shake the hands of all men old enough to vote in the crowd.

He said, "I will hold a forum in the church this evening if the Reverend will allow us to use it."

The Reverend nodded his head in agreement and a satisfied Russell Aimsley sauntered down the boardwalk nodding and smiling to everyone. He was very pleased with himself, as he made his way to the boarding house for supper.

Howard Whipley had been generous in paying Hilda and she had hired Louise and Lucy Jones, Grace Tyson and Greg Wilson, a boy from the ranch to help deal with feeding not only the dignitaries themselves, but their help as well.

The Parties helpers had already unloaded the luggage and were busy preparing the rooms. The back enclosed veranda had ten temporary cots set up. It was not very cold at night now so many of the staff could be accommodated there for the evening.

The supper was ready as they waited for the dignitaries to arrive. Greg was antsy. He wiggled and squirmed while he waited to serve the dinner. All of them were nervous and even Louise was trembling a little with so many important people coming so Greg's twitching largely remained unnoticed. Greg was an avid bug collector and he had caught a particularly large specimen of a Grasshopper in the back yard of the boarding house. He had put him safely in his pocket. However it had exited the pocket by a hole in the back of it. It was crawling around inside his shirt next to Greg's skin. Its legs tickled Greg. However it was too late to find a new home for the bug as the guests arrived.

Sir Aimsley followed by the other dignitaries stomped into the house and sat down at the various tables for the meal. Once seated, the plates of food were taken in one at a time and placed in front of the visitors. Hilda had fried her special chicken and there was mashed potatoes, gravy and creamed peas.

Obviously, Sir Aimsley was to be the first one served. Greg did the honours. He marched forward to give the steaming plate to him. Three things happened at once. Russell Aimsley flung out his arm in one of his gestures to emphasize what he was saying to his associates. Greg was coming up behind him and the flailing arm hit the plate. Greg made a heroic grab for control and perhaps could have saved the situation, if the reason for his earlier squirming hadn't put in an appearance. The grasshopper crawled out of the shirt collar and immediately jumped into the middle of the swaying plate. Greg froze in horror and the whole plate, Grasshopper and all did a graceful arc to land on Russell Aimsley's shoulder. The contents of the plate dripped down the front of his suit. It was the first time anyone including his own entourage, had ever seen the man speechless with shock. This state of affairs only lasted a couple of seconds. With a roar of pain from the hot food, Russell Aimsley stood up his chair crashing over. Then the real diatribe started. Just after Russell started his tirade, Greg white with terror fled to the kitchen for safety.

Hilda and Louise rushed to the apoplectic politician's side apologizing profusely. They wiped the food off the irate man and Lucy picked up the overturned chair. Russell waved them away, even more annoyed at their solicitude. The rest of the guests remained silent staring at the angry politician in wonder. Perhaps they had never seen this side of the debonair gentleman. However Louise noted one of them had a mischievous grin that he was hiding behind a hand covering his mouth.

Louise offered to clean the suit overnight so that he could have it in the morning. With vague attempt to control his temper and a glare for both of them, Russell sat down again, very aware of the stain on his suit and the amused glances from his acquaintances. Hilda hurried to serve him another plateful. She brought it out herself and placed it safely before him. Lucy and Louise quickly served the rest of them.

No one complained about the meal. They certainly seemed to enjoy it, according to the number of seconds the entourage asked for. Fortunately Hilda had anticipated something of the sort and had prepared enough for a small army. However, not one thank-you did Hilda get from them. Once the dignitaries had retreated to their rooms, the rest of the hungry helpers and aides took turns sitting and eating. By the time they were finished not one scrap of the meal was left Hilda was pleased because all of them were very verbal in their thanks for the wonderful meal.

"Altogether," Hilda thought, "I would rather vote for the help as the politicians. At least they are polite." She giggled as she remembered that wonderful sight of gravy dripping down the honourable Russell Aimsley.

When she returned to the kitchen, she saw the contrite Greg scrubbing dishes for all he was worth. His face was still white. He faced her bravely when she went over to him. He held his head high, shoulders back waiting for her punishment. He fully expected to be fired.

To his utter astonishment, Hilda hugged him and started to laugh. Louise, Grace and Lucy joined in the laughter. Once Greg realized that he was not going to be punished, a small grin appeared and he too joined in the gayety.

"That was the funniest thing I have ever seen," Hilda said, tears rolling down her cheeks. "I know we have to cater to these people, but that man was so officious and arrogant that he deserved what happened. But please Greg no more insects come into this house when you are working, okay?"

"Yes ma'am," Greg said. "I am really sorry, but that grasshopper was a whopper. I really wanted him for my collection, but I promise I won't do it again when I am working." He stated solemnly.

She sniffed, "If I had a vote, he certainly wouldn't get it!" she said to Louise who was helping her." Louise laughed and both of them got busy cleaning up after the annoying tenants.

Howard Whipley came storming in to talk to Hilda. "Where is the Mayor, I was told he would be here to meet Sir Aimsley. I was horrified when he didn't show up at Sir Aimsley's arrival."

Hilda eyed the thin young man with distaste. "He was there! Just because your candidate didn't recognise him was not our fault!"

"He, he was there?" Howard sputtered. "But why didn't he announce himself. This is deplorable. "Please have someone introduce him at the forum tonight!" He demanded.

Without waiting for an answer, Howard flounced out again.

"Well I never!" Hilda said furiously. Her hands were on her hips in agitation.

They were just finishing up the chores, when the sound of boots on the stairs were heard as the candidate and followers, headed for the church. Sir Aimsley had a clean suit on and didn't even glance their way. A servant of the politician came in later and asked Louise if the suit could be cleaned, as he did not know how.

Louise assured him it could be done and she left to find Charles to get the water heating for the special laundry job.

That evening most of the community and surrounding area arrived to take in the Candidates election speech. The church was packed. Some women were there, but most were noticeably absent. Most women found no point to going when they had no vote.

"One of these days", Jenny said to Janet, "One of these days women will have a say in who gets into the government. We will have the vote."

Janet looked at her upset friend and said. "Well one thing about it, he will never forget, our town." Of course the whole town was in the know, about the fiasco at the boarding house supper.

"Well I will attend anyway!" Jenny said. She stood in the back, because all seats were taken. Mayor like usual accompanied her.

In the church, the men waited restlessly for the meeting to start. The politician and his followers entered the building and marched to the front.

"But where is the Mayor? I understood he would be here to greet me!" He looked around rather annoyed that the head of the town was not upfront to meet him. It was obvious that the men sitting there in their homespun shirts and trousers were not the head of this community. He took a second glance at James, sitting in the third row. He seemed like an important person, because he was dressed neatly, but Russell remained uncertain.

Joe Walters then mischievously stepped forward. "But Mayor is here to greet you Sir Aimsley!"

"Well I should hope so!" Sir Russell Aimsley said with a feral smile.

Joe then made a show of pointing to the dog beside Jenny. "I would like to introduce you to the Honourable Mayor of Water Valley." Russell's eyes followed the direction of Joe's finger. He mistook the precise direction of the point and thought he was indicating Jenny.

"A woman!" He gasped. "You have a woman Mayor? This is outrageous, unheard of!" He sputtered.

"Oh no, Sir Aimsley," Jenny said sweetly, bending down to indicate the dog. "Mayor, meet Sir Russell Aimsley, candidate for the Republican Party of Montana." Mayor's growl strengthened and he gave a bark.

Russell tried valiantly to maintain his composure when the whole community roared with laughter at his expense. With his poise gone and His face red, he attempted to gain control of the situation. He started in on his prepared speech.

The speech was an arrogant criticism of the Governor. Russell tried in every way to convince the gathering that he was best for the leadership. He did have some good points, but it was really an atrocious amount of doggerel.

Janet was outside in her lawn chair listening to the drone of voices, the occasional shout and once in a while some clapping. The meeting seemed to go on forever, but really it was just a little after nine o'clock when the forum dismissed. James and Jenny came over and joined Janet on the lawn furniture. They updated her on the meeting. James candidly answered her queries. He told her about the Mayor incident. Everyone laughed with glee.

James continued more soberly. "Russell Aimsley has some very good ideas, but there is little chance of him getting elected. It seems he irritated a lot of the voters with his arrogant attitude. His outburst at supper did not endear him to a lot of the folks. In fact most feel he is a figure of fun, especially after he was introduced to Jenny and the Mayor."

Jenny agreed with James. She wished she would have a say in the election. James then said goodnight and returned to the ranch. Jenny and Janet also gave each other a hug good night and returned to their homes.

The next morning the entire contingent was observed, as they got ready to leave Water Valley. They were minus Howard Whipley, who had gone on ahead to make arrangements for their arrival in Big Rock. Then Russell Aimsley finally hefted his bulk into the carriage and the whole parade started off on their journey to the next city. Their visit had certainly been an interesting break in the lives of the Water Valley citizens. It would give them something to talk and laugh about for a long time. Mayor too, was happy to see these strange people go. He could relax. All that day he could be seen napping in the shade of the oak tree across from the store.

Chapter 42

The Easter Holiday would begin on Good Friday. Jenny had the children working on the spring examinations most of that week. However she did have an Easter egg hunting party for them Thursday afternoon. Boiled eggs that the children had painted the afternoon before were hidden all over the schoolyard. With much giggling and shouting, all the children were able to find their two eggs. Jenny dismissed them just after lunch so that they could start their holiday immediately.

James had asked her to come out to the ranch to spend Easter with them. She was very excited about the prospect, but knew she had all the test papers to mark. Left alone in the schoolroom Jenny sat at her desk busily finishing her work. She had told James she would be at the ranch in time for supper. Task completed, she hurried home to prepare for her departure to the ranch.

She was looking forward to seeing Alice again. In spite of her promise to visit often, she had not found the time to go to the ranch since New Years.

She looked at her watch. It was just a little after three o'clock. She had plenty of time before she needed to leave.

Mayor had been acting very strange. He would not leave her side. When she had dismissed the class, Mayor was waiting outside. He kept close to her interfering with her movement. Never had she seen him so attentive. Usually he was roaming about, running on ahead or lagging behind. She was a bit tired and had little patience for the dog at this time. The physical labor of working on community repairs, had given her some blisters and her muscles ached. Jenny grew out of patience with Mayor when she tripped over him for the third time.

She told him "Go lie down Mayor! Leave me alone." Mayor looked at her reproachfully.

Jenny went into her house and firmly closed the door in Mayor's face. Jenny could hardly believe it when Mayor, scratched on her door and whined pathetically. Jenny yelled at him. "Stop it Mayor, what has gotten into you anyway?" The scratching subsided and she decided just to rest a few minutes in her chair. She started to read her book, but before she realized it she fell asleep, her book sliding unheeded to the floor.

Jenny awoke. Some sixth sense warned her that something was not right. She froze. Gus stood there in front of her. His clothes were torn and filthy. His face wore hatred in every line. Jenny tried to reach for the tiny gun on her thigh, but was stopped by the huge hunting knife thrust at her face.

Jenny was terrified. She was looking certain death in the face. This man had nothing to lose by killing her. She was shaking like a leaf, but she tried to control her face and voice, to hide the fact that she was petrified.

"Hello Gus," she said. "Is there something I can help you with?"

"Shad-up" Gus snarled. "Get up."

With shaking knees Jenny managed to get herself to her feet.

"Turn around," he said.

She did as she was told, her mind frantically trying to find a way out of this predicament. Now she wished she had gone straight to the ranch. How she wished she had not been mean to Mayor and let him come into the house. He tied her wrists behind her back, with cruel twists on the rope. Jenny winced. She had tried to hold her wrists a bit apart to prevent the rope from getting too tight, but Gus was too wise.

He took a dirty rag out of his pocket and stuffed it in her mouth. It tasted foul. Jenny gagged as it was forced to the back of her tongue.

Gus laughed and threw her back in the chair. He then took a sack and stripped her pantry of any food that could be carried easily. Once that was done he took great pleasure in her dismay, by smashing everything in the room that had little value. He threw any valuables and silver into a sack he carried with him. Jenny glanced at the mantle clock just before Gus smashed it. It was five o'clock in the afternoon; she must have been really tired to sleep so long.

Gus dragged Jenny with him into the bedroom. A howling, hissing and spitting Kally greeted Gus. Gus roared with anger and cursed as Kally attacked him. Jenny could only watch helplessly while Gus grabbed Kally and threw her against the wall. Jenny stared at Kally, tears streaming down her cheeks. Kally did not move. Gus continued to slash her clothes and bedding to ribbons. He hauled Jenny back to the kitchen with more items that he could sell and threw them in the sack as well.

Jenny was sending silent prayers heavenward. She prayed that Kally was all right and that someone would come. Gus's face and hands were covered with bloody scratches, showing where the kitten had made her marks. Her home was in a shambles.

Jenny was trying to remain calm, furiously thinking of how to escape. With the hedges around her house and school, she knew they wouldn't be spotted by anyone from the town.

Gus dragged her out the back way and found himself facing a formidable enemy. Mayor, who had been so uneasy all day sensing the danger to Jenny raced around the corner of the house and attacked Gus. Gus's cry of anguish as Mayor grabbed his arm caused him to let Jenny go. Jenny tried to run, but terror caused her legs to fail her. Gus with insane strength clutched Mayor by the scruff of his neck fur and threw him into the side of the house. Mayor just bounced. He was turning to leap again when Gus hit him with a piece of firewood that Jenny used to prop her back door open in nice weather. Mayor went down without a sound.

It all happened so fast. Jenny meanwhile, gathered strength scrambled around the side of the house. Gus was right behind her and the next thing she knew she was seeing stars. He had hit the back of her head with the same piece of wood.

He dragged her through the trees and bushes behind her house. They circled the community crossing the creek behind the livery barn. By staying in the bush, they were not seen. Jenny's feet were soaked, as she only had light shoes on. As they worked their way down to the river Jenny frantically tried to break branches and make marks in the ground to indicate their passage. However Gus was not trying to hide the trail. He wasn't even attempting to cover his tracks.

Gus forced Jenny along until they came to a broken down old horse. He lifted her up and threw her across the front of the saddle on the horse's neck. Her head hung down one way and her feet the other.

He then mounted behind her. Gus hit the poor horse with the reins, and the animal shuffled forward. They forced their way along the bank of the river and into the mountains. Jenny became dizzy as the blood went to her head; her stomach ached from the punishment the horse's bony neck was giving her. She tried to think, but each step the horse took disoriented her more. She had trouble breathing, as the gag was shoved so far into her mouth. Bushes and branches beat across her legs, back, and head. Each time Gus would laugh hysterically. Gus was alternately, mumbling and then cursing her. For the most part he kept up a solid stream of expletives. He threatened to kill her and everyone else in the community. Jenny's ears burned red at the horrible language.

"We must be on some animal or trapping trail," she thought. The horse was definitely climbing. When a large branch slapped him across the chest, Gus roared with anger and his cursing became louder and more erratic.

With every passing step, Jenny's hope of a quick rescue faded. It was not likely anyone in town would miss her, at least for a while. James would, when she didn't show up for supper. They would wait a bit of course and then James would ride to meet her.

In her despair, she estimated they would discover her missing by maybe eight o'clock or nine o'clock. It would be too late to track her very far until morning. Jenny's heart sank. Any rescue would probably have to be left until daylight. The mad light in Gus's eyes told her he had full intentions of destroying her, probably long before anyone could find her. She kept up a silent prayer for her soul. Jenny knew she was going to die.

Still, she had the comfort of the little gun. Gus had not searched her. She would have to be patient choosing just the right time to use it. It was slow going through the deep brush. It was harder still when it got dark. Gus kept the horse moving. James would probably know by now that she was kidnapped. It was small consolation. Jenny had lost track of the time. She was sure it was hours. Gus's cursing finally abated. He said nothing, except to swear as a branch from some trees swatted him as they rode by. Her head felt heavy and ready to explode. Her whole body felt numb. She could not feel her feet.

Jenny blacked out a little and only aroused when water splashed her face. They were crossing the river. It was surprisingly narrow at this point indicating it was high up in the mountain range, if it was even the same river. Her body ached, that is, what she could feel of it. They stopped and he threw her to the ground, there was no way her numb feet would allow her to stand let alone run.

He left the exhausted horse to fend for itself as he dragged her upright. He let go expecting her to remain standing, but she didn't. She collapsed when her legs would not hold her. Cursing he grabbed her by the hair and dragged her across the rough ground. They reached some sort of shelter, and he threw her inside. It was very dark. He then lit a fire in the broken down fireplace.

In the faint light Jenny could see she was in a one-room hut, with a rickety table, one chair, and a cot. Gus threw the sack of food onto the table. There was dirt and junk all over the floor and piled up in corners. There was a vertical support beam in the centre of the room. He retied her hands behind her back and around the beam. Jenny was truly trapped now. He pulled the gag from her mouth and Jenny gratefully gulped in fresh air.

He went out the door then, and Jenny tried to get at the gun. Her legs were a mass of pins and needles, as the circulation started to return in them. She frantically tried to work her leg around and toward her hands. It almost worked, but Gus returned too soon.

He had a jug of moonshine with him. He frequently took huge gulps. He talked to himself and laughed at some private joke.

"The man is mad and the liquor is not helping matters," Jenny thought.

Gus dumped the sack out on the table and grabbed some food. He stuffed his face like he had not eaten in weeks. He alternated mouthfuls with a swig of liquor. While he concentrated on his stomach, time was passing which was to Jenny's advantage, as least she hoped so.

Jenny needed to buy more time. She knew Gus was bent on revenge, but maybe she could interest him. "Gus, I have lots of money, I'll give it all to you if you let me go."

Gus just snorted and continued eating and drinking. "Honest, I have lots of money in the bank at Big Rock. I promise you can have it all if you take me there."

Gus lurched to his feet and came to her. "What ya take me for, a fool?!" He slapped her hard. Her head snapped back and hit the pole. His outraged yelling became indecipherable again. Jenny subsided into silence. Her eyes were blurry and she saw blackness with flashes of white light. Gus went back to his seat by the fire.

Gus was totally drunk by the time the faint predawn light started to show. Jenny hoped he would pass out, but her luck had ended. With mumbles mixed with the odd shout, he started to berate Jenny. His words were so slurred with drink that Jenny couldn't make out what he was saying.

He came up face to face with her, and started yelling. His sour breath caused her to gag again in revulsion. Each word was accompanied by a slap to her face. Gus grabbed the front of her dress and pulled. The fabric ripped. It startled him. Then he got a gleam in his eyes and he started tearing the rest of her clothes off. Jenny panicked and kicked out at him. She managed to hit him in the groin. He folded over for a few seconds his eyes bulging and he groaned. He bit his lip.

When he arose he was completely beside himself in anger. Blood from his cut lip spattered her. He hit her across the face, hard with his fist. Jenny's head snapped around and her vision blurred again. She had a hard time keeping a grip on reality. Her knees sagged but she managed to remain upright. He rained blows down on her. Her body was in total agony.

He found the tiny gun. He tore the holster off of her leaving a red welt where the leather strap cut her. He threw the gun into the corner laughing at her futile attempt at protection. It also angered him that she would even try to use that gun on him. It was obvious that he intended to kill her, but he was going to torture her before the end. He beat her with a short leather whip used for horses. With her body on fire Jenny's tried her hardest to be stoic. It was becoming more difficult all the time. This bravery seemed to anger him still more, and he looked around for some other way of making her hurt.

"You'll scream, bitch before I'm through with you!" he grunted.

A few sparks from a log in the fire attracted his attention. Grinning evilly he grabbed a burning stick and came toward her. Jenny cringed as he slowly, oh so slowly advanced it toward her chest. Her eyes focused horribly on the glowing end of the brand. He touched her on the shoulder and drew it down toward her navel. Her bravery completely disappeared; all she could do was scream in anguish. She jerked herself around trying to escape. The pole she was tied too was moving. Dust poured down on her from the rickety roof. Jenny jerked harder. Maybe she could pull the roof down on them. Gus hit her again hard. He was laughing in triumph, over making her scream. This time the blow disoriented her completely. Gus pressed the burning brand into her abdomen slowly working it sadistically deeper. The pain was excruciating. Gus just kept pressing in harder and harder. Blackness was coming over her when time seemed to stop.

The door crashed in. Gus whirled. Jake stood there with a rifle in his hand, Mayor right beside him growling. Anger suffused Jake's face as he got a glance at Jenny. He was aghast. He lifted the rifle to his shoulder as Gus dived for him. Jake's gun went off. Gus hit Jake and they both fell back out the door. Then it was quiet. Mayor dodged the men and headed for Jenny.

Jenny fought off unconsciousness and watched the door, wondering what happened. The pain in her stomach caused her to sink to the floor, the brand was still inside her. She tried to curl up to ease the pain. Mayor was licking her face. She was glad to see him too. But for some reason her eyes kept losing focus and she couldn't seem to think straight. At last the burning branch fell away, leaving a gaping wound. Blood was leaking from the wound. Weakened Jenny gave up and passed out.

Outside Jake pushed his father off of him. He sat up and realized his father was dead. The bullet had hit the heart. He got violently sick. When he finally stopped retching, Jake was shaking in shock. "You bastard, you finally got what you deserve. I hope Ma can see us from heaven right now!" He threw the rifle down and backed away from the body.

Remembering Jenny he dashed for the door and saw Jenny in a crumpled heap at the bottom of the pillar. Mayor was anxiously trying to revive her by licking her face. There was blood coming from somewhere. He grabbed the hunting knife from the table and cut Jenny's hands loose. He laid her out and tore a piece of her dress up for a bandage on her stab wound. He couldn't tell how deep it was but it was certainly huge although not much blood was coming out of it. Realizing her nudity, he grabbed an old blanket from the cot, and covered her. Mayor was upset and he licked and whined, trying to wake Jenny up.

Jake had covered Jenny up just in time. The rest of the rescue team arrived. He had been working at the stable with Soot, when Mayor had alerted the town. He was howling at the top of his lungs. People rushed to Jenny's cabin. Once they discovered that Jenny was gone, Jake didn't hesitate. He had grabbed a rifle from a startled David Olson ran to get Soot, mounted and started to follow the trail. Mayor was racing ahead, his nose following Jenny's scent. He had raced off, Mayor beside him shouting directions back to the others.

It was everyone's assumption that Gus was the cause of the disappearance. James was just crossing the bridge to escort Jenny to the ranch when he heard the church bell start to ring. James hurried up the hill to find out what was going on. The rest of the men were hurrying to saddle the horses and follow Jake. His trail would not be hard to follow.

James was the first in the hut door, after assuring himself that Gus was indeed dead. He dropped down beside Jenny. She was so still and her face was so white. Fear just about stopped his heart. Cradling her head on his lap his tears flowed. Jenny regained consciousness and was very happy at seeing him holding her. She smiled wanly and sighed in relief. Her stomach seemed to be on fire and the rest of her ached. She was covered in scratches, bruises and whip marks. One eye was swollen shut. Jenny gave up the fight to remain conscious and she let herself pass out.

Doctor Ben was the second one in through the door. He ordered everyone out. James would not budge, but Jake left in a hurry. Ben examined her main wound. He said that Jake had done a good job of stopping what bleeding there was. To James' mute inquiry he said that Jenny's wound would be touch and go and that they had to get her to the clinic as fast as possible. Then James gathered her up in the blanket and carried her out to his horse. He handed her to the doctor while he climbed into the saddle. Ben handed Jenny up to him. His quick glance saw Gus Appleby tied to the back of his own decrepit horse. Then the race began. James and Ben kicked the horses into a run down the hill at breakneck speed. It was a trip neither of them ever wanted to repeat. It was a wonder they were not killed, as they careened around corners and jumped fallen logs and creeks.

The rest of the team made their way down the mountain to the settlement at a saner pace. They had gathered all of Jenny's things back into the sack. They were all frightfully worried about her. True the perpetrator was dead, but there were many of them that wished he were still alive so they could hang him.

Chapter 43

Jenny never woke up on that horrendous journey to the clinic. She was so still, that James panicked and thought she was dead. When the two of them reached the doctor's office, James held her close and carried her into the infirmary.

James was relieved when Jenny roused a bit as he laid her on the new examination table. She gasped when she was jostled. She couldn't remember a time when she hurt so badly. James hung onto her hand. Nellie breathless from the run appeared and prepared to assist Ben with fixing Jenny up. Ben said, "James I want you to wait outside, please. This won't be pleasant and I can't afford to be distracted when I work on her."

James started to object, when he saw the sober look on Ben's face. He held his tongue and went quietly to the waiting room. He put a kettle on for hot water, at Nellie's request. It at least gave him something to do.

The ash and splinters from the rough wood had contaminated her wound deep into her abdomen. It needed a thorough cleaning. Infection could set in very quickly. The doctor put a cloth dampened with ether over her mouth and nose.

"Breathe as deep as you can, Jenny," he said.

Jenny tried, but the pain seemed to prevent her from breathing very much at all. Gradually, however, the ether did its work and her body relaxed. Jenny slept.

James was scared. Abdominal wounds were bad news. He paced back and forth across the floor. Reverend was there, saying constant prayers. Jake sat mutely in one corner, shivering in shock.

The doctor and Nellie worked furiously, cleaning all the dirt and ash from the stab wound. The edge was so ragged. A knife would have left a cleaner cut. The branch had been dirty as well as hot and that doubled their problem. The bleeding had stopped fairly quickly due to the burned ends of blood vessels. However there was dirt in each and every one. The wound had missed all the vital organs, but had damaged some of Jenny's intestines. Ben was heart sick, but worked carefully and skilfully to repair every bit of damage.

When the doctor finished the main wound they looked after the more minor burns and cuts. Jenny's body was a mass of bruises. Her eye was completely shut and the one side of her face swollen from the blows Gus had given her.

Jake sat hat in hand just inside the office door. His mind was going in circles. The shock of killing a person was gut wrenching to anyone and having that person be one's father was even worse. The Reverend came to sit beside him.

"Jake, everything will work out. The Lord will help Jenny recover from this. As for your father, he lent himself to the devil. You saved Jenny from him. No one will blame you for what you have done and the Lord forgives."

"I didn't do it on purpose sir, the gun went off when he jumped for me. But Reverend, what's taking so long in there?!" Jake said pointing at the infirmary door.

Reverend said, "Jenny was badly injured and it will take the doctor some time to fix every wound. As I said, the Lord will help her to get better."

A gentle touch on his shoulder made him jump. Janet was there. She smiled at the Reverend and asked Jake to come with her. Jake did not want to leave but Janet insisted.

Janet of course had heard what happened and had a good idea of what Jake might be going through. They walked up the hill to her house. She led him into her living room. She poured him a good stiff drink of brandy. He didn't know how to tell her no and didn't even try. He forced himself to drink it. He choked and sputtered as the strong liquid burned its way down his throat. He stared at Janet just a bit resentfully.

Janet just smiled sympathetically and told him, "Have another swallow."

That was all it took and the warmth of it started to spread throughout his body. He relaxed a bit. Janet talked to him, on many subjects, but stayed away from Jenny and what happened. Finally the drink had done its work, and Jake's mind had relaxed just enough. Janet and he talked for over an hour.

Janet told him, "You did the right thing, even though it was horrible. Jenny would have been dead very shortly if you had not interfered. You did well under the circumstances."

Jake knew that, but it helped to hear it from someone else. Ray came in and told them that Ben was finished with Jenny. She had just been put into the bed of the Clinic. Janet and Jake hurried there, where the exhausted doctor tried to assure them Jenny was doing fine at the moment.

Uneasy thoughts went through everyone's mind. The situation was grave, but they had high hopes.

Janet and Jake looked in on Jenny who was still sleeping. James was there, holding her hand. He had every intention of staying with her for the duration of her recovery.

James's mind kept going over the scene at the cabin, again and again. He too was as tight with worry, as Jake had been. The doc brought him a glass of whiskey. James took a big swallow. He sipped the rest. Joe and David brought in sandwiches. James ate, realizing that he and the whole rescue party had not eaten since the night before. The whiskey was working too fast, on an empty stomach. His eyes never left Jenny's face all the while he ate.

"David, could you send word to the ranch about the happenings here? My grandmother will be worried about our non-appearance at the ranch. Tell her I'll not be home for a while."

"Sure, I'll do that right away, James," David said turned toward the door. He hesitated for a minute and turned back to James. "Ben is a good doctor, Jenny will be all right. The whole town is praying for her recovery." He then hurried out the door before James could reply.

Nellie, after assuring herself Jenny was as comfortable as she could make her, left James alone with her.

James had never felt this helpless. There was nothing at the moment he could do. It was a waiting game now. His every thought became a prayer. Jenny remained asleep. Nellie popped back in to bring a basin. She told James that Jenny would likely be nauseous from the ether.

Jenny woke up around midnight. James and Nellie were dozing in chairs next to the bed. She felt light headed and her stomach was churning. She barely gasped out Nellie's name, when that lady leaped to her side. She held the basin, when Jenny lost control. Nellie supported her head, as she retched and retched. The pain in her stomached doubled each time she did. She didn't have much in her stomach, but that didn't stop her from wanting to throw up her shoes. James had politely left the room to prevent Jenny acute embarrassment.

When her stomach finally settled down, Jenny was spent and limp. Her wound was bleeding again. Ben returned to see how much damage was done. He put fresh bandages on it to absorb the blood. Some of the stitches were pulled, but fortunately none were broken. He left the two of them alone again. Her pale wan face flushed. Nellie just smiled at her and cleaned her face with gentleness. Nellie told Jenny that her stomach's reaction was expected and she was used to it. Her one eye flashed her thanks. The other was swollen and it hurt to smile, or even move her jaw.

James came back in when Jenny was settled again. She blushed when he sat in the chair beside her. She was not quite sure she wanted him this close in her condition. It made her feel a bit uneasy. She could tell he cared for her very much and didn't know how to react. Then she just didn't care. She was just in too much misery. Jenny was aware of each and every wound. Her body was hurting badly. The retching had made it worse.

She tried to make her swollen mouth work. Tremblingly Jenny whispered, "Gus?"

James told her "Gus is dead, Jenny, he can't hurt you anymore. Don't try to talk, you just rest and get better." He added silently to himself "I can't lose you."

Jenny shuddered in relief. She was glad she did not have to worry any more. Jake and her were both safe. She mumbled around her swollen mouth. "I'm kind of thirsty."

James gave her a sip of water. Nellie had some chicken broth on the stove, and Nellie patiently gave her a spoonful at a time. To Jenny, it was the best tasting soup she had ever had. Nellie also had had her take some of the horrid tasting liquid, next to the bed. It was the same medicine she had given Jake countless times when he was ill.

Jenny endured the pain until the medicine caused her to drift off into sleep.

It was hot. She was walking over desert sand. There was a cool lake ahead of her. She started to run, but as hard as she ran, she could not reach it. It kept in front of her. Then there was the taste of water. She roused, and realized there was a glass full of cold water at her lips. She drank greedily.

After, she dreamed again. They turned nasty. She was running again, this time away from a demented face. It was black and bleeding. It chased her. She couldn't make her legs run any faster. It was going to catch her. She screamed in terror. Then she was cold. She was falling down an ice shaft.

There were sharp jagged points of ice facing upward. She was going to hit them. She was going to die and she knew it. As she hit the first spire of ice, it melted beneath her. Jenny looked around and saw all the ice melting away. There was no heat. Or was there? She was again falling though the melted ice right into the sun. Heat again seared her."

Jenny became aware of something cool on her forehead and she opened her eyes. Nellie was putting a cold compress on her forehead. It felt good. She was hot, but why was her body shivering? Jenny looked around. She couldn't figure out where she was. Nellie gave her something to drink and Jenny drifted into sleep again. Time was meaningless to her, but to James and Nellie and all the people of Water Valley and the ranch the days passed slowly. Alternating between fevers and chills, Jenny was very, very ill.

She was floating, she laughed, "I'm a bird," she said. She saw the blue sky, and looked down, there were fluffy white clouds underneath her. She spread her arms, and flew down between them. There was land far beneath her. She didn't want to go there. She hummed as she flew. She soared; she climbed high and dropped low in the air currents. She could feel them. Jenny opened her eyes, it was bright and she squinted as she came closer to the earth. "What is that?" she said as she saw a rectangular white thing on a hill. She swooped down closer. "It was a bed and she startled herself. It was her lying in the bed. "Now that doesn't make sense, how can I be here and there too?" She moved even closer, the face on the bed changed from hers, to Gus Appleby's! She screamed silently, as the vision stood up and started to come after her. She flew away in terror, but Gus was right behind her. He was juggling burning brands in his blood stained hands. She flew toward a light, and reached for it, straining with every muscle in her body. It did not seem to get any closer. A wailing cry sounded from behind her and she strived harder. The light changed. James face appeared in the bright cloud. He was holding his hands out to her. Would she reach him in time? She reached toward him, but couldn't get closer. Pain doubled her over, but she kept her eyes focused on James face.

Then time seemed to stand still as James blew a mighty wind from his mouth, and the apparition behind her disintegrated, and was gone. She felt every ache in her body, and heard dim voices. They were calling her. She wanted to sleep not wake up. She was tired and they wouldn't let her go to sleep. She became annoyed with the voices. Then everything faded away, and she relaxed into sleep.

When Jenny's dreams turned nasty, James remained with her trying to soothe her. Sometimes it worked, sometimes it didn't. Nightmares would have her screaming. James held her by the hour talking to her. His words seemed to settle her down for a bit, but never long.

Dr. Ben was fighting a battle. Her wound was red and swollen. It looked nasty and the infection was growing. He tried everything to stop the infection.

Easter came and went. People would drop in to the clinic, but visitors were not allowed into the bedroom.

Ben and Nellie watched her wound with great concern. Reluctantly they took her back to the operating table and tried to remove all the infection that was lacing her wound. Ben was losing the fight to keep Jenny alive.

"James, the infection is spreading and getting worse. I don't have anything to stop it," Ben said helplessly.

James, with tears flowing freely down his cheeks said "I am going out for a while. Try to get her to hang on until I return."

Ben watched James rush from the clinic. He didn't know what to think of James's strange reaction. He felt the hopelessness of the situation but kept working on stopping the infection. He would never give up.

Time passed and Ben and Nellie became concerned. Where had James gone? It was several hours later when he returned. He had an old Indian man with him. He had a rifle in one hand. Ben could hardly believe his eyes, as James let the man go near his precious Jenny.

Reuben yelled, "No, don't go near her!"

Nellie shrieked and rushed to Jenny's side. She grabbed an empty basin and held it menacingly between the Indian and Jenny.

James set the rifle down and grabbed Nellie's arm with a grip of steel pulling her away. He also grabbed Ben and forced them to listen to him. He was frantic.

"You admitted to me that your methods can't help her and she will die, right?" He waited for the reluctant nod of Bens and Nellie's head. "I'll not let her go without trying every possible avenue to save her. This is a healer from the tribe at the lower end of our ranch. He has knowledge of herbs and cures long forgotten by the white man. Maybe he can do what your modern medicine can't," James said firmly and defiantly. "I want him to try."

Nellie cried out in anguish! "He is a filthy, heathen Indian. Why don't you let Jenny die in peace?" She turned and rushed out of the clinic. Obviously grief had addled James's senses.

Ben was in shock. He thought. "James has lost his reason. What can I do? I am just too new to medicine. I should not have taken this position. My first real trial and I have lost." Desperately he tried to observe what the man by the name of Thorn was doing. Thorn sat on the floor and chewed some leaves, making a paste. Reuben was horrified, when Thorn took this sodden sticky mess and put it directly into Jenny's wound. He left the room, not wanting to see any more. He was too young for this job. His first major crisis and he had lost the battle. Shoulders slumped in defeat, he retreated to his cabin totally depressed.

Outraged cries in the street alerted James to trouble. Nellie had told everyone what was happening. A mob was gathering outside the clinic. Angry settlers and townsfolk were about to storm the clinic. They had full intentions of hanging the Indian.

James had come prepared for this reaction. He knew that most people thought of the Indian's with suspicion and intolerance. He barricaded the back door. He walked out to the front door. The mob was in no mood to listen to him. He fired a shot into the air. When the angry murmuring subsided, James said. "I am not crazy even though you think so. Do you want to mourn Jenny's death in the morning or allow me to try and save her life?" His face looked like granite as he continued. "Anyone coming in through that door will find himself with an ounce of lead in him. Go back to your houses and pray hard that Thorn can do what our own doctor can't, save Jenny's life!" Returning to the clinic bedroom, he sat in a hard backed chair, rifle in hand and facing the inner clinic door. The noise of anger subsided from outside as the bewildered towns folk settled down to wait.

Thorn in the meantime, settled himself to wait the outcome of his poultice. He was aware of the situation, but it didn't seem to bother him. While he waited he chanted, in simple words of his people. It had a rhythmic sound to it. He was sending up prayers to the healing spirit. James lowered himself to sit beside the old man. When Thorn stopped his chanting and opened his eyes, he observed the disheartened face in front of him. He reached out to the sad young man. James looked up at him. The wrinkled face willed confidence into him. James found himself relaxing for the first time since Jenny was kidnapped.

Thorn said, "Have hope and faith young one. She who the spirits tell me is your partner will live." He then looked up at the ceiling, and closed his eyes. "Your family will prosper. Your grandfather once saved my life many years ago and if by something I do here, I can repay that life debt, my life will be complete."

James was surprised. "Grandfather never told me that story, will you tell me what happened?"

Thorn sighed as his thoughts returned to a day long ago. "I was on a journey to another tribe further west. I had to cross part of your land to get there. A band of cattle rustlers caught me and were about to hang me when your grandfather came along. He was tracking those same rustlers. He gained a good spot in some rocks and started shooting. Fortunately the first shot severed the rope around my neck. The horse I was tied to bolted at the shot and carried me out of danger. Your grandfather's men had been nearby. They arrived to help him round up the rustlers. Jim then came after me. The horse had run itself out, but I was still bound hand and foot to him." Thorn smiled. "I fully expected to be killed at the hands of your grandfather as well, but he just smiled and cut the ropes. He spoke a few words in my language telling me to go and live a long life in peace. I don't know and never did find out how he knew my language, but I told him that my life was his. We often met each other over the years. He taught me English and we became good friends."

"If grandmother knew this story she never told me," James said. "Thank you Thorn for again risking your life to come here. I was wondering how it was that I met you not far from the ranch house. You were coming to meet me weren't you?"

"I had a dream from the spirits saying that you needed me, so I started for the ranch," Thorn said simply.

James was amazed and resumed his seat on the chair. The mob outside could gain courage again, but he was not too worried.

Thorn, then chanted some more. He waited for an hour. He then cleaned off the sodden leaves, which had turned black. He threw them in a waste bucket. He chewed some more leaves putting them on the wound. This process was repeated for the next five hours. When Thorn took the last packet out, the leaves had not changed color. They stayed the same as when Thorn had put them in. He nodded and smiled at James who had never moved from his chair. Jenny moaned a little and tossed in her sleep. Color was returning to her cheeks. Thorn stood up.

The timing was just right as Doc Ben who couldn't stay in his cabin any more called out to James from the door. "May I come in James?" As James acquiesced, Ben accompanied by Nellie rushed in.

A hasty examination show the flesh of her wound was starting to turn a more normal color. Ben could not believe it. He looked at James, then Thorn in amazement. Ben breathed a huge sigh of relief. "I have got to learn what you use!" he stated.

The three of them escorted Thorn from the clinic. People waiting outside stood up with frowns on their faces.

Ben shouted, "Jenny is going to be all right. Thorn saved her life."

The crowd stared at Thorn in wonder. Then as the words sunk in they started to cheer. Thorn was pleased, mounted his pony and crossed the bridge toward his home.

Happy people dispersed to attend to their own affairs. Jenny was going to be fine. It put a spring in everyone's step.

Jenny slept more normally, that night. Her lacerated flesh was starting to heal. No dreams seemed to plague her and even James managed to get some sleep in the cot across the room. It was a total miracle and Ben learned something that day. He would never again question practices that he knew nothing about. Just because they were not taught in medical school did not rule them unworthy.

It was noon the Friday after Easter when Jenny woke up. Her eyes were clear and bright. She saw James standing over by the window. His back was to her. His shoulders were hunched as his mind wandered.

"James?" she whispered. Nothing seemed to come out. However she must have made some noise, because James whirled around. He stood there for a moment. Joy suffused his face and he ran to her. Taking her hand, he raised it to his lips, covering it with kisses. There were tears in his eyes, as he gazed at her. Her stomach didn't hurt as much as it had before and that alone made her feel better. She reached up and brushed a solitary tear off his cheek. He buried his head into her shoulder and let the tears flow. Jenny looked up to see Ben and Nellie on the other side of the bed. Nellie put a finger up to her mouth silencing what Jenny was going to say.

"James needs to do that." Nellie whispered. "He has been holding back his emotions too much. He was so worried over you."

Jenny looked down at the tousled head of hair next to her. Her heart gave a lurch. She so loved this man. Gently she took her other hand and stroked James head. When James became silent, his tears finished. She let him pull away. James was a bit embarrassed and his red face told her this.

Jenny smiled "James, thank you for chasing my nightmares away. At least my memory tells me it was you."

James smiled in return. "I am only glad I could." She reached for him and he obligingly kissed and hugged her.

Jenny was hungry and thirsty. A delighted James hurried for more soup for her. Nellie helped Jenny sit up in the bed a bit. Her wound hurt, but not as much as she remembered.

A tray was brought in so she could eat easily in bed. She managed to eat most of it. She then looked critically at James, "You had better get something to eat yourself, you've lost weight and you look horrible. You need sleep as well!" she told him bluntly.

He grinned at her and said, "Yes, ma'am." With that he walked across the room to a rumpled bed and fell in. Jenny yawned and settled down herself. Nellie and Rueben smiled at each other and left the two sleepers to themselves.

Jenny recovered fairly quickly after that. There were no more fevers, although nightmares still troubled her at night. These became fewer over time but it would still take years for them to stop completely.

It was a couple of days later before the doctor allowed Jenny to have visitors. Her first surprise and one to James too, was Alice leaning on her cane limping into the room. James rushed to greet her and found her a chair close to Jenny. Alice didn't sit immediately, but stood beside Jenny. She gently touched one of Jenny's hands and stroked it. Jenny lifted her arms and Alice hugged her. The two of them had tears in their eyes and the stoic grandmother sat down with great dignity. She took out a dainty handkerchief and wiped away her tears.

"I am so glad you are going to be alright," she whispered. "I could not bear the thought of anything happening to you, Jenny. You have become a very good friend."

Jenny was touched and thanked her. James stood proudly beside his grandmother. He was happy that is grandmother liked

Jenny. He knew he had lost his heart to her. He was very much in love with Jenny. Alice soon left for the trip back to the ranch.

Many people came to visit with good wishes. No one outstayed his or her welcome, but by supper Jenny was exhausted. She ate her supper and fell asleep quickly. The next day Dr. Ben said she could get up if she felt like it.

She was ready too. It was boring staying in one spot for so long. Jenny hated the confinement.

James was gone somewhere for the moment and Jenny needed to talk to Ben alone. She had been secretly fretting ever since she had become aware of her injuries.

"Ben?" she said. He turned to her at the inquiry in her voice. "I have been a bit scared to ask, but I need to know. The damage to me, did it affect anything..." she blushed and stammered but determinedly kept going. "I mean...I'll be able to have children someday won't I?"

Ben sat down near Jenny, and smiled. "You were pretty torn up inside Jenny." He frowned a little then and went on. "You have many scars and most of them are not visible, but are inside you. We will have to watch you closely and it might hurt to carry a child, but I don't foresee anything to forbid you to get pregnant."

Jenny sighed with relief. Until Ben told her the situation, she hadn't realized how much she had worried about it. She sat on the side of the bed and touched her feet to the floor. Ben held her hand and she stood. It was good to be able to again, but her legs were sure shaking. Her stomach felt like it was going to fall to the floor, or the wounds re-open. She swung around and sat in the chair next to the bed. It felt good to sit up properly.

When James returned, the first thing she wanted to know was the damage report on her home.

"Why don't you bring Kally down to me, James," Jenny said with a smile, "I am dying to see her and miss her purring. She can stay with me on the bed."

James was silent for a minute, and cleared his throat. "Umm, Jenny, Kally is dead," he said slowly.

Jenny looked up at him, "Gus killed her didn't he. I was hoping she would be all right."

James sadly nodded and hurried to hold her hand. "Yes, she was a target of Gus's revenge," he said.

Tears welled up in Jenny's eyes and she fought to control her emotions. She wanted to ask more, but couldn't make herself. In reality she just didn't want to know.

"We have made a special graveyard for pets, just south of your cabin. We buried Kally there." James said. "The Reverend blessed it and Pops built a picket fence around a twenty foot area. The village decided it was a good idea. I believe most people were thinking of a place for Mayor, when it's his time. Not many people here have pets, but we decided to do it anyway for future needs."

Jenny stared at him in wonder. What a thoughtful man James was. She didn't know of many that would do something like this for people. It showed just how sensitive he was to everyone's feelings. Her stomach gave another flip and she bit her lip. She had lost her battle to remain neutral in her emotions regarding James. She just loved this rugged caring man. She sternly called her feelings to order.

She pushed herself hard to get back into shape and mobile. Ben cautioned her to take it easy, but she wanted to get back to normal and back to her friends and students.

When Ben allowed her to leave the clinic, James escorted her up the hill. The first thing Jenny wanted to do was go visit the new cemetery. Sure enough just south of her house was the special place set up by everyone. The picket fence standing only two feet high surrounded an area maybe ten feet by ten feet. In one corner was the freshly dug grave of Kally. Pops had carved a small tombstone. It simply said "Kally." Tears came again and the two of them went to her house. It would seem much lonelier now.

James opened the door and suddenly Jenny couldn't move. Panic seized her.

James went on in, not noticing Jenny's hesitation. Forcing herself to move Jenny entered the house. It was not the same. Her home had been violated.

She started to shake. James turned around and noticed her pale face and trembling body. He rushed to her and took her hand.

"It's going to be okay Jenny, you're safe now. Gus can never hurt you again."

Jenny's teeth were chattering, as she tried to force herself to calm down. The town had done a wonderful job of cleaning up her cabin. She willed herself to be brave. She did not want to show weakness to James or anyone.

Her mind was in turmoil, she could not stay here, at least not by herself. The thought of being alone was terrifying her. Then Mayor was there as if conjured. Jenny had seated herself in a chair and the dog came in uninvited. He sat down in front of Jenny and put his paw on her arm. He seemed to understand Jenny's terror. To regain her composure, Jenny reached down and hugged the dog.

She stood up then. James started a fire in the cold stove. He put a pot of water on. James sensed her apprehension. He vowed to make sure everyone in town would drop in and visit her. He was terribly worried. He was not entirely oblivious to Jenny's inner terror. If it hadn't been for the fact that Ben needed to have Jenny close for bandage changing, he thought he might kidnap her himself and take her to the ranch. However he had no right to do so, not yet anyway.

Jenny bravely bid farewell to James, as he left her to go back to the ranch. Mayor stood beside her. He seemed to instinctively know her need and in the next few days he never left her side, except when she was in school.

Jenny welcomed him and was grateful for his presence. She didn't feel so alone with the dog near her. She went out on the veranda and was greeted by an enthusiastic chatter. Squeaker came down to the lower branches of the Maple tree to beg for peanuts. Jenny smiled at her wild friend. She hurried inside to grab the peanuts she kept especially for Squeaker from her drawer. She took them out to the demanding squirrel.

It was a warm afternoon and Jenny sat on the veranda chair. Mayor sat beside her and the squirrel ignored them both as he daintily picked up a peanut and expertly removed the shell. It was a glorious day and it was good to be alive. Mayor sat up and put his head on Jenny's knee. She stroked him and burst into tears. Yes, she was alive, but the horror of her experience, was just too fresh. She stood up and went to the door of the cabin. Her heart started to pound and her body started to shake again. Mayor put his nose in her limp hand. Gathering her courage she entered the house. She was determined to put a good face on things.

She looked around. Yes, her house had been cleaned up and the furniture repaired but a lot of her mementos were gone. She was sad about that but thankful that the total damage had not been worse. She had very few clothes left that hadn't been shredded in Gus's fury. Jenny grew very depressed.

It took every ounce of her will power and many hugs of Mayor to throw off her terror and depression. "I will beat this," she told herself. "I will be fine, I do not need to be scared of being alone."

In spite of just about everyone objections, Jenny toddled to the school on Monday morning. She was still stiff and sore, but it was good to be busy again. The children all treated her like spun glass. They never let her lift a finger.

She laughed, "You are all spoiling me. If you don't watch it, I'll expect it from now on!"

The children would just smile and carry on with whatever task they were doing. They loved their "Miss Jenny."

Chapter 44

By May Day Jenny was much better and almost back to her old self. She had the occasional twinge in her stomach, but her bruises had faded. She would bear the scar of the burning brand across her body for life. "I'll never be able to wear a low cut gown again," she thought ruefully.

It would also be a long time before she could be alone without fear. She would jump at shadows and her heart would race. Jenny would berate herself for being such a weakling. It never seemed to help though. James noticed this, because such a phobia could not be completely hidden. He talked to Reuben about it, and was told that Jenny may never get completely over her trauma. James vowed he would help her in any way and quietly made sure that Jenny was never totally alone. James never worried when Mayor was with her because she seemed at ease with the dog.

She began to think about her lack of wardrobe and other items that had been destroyed. She needed to go to Big Rock. Reluctantly she realized she would just have to wait until school was completed.

She was fretting over this when James arrived. "How are you feeling?" he asked.

"Just fine," she said perkily. "But I wish I could go to Big Rock," she stated. "I have many things to replace."

James grinned and said, "A trip is just what you need; maybe it will take your mind off things. I think it's a splendid idea. You know I believe Jake would enjoy the trip also and he could help carry your booty," James suggested.

"Oh, that would be wonderful!" Then Jenny frowned. "But what about school, the children have missed enough school, what with my injuries and all."

"Umm, do you think I would make a good substitute teacher?" he asked.

"You would teach for me?" she asked in astonishment. When a firm nod answered her, she exclaimed. "Bless you, that would be terrific. You'll make a great teacher." With her fears laid to rest she became excited and swiftly made plans. "I wonder if Janet would like to come with me?" she said, "I believe she would enjoy the trip as well."

Nothing could deter her from hurrying to the store to put her proposal in front of Janet. James just smiled and followed her. He loved her enthusiasm.

"Oh my goodness, that sounds just delightful, it has been over a year since I was last away from the store here." Janet gushed when the plan was put to her. "Why don't we plan the trip for Monday morning?" she asked.

James said, "That is a good day, I'll have Jake bring a team and buckboard for you Monday." He added in a teasing voice "I'll make sure the seats are well cushioned just for you Jenny!" He knew Jenny's dislike of hard wooden seats.

Jenny's radiant smile was thanks enough for the smitten man. He told them "Jake will have a list of things to buy for the ranch if you ladies don't mind." The ladies were quite agreeable. When the rest of the town heard that they were going, Jenny was approached by many, asking her to pick up various items. Jenny carefully wrote them down so she wouldn't forget anything

Monday morning was turning out to be a beautiful spring day. The three of them laughed and chatted gaily as they drove. The buckboard seats had indeed been covered with cushions to make the trip more enjoyable. As they crossed under the towering canyon walls that had held Water Valley in isolation all winter, they noticed no sign of the avalanche remaining. They all yelled in exuberance, listening to the echoes bounce off the steep cliffs. They stopped at noon and ate the excellent lunch Janet had brought. Jenny laughed and wondered how James was doing at being a teacher. She had great confidence in him and imagined that her students were having a wonderful time.

The three of them arrived in Big Rock with as much enthusiasm as they had when they started out. Jenny took all three of them straight to Dora's boarding house. She was happy to accommodate all three of them. Janet and Jenny shared a room with two small beds.

After a wonderful supper Dora finished her chores and joined the three of them out on the veranda. She had heard vague rumours of the events in Water Valley, but she wanted first hand information. They told her of all the happenings in Water Valley and Dora could hardly believe her ears when told of Jenny's horrible experience.

Dora asked "Are you sure you're all right, Jenny?"

Jenny smiled, "I'm just fine, Dora. I just feel twinges now and again. They get fewer as time goes on."

All of them slept soundly that night and were up bright and early to tour the town. Jake's first task was to see that the horses had been looked after in John Frost's livery barn. Satisfied he took the list of supplies James had given him and spent the next few hours filling the order. He then started out to locate the women.

Janet and Jenny hardly noticed he was gone, in their delight of shopping. They scoured the town for items to complete the enormous shopping list. Much time was spent going over fabrics for Jenny's replacement wardrobe. Jenny had also brought the furs, which Jake had given her for Christmas. A jacket was going to be sewn from them with a matching hat. If any fur was left over, a beautiful muff would be made from it.

Satisfied that everything would be as she wished, Janet and Jenny left the dress shop. They laughed when they noticed the time and realized they had just spent three hours pondering materials and patterns. It was lunchtime. They spotted Jake coming along the street toward them.

"Just on time!" Jenny greeted Jake. "I hope you're hungry, because I sure am." She smiled at the enthusiastic grin Jake was giving her. "I told Dora not to bother with lunch for us, because I am treating you to something special." With that she led the puzzled couple, around a corner to a little cantina.

The adobe walls had arched windows, with red and white curtains. They entered the building, and were greeted by a tiny white haired lady. Senora Maria Alvarez showed them to a table beside one window. A red and white checked tablecloth graced the circular table. A huge candle with a flower beside it sat in the centre. Jake looked around him in wonder. He had never been in a café before. A younger version of the elderly lady came out with fresh bread in a basket. A pot of butter followed. It proved to be Senora Alvarez's granddaughter, Juanita. Maria followed with three large bowls of beef stew. The three of them enjoyed the delicious meal, and when they were finished. Jenny gave a wink to Maria, who was waiting for the signal.

Unbeknownst to Janet and Jake, Jenny had sent Tommy Spinks with a message to Maria early that same morning. On her previous visit in August, Jenny had noticed a little sign in the window. It said "Ice Cream available by special order."

It was with a very special flourish that Maria came with three huge dishes of vanilla ice cream. Jake and Janet were astonished. Janet had eaten it many years before, but this was Jake's first experience. It didn't take him long to polish it off though. Both of them thanked Jenny profusely. Jenny was so happy to have surprised her friends successfully. However the surprise was not over.

Jenny looked at Jake, and said solemnly. "Jake, you are very special to me. You are going to be a great man someday." Janet and Jake were both staring at her attentively. She continued. "I would like you to regard me as your big sister. I know you're almost too old for that, but I would still like to have you as a brother. You are an only child and so am I. Both of us have no parents and I would really like a brother. Please think about this, you do not have to answer right away."

Jake couldn't speak. He was not sure the ice cream was agreeing with him at the moment. Through a lump in his throat he managed to blurt out. "Miss Jenny," he said. "Nothing would make me happier than having a big sister like you. Yes I accept." He stood up then accidentally knocking the chair over in his spontaneous movement. Ignoring it he flew around the table lifting Jenny right out of her chair, hugging her hard.

Jenny laughed rather breathlessly. Janet retrieved the fallen chair and the three of them left the café very satisfied.

"To you Jake, except in the classroom, I would like you to call me just Jenny. Your sister Jenny," she said smiling at the beaming boy.

Jenny entered the gold merchant's store. She asked to see the men's pocket watches. She found one she liked and whispered to the proprietor. "Please engrave this right now if you can." She wrote something down on a piece of paper and handed it to him. He hurried to do her bidding and the three of them waited patiently for him to finish. When he returned with the piece, Jenny pointed out a chain. The goldsmith attached it to the watch.

The trio left the store. Jenny handed the watch to Jake. His eyes got big and round as he read the words engraved inside the cover. "To my best brother, Love your sister Jenny," was inscribed there. Jake never said a word but hugged Jenny so hard, she heard her ribs creak. Laughing, they walked on.

Jenny told Jake to go to the dry goods store and try on some new trousers and shirts. It was going to be a welcome to the family present for him. She told them that she needed to go to the bank. Janet and Jake did as they were asked. When she finished her banking she returned to the dry goods store. She bought Jake three pairs of dungarees and five shirts. She also bought a shirt for special occasions. A black pair of cotton trousers joined the special shirt. Jake didn't know what to say. He was so happy he never wanted this day to end. She had him go and pick out some underwear too, for she would not embarrass him by doing so for him.

With that all completed, the tired trio returned to the boarding house for the evening. Jake was antsy, he couldn't sit still.

Finally Jake asked politely, "Miss Jenny, umm... Jenny, I mean, can I go out for the evening? I would like to see the town at night." He inquired hopefully.

Jenny said with a grin, "Sure, I think it's all right, but please try not to get into any trouble," she warned him lightly.

Jake donned one of his new outfits and left the house in high spirits. When he returned his grin told Jenny and Janet that he had a wonderful time.

Jenny had been a bit worried, but Jake was able to take care of himself. Jake told them he had gotten together with another lad and they had toured the town ending up playing cards in one of the cantinas. When the cantina closed he had come back to the boarding house.

Early the next morning they started out for home with packages piled high.

They were all feeling chipper. Jenny was enjoying this outing tremendously. She feared she had become a lover of travelling. She enjoyed seeing new places. Dora's lunch came in handy as well.

They arrived at the Water Valley General Store just past seven o'clock. James was waiting for their arrival and he and Ray helped Jake unload the wagon with Janet's packages and the items requested by the various people. Jenny and James walked while Jake drove to Jenny's house where her goodies were soon ensconced safely into their proper places.

Jenny said farewell to Jake who still had to drive to the ranch. James told him he would be along in a little bit. They watched Jake skilfully turn the wagon around and head for Main Street.

Jenny turned twinkling eyes on James. "Well, James how was teaching?" Jenny asked gaily.

James laughed. "The teaching part was easy, it was the romance I had a hard time handling."

Jenny frowned "What do you mean romance?" she asked curiously.

James said with a smile "Sit down here, and I'll tell you all about it." He indicated one of Jenny's veranda chairs.

Jenny sat, waiting with anticipation James's story.

"It seems that little Barbara Jones, has a crush on Johnny Breckinridge," he said. "She follows him around and teases him unmercifully. Johnny's face would sometimes get the look of a hunted deer. Well Tuesday was extremely hot and Johnny did not show up after lunch hour. All of the students, with the possible exception of Barbara, did not know what happened to him. One of the older boys suggested he might have played hooky and went to the swimming hole. I wouldn't have blamed him; the school was like an oven. Anyway, I didn't become too concerned and kept on with the lessons. At three o'clock I dismissed the class and we went outside. Greg had to go to the outhouse, and he was the one that discovered our missing boy. Poor Johnny had been locked into the shack, where he had retreated for refuge. Barbara in a fit of pique had locked the door on him. The poor lad was weak, from lack of fresh air and it was even worse than the school for heat. And oh, the smell of the boy! No one wanted to get too close to him. He headed straight for the watering trough in the park and jumped in clothes and all. It was hard for me to keep a straight face, I can tell you. I sentenced Barbara to clean the outhouses for one week, every day. She was not pleased. I don't think her ardour extended to latrine duty. Anyway she has left poor Johnny alone since then!"

Jenny laughed, and wished she could have seen it herself. She hugged James. "I enjoyed Big Rock and shopping so much, thank you for taking over the teaching for me. I appreciate it more than you would believe. I think I am all set until at least the summer."

He kissed her hand, then left for home. It was lucky his horse knew the way because his head was too full of dreams for him to pay attention to where he was going.

Chapter 45

Jenny's students were busy preparing for final examinations. It was hard to keep them on track because of the gorgeous weather. Trees were beautiful in the varying shades of green that spring and summer always displayed. The sun shone relentlessly causing the children to dream of the swimming hole, not school work.

The heat of the schoolroom was stifling, so that Jenny had blankets set out just behind the school and most of their lessons were conducted outdoors. The school had an unexpected visitor, on one of these beautiful days. It was the fifteenth of June and a large robust man walked around the school to the back where the students had just started their day's studies. Jenny stood up to greet the stranger.

"My name is Ben Moss," he said holding out his hand to be shaken, "Superintendent of the Montana Board of Education."

Jenny smiled. "Welcome to Water Valley, Mr. Moss. As you can see we're enjoying the beautiful weather by sitting out here for our studies instead of the schoolhouse. It's very hot in there," she explained. Her heart was beating a bit faster and she was apprehensive.

It is true that he was rather surprised at the unorthodox manner of teaching, but he was an open-minded man and patient.

He sat down at the rear of their makeshift school and listened. He spent the entire day with Jenny and the students.

The students had a hard time curbing their curiosity about the gentleman and concentrate on their studies. Strangers had a tendency to make them nervous. Ben Moss was quite used to this reaction and sat in the background not saying a word.

By the end of the day, he was well satisfied that the students were doing well. He handed Jenny a sealed package of papers. These were the State Ninth Grade examinations. To go on to college or other facility, the students needed to pass these tests.

"You are doing an excellent job of teaching these children." He hesitated a second or two causing Jenny to become apprehensive. "I am in hopes that you'll be staying for another year?"

Jenny relaxed, "Yes I do plan to, I love the position here and I love my students."

Ben Moss, in turn breathed a sigh of relief. "I am so happy that you will. There are so many lady teachers that only stay one year because of finding a young man to marry."

"Why would that be a problem?" Jenny asked puzzled. "Don't they want to teach after they marry?"

"Well, it is not a question of whether they want to or not," he said a bit uncomfortably "You realize the rules that state a married lady can't be a school teacher, don't you?"

Jenny was horrified. "N-no," she said faintly. "Why on earth would marriage make a difference? It doesn't change a woman's teaching abilities!"

"It is a rule, probably out dated by now stating that a married woman's place is in the home. The jobs are to be left to men and single ladies," he finished lamely.

Jenny could only stare at him helplessly.

"Well, I will bid you goodbye for now, Miss Stockton. I will return around the same time next year. Your upcoming curriculum will be sent in the mail sometime in August."

"Thank you," Jenny managed to whisper. She watched Ben Moss round the corner of the school and disappear. "What a stupid law!" she fumed.

Jenny kept Bill Storm, Irene Summers and Mary Barns after school to tell them of the examinations. She and told them that on

Monday June twenty-first, the examinations would be administered to them. It gave them a week of study. She was not allowed to open the sealed envelopes so she did not know if all the questions on the test had been previously taught. She was still confident of the students' ability to pass.

Due to these examinations, all the other students were told that there would be no school on Monday. This was greeted with varying degrees of enthusiasm. The three grade nines were petrified. Jenny tried to inspire confidence in their abilities.

Monday morning Bill, Irene and Mary were on time. It seemed empty in the classroom without the other students. They were surprised to see Reverend Chase sitting near Jenny at the front of the room.

"I am here as an observer to make sure that these tests are administered fairly," the Reverend said. He offered a short blessing on the three of them. He handed out the sealed envelopes containing the exams. He was the official timer and would be gathering them up to send them by the mail wagon to Big Rock then on to Helena, where the State's Board of Education was located. The final results would not be known until August. It would be an anxious time for the three students and Jenny as well. Jenny if anything was more nervous than her students. She sat very still at her desk, clenching her hands together. The day passed slowly to her agonizing mind. When they were finished, Art took the examinations straight to the General Store. Ray was the Post Master of Water Valley. He would put the examinations in the safe until the mail wagon made his return trip from Butte on the Thursday.

The three children were exhausted and so was Jenny. The results of these tests would judge whether her teaching methods were correct. Ben Moss had liked her teaching, but would the results meet her own standards?

There was just the rest of this week and the next until the end of the school year. The three older students were a mass of nerves and the rest of them hated being confined to the curriculum. Jenny had an idea.

Jenny announced, "If all of you are willing to help me, I would like to hold a graduation ceremony on Saturday Night after the last day of school."

Jenny was pleased at the enthusiastic response of all the children. They cheered.

"I know that the examination results will take a long time to return, however I have great confidence in Bill, Irene and Mary. They will pass. I want to honour them and the rest of you for your cooperation and hard work." Jenny beamed.

The rest of the afternoon was spent making plans. Invitations to everyone in the area were made. Jenny managed to get them to do some schoolwork in between preparations for the celebration. After the children were dismissed, Jenny hurried over to the stables to consult with David. The barn was twice the size of the church and had a huge hayloft. It was mostly empty right now, because the new mown hay was still drying in the fields.

Jenny thought it was perfect and David scratching his head said that Jenny could use it. Jake had Soot, so she borrowed a horse and buggy from David and drove down the road about six miles to the Fredericks Farm. She had met Jock and Jim, the brothers at the New Year's dance out at the ranch. Jock and Jim were delighted to play and call at the barn dance.

Jenny returned home to make more plans for the party. The next few days flew by with the excited children making decorations and party treats. The whole class brought mops and buckets and the hayloft was scrubbed unmercifully. It looked wonderful when it was finished. The boys were sent to scavenge benches and chairs from where ever they could find them. There didn't seem to be anywhere near enough, so Jenny sent them out to root in woodpiles and scour the bush out back, for logs or stumps big enough to sit on. These they covered in blankets, so that no one got splinters by sitting on them.

By Friday afternoon everything was in place. The cookies, cakes and pies were finished. The children were tired and so was Jenny. She went home, and vowed herself a quiet evening. Mayor like usual was right beside her.

She was very surprised when a tentative knock sounded on her front door. She hurried to open it. James stood there. The setting sun framed his face. Jenny caught her breath. She was about to invite him in when he spoke first.

"Jenny, it is a beautiful evening and I know you're tired from your preparations for tomorrow night, but would you come for a walk with me?" he asked.

He sounded so meek and slightly nervous that Jenny grew alarmed. Why of course I will!" she said without hesitation. "Are you all right?"

"I- I'm fine," he said in a low voice. He then followed her out to the gate, where he steered her south. There was a narrow trail, which had been worn by many feet winding between the Poplar and Birch trees. The odd Pine and Spruce intermingled with the rest of the trees. They were steadily walking downhill. Jenny had often walked down the path to watch the children play in the water.

The two of them walked hand in hand where the path allowed them and single file where it narrowed. They didn't say anything, just enjoying each other's company. James hoped that the swimming hole would be deserted at this time of day.

It was and he took her to one side where the moss grew thick and soft. They sat down and looked at the quiet lagoon. It was part of the river system, which forked just north of where they were sitting. A small tributary was formed. A beaver dam had stopped its flow backing up the water to form the pool. The water then flowed over the dam, carrying on to rejoin the river a few hundred yards down stream. The island was home to many an overnight outing and the community youngsters played many games there. One huge oak tree, with branches spreading out over the pond, had a rope tied on it. The children would grab the rope and swing out over the lagoon and drop into the water.

As they sat there quietly, James mused over the dam. The beavers were used to the noise of the children by now and hid in their lodges until all became quiet again. Both James and Jenny were thrilled when a head popped out of the water observing them. The beaver seemed to know that they meant no harm and started to go about his or her daily business with little concern. Jenny and James watched quietly fascinated as three more heads popped up and started swimming around. Two of them were tiny kits. They followed their mother until she found something to eat. Then bored they started to play. They raced around, pushing one another as they dived and splashed. Father Beaver had got busy working on the dam. James knew that daily repairs were needed to keep the water from wrecking the construction.

Time passed, and James and Jenny sat without saying a word. It grew dark and the huge white moon rose over the mountain, bathing everything in a shimmering glow. James was uncharacteristically nervous. Jenny waited patiently knowing that James would eventually tell her what was wrong.

Finally James turned toward her. "Jenny I need… I have something very important to ask you." He lapsed into silence for a minute and Jenny felt compelled to say something.

"James, I can tell something is troubling you, please tell me or ask me. Are we not friends?"

James took a deep breath and plunged forward. He stood up and helped her to stand. James dropped down on one knee, and took one of Jenny's hands and looked up at her beseechingly.

"Will you marry me?" He asked, holding her gaze.

Jenny was in shock! She thought of all the platitudes she had been taught to say in all such circumstances. Then it simply didn't matter. Her heart reached out to his. "Yes!" she said simply. "Oh yes."

They kissed again fervently and he took out a small box that had been in his pocket. He opened it, and took out a gold ring. It had a sapphire set in the middle of a circle of tiny diamonds. To her surprise, the ring came apart. A simple gold band pulled away from the sapphire. The larger ring with the sapphire and diamonds he put on her finger, and the other he put on his own little finger. This is a family heirloom he said. My father gave it to me, when I turned eighteen. The first part was to be given to my bride to be, while I wear the second part until our marriage. I then give my part of the ring back to you as a wedding band. It shows my fidelity to you. On our oldest son's eighteenth birthday, the whole ring will be given to him."

Jenny was silent for a couple of minutes. Then she looked up at him and whispered, "I love you James."

He hugged her close, a murmured emotionally, "I love you too, my darling."

James looked down into her sparkling eyes and he clasped her close. He lowered his head and he kissed her. Warmth radiated from Jenny's mouth all the way through her body, she never wanted the kiss to stop. James lifted his head and looked at his wonderful lady. She was breathing hard, and her eyes were closed. She slowly opened them and gazed in wonder at the handsome man staring down at her. She was trembling in reaction.

James decided it was time to make their way back to Jenny's cabin. They moved toward the path, startling the beaver family. Father Beaver slapped the water with his tail and all four of them disappeared beneath the surface.

Jenny never did remember that walk back to her cabin. Her heart was too full of emotions. At the door, he kissed her again and bid her sweet dreams. She watched as he made his way toward the stables. Jenny entered her kitchen trembling in a state of shock. She sat in her chair and clasped her hands together. Could this really have happened to her? She raised her hands up to her face covering her mouth as she cried in happiness. Her parents would have been proud. At least she thought they would. Jenny would like to think they would have loved James as well. Perhaps he could have been what they wished for her.

Jenny tore her mind away from thoughts of her parents. She got up and took her dress off. As she slowly changed into her nightgown her thoughts raced with various exciting ideas and plans. She had to write a letter to Frances.

Frances would be thrilled. Maybe she would be able to come out for the wedding. Surely a job could be found for her somewhere on the ranch. After all, she would be needed when her children came. Jenny hugged herself and danced around the room. This was the best day of Jenny's life. Gradually her excitement toned down and she crawled into the comfortable bed. Mayor had been watching her from the rug near the stove. He paced toward the bed, trying to figure out why Jenny was both crying and happy. He was extremely puzzled. Jenny saw him and gave him a big hug. He settled down near the bed, but never took his eyes off of her. Now Jenny knew how all her Boston friends must have felt when they got engaged. Indeed she had been missing something.

It was just possible her bridges, were not quite burned after all. She giggled at the thought. It took her a while to actually close her eyes and composed herself for sleep. Jenny had wonderful happy dreams.

Chapter 46

The next morning she was up early, sitting at her kitchen table working on the awards for all of her students. She was a firm believer in positive reinforcement. No one in her class would go home without some sort of award.

That evening James arrived and knocked on the door. After entering, he took his hat off and politely asked if he could escort her to the dance that evening.

Jenny made a great pretence of examining every inch of him. "Umm," she said cocking her head. "I never go out on a date with strangers."

"Who me? I am no stranger, I creep and crawl into your dreams every night," he said loftily.

Jenny growled playfully. "You sound like some sort of disease! I think I'll find someone more sanitary to go to the dance with."

James scowled and with deliberate slowness curled his hands into claws and started to wiggle the fingers. "Then I guess I'll just have to tickle you," he threatened, advancing toward her. With a squeal, Jenny retreated behind one of the big chairs. James chased her and the two of them ran around the room. Jenny was dreadfully ticklish. James took a shortcut between the chairs and caught her. He clutched her close and she couldn't escape. He promptly gave her a big smooch.

"So you are going to be like that, are you?" Jenny retorted. "I guess I have no choice then, I'll just have to go with you." She sighed dramatically as if it was going to be torture.

He did tickle her then, until she laughed herself breathless. "No, you have no choice at all," he said with deceptive mildness.

Jenny tried to keep a straight face, but again dissolved into laughter. James seriousness lasted a few seconds more, but soon joined her. Laughing gaily in perfect accord Jenny gathered all her papers and they left the house for the barn.

"My goodness everyone seems to be here!" Jenny stated as she looked in amazement at the rows and rows of horses and wagons parked all along the street. The park across from the Store was packed as well. There was a festive mood in the air. Laughter and boisterous greetings were flying about the town. Everyone loved a barn dance.

The ceremony was due to start at seven o'clock, but the barn was full before six-thirty.

At precisely the right time, Jenny in her turquoise cotton dress with dark blue lace made her way down the aisle. When she reached the front she turned and asked everyone to stand. Jock struck up the fiddle, and he played a marching tune, and the three young graduates marched single file toward the stage. As they took their place on the appointed chairs facing the audience, Jenny had the two littlest students bring in the American Flag.

The whole class sang the Star Spangled Banner and recited the Pledge of Allegiance. With that ritual completed, Jenny said. "I would like to welcome you all here for this very special occasion. All my students have worked hard and it is a special pleasure for me to see the accomplishments of these dedicated students. It is a credit to their hard work that all three of these graduates, I am certain will pass their exams. I do not hesitate in the least to state that they will qualify to continue their educations' in Helena or any other state they may choose to go to." Jenny then turned toward the graduates. "Irene Summers, please come forward."

Irene with trembling feet came forward to receive the paper that Jenny had drawn up. It was rolled up and held with a red ribbon. She curtsied to Jenny and then went into the audience. She pinned a small bouquet of flowers to her mothers dress. She then rejoined the small group on stage.

Then it was Mary Barnes turn. She repeated the same moves as Irene had. Bill also bowed to Jenny when he received his diploma and gave his mother some flowers. He returned to the stage and faced the large gathering. He gave a resounding speech, on the appreciation of the teaching and the goals the three of them had to look forward too. He told everyone that he was heading for San Francisco to the college there. It was a very stirring speech greeted with cheers and applause.

Jenny then called all the children up one at a time to receive their special awards. Then with great pride Jenny announced Jake's award. She called him up to the front.

Jenny said. "Ladies and Gentlemen, it is with great pride that I give this award to Jake. He has worked hard, I felt he was doing extremely well. I did not tell him that the exams he completed with good marks weren't the usual sixth grade tests, but were actually the eighth grade examinations. Through hard work he has accomplished a great deal this year. He will be admitted to the ninth grade next year."

A stunned Jake got his share of back slaps at this coupe. The formal ceremony was over and everyone helped move the chairs to the sides of the barn. Jock started the fiddling.

Jenny's first dance was with James, but Jake was second. After that Jenny danced with all the young men in her class. James was doing the same for all the girls. It was a wonderful evening, but to Jenny one of the highlights of the evening was watching Jake and Lucy, spending more time dancing with each other than the rest put together.

James embarrassed Jenny in between dances near the end of the evening.

When he had everyone's attention, he announced.

"My friends and neighbours," he said, "It is with great pleasure, that I give you the news that, Miss Jennifer Stockton, has granted me the honour of becoming her husband."

Roars of approval and delight resounded from the gathered crowd. Jenny was sure everyone hugged and kissed her. James was beaming as everyone congratulated him. It was quite a while before the furor died down and the dancing resumed. James escorted Jenny onto the floor for their first formal engagement dance. Jenny was in heaven.

Everyone was reluctant to leave. They closed up the barn at ten-thirty, and James and Jenny started the walk to her house.

It was a beautiful evening, and the both of them took some time and sat in the veranda's chairs. Jenny closed her eyes and sighed. She was truly sorry the school term was over.

James said softly "You know it *is* your choice to name the wedding day." Jenny opened her large luminous eyes and looked at him.

"I suppose it *is* too late to change my mind," she said teasingly.

James said. "I think the whole town would lynch us if we disappointed them now!" he grinned.

"Oh, well I guess we had better go through with this then. I think the rope would ruin my dress," she said soberly as if in intense misery.

James bounded out of his chair and lifted Jenny out of hers. "I'll never let you get away from me and I especially never want to come that close to losing you ever again," he whispered passionately. Blue eyes stared into green. He lowered his lips and touched hers very lightly. Her eyes widened, as a fire seemed to spread from her burning lips.

James kissed her again crushing her against him. He never wanted to let her go. She was his life. Emotions crashed within their bodies. Jenny felt her body grow warm. Her knees felt weak. She never wanted the kiss to stop. She was breathing hard. So was James. He kissed her again lightly, as her wobbly legs regained their strength.

He whispered "You had better not make that wedding date too far in the future, because I never want to let you out of my sight." He buried his head in her shoulder.

Jenny had the look of a cat that had been into the cream. She grinned in anticipation and longing. Oh how she loved this man. She had found the very thing that had caused her to run away from Boston. She had come here to change her life and had accomplished much of what she wanted to do. Jenny loved being a teacher and she loved her students. Water Valley was a place where dreams seemed to come true, not only for Jenny but everyone who came here. Just look at how far she had come. She was in the arms of one who truly loved her. It was indescribable.

She longed to be with James, but she knew she wanted to teach at least one more year. The two of them decided the wedding would take place a week after the school year closed the next year. That part settled, Jenny looked forward to a wonderful life ahead. She thought she had burned her bridges behind her, but now found herself building one instead. With her head spinning in wonder, she held James close to her. This was definitely not the end, but...

A New Beginning

S hiloh J. Manley was born in Alberta Canada in the late 1940's. Raised on a farm with her parents and three brothers, the family worked hard to make a living. Her father, aunts and many other senior citizens told her stories of the one room school, and all the different happenings throughout their years there. Many of these stories along with Shiloh's own life experiences growing up in the rural west are incorporated into this book.

Shiloh is married and along with her husband and daughter are now living in beautiful British Columbia's Okanagan Valley. She continues to write and has begun working on the sequel to Burning Bridges.

Proof

Made in the USA
Charleston, SC
17 March 2010